PENGUIN CLASSICS

DEATH OF A HERO

RICHARD ALDINGTON was born in 1892 and was educated at Dover College and London University. Before World War I he was known as a poet of distinction, as a translator, and as a critic. He was a founding member of the Imagist movement in poetry along with Ezra Pound and Aldington's then-wife, Hilda Doolittle (H.D.). Aldington joined the British army in 1916, served in France and Flanders, and was wounded in 1918. His first novel was *Death of a Hero*, which was published in 1929, a full ten years after his discharge from the army. This was followed by the satirical *The Colonel's Daughter* and by *Women Must Work*. He also published collections of short stories, a study of Voltaire, and biographies of contemporaries such as T. E. Lawrence, Robert Louis Stevenson, and D. H. Lawrence. Aldington died in France in 1962.

JAMES H. MEREDITH is an internationally respected scholar on the literature and films of twentieth-century wars. He is a retired U.S. Air Force lieutenant colonel, the president of the Ernest Hemingway Foundation and Society, and is a contributing editor of *War, Literature, and the Arts: An International Journal of the Humanities.*

RICHARD ALDINGTON

Death of a Hero

Introduction by
JAMES H. MEREDITH

PENGUIN BOOKS

PENGUIN BOOKS

Published by the Penguin Group

Penguin Group (USA) Inc., 375 Hudson Street, New York, New York 10014, USA

Penguin Group (Canada), 90 Eglinton Avenue East, Suite 700, Toronto, Ontario M4P 2Y3,
Canada (a division of Pearson Penguin Canada Inc.)

Penguin Books Ltd, 80 Strand, London WC2R 0RL, England

Penguin Ireland, 25 St Stephen's Green, Dublin 2, Ireland (a division of Penguin Books Ltd)

Penguin Group (Australia), 707 Collins Street, Melbourne, Victoria 3008, Australia
(a division of Pearson Australia Group Pty Ltd)

Penguin Books India Pvt Ltd, 11 Community Centre, Panchsheel Park,
New Delhi – 110 017, India

Penguin Group (NZ), 67 Apollo Drive, Rosedale, Auckland 0632, New Zealand
(a division of Pearson New Zealand Ltd)

Penguin Books, Rosebank Office Park, 181 Jan Smuts Avenue, Parktown North 2193, South Africa

Penguin China, B7 Jaiming Center, 27 East Third Ring Road North, Chaoyang
District, Beijing 100020, China

Penguin Books Ltd, Registered Offices:
80 Strand, London WC2R 0RL, England

First published in the United States of America by Covici, Friede, Inc. 1929
First published in Great Britain by Chatto & Windus 1929
This edition with an introduction by James H. Meredith published in Penguin Books 2013

1 3 5 7 9 10 8 6 4 2

Copyright Richard Aldington, 1929
Copyright renewed Richard Aldington, 1957
Introduction copyright © James H. Meredith, 2013
All rights reserved

Published by arrangement with the Estate of Richard Aldington

LIBRARY OF CONGRESS CATALOGING-IN-PUBLICATION DATA
Aldington, Richard, 1892–1962.
Death of a hero / Richard Aldington ; introduction by James H. Meredith.
p. cm.—(Penguin classics)
ISBN 978-0-14-310687-6 (pbk.)
1. World War, 1914–1918—Fiction. I. Title.
PR6001.L4D4 2013
823'.912—dc23   2012036338

Printed in the United States of America

"See how we trifle! but one can't pass one's youth too amusingly; for one must grow old, and that in England; two most serious circumstances, either of which makes people grey in the twinkling of a bedstaff; for know you, there is not a country upon earth where there are so many old fools and so few young ones."

—HORACE WALPOLE

Contents

Introduction

World War I was the first truly global conflict—a revolutionary awakening from romantic old-world values to the realities of modern life. The Great War was the first modern war in which the soldier became noticeably alienated due to dehumanized and mechanized battlefield conditions. Richard Aldington's classic World War I novel, *Death of a Hero* (1929), artfully conveys the soldier's transforming alienation in a straightforward, unsentimental, and accurate depiction of combat on the western front.

George Winterbourne, of the intellectual and artistic segment of the British middle class that was already noticeably out of sorts in England even before the war began, is an unusual Everyman for this genre. The physical pain and moral agony that was a British soldier's life on the western front is effectively rendered without employing the self-pitying pathos that could have limited it.

Winterbourne, a striving artist, is reminiscent of the protagonist of T. S. Eliot's poem "The Love Song of J. Alfred Prufrock." Eliot's Prufrock is modernist poetry's most well-known intellectual dilettante. Aldington, himself a modernist like Eliot, was an imagist poet, a friend of Ezra Pound, and husband to Hilda Doolittle (H.D.), both prominent poets in their own right. In the modernist caste, before the war both Prufrock and Winterbourne were living (as it were) at a time when the British Empire had produced enough wealth and leisure for large numbers of the educated middle class to strive for intellectual and artistic pursuits professionally. This class now had access to endeavors that had once been reserved solely for the landed gentry.

In 1914, the continuation of Great Britain as an empire

meant that these would-be intellectuals and artists ultimately would have to fight as common soldiers. The educated middle class would not have been wealthy enough to obtain shelter from the demands of the empire. Prufrock measures every moment—every step—as he navigates the checks and balances of his modernist world, while Winterbourne falls into the ranks of soldiers sent to the front lines to preserve modernist ideals. Over the course of the war, Great Britain would need a lot more manpower, and the largest segment of population, logically, was the middle class, from tradesmen to intellectuals. By the end of the war, Great Britain would lose 743,000 men, approximately seven times the number of soldiers who were in uniform when the conflict began.[1]

A great paradox of this situation is that these middle-class intellectuals and artists, who generally were sensitive, educated, intelligent, and aggressively individualistic, also wrote about their experiences after the war. Their narratives became the history—the archive—for readers seeking to experience the Great War. Having such a large educated class on the battlefield was a first for the Western world. With so many writers and artists in the ranks, very much has been written and recorded about the war throughout all levels of the experience.

Aldington's novel is about Winterbourne, but the story is told in the first person by an unnamed narrator who knew Winterbourne from his last days on the western front. First-person war narratives typically tell a story with exciting immediacy. However, if the first-person narrator is killed in battle, it becomes awkward to explain how the story was put into publication. A first-person war narrative has to be told retrospectively, and that presents a logical problem: If the narrator is already dead or severely incapacitated, the story must die with the teller, yes? And yet it is a pattern we see more than once in the literature of the Great War. In Erich Maria Remarque's *All Quiet on the Western Front,* which was published in 1929, the same year as *Death of a Hero,* the story continues after the narrator is killed, but without explanation as to how the story is ultimately fashioned into a published novel. What Remarque gains in pathos and in emotional immediacy, he loses in logos, or logic. Aldington's *Death of a*

Hero avoids this irreducible awkwardness by having another soldier step in to tell Winterbourne's story, making the narrative more consistent, more powerful, and more convincing than Remarque's oft-studied novel. Frederic Henry, Ernest Hemingway's narrator in *A Farewell to Arms*, also published in 1929, is a noncombatant ambulance driver who manages to escape the day-to-day horrors of trench warfare even before he deserts the Italian army. Hemingway's great World War I classic is more of a love story between Henry and the English nurse Catherine Barkley than the comprehensive combat story captured in Aldington's complex narrative.

In *Death of a Hero,* the narrator is sympathetic to Winterbourne's station: "Winterbourne's death is a symbol to me of the whole sickening bloody waste of it, the damnable stupid waste and torture of it."[2] In the eyes the narrator—a fellow soldier and fellow intellectual—Winterbourne dies a hero's death. After Winterbourne is killed while fighting in the last stages of the war, the narrator is compelled to relate not only the events leading up to his death, but also to describe the people in his life that emotionally helped put him in that moral spot on the battlefield:

> I think that George committed suicide in that last battle of the war. I don't mean shot himself, but it was so very easy for a company commander to stand up when an enemy was traversing. The situation he had got into with Elizabeth and Fanny Welford was not inextricable but it would have needed a certain amount of patience and energy and determination and common sense to put right. But by November '18 poor old George was whacked, whacked to the wide. He was a bit off his head, as nearly all the troops were after six months on the line.[3]

Winterbourne's home front was decidedly a middle-class family that deluded itself with aristocratic pretensions, and his parents were aggressively dysfunctional. According to the narrator, Winterbourne's parents, always primarily concerned with their own condition, never seemed engaged with Winterbourne's economic and social development as a child. He haphazardly drifted into the intellectual milieu of his wife,

Elizabeth, and his mistress, Fanny, expecting to be able to pursue his artistic development unfettered. Yet the demands of the empire in wartime changed all of that. The narrator stresses that while Winterbourne's "nerves were certainly all to pieces," Elizabeth and Fanny "adjusted to the war with marvelous precision and speed, just as they afterwards adapted themselves to the post war."[4] Like so many in that milieu on the home front, they experimented with all the new social trends: "the Zion of sex, abounding in inhibitions, dream symbolism, complexes, sadism, representations, masochism, Lesbianism, sodomy, etcetera." However, while Elizabeth and Fanny were getting on with their lives during the war, Winterbourne was getting on with his death.

Aldington, the poet and writer, intended for the novel to be a social satire and critique of the smug and self-satisfied British culture that sent Winterbourne, and so many others like him, to war without first psychologically preparing them for the carnage ahead. Until that point, British culture had molded Winterbourne's character into that of a freethinking intellectual, not a tough-minded soldier. And tragically, at this historical moment, Great Britain needed a lot more soldiers than it did writers and artists. In retrospect, the novel conveys, more than anything else, the way this society set Winterbourne up to fail spiritually on the battlefield by demonstrating the debilitating effects on the human spirit of long-term battlefield exposure. Perhaps a still more tragic backdrop to these battlefield enigmas was the reality of a home front seemingly unaffected by and uncaring about the soldier's condition.

As the contemporary reader approaches this story of a war begun nearly 100 years ago, in order to appreciate the details that would have been common knowledge and chronicled in daily newspapers for Aldington's initial audience, it is necessary that he or she understand the historical context of the war.

World War I began in the summer of 1914 following the assassination on June 28 of Archduke Franz Ferdinand by Gavrilo Princip, a radical Serbian terrorist, in Sarajevo. The political aftermath of that assassination created a diplomatic situation so poisoned (and bungled) that the major nations of

Europe would end up at war with each other by midnight, August 4. On one side of the conflict were Germany, ruled by Kaiser Wilhelm II, and the Austro-Hungarian Empire, ruled by Emperor Franz Josef. On the other side were France; Russia, ruled by Tsar Nicholas II; and Great Britain. The United States would not enter into the war until 1917.

The initial stage of the war largely followed the implementation of the German Schlieffen Plan and the counter-response by the allied nations. The Schlieffen Plan established a schedule in which the German army would drive through neutral Belgium and invade northern France before France could fully mobilize its large conscript army; defeat the French within six weeks; and then move east to defeat Russia. The plan ignored Great Britain because it had no army on the continent. By following this plan, Germany would be able to avoid a two-front war. But the plan failed.

Great Britain's position in the war changed when Germany marched across the Belgian border on August 2. Due to the 1839 Treaty of London that guaranteed Belgium's neutrality in all European wars, Great Britain was forced to declare war against Germany. Before the English arrived, Belgium's armed resistance to the invasion slowed the German army's advance toward France. Soon after, and much to the surprise of German military strategists, by the end of the month Great Britain managed to field a small force against the German advance at Mons, Belgium. But the British soon retreated against the much larger German force.

But in September the British and French forces united to oppose the German invasion on the Marne River in northern France. In four days, the mighty German army was defeated and was forced to dig entrenchments, thereby triggering what would be one of the greatest horrors of this Great War—the trench warfare that would become synonymous with fighting along the western front. Simultaneously, on the eastern front, while Germany would be much more successful against the large but severely antiquated Russian army, its forces were still now deeply entrenched in a two-front war.

However, at the beginning of the war, Great Britain had no soldiers on the European continent. Therefore, a British

Expeditionary Force had to be formed, organized, and equipped in a very short time. At first, the British could send only a relatively small army of 160,000 troops over to Europe—the rest of the army was scattered throughout the empire and had to be brought home—compared with the three million in the Austro-Hungarian army, four million in the French army, and four and half million in the German army.[5]

Except for Germany, most of these larger armies were built on ordinary civilian conscripts. Although in the beginning there was some conscription to fill in the ranks, most of Germany's large army were professional soldiers; Germany had been building its military might during the decades leading up to the war. While most of Europe's military strategists thought the war would be a brief affair, Great Britain's Lord Kitchener, the secretary of state for war, argued that this war would be long and that many British men would be needed to sustain the fight. Until this moment in history, Great Britain had primarily ruled and controlled its vast global empire with an enormous navy and a small professional army.

Foreseeing that circumstances had radically changed, Kitchener immediately called for 100,000 citizen volunteers to join the professional ranks, and got them easily. By September 1914, only six weeks from the war's start, 478,893 volunteers from among the young, male citizens of Great Britain would respond to Kitchener's appeal. Unlike the other European nations, Great Britain was able to field enough men for battle during the first phase of the war without conscription. The first of Kitchener's New Army, as it soon became known, would not leave for active service until May 9, 1915. Winterbourne, along with so many other ordinary British men, would eventually become a part of Kitchener's New Army on the western front. Moreover, the technological and industrial might of the British Empire, financed by American capital, would produce mountains of ammunition and artillery, so much so that the nature of battle would change drastically in 1916. It would become a war of statistics.

One battle alone represents this drastic change in warfare for the British—the Battle of the Somme, which began on July 1,

1916. On that fateful day alone, the British army would suffer 20,000 soldiers killed and 25,000 wounded. The battle would last for four more months and cost the British 95,675 more soldiers killed.[6] By the end of 1916, around the time that Winterbourne would have joined the army, the British Expeditionary Army consisted of 1,591,745 men, ten times the number it had held at the war's start.[7] The narrator of the novel roughly dates Winterbourne's engagement in the war from April 1917 to November 1918, when he is killed in fighting around Cambrai.

Winterbourne begins his active service as a common soldier, but because of the high attrition rates, especially among junior officers, he is eventually promoted to the rank of captain, the rank he holds when he dies. When Winterbourne is promoted to junior officer status, he is sent back to England for training and subsequently back to the same unit at the same location on the western front. Winterbourne's first major engagement, the Battle of Arras, started on April 9, 1917 and lasted until the 15th and featured the first penetration by British forces of the Hindenburg Line, a complex series of strong German defensive fortifications.

The battle also marked the first use of a technological advance called "creeping barrage," which allowed the British to move their artillery forward ahead of their advancing soldiers. This led to dramatic successes in capturing the first two sets of German trenches. The British soon found that the third and last set of trenches were much more fortified and better prepared for their assault. Despite the use of the tank, another new technology, the British were not able to overwhelm this third and last set of German trenches.[8] In the end, the British had driven four miles deep into a ten-mile stretch of German trenches—a major success, but bought at a terrible price. As an example of the costs, in Arras, France, there stands a British war memorial with the names of the 35,928 British soldiers who died in that battle but who have no known graves.

That is how the experience of the battle is told statistically and historically. Here is a sample of how Aldington tells the story of the battle personally.

"There is nothing here but a network of Boche trenches; look how deep they are. I couldn't see a soul and there are still Boche trench-notices up. I'm hanged if I know where we are. For all I know we're in the Boche lines."[9]

Lost in the maze of German trenches, Winterbourne is disoriented. He walks and talks with his commanding officer, Evans. Aldington goes on to write that "they wandered about until nearly dawn, without finding the Front line." After the battle, Winterbourne and his fellow soldiers "shambled heavily along, not keeping step or attempting to; bent wearily forward under the weight of their equipment, their unseeing eyes turned to the muddy ground."[10]

Winterbourne's life ends in the closing days of the war. His company was part of the larger British force that was pushing the Germans back toward their own borders. Winterbourne had been relentlessly driving his men forward into battle, and as the narrator describes it, "something seemed to break in Winterbourne's head."[11] The narrator goes on to observe: "He felt he was going mad, and sprang to his feet. The line of bullets smashed across his chest like a savage steel whip. The universe exploded in his head."[12] His body riddled with lead and steel, Winterbourne dies as a part of the war machine instead of continuing to live in the age that had produced those machines.

Winterbourne's fictional life ends thus, just days before the war actually ended on the eleventh hour of the eleventh day of the eleventh month, 1918. And soon after the war, the writers who survived would begin relating their various narratives of this great conflict. While both Remarque's and Hemingway's classic World War I narratives convey their war perspectives quite vigorously, neither novel drills down as deeply into the granite core of the trench soldier's experience as Aldington's *Death of a Hero*.

JAMES H. MEREDITH

Notes

1. Martin Gilbert, *The First World War: A Complete History* (New York: Henry Holt and Company, 1994), p. 37.
2. Richard Aldington, *Death of a Hero*, p. xxx.
3. Ibid, p. xxx.
4. Ibid, p. xxx.
5. Gilbert, *The First World War*, p. 541.
6. Ibid, p. 299.
7. Ibid, p. 300.
8. Ibid, pp. 320–323.
9. Aldington, *Death of a Hero*, p. xxx.
10. Ibid, p. xxx.
11. Ibid, p. xxx.
12. Ibid, p. xxx.

A Note from the Author

This novel in print differs in some particulars from the same book in manuscript. To my astonishment, my publishers informed me that certain words, phrases, sentences, and even passages, are at present taboo in England. I have recorded nothing which I have not observed in human life, said nothing I do not believe to be true. I had not the slightest intention of appealing to any one's salacious instincts; if I had wanted to do that, I should have chosen a theme less seriously tragic. But I am bound to accept the opinion of those who are better acquainted with popular feelings than I am. At my request the publishers are removing what they believe would be considered objectionable, and are placing asterisks to show where omissions have been made. If anything "objectional" remains, the responsibility is, of course, mine. In my opinion it is better for the book to appear mutilated than for me to say what I don't believe.

En attendant mieux,

R. A.

Preface

To
Halcott Glover

My dear Hal,—Remembering George Moore's denunciation of prefaces, I felt that what I wanted to say here could be best expressed in a letter to you. Although you are a little older than I, you belong essentially to the same generation—those who spent their childhood and adolescence struggling, like young Samsons, in the toils of the Victorians; whose early manhood coincided with the European War. A great number of the men of our generation died prematurely. We are unlucky or lucky enough to remain.

I began this book almost immediately after the Armistice, in a little Belgian cottage—my billet. I remember the landscape was buried deep in snow, and that we had very little fuel. Then came demobilisation, and the effort of readjustment cost my manuscript its life. I threw it aside, and never picked it up again. The attempt was premature. Then, ten years later, almost day for day, I felt the impulse return and began this book. You, I know, will read it sympathetically for many reasons. But I cannot expect the same favour from others.

This book is not the work of a professional novelist. It is, apparently, not a novel at all. Certain conventions of form and method in the novel have been erected, I gather, into immutable laws, and are looked upon with quite superstitious reverence. They are entirely disregarded here. To me the excuse for the novel is that one can do any damn thing one pleases. I am told I have done things as terrible as if you introduced asides and soliloquies into your plays, and came on to the stage in the middle of a scene to take part in the action. You know how much I should be interested if you did that—I am all for disregarding artistic rules of thumb. I dislike standardised art as much as standardised life. Whether I have been guilty of Expressionism or Super-realism or not, I don't know and don't care. I knew what I wanted to say, and said it. And I know I have not tried to be "original."

The technique of this book, if it can be said to have one, is that which I evolved for myself in writing a longish modern poem (which you liked) called "A Fool i' th' Forest." Some people said that was "jazz poetry"; so I suppose this is a jazz novel. You will see how appropriate that is to the theme.

I believe you at least will be sympathetic to the implied or expressed idealism of this book. Through a good many doubts and hesitations and changes I have always preserved a certain idealism. I believe in men, I believe in a certain fundamental integrity and comradeship, without which society could not endure. How often that integrity is perverted, how often that comradeship betrayed, there is no need to tell you. I disbelieve in bunk and despotism, even in a dictatorship of the intelligentsia. I think you and I are not wholly unacquainted with the intelligentsia?

Some of the young, they who will "do the noble things that we forgot," think differently. According to them, bunk must be parried by super-bunk. Sincerity is superannuated. It doesn't matter what you have to say; what matters is whether you can put it across successfully. And the only hope is to forbid everybody to read except a few privileged persons (chosen how and by whom?) who will autocratically tell the rest of us what to do. Well, do we believe that? I answer on your behalf as well as my own that we emphatically do not. Of course, these young men may be Swiftian ironists.

But, as you will see, this book is really a threnody, a memorial in its ineffective way to a generation which hoped much, strove honestly, and suffered deeply. Others, of course, may see it all very differently. Why should they not? I believe that all we claim is that we try to say what appears to be the truth, and that we are not afraid either to contradict ourselves or to retract an error.

Always yours,
RICHARD ALDINGTON.
Paris 1929.

Death of a Hero

PROLOGUE

MORTE D'UN ERÖE

allegretto

The casualty lists went on appearing for a long time after the Armistice—last spasms of Europe's severed arteries. Of course, nobody much bothered to read the lists. Why should they? The living must protect themselves from the dead, especially the intrusive dead. But the twentieth century had lost its Spring with a vengeance. So a good deal of forgetting had to be done.

Under the heading "Killed in Action," one of these later lists contained the words:

"Winterbourne, Edward Frederick George, A/Capt., 2/9 Battn. R. Foddershire Regt."

The small interest created by this item of news and the rapidity with which he was forgotten would have surprised even George Winterbourne; and he had that bottomless cynicism of the infantry subaltern which veiled itself in imbecile cheerfulness, and thereby misled a good many not very acute people. Winterbourne had rather hoped he would be killed, and knew that his premature demise in the middle twenties would be borne with easy stoicism by those who survived him. But his vanity would have been a little shocked by what actually happened.

A life, they say, may be considered as a point of light which suddenly appears from nowhere, out of the blue. The point describes a luminous geometrical figure in space-time; and then just as suddenly disappears. (Interesting to have seen the lights disappearing from Space-Time during one of the big battles—Death dowses the glims.) Well, it happens to us all; but our vanity is interested by the hope that the rather tangled and not very luminous track we made will continue to shine for a few people for a few years. I suppose Winterbourne's name does appear on some War Memorial, probably in the Chapel of his Public School; and, of course, he's got his neat ration of headstone in France. But that's about all. Nobody much minded that he was killed. Unassertive people with no money have few friends; and Winterbourne hadn't counted much on his scanty flock, least of all on me. But I know—because he told me himself—that he had rather relied on four people to take some interest in him and his fate. They were his father and mother, his wife and his mistress. If he had known what actually occurred with these four at the news of his death I think he would have been a little shocked, as well as heartily amused and perhaps a bit relieved. It would have freed him from certain feelings of responsibility.

Winterbourne's father, whom I knew slightly, was an inadequate sentimentalist. Mild, with an affectation of gentility, incompetent, selfishly unselfish (*i.e.* always patting himself on the back for "renouncing" something he was afraid to do or be or take), he had a genius for messing up other people's lives. The amount of irreparable harm which can be done by a really good man is astounding. Ten astute rogues do less. He messed up his wife's life by being weak with her; messed up his children's lives by being weak and sentimentalish with them and by losing his money—the unforgivable sin in a parent; messed up the lives of his friends and clients by honestly losing their money for them; and messed up his own most completely. That was the one thing he ever did with complete and satisfactory thoroughness. The mess he got his life into would have baffled an army of psychologists to unravel.

When I told Winterbourne what I thought of his father, he admitted it was mostly true. But he rather liked the man, probably disarmed by the mildness, and not sufficiently hard to his father's soft, selfish sentimentality. Possibly old Winterbourne would have felt and have acted differently in his reactions to George's death, if circumstances had been different. But he was so scared by the war, so unable to adjust himself to a harsh, intruding reality—he had spent his life avoiding realities—that he took refuge in a drivelling religiosity. He got to know some rather slimy Roman Catholics, and read the slimy religious tracts they showered on him, and talked and sobbed to the exceedingly slimy priest they found for him. So about the middle of the war he was "received," and found—let us hope—comfort in much prayer and Massgoing and writing rules for Future Conduct and rather suspecting he was like François de Sales and praying for the beatification of the super-slimy Thérèse of Lisieux.

Old Winterbourne was in London, "doing war work," when the news of George's death came. He would never have done anything so positive and energetic if he had not been nagged and goaded into it by his wife. She was animated less by motives of disinterested patriotism than by exasperation with him for existing at all and for interrupting her love affairs. Old Winterbourne always said with proud, sad dignity that his "religious convictions forbade" him to divorce her. Religious convictions are such an easy excuse for being nasty. So she found a war job for him in London, and put him into a position where it was impossible for him to refuse.

The telegram from the War Office—"regret to inform . . . killed in action. . . . Their Majesties' sympathy . . ."—went to the home address in the country, and was opened by Mrs. Winterbourne. Such an excitement for her, almost a pleasant change, for it was pretty dull in the country just after the Armistice. She was sitting by the fire, yawning over her twenty-second lover—the affair had lasted nearly a year—when the servant brought the telegram. It was addressed to Mr. Winterbourne, but of course she opened it; she had an idea that "one of *those* women" was "after" her husband, who, however, was regrettably chaste, from cowardice.

Mrs. Winterbourne liked drama in private life. She uttered a most creditable shriek, clasped both hands to her rather soggy bosom, and pretended to faint. The lover, one of those nice, clean, sporting Englishmen with a minimum of intelligence and an infinite capacity for being gulled by females, especially the clean English sort, clutched her unwillingly and automatically but with quite an Ethel M. Dell appearance of emotion, and exclaimed:

"Darling, what is it? Has *he* insulted you again?"

Poor old Winterbourne was incapable of insulting any one, but it was a convention always established between Mrs. Winterbourne and her lovers that Winterbourne had "insulted" her, when his worst taunt had been to pray earnestly for her conversion to the True Faith, along with the rest of "poor misguided England."

In low, moaning tones, founded on the best tradition of sensational fiction, Mrs. Winterbourne feebly ejaculated:

"Dead, dead, dead!"

"Who's dead? Winterbourne?"

(Some apprehension perhaps in the attendant Sam Browne—he would have to propose, of course, and might be accepted.)

"They've killed him, those vile, *filthy* foreigners. My *baby* son."

Sam Browne, still mystified, read the telegram. He then stood to attention, saluted (although not wearing a cap), and said solemnly:

"A clean, sportin' death, an *Englishman's* death."

(When Huns were killed it was neither clean nor sportin', but served the beggars—("*******," among men)—right.)

The tears Mrs. Winterbourne shed were not very natural, but they did not take long to dry. Dramatically, she ran to the telephone. Dramatically, she called to the local exchange:

"Trrrunks. (Sob.) Give me Kensington 1030. Mr. Winterbourne's number, you know. (Sob.) Our *darling* son—Captain Winterbourne—has been killed by those (sob) beasts. (Sob. Pause.) Oh, thank you *so* much, Mr. Crump, I *knew* you would feel for us in our trouble. (Sob. Sob.) But the blow is so sudden. I *must* speak to Mr. Winterbourne. Our hearts are *breaking* here. (Sobissimo.) Thank you. I'll wait till you ring me."

Mrs. Winterbourne's effort on the telephone to her husband was not unworthy of her:

"Is that you, George? Yes, Isabel speaking. I have just had *rather* bad news. No, about George. You must be prepared, darling. I fear he is seriously ill. What? No. *George.* GEORGE. Can't you hear? Yes, that's better. Now, listen, darling, you must prepare for a *great* shock. George is seriously ill. Yes, *our* George, our *baby* son. What? Wounded? No, not wounded, very *dangerously* ill. No, darling, there is little hope. (Sob.) Yes, darling, a telegram from the *King* and *Queen*. Shall I read it? You are prepared for the shock (sob), George, aren't you? 'Deeply regret . . . killed in action. . . . Their Majesties' sympathy. . . .' (Sob. Long pause.) Are you there, George? Hullo, hullo. (Sob.) Hullo, hullo. HULLO. (Aside to Sam Browne.) He's rung off! How that man *insults* me! how can I bear it in my sorrow? After I bad prepared him for the shock! (Sob. Sob.) But I have always had to *fight* for my children, while he squatted over his books—and *prayed*."

To Mrs. Winterbourne's credit, let it be said, she had very little belief in the value of prayer in practical affairs. But then, her real objection to religion was founded upon her dislike for doing anything she didn't want to do, and a profound hatred for everything distantly resembling thought.

At the fatal news Mr. Winterbourne had fallen upon his knees (not forgetting, however, to ring off the harpy), ejaculating: "Lord Jesus, receive his soul!" Mr. Winterbourne then prayed a good deal, for George's soul, for himself, for "my erring but beloved spouse," for his other children, "may they be spared and by Thy Mercy brought to the True Faith," for England (ditto), for his enemies, "though Thou knowest, Dear Lord Jesus, the enmity was none of my seeking, sinner though I be, mea culpa, mea culpa, mea maxima culpa, Ave Maria. . . ."

Mr. Winterbourne remained on his knees for some time. But, as the hall tiles hurt his knees, he went and knelt on a hassock at the *prie-dieu* in his bedroom. On the top of this was an open Breviary in very ecclesiastical binding with a florid ecclesiastical book-marker, all lying on an ecclesiastical bit of embroidery, the "gift of a Catholic sister in Christ." Above, on a bracket, was a coloured B.V.M. from the Place St. Sulpice, holding a nauseating Infant Jesus dangling a bloody and sunrayed Sacred Heart. Over this again was a large but rather cheap-looking imitation bronze Crucifix, with a reproduction (coloured) of Leonardo's *Last Supper* to the right, and another reproduction (uncoloured) of Holman Hunt's (heretical) *Light of the World* to the left. All of which gave Mr. Winterbourne the deepest spiritual comfort.

After dinner, of which he ate sparingly, thinking with dreary satisfaction how grief destroys appetite, he went round to see his confessor, Father Slack. He spent a pleasantly emotional evening. Mr. Winterbourne cried a good deal, and they both prayed; Father Slack said perhaps George had been influenced by his father's prayers and virtues and had made an act of contrition before he died; and Mr. Winterbourne said that although George had not been "received" he had "a true Catholic spirit" and had once read a sermon of Bossuet; and Father Slack said he would pray for George's soul, and Mr. Winterbourne left £5 for Masses for the repose of George, which was generous (if foolish), for he didn't earn much.

And then Mr. Winterbourne used to pray ten minutes longer every night and morning for George's soul, but unfortunately he went and got himself run over just by the Marble Arch as he was meditating on that blessed martyr, Father Parsons, and that other more blessed martyr, Father Garnet of Gunpowder fame. So, as the £5 was soon exhausted, there was nobody to pray for George's soul; and for all the Holy Roman and Apostolic Church knows or cares, poor old George is in Hell, and likely to remain there. But, after the last few years of his life, George probably doesn't find any difference.

So much for George's father and George's death. The "reactions" (as they are called) of Mrs. Winterbourne were different. She found it rather exciting and stimulating at first, especially erotically stimulating. She was a woman who constantly dramatised herself and her life. She was as avid of public consideration as an Italian lieutenant, no matter what the quality of the praise. The only servants who ever stayed more than a trial month with her were those who bowed themselves to an abject discipline of adulation for Mrs. Winterbourne, Mrs. Winterbourne's doings and sayings and possessions and whims and friends. Only, since Mrs. Winterbourne was exceedingly fickle and quarrelsome, and was always changing friends into enemies and vowed enemies into hollow friends, a more than diplomatic suppleness was exacted of these mercenary retainers, who only stayed with her because she gave them presents or raised their wages whenever the praise was really gratifying.

Although a lady of "mature charms," Mrs. Winterbourne

loved to fancy herself as a delicious young thing of seventeen, passionately beloved by a sheik-like but nevertheless "clean" (not to say "straight") Englishman. She was a mistress of would-be revolutionary platitudes about marriage and property (rather like the talk of an "enlightened" parson), but, in fact, was as sordid, avaricious, conventional, and spiteful a middle-class woman as you could dread to meet. Like all her class, she toadied to her betters and bullied her inferiors. But, with her conventionality, she was, of course, a hypocrite. In her kitten-ish moods, which she cultivated with a strange lack of a sense of congruity, she liked to throw out hints about "kicking over the traces." But, as a matter of fact, she never soared much above tippling, financial dishonesty, squabbling, lying, bet-ting, and affairs with bounderish young men whom only her romantic effrontery could have dared describe as "clean and straight," although there was no doubt whatever about their being English, and indeed sportin' in a more or less bounder-ish way.

She had had so many of these clean, straight young sheiks, that even poor Mr. Winterbourne got mixed up, and when he used to write dramatic letters beginning, "Sir,—You have robbed me of my wife's affection like a low hound—be it said in no un-Christian spirit," the letters were always getting addressed to the penultimate or ante-penultimate sheik, instead of the straight, clean one of the moment. However, rendered serious by the exhortations of the war Press and still more by the ever-ripening maturity of her charms, Mrs. Winterbourne made an instinctive and firm clutch at Sam Browne—so suc-cessfully that she clutched the poor devil for the remainder of his abbreviated life. (She did the abbreviation.) Sam Browne, of course, was almost too good to be true. If I hadn't seen him myself I should never have believed in him. He was an ani-mated—and not so very animated—stereotype. His knowl-edge of life was rudimentary to the point of being quadruped, and intelligence had been bestowed upon him with rigid parsi-mony. An adult Boy Scout, a Public School fag in shining armour—the armour of obtuseness. He met every situation in life with a formula, and no situation in life ever reached him except in the shape imposed upon it by the appropriate and predetermined formula. So, though he wasn't very successful at anything, he got along all right, sliding almost decorously down grooves which had nothing ringing about them. Unless urged, he never mentioned his wound, his decoration, or the fact that he had "rolled up" on August 4th. The modest, well-bred, etcetera, English gentleman.

The formula for the death of a married mistress's son was stern heroism, and gentle consolation to the wounded mother-heart. Mrs. Winterbourne played up at first—it was the sort of thing that the sheik always did with his passionate but tender love. But the effect of George's death on her temperament was, strangely enough, almost wholly erotic. The war did that to lots of women. All the dying and wounds and mud and bloodiness—at a safe distance—gave them a great kick, and excited them to an almost unbearable pitch of amorousness. Of course, in that eternity of 1914-18 they must have come to feel that men alone were mortal, and they immortals; where-fore they tried to behave like houris with all available sheiks—hence the lure of "war work" with its unbounded opportunities. And then there was the deep primitive physiological instinct—men to kill and be killed; women to produce more men to con-tinue the process. (This, however, was often frustrated by the march of Science, viz. anti-conceptives; for which, much thanks.)

So you must not be surprised if Mrs. Winterbourne's emo-tion at the death of George almost immediately took an erotic form. She was lying on her bed in an ample pair of white draw-ers with very long ruffles and a remarkably florid, if chaste, chemise. And the sheik, strong, silent, restrained, tender, was dabbing her forehead and nose with eau-de-cologne, while she took large sips of brandy at increasingly frequent intervals. It was, of course, proper and even pleasant to have her grief so much respected; but she did wish Sam hadn't to be poked always into taking the initiative. Couldn't the man see that tender nerves like hers needed to be soothed with a little Real Love *at once*?

"He was so much to me, Sam," she said in low, indeed trem-ulous tones, subtly calculated. "I was only a child when he was born—a child *with* a child, people used to say—and we grew up together. I was so young that I did not put up my hair until two years after he was born." (Mrs. Winterbourne's propaganda about her perennial youth was so obvious that it would hardly have deceived the readers of "John Blunt"—but the sheiks all fell for it. God knows how young they thought she was—probably imagined Winterbourne had "insulted" her when she was ten.)

"We were always together, such pals, Sam, and he told me everything."

(Poor old George! He had such a dislike for his mother that he hadn't seen her five times in the last five years of his life. And as for telling her anything—why, the most noble of noble savages would immediately have suspected *her*. She had let George down so badly time after time when he was a boy that he was all tight inside, and couldn't give confidence to his wife or his mistresses or a man.)

"But now he's gone"—and somehow Mrs. Winterbourne's voice became so erotically suggestive that even the obtuse sheik noticed it and was vaguely troubled—"now he's gone, I've nothing in the world but *you*, Sam. You heard how that vile man insulted me on the telephone to-day. Kiss me, Sam, and promise you'll always be a pal, a *real* pal."

Active love-making was not in the sheik's formula for that day; consolation there was to be, but the "sacredness" of mother-grief was not to be profaned by sexual intercourse; although that too, oddly enough, was "sacred" between a "clean" Englishman and a "pure" woman who had only had one husband and twenty-two lovers. But what can the Sam Brownes of the world do against the wills, especially the will to copulate, of the Mrs. Winterbournes? ** **** ********** ** *** *********. He, too, found a certain queer, perverse satisfaction in honeying and making love over a nasty corpse; while, if he had been capable of making the reflection, he would have realised that Mrs. Winterbourne was not only a sadist, but a necrophilous one.

In the succeeding weeks George's death was the source of other, almost unclouded, joys to Mrs. Winterbourne. She pardoned—temporarily—the most offending of her enemies to

increase the number of artistically tear-blotched letters of
bereavement she composed. Quite a few of the nearly gentry,
who usually avoided Mrs. Winterbourne as a particularly vir-
ulent specimen of the human scorpion, paid calls—very brief
calls—of condolence. Even the Vicar appeared, and was greeted
with effusive sweetness; for though Mrs. Winterbourne pro-
fessed herself a social rebel and an "Agnostic" (not, however,
until she had been more or less kicked out of middle-class and
Church society), she retained a superstitious reverence for parsons of the Established Church.

Another joy was squabbling with Elizabeth Winterbourne,
George's wife, about his poor little "estate" and military
effects. When George joined up, he thought he had to give his
father as his next-of-kin. Later, he found his mistake, and
when he went out to France the second time he gave his wife.
The War Office carefully preserved both records, either under
the impression that there were two George Winterbournes, or
because the original record was never erased and so became
law. At any rate, some of George's possessions were sent to the
country address, and, although directed to his father, were
unscrupulously seized by his mother. And the remainder of his
military kit and the pay due him went to his wife. Old Mrs.
Winterbourne was fearfully enraged at this. Stupid red tape,
she said it was. Why! wasn't her baby son *hers*? Hadn't she
borne him, and therefore established complete possession of
him and his for the rest of her natural life? What can any
woman mean to a *Man* in comparison with his *Mother*? Therefore, it was plain that she was the next-of-kin, and that all
George's possessions, including the widow's pension, should
come to her and her only: Q.E.D. She bothered her harassed
husband about it, tried to stimulate Sam Browne to action—
but he evaporated in a would-be straight, clean letter to
Elizabeth, who knocked him out in the first round—and even
consulted a lawyer in London. Old Mrs. Winterbourne came
back from London in a spluttering temper. "That man" (*i.e.*
her husband) had "insulted" her again, by timidly stating that
all George's possessions ought to be given to his wife, who
would doubtless allow them to keep a few "mementoes." And
the lawyer—foul brute—had un-sympathetically said that

George's wife had a perfect right to sue her mother-in-law for detaining her (Elizabeth's) property. George's will was perfectly plain—he had left everything he had to his wife. However, that small amount of George's property which his mother got hold of she kept, in defiance of all the King's horses and writs. And she took, she embraced, the opportunity of telling "that woman" (*i.e.* Elizabeth) what she thought of her—which, if believed, meant that poor Elizabeth was a composition of Catherine of Russia, Lucrezia Borgia, Mme. de Brinvilliers, Moll Flanders, a *tricoteuse*, and a hissing villainess from the Surrey side.

But George only lasted his mother as a source of posthumous excitement for about two months. Just as the quarrel with Elizabeth reached stupendous heights of vulgar invective (on her side), old Winterbourne got himself run over. So there was the excitement of the inquest and a real funeral, and widow's weeds and more tear-blotched letters. She even sent a tear-blotched letter to Elizabeth, which I saw, saying that "twenty years"—it was really almost thirty—"of happy married life were over, both father and son were now happily united, and, whatever Mr. Winterbourne's faults, he was a *gentleman*." (Heavily underlined and followed by several exclamation marks, the insinuation being apparently that Elizabeth was no lady.)

A month later Mrs. Winterbourne married the sheik—alas, no sheik now!—at a London registry office, whence they departed to Australia to live a clean, sportin' life. Peace be with them both—they were too clean and sportin' for a corrupt and unclean Europe.

George's parents, of course, were grotesques. When, in a mood of cynical merriment, he used to tell his friends the exact truth about his parents, he was always accused—even by quite intelligent people—of creating a monstrous legend. Unless all the accepted ideas about heredity and environment are false—which they probably are—it is a regular mystery of Udolpho how George managed to be so different from his parents and the family *milieu*. Physically he looked like them both—in every other respect, he might have dropped from the moon for all the resemblance he had to them. Perhaps they

seemed so grotesque because neither of them could adjust to
the tremendous revolution in everything, of which the war was
a cause or symptom. The whole immense drama went on in
front of their noses, and they never perceived it. They only
worried about their rations. Old Winterbourne also worried a
good deal about "the country," and wrote letters of advice to
The Times (which didn't publish them), and then rewrote them
on Club notepaper to the Prime Minister. They were invariably politely acknowledged by a secretary. But Mrs. Winterbourne only cared spasmodically about "the country." Her
view of the British Empire was that it should continue the war
as a holy crusade for the extermination of all "filthy, vile foreigners," making the world safe for straight, clean sheiks and
pure, sweet, kittenish Englishwomen of fifty. Grotesques
indeed, fanciful, unbelievable, like men's fashions of 1840. To
me, who only saw them a few times, either in company with
George or as his executor, they seemed as fantastic, as ridiculous, as prehistoric as the returning *émigrés* seemed to Paris in
1815. Like the Bourbons, the elder Winterbournes learned
nothing from the war, and forgot nothing. It is the tragedy of
England that the war has taught its Winterbournes nothing,
and that it has been ruled by grotesques and a groaning Civil
Service of disheartened men and women, while the young have
simply chucked up the job in despair. *Gott strafe England* is a
prayer that has been fully answered—by the insanity of retain-
ing the old Winterbourne grotesques and pretending they are
alive. And we go on acquiescing, we go on without even the guts
to kick the grotesque Aunt Sallies of England into the Limbo
they deserve. *Pero, paciencia. Mañana. Mañana. . . .*

I think that George committed suicide in that last battle of the
war. I don't mean shot himself, but it was so very easy for a
company commander to stand up when an enemy machine-
gun was traversing. The situation he had got into with Elizabeth and Fanny Welford was not inextricable, but it would
have needed a certain amount of patience and energy and
determination and common sense to put right. But by November '18 poor old George was whacked, whacked to the wide.
He was a bit off his head, as nearly all the troops were after six

months in the line. Since Arras (April '17) he had lived on his
nerves, and when I saw him at the Divisional Rest Camp in
October '18 he struck me as a man who was done for, used up.
He ought to have gone to the Brigadier and got sent down for
a bit. But he was so horribly afraid of being afraid. He told me
that last night I saw him that he was afraid even of whizz-bangs
now, and that he didn't see how he would face another barrage. But he was damned obstinate, and insisted on going back
to the battalion, although he knew they were due for another
battle. We lay awake half the night, and he went over Elizabeth
and Fanny and himself, and himself and Fanny and Elizabeth,
until it was such a nightmare, such a portentous House of
Atrides tragedy, that I began to think myself that it was hopeless. There was a series of night-bombing attacks going on,
and we lay in the darkness on sacking-beds, muttering to each
other—or rather George went on and on muttering, and I tried
to interrupt and couldn't. And every time a bomb fell anywhere near the camp, I could feel George start in the darkness.
His nerves were certainly all to pieces.

Elizabeth and Fanny were not grotesques. They adjusted to the
war with marvellous precision and speed, just as they afterwards adapted themselves to the post-war. They both had that
rather hard efficiency of the war and post-war female, veiling
the ancient predatory and possessive instincts of the sex under
a skilful smoke-barrage of Freudian and Havelock Ellis theories. To hear them talk theoretically was most impressive.
They were terribly at ease upon the Zion of sex, abounding in
inhibitions, dream symbolism, complexes, sadism, repres-
sions, masochism, Lesbianism, sodomy, etcetera. Such wise
young women! you thought; no sentimental nonsense about
them. No silly emotional slip-slop messes would ever come *their*
way. They knew all about the sexual problem, and how to set-
tle it. There was the physical relationship and the emotional
relationship and the intellectual relationship; and they knew
how to manage all three, as easily as a pilot with twenty years'
experience brings a handy ship to anchor in the Pool of London. They knew that freedom, complete freedom, was the only
solution. The man had his lovers, and the woman had hers.

But where there was a "proper relationship," nothing could break it. Jealousy? it was impossible that so primitive a passion could inhabit those enlightened and rather flat bosoms. Female wiles and underhand tricks? Insulting to make such a suggestion. No, no. Men must be "free" and women must be "free."

Well, George had simple-Simonly believed all this. He "had an affair" with Elizabeth, and then he "had an affair" with Fanny, her best friend. George thought they ought to tell Elizabeth. But Fanny said why bother? Elizabeth *must* know instinctively, and it was so much better to trust to the deeper instincts than to talk about things with "the inferior intelligence." So they said nothing to Elizabeth, who didn't know instinctively, and thought that George and Fanny were "sexually antipathetic." That was just before the war. But in 1914 something went wrong with Elizabeth's period, and she thought she was going to have a baby. And then, my hat, what a pother! Elizabeth lost her head entirely. Freud and Ellis went to the devil in a twinkling. No more talk of "freedom" *then*! If she had a baby, her father would cut off her allowance, people would cut her, she wouldn't be asked to Lady Saint-Lawrence's dinners, she . . . Well, she "went at" George in a way which threw him on his beam-ends. She made him use up a lot of money on a special licence, and they were married at a Registry office in the presence of Elizabeth's parents, who were also swept bewildered into this sudden match, they knew not how or why. Elizabeth's father had feebly protested that George hadn't any money, and Mrs. Winterbourne senior wrote a marvellous, tear-blotched, dramatic epistle, in which she said that George was a feeble-minded degenerate who had broken his mother's tender heart and insultingly trampled upon it, in a low, sensual lust for a vile woman who was only "after" the Winterbourne money. As there wasn't any Winterbourne money left, and the elder Winterbournes lived on tick and shifts, the accusation was, to say the least, fanciful. But Elizabeth bore down all opposition, and she and George were married.

After the marriage, Elizabeth breathed again and became almost human. Then and only then did she think of consulting a doctor, who diagnosed some minor female malady, told her to "avoid cohabitation" for a few weeks, and poofed with laughter at her pregnancy. George and Elizabeth took a flat in Chelsea, and within three months Elizabeth was just as "enlightened" as before and fuller of "freedom" than ever. Relieved by the doctor's assurance that only an operation could enable her to have a child, she "had an affair" with a young man from Cambridge, and told George about it. George was rather surprised and peeved, but played the game nobly, and most gallantly yielded the flat up for the night whenever Elizabeth dropped a hint. Of course, he didn't suffer as much deprivation as Elizabeth thought, because he invariably spent those nights with Fanny.

This went on until about the end of 1915. George, though attractive to women, had a first-rate talent for the malapropos in dealing with them. If he had told Elizabeth about his affair with Fanny at the moment when she was full-flushed with the young man from Cambridge, she would no doubt have acquiesced, and the thing would have been smoothed over. Unluckily for George, he felt so certain that Fanny was right and so certain that Elizabeth was right. He was perfectly convinced that Elizabeth knew all about him and Fanny, and that if they didn't speak of it together the only reason was that "one took such things for granted," no need to "cerebrise" about them. Then one night, when Elizabeth was getting tired of the young man from Cambridge, she was struck by the extraordinary alacrity George showed in "getting out."

"But, darling," she said, "isn't it very expensive always going to an hotel? Can we afford it? And don't you mind?"

"Oh no," said the innocent George; "I shall run round and spend the night with Fanny as usual, you know."

Then there was a blazing row, Elizabeth at George, and then Fanny at George, and then—epic contest—Elizabeth at Fanny. Poor old George got so fed up, he went off and joined the infantry, fell into the first recruiting office he came to, and was whisked off to a training camp in the Midlands. But, of course, that didn't solve the situation. Elizabeth's blood was up, and Fanny's blood was up. It was Achilles against Hector, with George as the body of Patroclus. Not that either of them so horribly wanted George, but it was essential to each to come off victorious and "bag" him, with the not improbable epilogue of dropping him pretty quickly after he had been "bagged" away from the other woman. So they each wrote him tender and emotional and "understanding" letters, and sympathised with his sufferings under military discipline. Elizabeth came down to the Midlands to bag him for week-ends; and then one week when she was "having an affair" with a young American in the Flying Corps, George got his "firing leave" and spent it with Fanny. George was a bit obtuse with women. He was very fond of Elizabeth, but he was also very fond of Fanny. If he hadn't been taken in with the "freedom" talk and had kept Elizabeth permanently in the dark about Fanny, he might have lived an enviable double life. Unfortunately for him, he couldn't, and never did, see that the "freedom" talk was only talk with the two women, although it was real enough to him. So he wrote them both the most imbecile and provocative letters, praised Elizabeth to Fanny, and Fanny to Elizabeth, and said how much he cared for them both; and he was like Shelley, and Elizabeth was like Mary, and Fanny was like Emilia Viviani. And he went on doing that even in France, right up to the end. And he never even suspected what an ass he was.

Of course, George had not set foot on the boat which took him to the Boulogne Base-Camp for the first time, before both Elizabeth and Fanny had become absorbed in other "affairs." They only fought for George in a desultory way as a symbol, more to spite each other than because they wanted to saddle themselves with him.

Elizabeth was out when her telegram came from the War Office. She did not get it until nearly midnight, when she came back to the flat with a fascinating young Swedish painter she had met at a Chelsea "rag" that evening. She was a bit sozzled, and the young Swede—tall, blond, and handsome—was more than a little fired with love and whisky. The telegram was lying on the door-mat with two or three letters. Elizabeth picked them up, and opened the telegram mechanically as she switched on the electric light. The Swede stood watching her drunkenly and amorously. She could not avoid a slight start, and turned a little pale.

"What's the matter?"

Elizabeth laughed her high little nervous laugh, and laid the telegram and letters on the table.

"The War Office regrets that my husband has been killed in action."

It was now the Swede's turn to be startled.

"Your husband? . . . Perhaps I'd better . . ."

"Don't be a bloody fool," said Elizabeth sharply; "he went out of my life years ago. *She'll* mind, but I shan't."

She cried a bit in the bathroom, however; but the Swede was certainly a very attentive lover. They drank a good deal of brandy, too.

Next day Elizabeth wrote to Fanny the first letter she had sent her for months:

> "Only a line, darling, to tell you that I have a telegram from the W.O. to say George was killed in France on the 4th. I thought it would be less of a shock for you to hear it from me than accidentally. Come and see me when you get your weeps over, and we can hold a post-mortem."

Fanny didn't reply to the letter. She had been rather fond of George, and thought Elizabeth heartless. But Elizabeth too had been fond of George; only, she wasn't going to give it away to Fanny. I saw a good deal of Elizabeth while settling up George's scanty estate—mostly furniture and books in the flat, his credit at Cox's, a few War Bonds, a little money due to him from civilian sources, and Elizabeth's pension. However, it meant a certain amount of letter-writing, which Elizabeth was glad to have me do. I also saw Fanny once or twice, and took her the trifles George had left her. But I never saw the two women together—they avoided each other; and when my duties as executor were done, I saw very little of either. Fanny went to Paris in 1919, and soon married an American painter. I saw her in the Dome one night in 1924, pretty well rouged and quite nicely dressed, with a party. She was laughing and flirting with a middle-aged American—possibly an art patron—and didn't look as if she mourned much for George. Why indeed should she?

As for Elizabeth, she rather went to pieces. With her father's allowance, which doubled and became her own income when he died, and her widow's pension, she was quite well off as poor people of the "artistic" sort go. She travelled a good deal, always with a pretty large brandy-flask, and had more lovers than were good for her—or them. I hadn't seen her for years, until about a month ago I ran into her on the corner of the Piazzetta in Venice. She was with Stanley Hopkins, one of these extremely clever young novelists who oscillate between women and homosexuality. He had recently published a novel so exceedingly clever, so stupendously smart and up-to-date and witty and full of personalities about well-known people, that he was quite famous, especially in America, where all Hopkins's brilliantly quacking and hissing and kissing geese were taken as melodious swans and (*vide* Press) as a "startling revelation of the corruption of the British Aristocracy." We went and had ices together, all three, at Florian's; and then Hopkins went off to get something, and left us together for half an hour. Elizabeth chattered very wittily—you had to be witty with Hopkins or die of shame and humiliation—but never mentioned George. George was a drab bird from a drab past. She told me that she and Hopkins would not marry; they had both determined never to pollute themselves with the farce of "legalised copulation," but they would "probably go on living with each other." Hopkins, who was a very rich young man as well as a successful novelist, had settled a thousand a year on her, so that they could both be "free." She looked as nearly un-miserable as our cynical and battered generation can look; but she still had the brandy-flask.

Like a fool, I allowed myself to be persuaded to drink liqueur brandies after dinner that evening; and paid for it with a sleepless night. No doubt it was the unexpected meeting with Elizabeth which made me think a lot about George during those ghastly wakeful hours. I can't claim that I had set up any altar to the deceased George in my heart, but I truly believe that I am the only person left alive who ever thinks of him. Perhaps because I was the only person who cared for George for his own sake, disinterestedly. Naturally, his death meant very little to me at the time—there were eighty deaths in my own battalion on the day George was killed, and the Armistice and getting out of the blasted Army and settling my own problems and starting civilian life again and getting to work, all occupied my attention. In fact, it was not until two or three years after the war that I began to think much, if at all, about George. Then, although I didn't in the least believe in it, I got a half-superstitious, half-sentimental idea that "he" (poor old bag of decaying bones) wanted me to think about him. I half knew, half guessed that the people on whom he had counted had forgotten him, at least no longer cared that he had existed, and would have been merely surprised and rather annoyed if he had suddenly come back, like one of those shell-shocked heroes of fiction who recover their wits seven years after the Armistice. His father had taken it out in religiosity, his mother in the sheik, Elizabeth in "unlicensed copulation" and brandy, and Fanny in tears and marrying a painter. But I hadn't taken it out in anything, I hadn't been conscious that George's death meant anything in particular to me; and so it was waiting inside patiently to be dealt with in due course.

Friendships between soldiers during the war were a real and beautiful and unique relationship which has now entirely vanished, at least from Western Europe. Let me at once disabuse the eager-eyed Sodomites among my readers by stating emphatically once and for all that there was nothing sodomitical in these friendships. I have lived and slept for months, indeed years, with "the troops," and had several such companionships. But no vaguest proposal was ever made to me; I never saw any signs of sodomy, and never heard anything to make me suppose it existed. However, I was with the fighting troops. I can't answer for what went on behind the lines.

No, no. There was no sodomy about it. It was just a human relation, a comradeship, an undemonstrative exchange of sympathies between ordinary men racked to extremity under a great common strain in a great common danger. There was nothing dramatic about it. Bill and Tom would be in the same section, or Jones and Smith subalterns in the same company. They'd go on fatigues and patrols together, march behind each other on trench reliefs, booze at the same estaminet, and show each other the "photos" of "Ma" and "my tart," if Tommies. Or they'd meet on trench duty, and volunteer for the same trench raid, and back up each other's lies to the inspecting Brigadier, and share a servant, and stick together in a battle, and ride together when on rest and talk shyly about their "fiancées" or wives in England, if officers. When they separated, they would be glum for a bit, and then, in the course of a month or two or three, strike up another friendship. Only, the companionship was generally a real one, pretty unselfish. Of course, this sort of friendship was stronger in France than in England, more vivid in the line than out of it. Probably a man must have something to love—quite apart from the "love" of sexual desire. (Prisoners are supposed to love rats and spiders.) Soldiers, especially soldiers overseas in the last war, entirely cut off from women and friends, had perforce to love another soldier, there being no dogs available. Very few of these friendships survived the Peace.

After several months in France and a month's leave, I felt pretty glum when I was sent to an Officer's Training Camp in a beautiful but very remote part of Dorset. I was mooning about in a gloomy way before my first dinner as a potential though temporary gentleman, when I ran into another fellow similarly mooning. He was George, who had been seen off that day from Waterloo by Elizabeth and Fanny (although I did not then know it), and who was also feeling very glum about it. We exchanged a few words, found we were both B.E.F. (most of the others were not) and that we were allotted to the same barrack-room. We found we had certain tastes in common, and we became friends.

I liked George. For one thing, he was the only person in the whole of that hellish camp with whom I could exchange one word on any topic but booze, "tarts," "square-pushing," smut, the war, and camp gossip. George was very enthusiastic about modern painting. His own painting, he told me, was "pretty dud," but in peace time he made a good living by writing art criticism for various papers and by buying modern pictures, chiefly French and German, on commission for wealthy collectors. We lent each other books from our scanty store, and George was quite thrilled to know that I had published one or two little books of poetry and had met Yeats and Marinetti. I talked to him about modern poetry, and he talked to me about modern painting; and I think we helped to keep each other's "souls" alive. In the evenings we played chess or strolled about, if it was fine. George didn't go square-pushing with tarts, and I didn't go square-pushing with tarts. So on Saturday afternoons and Sundays we took long walks over that barren but rather beautiful Dorset down country, and had a quiet dinner with a bottle of wine in one or other of the better country inns. And all that kept up our own particular "morale," which each of us had determined not to yield to the Army swinishness. Poor George had suffered more than I. He had been more bullied as a Tommy, had a worse time in France, and suffered horribly from that "tightness" inside, that inability to confide himself, induced by his singular home life and appalling mother. I feel quite sure he told me more about himself, far more, than he ever told any one else, so that eventually I knew quite a lot about him. He told me all about his parents and about Elizabeth and Fanny, and about his childhood and his life in London and Paris.

As I say, I liked George, and I'm grateful to him because he helped me to keep alive when a legion of the swine were trying to destroy me. And, of course, I helped him. He had a strong dose of shyness—his mother had sapped his self-confidence abominably—which made him seem rather conceited and very aloof. But *au fond* he was extraordinarily generous, spontaneous, rather Quixotish. It was that which made him so helpless with women, who neither want nor understand Quixotic behaviour and scrupulousness, and who either think they mean weakness or are veils for some devilish calculation. But with another man, who wanted nothing from him but a frank exchange of friendliness, he was a charming and inexhaustible companion. I was damned glad to get my commission and leave that stinking hole of a Camp, but I was really sorry to part from George. We agreed to write, and applied for commissions in the same regiment. Needless to say, we were gazetted to completely different regiments from those we had applied for. We exchanged one or two letters while waiting in depôts in England, and then ceased writing. But by an odd freak of the War Office we were both sent to different battalions in the same Brigade. It was nearly two months before we found this out, when we met by accident at Brigade Headquarters.

I was rather startled at George's appearance, he looked so worried and almost scared. I saw him on reliefs or at Brigade H.Q. or at Divisional Rest Camp several times. He looked whacked in May '18. In July the Division moved down to the Somme, but George's company front was raided the night before we left, and he was badly rattled by it. I had watched the box barrage from the top of Battalion H.Q. dugout (I was then signal officer), but I never thought that George was in it. He lost several men as prisoners, and the Brigadier was a bit nasty about it, which made George more rattled and jumpy than ever. I told him then that he ought to apply for a rest, but he was in an agony of feeling that he was disgraced and a coward, and wouldn't listen to me.

The last time I saw him was at Hermies, in October '18, as I mentioned before. I had come up from a course and found George had been "left out" at Divisional Rest Camp for that tour. There were some sacking-beds in the Orderly room, and George got me one. He talked on in the dark for what seemed hours during the air-raids, and I really thought he was demented. Next morning we rejoined our battalions, and I never saw him again.

George was killed soon after dawn on the 4th November 1918, at a place called Maison Blanche, on the road from Le Cateau to Bavay. He was the only officer in his battalion killed in that action, for the Germans surrendered or ran away in less than an hour. I heard about it that night, and, as the Brigade was "resting" on the 5th, I got permission from my Colonel to ride back to George's funeral. I heard from George's Colonel that he had got enfiladed by a machine-gun. The whole of his company were lying down, waiting for the flying trench-mortar squad to deal with the machine-gun, when for some unexplained reason George had stood up, and a dozen bullets had gone through him. "Silly ass," was the Colonel's comment, as he nodded and left me.

No coffins were available, so they wrapped George in a blanket and the Union Jack. The parson stood at the head of the grave, a mourning party of Tommies and N.C.O.'s from his company on one side, and, facing them, the officers of his battalion. I was on the extreme left of the line. The Chaplain read the military burial service in a clear voice, and read it well. There was very little artillery fire. Only one battery of our own heavies, about a mile nearer the enemy, was shelling at regular intervals like a last salute. We stood to attention, and the body was lowered. Each of the officers in turn stepped up to the graveside, saluted and turned away. Then the battalion buglers blew that soul-shattering, heart-rending Last Post, with its inexorable chains of rapid, sobbing notes and drawn-out piercing wails. I admit I did a lot of swallowing those few minutes. You can say what you like against the Army, but they treat you like a gentleman, when you're dead. . . . The Tommies were numbered, formed fours, right turned and marched away; and the officers strolled over to the mess for a drink. . . .

The death of a hero! What mockery, what bloody cant! What sickening, putrid cant! George's death is a symbol to me of the whole sickening bloody waste of it, the damnable stupid waste and torture of it. You've seen how George's own people—the makers of his body, the women who held his body to theirs— were affected by his death. The Army did its bit, but how could the Army individually mourn a million "heroes"? How could the little bit of Army which knew George mourn him? At dawn next morning we were hot-foot after the retreating enemy, and did not pause until the Armistice—and then we had our own lives to struggle with and disentangle.

That night in Venice, George and his death became a symbol to me—and still remain a symbol. Somehow or other we have to make these dead acceptable, we have to atone for them, we have to appease them. How, I don't quite know. I know there's the Two Minutes' Silence. But after all, a Two Minutes' Silence once a year isn't doing much—in fact, it's doing

nothing. Atonement—how can we atone? How can we atone
for the lost millions and millions of years of life, how atone for
those lakes and seas of blood? Something is unfulfilled, and
that is poisoning us. It is poisoning me, at any rate, though I
have agonised over it, as I now agonise over poor George, for
whose death no other human being has agonised. What can
we do? Headstones and wreaths and memorials and speeches
and the Cenotaph—no, no; it has got to be something *in* us.
Somehow we must atone to the dead—the dead, murdered,
violently-dead soldiers. The reproach is not from them, but in
ourselves. Most of us don't know it, but it is there, and poisons
us. It is the poison that makes us heartless and hopeless and
lifeless—us, the war generation, and the new generation too.
The whole world is blood-guilty, cursed like Orestes, and mad,
and destroying itself, as if pursued by an infinite legion of
Eumenides. Somehow we must atone, somehow we must free
ourselves from the curse—the blood-guiltiness. We must find—
where? how?—the greater Pallas who will absolve us on some
Acropolis of Justice. But meanwhile the dead poison us and
those who come after us.

That is why I am writing the life of George Winterbourne, a
unit, one human body murdered, but to me a symbol. It is an
atonement, a desperate effort to wipe off the blood-guiltiness.
Perhaps it is the wrong way. Perhaps the poison will still be in
me. If so, I shall search for some other way. But I shall search.
I know what is poisoning me. I do not know what is poisoning
you, but you are poisoned. Perhaps you too must atone.

PART I

I

A very different England, that of 1890, and yet curiously the
same. In some ways so fabulous, so remote from us; in others
so near, terrifyingly near and like us. An England morally buried in great foggy wrappings of hypocrisy and prosperity and
cheapness. The wealth of that England, the maritime power of
that England, its worse than R. L. S. optimism, its righteous
cant! Victoria, broad-bottomed on her people's will; the pos-
sessing class, heavy-bottomed on the people's neck. The working class beginning to heave restively, but still Moody and
Sankeyish, still under the Golden Rule of "Ever remember, my
dear Bert, you may one day be manager of that concern." The
middle classes, especially the traders, making money hand
over fist, and still "praying that our unexampled prosperity
may last." The aristocracy still pretty flip, keeping its tail up.
Still lots of respect for Rank and Property—Dizzy not long
dead and his novels not yet grotesques, not yet wholly a fossil
parody. The intellectuals æsthetic and Oscarish, or æsthetic
and Burne-Morrisy, or Utilitarian and Huxley-Darwinish.

Come where the booze is cheaper.

Where I could live on a pound a week in lux-u-ry.

The world is so full of a number of things, I am *sure* we
should ALL be as Happy as KINGS.

Consols over par.

Lord Claud Hamilton and White at the Admiralty, building,
building, building.

Building a majestic ruin.

George Moore an elegant scandal in a hansom; Hardy a rural
atheistic scandal, not yet discovered to be an intolerable bore;
Oscar prancing negligently, O so clever! O so la-di-dah!

Rummy old England. Pox on you, you old bitch, you've made worms' meat of us. (We've made worms' meat of ourselves.) But still, let me look back upon thee. Timon knew thee.

The Winterbournes were not gentry, but nourished vague and unfounded traditions of past genteel splendours. They were, however, pretty comfortable middle-class. Worcestershire, migrated to Sheffield. Methodist on female side; C. of E. on the Winterbourne side. Young George Augustus—father of our George—was pretty comfortable. His mother was a dominating old bitch who destroyed his initiative and courage, but in the 'eighties hardly any one had the sense to tell dominating bitch-mothers to go to hell. George Augustus didn't. At fifteen he wrote a Nonconformist tract (which was published) expressing nothing but his dear Mamma's views. He became top of his school, in conformity with dear Mamma's views also. He did not go to Oxford, as he wanted, because dear Mamma thought it unpractical. And he did pass his examinations as a lawyer, because dear Mamma thought it so eminently right that he should have a profession and that there should be a lawyer in the family. George Augustus was a third son. The eldest son became a Nonconformist parson, because dear Mamma had prayed for guidance on her marriage night and during her first pregnancy (only, she never mentioned such horrid occurrences, even to her husband, but—she had "prayed for guidance"), and it had been revealed to her that her firstborn must take up The Ministry. And take it up, poor devil, he did. The second son had a little bit of spunk, and his dear Mamma made him a waster. Remained George Augustus, dear Mamma's darling chick, who prayed at her knee, and was flogged regularly once a month by dear Papa, because the Scripture says: Spare the rod, spoil the child. Dear Papa had never done anything in particular, lived on his "means," was generally rather in debt, and spent the last fifteen years of his life praying to the C. of E. God in the garden, while dear Mamma prayed to John Wesley's God in her bedroom. Dear Mamma admired dear, pious Mr. Bright and grand Mr. Gladstone; but dear Papa collected and even read all the Works of the Right Hnble. the Earl of Beaconsfield, K.G.

Still, George Augustus was pretty comfortable. The one thing he wanted in life was to be pretty comfortable. After he became a full-blown solicitor, at the age of twenty-four, a family council was held. Present: Dear Mamma, dear Papa, George Augustus. Nothing formal, *of course*, just a cosy little family gathering after tea, round the blazing hearth (coal was cheap in Sheffield then), rep curtains drawn, and sweet domestic peace. Dear Papa opened the proceedings:

"George, you are now come to man's estate. At considerable sacrifice, your dear Mamma and I have given you a Profession. You are an Admitted Solicitor, and we are proud—I think we may say 'proud,' Mamma?—that we have a legal luminary in the family . . ."

But dear Mamma could not allow dear Papa even the semblance of authority, respected not even the forms of Limited Domestic Monarchy, and cut in:

"Your Papa is right, George. The question is now, what are you going to *do* in your Profession?"

Did a feeble hope of escape cross the bright young mind of George Augustus? Or was that supine love of being pretty comfortable, added to the terror of disobeying dear Mamma, already dominant? He murmured something about "getting in with a respectable and old-established firm in London." At the word "London" dear Mamma bridled. Although Mr. Gladstone spent much of his time in London, it was notorious in Sheffield Nonconformist circles that London was a haunt of vice, filled with theatres and unmentionable women. Besides, dear Mamma was not going to let George Augustus off so easily; she still meant he should plough a deuce of a long furrow of filial obedience.

"I cannot hear of *London*, George. It would break my heart and bring your dear Papa's grey hairs" (dear Papa hated to be reminded that he was bald) "in sorrow to the grave, if you went to the *bad* in that dreadful town. Think how we should feel if we heard you had visited a *theatre*! No, George, we shall not fail in our duty. We have brought you up to be a God-fearing Christian man . . ." *et patata et patati*.

The upshot was, of course, that dear George Augustus did not go to London. He didn't even get an office of his own in

Sheffield. It was agreed that George Augustus would never marry (except for a whore or two, furtively and ineffectually possessed on furtive ineffectual sprees in London, George Augustus was a virgin), but would spend his life with dear Mamma, and (afterthought) dear Papa. So some structural alterations were made in the house. Another entrance was made, with a new brass plate engraved in copperplate:

G. A. WINTERBOURNE SOLICITOR

Three rooms, somewhat separated from the rest of the house, were allotted to George Augustus—a bedroom, an "Office," and a "cosy study." Needless to say, George Augustus did very little practice, except when his dear Mamma in an access of ambition procured him the job of making the will of some female friend or of drawing up the conveyance of the land for a new Wesleyan Chapel. What George Augustus did with most of his time is a bit of a puzzle—twiddled his thumbs, and read Dickens and Thackeray and Bulwer and George Augustus Sala mostly.

This lasted three or four years. Dear Mamma had her talons deep into George Augustus, vamped on him hideously; and was content. Dear Papa prayed in the garden and read the Right Hnble. etcetera's novels, and was uneasily content. George Augustus was pretty comfortable, and thought himself rather a hell of a boy because he occasionally sneaked off to a play or a whore, and bought some of the Vizetelly books on the sly. But there was one snag dear Mamma had not foreseen. Dear Papa had been fairly decently educated and brought up; he had, when a young man, travelled annually for several weeks, and had seen the Fields of Waterloo, Paris, and Ramsgate. After he married dear Mamma, he had to be content with Malvern and Ramsgate, for he was never allowed again to behold that wicked Continent. However, such is the force of Tradition, George Augustus was annually allowed a month's holiday. In 1887 he visited Ireland; in 1888, Scotland; in 1889, the Lake District, with "pilgrimages" to the "shrines" of those unblemished geniuses, Wordsworth and Southey. But in 1890 George Augustus went to "rural Kent," with "pilgrimages" to the Dingley Dell country and to the "shrine" of Sir Philip Sidney. But there were sirens awaiting our Odysseus in rural Kent. George Augustus met Isabel Hartly, and, before he knew where he was, had arranged irrevocably a marriage with her— *without* telling dear Mamma. *Hic incipit vita nova.* Thus was George, young George, generated.

The Hartlys must have been more fun than the Winterbournes. The Winterbournes had never done a damn thing in their lives, and were as stuffily, frowsily, mawkish-religiously boring as a family could be and still remain—I won't say alive or even sentient, but—able to digest their very puddingly meals. The Hartlys were different. They were poor Army. Pa Hartly had chased all round the Empire, dragging with him Ma Hartly, always in pod and always pupping in incongruous and inconvenient spots—the Egyptian desert, a shipwrecked troopship, a malarial morass in the West Indies, on the road to Kandahar. They had an inconceivable number of children, dead, dying, and alive, of all ages and sexes. Finally, old Hartly settled down near his wife's family in rural Kent, with a smallish pension, a tiny "private" income, and the world of his swarming progeny on his less than Atlantean shoulders. I believe he had had two or three wives, all horribly fertile. No doubt the earlier Mrs. Hartlys had perished of superfluous childbearing, "superfœtation of τὸ ἕν."

Isabel Hartly was one—don't ask which in numerical order, or by which wife—of Captain Hartly's daughters. She was very pretty, in a florid, vulgarish way, with her artful-innocent dark eyes, and flashing smiles, and pretty little bustle and frills, and "fresh complexion" and "abounding health." She was fascinatingly ignorant, even to the none too sophisticated George Augustus. And she had a strength of character superior even to dear Mamma's, added to a superb, an admirable vitality, which bewitched, bewildered, electrified the somewhat sluggish and pretty comfortable George Augustus. He had never

met any one like her. In fact, dear Mamma had never allowed
him to meet any one but rather soggy Nonconformists of
mature years, and "nice" youths and maidens of exemplary
Nonconformist stupidity and lifelessness.

George Augustus fell horribly in love.

He abode at the village inn, which was cheap and pretty
comfortable; and he did himself well. On these holidays he
had such a mood of exultation (subconscious) in getting away
from dear Mamma that he felt like a hero in Bulwer Lytton.
We should say he swanked; probably the early 'nineties would
have said he came the masher. He certainly mashed Isabel.

The Hartlys didn't swank. They made no effort to conceal
their poverty or the vulgarity imported into the family by the
third (or fourth) Mrs. Hartly. They were fond of pork, and
gratefully accepted the gifts of vegetables and fruit which the
kind-hearted English country-people force on those they know
are none too well off. They grew lots of vegetables and fruit
themselves, and kept pigs. They made blackberry jam and
damson jam, and scoured the country for mushrooms; and the
only "drink" ever allowed in the family was Pa Hartly's "drop
o' grog" secretly consumed after the innumerable children had
gone to bed in threes and fours.

So it wasn't hard for George Augustus to swank. He took
the Hartlys—even Isabel—in completely. He talked about
"my people" and "our place." He talked about his Profession.
He gave them copies of the Nonconformist tract he had published at fifteen. He gave Ma Hartly a fourteen-pound tin of
that expensive (2s. 3d. a pound) tea she had always pined for
since they had left Ceylon. He bought fantastic things for
Isabel—a coral brooch, a copy of the *Pilgrim's Progress* bound
in wood from the door of Bunyan's parish church, a turkey, a
year's subscription to the *Family Herald Supplement*, a new
shawl, boxes of 1s. 6d. a pound chocolates, and took her for
drives in an open landau smelling of horse-piss and oats.

The Hartlys thought he was "rich." George Augustus was
so very comfortable and *exalté* that he too really thought he
was "rich."

One night, a sweet rural night, with a lemon moon over the

sweet, breast-round, soft English country, with the nightin-
gales jug-jugging and twit-twitting like mad in the leafy lanes,
George Augustus kissed Isabel by a stile, and—manly fellow—
asked her to marry him. Isabel—she had a pretty fiery temperament even then—had just sense enough not to kiss back and
let him know that other "fellows" had kissed her, and perhaps
fumbled further. She turned away her pretty head with its
Pompadour knot of dark hair, and murmured—yes, she did,
because she *had* read the stories in the *Quiver* and the *Family
Herald*:

"O Mr. Winterbourne, this is so unexpected!"

But then her common sense and the eagerness to be "rich"
got the better of her *Quiver* artificiality, and she said, oh so
softly and moderately:

"*Yes!*"

George Augustus quivered dramatically, clasped her, and
they kissed a long time. He liked her ever so much more than
the London whores, but he didn't dare do any more than kiss
her, and exclaim:

"Isabel! I love you. Be mine. Be my wife and build a home
for me. Let us pass our lives in a delirium of joy. Oh that I need
not leave you to-night!"

On the way home Isabel said:

"You must speak to father to-morrow."

And George Augustus, who was nothing if not the gent,
replied:

> "I could not love thee, dear, so much,
> Loved I not honour more."

Next morning, according to schedule, George Augustus
called on Pa Hartly with a bottle of 3s. 6d. port and a leg of
fresh pork; and after a good deal of hemming and blushing and
talking round the subject (as if old Hartly hadn't heard from
Isabel what was coming!), formally and with immense solem-
nity applied for the job of supporting Isabel for the rest of his
and her natural lives.

Did Pa Hartly refuse? Did he hesitate? Eagerly, gratefully,

effusively, enthusiastically, he granted the request. He slapped George Augustus on the shoulder, which military expression of goodwill startled and slightly annoyed the prim George Augustus. He said George Augustus was a man after his own heart, the man he would have chosen to make his daughter happy, the man he longed to have as a son-in-law. He told two barrack-room stories, which made George Augustus exquisitely uneasy; drank two large glasses of port; and then launched out on a long story about how he had saved the British Army when he was an Ensign during the Crimea. George Augustus listened patiently and filially; but as hour after hour went by and the story showed no signs of ending, he ventured to suggest that the good news should be broken to Isabel and Ma Hartly, who (unknown to the gentlemen) were listening at the keyhole in an agony of impatience.

So they were called in, and Pa Hartly made a little speech founded on the style of old General Snooter, K.C.B., and then Pa kissed Isabel, and Ma embraced Isabel tearfully but enthusiastically and admiringly, and Pa pecked at Ma, and George Augustus kissed Isabel; and they were left alone for half an hour before "dinner"—1.30 P.M., chops, potatoes, greens, a fruit suet-pudding, and beer.

The Hartlys still thought George Augustus was "rich."

But before he left rural Kent he had to write home to his father for ten pounds to pay his inn bill and his fare. He told dear Papa about Isabel, and asked him to break the news to dear Mamma. "An old Army family," George Augustus wrote, and "a sweet, pure girl who loves me dearly and for whom I would fight like a TIGER and willingly lay down my life." He didn't mention the poverty and the vulgarity and the catch-as-catch-can atmosphere of the Hartly family, or the innumerable progeny. Dear Papa almost thought George Augustus was marrying into the gentry.

Dear Papa sent George Augustus his ten pounds, and broke the news to dear Mamma. Strangely enough, she did not cut up as rough as you might have expected. Did she feel the force of Isabel's character and determination even at that distance? Had she a suspicion of the furtive whoring, and did she think

it better to marry than to burn? Perhaps she thought she could
vamp George Augustus's wife as well as George Augustus, and
so enjoy two victims.

She wept a bit and prayed more than ever.

"I think, Papa," she said, "that the Hand of Providence
must have led Augustus. I hope Miss Isabel will make him a
good wife, and not be too grand with her Army ways to darn
his socks and overlook the maids. Of course, the young couple
must live here, and I shall be able to give kindly guidance to
their early married life as well as religious instruction to the
bride. I pray GOD may bless them."

Dear Papa, who was not a bad sort, said "Umph," and
wrote George Augustus a very decent letter, promising him
£200 to start married life, and suggesting that the honeymoon
should take place either in Paris or on the Plains of Waterloo.

The wedding took place in spring in "rural Kent." A lot of
Winterbournes, including, of course, George's parents, came
down. Dear Mamma was horribly shocked, not to say disgusted, by the *unseemly* behaviour of the Hartlys; and even
dear Papa was a bit staggered. But it was then too late to
retreat with honour.

A village wedding in 1890! Gods of our fathers known of
old, what a sight! Alas, that there were no cinemas then! Can't
you see it? Old men in bug-whiskers and top-hats; old ladies in
bustles and bonnets. Young men in drooping moustaches,
"artistic" flowing ties, and probably grey toppers. Young
women in small bustles and small flowery hats. And brides-
maids in white. And a best man. And George Augustus a bit
sweaty in a new morning suit. And Isabel, of course, "radiant"
in white and orange-blossoms. And the parson, and signing
the register, and the wedding-breakfast, and the double peal
on the bells, and the "going away." . . . No, it's too painful, it's
so horrible it isn't even funny. It's indecent. I'm positively sorry
for George Augustus and Isabel, especially for Isabel. What
said the bells? "Come and see the ✳✳✳✳✳✳. Come and see the
✳✳✳✳✳✳✳."

But Isabel enjoyed the whole ghastly ceremony, little beast.

She wrote a long description of it to one of her "fellows," whom she really loved but had jilted for George Augustus's "riches."

". . . It was a cloudy day, but as we knelt at the altar a long ray of sunshine came through the church window and rested lovingly on our bowed heads. . . ."

How could they rise to such bilge? But they did, they did, they did. And they believed in it. If only they'd had their tongues in their cheeks there might have been some hope. But they hadn't. They believed in the sickish, sweetish, canting bilge; they believed in it. Believed in it with all the superhuman force of ignorance.

Can one tabulate the ignorances, the relevant ignorances, of George Augustus and Isabel when they pledged themselves until death do us part?

George Augustus did not know how to make a living; he did not know in the very least how to treat a woman; he did not know how to live with a woman; he did not know how to make love to a woman—in fact, he was all minus there, for his experience with whores had been sordid, dismal, and repulsive; he did not know the anatomy of his own body, let alone the anatomy of a woman's body;

*   *   *   *   *   *

he did not know that pregnancy is a nine-months' illness; he had not the least idea that childbirth costs money if the woman is not to suffer vilely; he did not know that a married man dependent on his and his wife's parents is an abject, helpless, and contemptible figure; he did not know that it is hard to earn a decent living even when you have "a Profession"; he knew damn little about even his profession; he knew very little indeed about the conditions of life and nothing about business and about money, except how to spend it; he knew nothing about indoor sanitation, food values, carpentry, house-furnishing, shopping, fire-lighting, chimney-sweeping, higher mathematics, Greek, domestic invective, making the worse appear the better cause, how to feed a baby, music, dancing, Swedish drill, opening sardine-tins, boiling eggs, which side of the bed to sleep with a woman, charades, gas stoves, and an infinity of other things all indispensable to a married man.

He must have been rather a dull dog.

As for Isabel—what she didn't know includes almost the whole range of human knowledge. The puzzle is to find out what she *did* know. She didn't even know how to buy her own clothes—-Ma Hartly had always done that for her. Among the things she did not know were: How babies are made and come; how to make love; how to pretend she was enjoying it even when she wasn't; how to sew, wash, cook, scrub, run a house, purchase provisions, keep household accounts, domineer over a housemaid, order a dinner, dismiss a cook, know when a room was clean, manage George Augustus when he was in a bad temper, give George Augustus a pill when he was liverish, feed and wash a baby and pin on its napkins, pay and receive calls, knit, crochet, make pastry, how to tell a fresh herring is stale, the difference between pork and veal, never to use margarine, how to make a bed comfortable, look after her health, especially in pregnancy, produce the soft answer which turneth away wrath, keep the home fires burning, and an infinity of other things indispensable to a married woman.

(I really wonder how poor old George managed to get born at all.)

On the other hand, both George Augustus and Isabel knew how to read and write, pray, eat, drink, wash themselves, and dress up on Sundays. They were both pretty well acquainted with the Bible and Hymns A. and M.

And then they had luv. They "luved" each other. Luv was enough, luv covered a multitude of ignorances, luv would provide, luv would strew their path with roses and primroses. Luv and God. Failing Luv there was God, and failing God there was Luv. I suppose, orthodoxly, God ought to come first, but in an 1890 marriage there was such a lot of Luv and God that there was no room for common sense, or common sex knowledge, or any of the knowledge we vile modern decadents think necessary in men and women. Sweet Isabel, dear George Augustus! They were *so* young, *so* innocent, *so* pure. And what hell do you think is befitting the narrow-minded, slush-gutted, bug-whiskered or jet-bonneted he- and she-hypocrites who sent them to their doom? O Timon, Timon, had I thy rhetoric! Who dares, who dares in purity of manhood stand upright, and say . . . ? Let me not rave, sweet gods, let me not rave!

The honeymoon did not take place in Paris or on the Plains of Waterloo, but in a South Coast watering-place, a sweetly pretty spot Isabel had always wanted to visit. They had a ten-mile drive from the village to the railway, and a two hours' journey in a train which stopped at every station. They arrived tired, shy, and disappointed at the small but respectable hotel where a double room had been booked.

The marriage night was a failure. One might *almost* have foreseen it. George Augustus tried to be passionate and ecstatic, and merely succeeded in being clumsy and brutal. Isabel tried to be modestly yielding and complying, and was only *gauche*. ✳✳✳ ✳✳✳✳✳✳✳✳ ✳ ✳✳✳✳ ✳✳✳✳ ✳✳✳✳ ✳✳✳✳✳✳ ✳✳✳✳✳✳✳✳ ✳✳✳✳✳✳✳ ✳✳✳✳✳✳✳✳✳✳✳✳✳. And, as many a sweet Victorian bride of dear old England in the golden days of Good Queen Vicky, she lay awake hour after hour, while George Augustus slept stertorously, thinking, thinking, while the tears ran out of her eyes, as she lay on her back, and trickled slowly down her temples on to the bridal pillow. . . .

It's too painful, it's really too painful—all this damn silly "purity" and cant and Luv and ignorance. And silly, ignorant girls handed over in their ignorance and sweetly-prettiness to ignorant and clumsy young men for them to brutalise and wound in their ignorance. It's too painful to think of. Poor Isabel! What an initiation!

But, of course, that ghastly night had its consequences. In the first place, it meant that the marriage was legally consummated, and could not be broken without an appeal to the Divorce Courts—and I don't know if you could even get divorced in the golden days of grand old Mr. Gladstone, bless his heart, may hell be hot for him. And then it meant that Isabel shrank from sexual intercourse with George Augustus for the rest of her days; and, since she was a woman of considerable temperament, *that* implied the twenty-two lovers already stirring in the womb of futurity. And finally, since Isabel was as healthy as a young woman could be who had to wear madly tight corsets and long insanitary hair and long insanitary skirts, and who had rudimentary ideas of sex hygiene—finally, that *nuit de rêve* gave Isabel her first baby.

2

The baby was christened Edward Frederick George—Edward after the Prince of Wales (later H.M. King Edward VII), Frederick after his grandfather, George after his father.

Isabel wanted to call him George Hartly, but dear Mamma saw to it that there was as little Hartly as possible about *her* grandson.

The early years of the Isabel George Augustus *ménage* are really very dismal to contemplate. Largely because it was forced upon them by their elders and social convention, they began on a basis of humbug; unfortunately, they continued on a basis of humbug. Not only were they shattered by the awful experience of the wedding-night, but they were a good deal bored by the honeymoon generally. There wasn't much to do at Isabel's sweetly-pretty watering-place. George Augustus wouldn't admit even to himself that he was about as competent to be a husband as to teach white mice to perform military evolutions. Isabel knew in herself that they had begun with a ghastly failure, knew it with her instincts rather than her mind, but she had her pride. She knew perfectly well that failure would be attributed to her, and that she could expect no sympathy from any one, least of all her own family. Wasn't she "happily" married to a man who "luved" her—a "luv" match—and to a "rich" man? So Isabel consoled herself with the thought that George Augustus was "rich," and they both wrote ecstatic humbugging honeymoon letters to families and friends. And once they had started on the opposite road to honesty and facing facts, they were dished for life—condemned, they too, to the dreary landscape of humbug and "luv." Oh that God and Luv business! Isn't it mysterious that Isabel didn't take warning from the wretched cat-and-dog life of Ma and Pa, and that George Augustus hadn't noticed the hatred which surged between dear Mamma and dear Papa under the viscid surface of domestic peace and religion; and that they didn't try to break away to something a little better? But no; they accepted the standards, they had *Luv* and they had *God*, so of course all would be for the best in this best of all possible worlds.

George Augustus continued to play at being "rich" on his honeymoon. A week before his wedding he was allowed a banking account for the first time in his life. Dear Papa paid in £200, and, by arrangement with George Augustus, dear Mamma was made to believe it was £20. To this dear Mamma added a generous £5 from her own jointure, "a little nest-egg for a rainy day"—though what on earth you want with a "nest-egg" on "a rainy day," God and Luv only know. So the happy young couple started out with £205, and not the slightest chance of earning a penny until George Augustus gave up being "rich" and "pretty comfortable" and settled down to face facts and do a little work.

They spent a good deal—for them—on the honeymoon. George Augustus had a purse containing a lot of sovereigns and two £5 notes, with which he swanked intolerably. Isabel had never seen so much money at once and thought George Augustus was richer than ever. So she immediately began sending "useful presents" to the innumerable members of the impoverished Hartly family; and George Augustus, though annoyed— for he was fundamentally mean—let her. Altogether they spent £30 in a fortnight, and the first-class fares back to Sheffield left mighty little change out of another £5 note.

The first great shock of Isabel's life was her wedding-night. The second was when she saw the dingy little, smoke-blacked house of the "rich" Winterbournes, one of a row of highly desirable, yellow-brick, ten-roomed villas. The third was when she found that George Augustus earned nothing by his Profession, that he had no money but the balance of his £205, and that the Winterbournes were nearly as poor as the Hartlys.

Ghastly days that poor girl spent in that dreary little house during her first pregnancy, while George Augustus twiddled his thumbs in "the Office" (instead of in his "cosy study" as in his bachelor days) under pretence of "working"; while dear Papa prayed, and dear Mamma acid-sweetly nagged and humiliated her. Ghastly days when her morning sickness was treated as "a bilious attack."

"Too much rich food," said dear Mamma; "of course, darling Isabel, *you* were not used to such a plentiful table at home,"— and then playful-coyly-cattish—"we must really ask your dear husband to use his *authority* to restrain your appetite."

In fact, the Hartlys, in a scratchy, vulgarish way, enjoyed much more ample and varied food than that provided by dear Mamma's cheeseparing, genteelly meagre table.

Then, of course, there were rows. Isabel revolted, and displayed signs of that indomitable personality and talent for violent invective she afterwards developed to such Everest peaks of unpleasantness. Even dear Mamma found her match, but not before she had made Isabel miserably wretched for nearly two years and had permanently warped her character. Blessings upon you, dear Mamma, you "prayed for guidance," you "did all for the best"—and you made Isabel into a first-class bitch.

George Augustus was pained, deeply pained and surprised, by these rows. He was still pretty comfortable, and couldn't see why Isabel wasn't.

"Let us continue to be a loving, united family," he would say, "let us bear with one another. We all have our burdens"— (*e.g.* thumb-twiddling and reading novels)—"and all we need is a little more Luv, a little more Forbearance. We must pray for Strength and Guidance."

At first Isabel took these homilies pretty meekly. She believed she had to "respect" her husband, and she was still a little intimidated by George Augustus's superior Bulwer Lytton airs. But one day she lost her not very well-controlled temper

and let the Winterbournes have it. George Augustus was a
sneak and a cad and a liar! He wasn't "rich"! He was "pore as
a church mouse"! Him and his airs, pretending to her father
he was a rich gentleman with a Profession, when he didn't
earn a penny and got married on the £200 his father gave him!
She wouldn't have married him, she wouldn't, if he hadn't
come smarming round with his presents and his drives and
pretending she would be a lady! And she wished she was dead,
she did! And she wished she'd never set eyes on them!

Then the fat was in the fire! Dear Mamma took up the tale.
Reserving *in petto* a denunciation of the guilt-stricken and
consternated father and son in the matter of their deception
over the £200, she directed a skilful enfilade fire on the disarmed Isabel. Isabel was vulgar and irreligious, she was ill-bred
and uneducated, she was mercenary on her own showing, and
had ruined the hopeful life of George Augustus by seducing
him into a disastrous marriage. . . .

At that moment Isabel fainted, and most unfortunately for
our George the threatened miscarriage was averted—thanks
more to Isabel's health and vitality than to the ministrations of
her inept husband and in-laws. Only dear Papa was genuinely
distressed, and used what shred of influence he had to protect
Isabel. As for George Augustus, he simply collapsed, and did
nothing but ejaculate:

"Dear Mamma! Isabel! Let us be loving and united. Let us
bear one another's burdens!"

But he was swept away in the torrent of genuine hatred
revealed by this instructive scene. Even dear Mamma dropped
her Nonconformist tract hypocrisy, and only picked it up
again when Isabel fainted.

On dear Papa's suggestion George Augustus took Isabel away
to the seaside on what was left of the £200; and thus it happened that George was born in a seaside hotel.

It was a difficult birth, clumsily doctored. Isabel suffered
tortures for nearly forty hours. If she had not been as strong as
a young mare, she would inevitably have died. During this
agonising labour, George Augustus prayed freely, took short
walks, read *Lorna Doone*, had a half-bottle of claret with his

lunch and dinner, and slept tranquilly o' nights. When, finally, he was admitted on tiptoe to a glance at the half-dead woman with the horrid little packet of red infant by her side, he—raised his hand and gave them his blessing. He then tiptoed down to dinner, and ordered a whole bottle of claret in honour of the event.

3

Isabel and George Augustus depress me so much that I am anxious to get rid of them. On the other hand, it is impossible to understand George unless you know his parents. And then the older Winterbourne *ménage* rather fascinated me, with a fascination of loathing and contempt. I cannot help wondering how they could have been such ignorant fools, how they came to make so little effort to break free from the humbug, how less than nothing they cared about being themselves. Of course, I tell myself that our own magnanimous nephews will ask themselves precisely the same questions about *us*; but then I also tell myself that they must see we *did* struggle, we did fight against the humbug and the squelching of life and the worn-out formulæ, as young George fought. Perhaps Isabel did fight a little, but the forces of inertia and active spite were too much for her. Perhaps the twenty-two lovers and the talk about Agnosticism and Socialism (of which Isabel at all periods of her life knew rather less than nothing) were a sort of protest. But she was beaten by the economic factor—by the economic factor *and* the child. You can say what you please, but poverty and a child will quench any woman's instinct for self-development and self-assertion—or turn it sour. It turned Isabel's sour and sharp. As for George Augustus, I doubt if he had any instincts left, except the instinct to be pretty comfortable. Whatever he achieved in and with his life was entirely the product of Isabel's will and Isabel's goading. He was a born mucker. And, since Isabel was ignorant, self-willed, and over-ambitious, and turned sour and sharp under the tender mercies of dear Mamma, she came a mucker too—through George

Augustus. Yet I have far more sympathy for Isabel than for George Augustus. She was at least the wreck of a human being. He was a thumb-twiddler, a harmless praying-Mantis, a zero of no value except in combination with her integer.

When Isabel was well enough to travel—perhaps a little before—they, who had gone out two, returned home three. They had acquired the link which divides. They had become a "family," the eternal triangle of father, mother, child, which is so much more difficult and disagreeable and hard to deal with, and so much more productive of misery, than the other triangle of husband, wife, lover. After nine months of intimacy, Isabel and George Augustus were just getting used to each other and the "luv" situation, when this new complication appeared. Isabel was instinctively aware that yet another readjustment was needed, and, through her, George Augustus became dimly apprehensive that something was going on. So he prayed earnestly for Guidance, and all the way from the South Coast to Sheffield urged Isabel to remember that they must be a loving and united family, that they must bear one another's burdens, that they had "Luv" but must acquire "Forbearance." I don't wish—Heaven forfend!—that I had been in Isabel's place, but I should have liked to reply for five minutes on her behalf to George Augustus's angel-in-the-house, idiot-in-the-world cant.

So they returned three, and there was much sobbing and praying, and asking for guidance, and benediction of the unconscious George. (He was too little to make a long nose at them—let us do it for him, as his posthumous godfathers and godmothers.) Isabel's thwarted sex and idealism and ambition, her physical health and complete lack of intellectual complexity, made her an excellent mother. She really loved that miserable little packet of babydom begotten in disappointment and woe by George Augustus and herself in a hired bedroom of a dull hotel in a dull little town on the dull South Coast of dull England. She lavished herself on the infant George. The child tugging at her nipples gave her a physical satisfaction a thousand times more acute and exquisite than the clumsy caresses of George Augustus. She was like an animal with a cub.

George Augustus might swank to dear Papa that he would "fight for dear Isabel like a TIGER," but Isabel really would have fought, and did fight, for her baby, like a hot-headed, impetuous, pathetic, ignorant cow. If that was any achievement, she saved young George's life—saved him for a German machine-gun.

For a time there was peace in the smoke-blacked little house in Sheffield. Isabel was obviously still very weak. And the first grandson was an event. Dear Papa was enchanted with young George. He bought five dozen bottles of port to lay down for George's twenty-first birthday, and then began prudently drinking them at once "to see that they were the right vintage." He gave George Augustus £50 he hadn't got. He gave young George his solemn, grandfatherly, and valedictory blessing every night when Isabel put the infant to bed.

"God *will* bless him," said dear Papa impressively. "God will bless *all* my children *and* my posterity," as if he had been Abraham or God's Privy Councillor, as indeed he probably thought he was.

Even dear Mamma was quelled for a time. "A little che-ild shall lead them," she quoted venomously; and George Augustus wrote another Nonconformist tract on loving and united families, taking these holy and inspiring words as his text.

The first four years of George's life passed in a welter of squabbling, incompetence, and poverty, of which he was quite unconscious, though what harm was done to his subconscious would take a better psychologist than I to determine. I imagine that the combined influence of dear Papa, dear Mamma, Ma and Pa Hartly, George Augustus, and Isabel started him off on the race of life with a pretty heavy handicap weight. I should say that George was always an outsider in the Tattersall's Ring of Life—about 100 to 7 against. However, one can but stick to the events as closely as possible, and leave the reader to form conclusions and lay his own odds.

Before George was six months old the rows had begun again in the Sheffield house, and this time more virulently and fiercely than ever. Dear Mamma felt she was fighting for her authority and John Wesley against the intruder. Isabel was

fighting for herself and her child and—though she didn't know
it—any vestige of genuine humanity there might have been in
George Augustus.

About that time George Augustus became really intolerable.
A man he had known as a law student returned to Sheffield,
bought a practice, and did rather well. Henry Bulburry came it
over George Augustus pretty thick. He had spent three years
in a London solicitor's office, and to hear him talk you would
have thought Mr. Bulburry was the Lord Chancellor, the Beau
Brummell, and the Count d'Orsay of the year 1891. Bulburry
patronised George Augustus, and George Augustus lapped his
patronage up gratefully. Bulburry knew all the latest plays,
all the latest actresses, all the latest books. He roared with
laughter at George Augustus's Dickens and *Lorna Doone*, and
introduced him to Morris, Swinburne, Rossetti, Ruskin, Hardy,
Mr. Moore, and young Mr. Wilde. George Augustus got fearfully excited, and became an æsthete. Once when Pater came
to lecture at Sheffield he was so much moved at the spectacle
of those wonderful moustaches that he fainted, and had to be
taken home in a four-wheeler. George Augustus at last found
his *métier*. He realised that he was a dreamer of dreams born
out of his due time, that he should have floated Antinoüs-like
with the Emperor Hadrian to the music of flutes and viols on
the subtly-drifting waters of the immemorial Nile. Under a
canopy of perfumed silk he should have sat enthroned with
Zenobia while trains of naked, thewed Ethiopian slaves, glis-
tening with oil and nard, laid at his feet jewels of the opulent
East. He was older than the rocks among which he sat. He was
subtler than delicate music; and there was no change of light,
no shifting of the shadows, no change in the tumultuous outlines of wind-swept clouds, but had a meaning for him. Baby-
lon and Tyre were in him, and he too wept for beautiful Bion.
In Athens he had reclined, violet-crowned, at the banquet
where Socrates reasoned of love with Alcibiades. But above
all, he felt a stupendous passion for mediæval and Renaissance
Florence. He had never been to Italy, but he was wont to boast
that he had studied the plan of the city so carefully and so frequently that he could find his way about Florence blindfold.
He knew not one word of Italian, but he spoke ecstatically of

Dante and "his Circle," criticised the accuracy of Guicciardini, refuted Machiavelli, and was an authority—after Roscoe—on the life and times of Lorenzo and Leo X.

One day George Augustus announced to the family that he should abandon his Profession and WRITE.

There may be little differences in an English family, for the best of friends fall out at times, but in all serious crises they may be depended upon to show a united front. Thank God, there can still be no doubt about it—apart from pure literature of the sheik brand and refining pictures in the revived Millais tradition, an English family can still be relied upon to present a united front against any of its members indulging in the obscene pursuits of Literature or Art. Such things may be left to the obscene Continent and our own degenerates and decadents, though it would be well if stern methods were adopted by the police to cleanse our public life of the scandal brought upon Us by the latter. The great English middle-class mass, that dreadful squat pillar of the nation, will only tolerate art and literature that are fifty years out of date, eviscerated, detesticulated, bowdlerised, humbuggered, slip-slopped, subject to their anglicised Jehovah. They are still that unbroken rampart of Philistia against which Byron broke himself in vain, and which even the wings of Ariel were inadequate to surmount. So, look out, my friend. Hasten to adopt the slimy mask of British humbug and British fear of life, or expect to be smashed. You may escape for a time. You may think you can compromise. You can't. You've either got to lose your soul to them or have it smashed by them. Or you can exile yourself.

It was probably worse in the days of George Augustus, and anyway he was only a grotesque and didn't much matter. Still, the vitality of Isabel was real and should have found an outlet instead of being forced back into her and turned into a sharp, sour poison. And the pathetic efforts of George Augustus to be an æsthete and WRITE meant something, some inner struggle, some effort to create a life of his own. It was an evasion, of course, a feeble, flapping desire to escape into a dream world; but if you had been George Augustus, living under the sceptre of dear Mamma in the Sheffield of 1891, you too would have

yearned to escape. Isabel opposed this new freak of George
Augustus, because she also wanted to escape. And for her,
escape was only possible if George Augustus earned enough
money to take her and her baby away. She thought the Pre-
Raphaelites rather nonsensical and drivelling—and she wasn't
far wrong. She thought Mr. Hardy very gloomy and immoral,
and Mr. George Moore very frivolous and immoral, and
young Mr. Wilde very unhealthy and immoral. But her reading in the works of all these immortals was very sketchy and
snatchy—what really animated her was her immovable instinct
that George Augustus's only motive in life henceforth should
be to provide for her and her child, and to get them away from
Sheffield and dear Mamma.

Dear Papa and dear Mamma also thought these new crazes
of George Augustus nonsensical and immoral. Dear Mamma
read the opening pages of one of Mr. Hardy's novels, and then
burned the Obscene Thing in the kitchen copper. Whereupon
there was a blazing row with George Augustus. Backed by the
malicious Bulburry (who hated dear Mamma so much that he
put several little bits of business he didn't want into the hands
of George Augustus, who thereby made about £70 in six
months), George Augustus, who had never stood up for himself or his own integrity or Isabel or anything that mattered,
stood up for Mr. Hardy and his own false pathetic pose of
æstheticism. George Augustus locked all his priceless new
books into a cupboard, of which he jealously kept the key.
And he spent hours a day locked in his "cosy study" WRITING,
while the enraged thunder of the offended family rolled impo-
tently outside. But George Augustus was firm. He bought arty
ties, and saw Bulburry nearly every evening, and went on WRIT-
ING. Bulburry was so malevolent that he persuaded a friend,
who was editing an amateurish æsthetic review in London, to
publish an article by George Augustus entitled "The Wonder
of Cleopatra throughout the Ages." George Augustus got a
guinea for the article, and for a week the family was hushed
and awed.

But in that atmosphere of exasperation and dread of the
Unknown Obscene, rows were inevitable. And, since George
Augustus remained almost hermetically sealed in his cosy

study, and refused to come out and be rowed with, even when
dear Mamma tapped imperiously at the door and reminded
him, through the panels, of his Duties to God, his Mamma,
and Society, the rows inevitably took place between dear
Mamma and Isabel.

One night, after George Augustus was asleep, Isabel got up
and stole £5 from his sovereign-purse. Next morning, she took
the baby for a walk as usual, but took it to the railway station
and fled to the Hartly home in rural Kent. This was certainly
not the boldest thing Isabel ever did—she afterwards did
things of incredible rashness—but it was one of the most sensible, from her point of view. It was the first of her big efforts
to force George Augustus to action. It reminded him that he
had taken on certain responsibilities, and that responsibilities
are realities which cannot always be avoided. She bombed him
out of the dug-out of dear Mamma's tyranny, and eventually
Archied him out of the empyrean of æstheticism and writing.

But she didn't let herself or George Augustus down to the
Hartly family. She reckoned—and reckoned rightly—that
George Augustus would follow her up pretty smartly, for fear
of "what people would say." So she sent a telegram to Pa and
Ma to say she was coming to see them for a few days—they
were pretty well accustomed to Isabel's impulsive moves by
this time—and she left a note, a dramatic and naturally (not
artistically) tear-stained note for George Augustus on the bedroom dressing-table. She took a few inexpensive presents
home, and played her part so well that at first even Ma Hartly
only vaguely suspected that something was wrong.

The loving and united home at Sheffield was in some conster-
nation when Isabel did not return for lunch; and the consterna-
tion almost became panic—it certainly became rage in dear
Mamma—when George Augustus found and communicated
Isabel's letter.

"She must be found and brought back here at once," said dear
Mamma decisively, already scenting carnage from afar; "she has
disgraced herself, disgraced her husband, and disgraced the family. I have long noticed that she is inattentive at family prayers.
She must be given a good lesson. It was an ill day for us all when

Augustus married so far beneath him. He must go and fetch her back from her low, vulgar family—to think of our dear little George being in such *immoral* surroundings!"

"Suppose she won't come?" said dear Papa, who had suffered so many years from dear Mamma that he had a fellow-feeling for Isabel.

"She must be *made* to come," said dear Mamma. "Augustus! You must do your duty and assert your authority as a *Husband*. You must leave to-night."

"But what will people *say?*" murmured George Augustus dejectedly.

At those fatal words even dear Mamma flushed beneath the pallor of fifty years' bad temper and cloistered malevolence. What would people say? What would people say! What indeed! What would the Minister say? What would Mrs. Standish say? And Mrs. Gregory? And Miss Stint, who was another Minister's niece? And Cousin Joan, who had an eye like a brace of buzzards, and a nose for scandal and other carrion which would have been surprising in a starving condor of the Andes? What would they say? Why, they would say that young Mrs. Winterbourne had run away with a ticket-collector on the G.W.R. They would say young George had turned out to have a touch of the tar-brush owing to the prolonged residence of Captain and Mrs. Hartly in the West Indies; and that, consequently, Mrs. Winterbourne and the infant had been spirited away "to a home." They would say that there was a "dreadful disease" in the Winterbourne family, and that Isabel had run away with an infected baby. They would also say things which, being nearer the truth, would be even more painful. They would say that dear Mamma had plagued Isabel beyond the verge of endurance—and so she had run away, with or without an accomplice. They would say that George Augustus was unable to support his family, and that Isabel had grown tired of thumb-twiddling and "all this nonsense about books." They would say—what would they not say? And the Winterbournes, unique in this among human beings, were sensitive to "what people said."

So when George Augustus said dejectedly, "What will people

say?" even the ranks of Tuscany—viz. dear Mamma—were
for a moment dismayed. But that undaunted spirit (which has
made the Empire famous) soon rallied, and dear Mamma
evolved a plan, and issued orders with a precision and clarity
which may be recommended to all Brigadiers, Battalion, Company, and Platoon commanders. The maids must be told at
once that Mrs. Winterbourne had been unexpectedly called
home by the illness of her father—which was immediately
done; but as the maids had been listening with delighted eagerness to the conference in the parlour, that bit of camouflage
was not very effective. Then dear Mamma would pay a round
of visits that afternoon, and casually let drop that "dear Isabel" had been unexpectedly etcetera; to which she would add
negligently that an "important conveyance" had detained her
son in Sheffield until the next morning, when he would follow
his wife—"such a devoted couple, and only my daughter-in-
law's earnest entreaties could prevail upon my dear son not to
neglect this important business to act as her cavalier." Then,
George Augustus would leave next morning for rural Kent,
and would hale Isabel home like the husband of patient Grissel, or some other hero of romance.

All of which was carried out according to schedule, with
one important exception. When George Augustus unexpectedly walked into the multitudinous and tumultuous Saturday
dinner of the Hartly family—loin of fresh pork, greens, potatoes, apple sauce, fruit suet-pudding, but no beer this time—
he found no patient Grissel awaiting him. And his very
impatient and aggrieved Grissel was backed up by an equally
aggrieved family, who by now had wormed out of her by no
means reticent mind something of the truth. The Hartlys were
simply furious with George Augustus for not being "rich."
The way he had come it over them! The way he had mashed
Isabel with his 1s. 6d. a pound chocolates! The way dear
Mamma had put on her airs of righteous disapproval at Captain Hartly's little jokes about a fellah in India (Ha! ha!) and a
couple of native women (He! he!)! The intolerable way in
which dear Papa had come it about '64 port and Paris and the
Plains of Waterloo! And after the Hartlys had endured all

those humiliations, to find that George Augustus was not "rich" after all! Oh, horrible, most horrible!

So when George Augustus, still half-armed with the bolts of thunder-compelling dear Mamma, walked in dramatically to that agape of roast pig, he found he had a tougher job to deal with than he had imagined.

He was greeted with very constrained and not very polite reticence by the elder Hartlys, and gazed at by such an inordinate number of round O-eyed youthful Hartlys that he felt all the reproachful juvenile eyes in the world must be directed upon him, as he struggled with an (intentionally) tough and disagreeable portion of the meal.

Need it be said? George Augustus was defeated by Isabel and the Hartlys, as he would have been defeated by any one with half an ounce of spunk and half a dram of real character.

He capitulated.

Without the honours of war.

He apologised to Isabel.

And to Ma Hartly.

And to "the Captain."

An Armistice was arranged, the terms of which were:

George Augustus surrendered unconditionally, and all the honours of war went to Isabel.

Isabel was not to return to dear Mamma or to Sheffield, not ever again.

They were to take a cottage in rural Kent, not far from the Hartlys.

George Augustus was to return to Sheffield and bring to rural Kent his precious æsthetes and as much furniture as he could cadge.

He was to sell his "practice" in Sheffield, and to start to "practise" in rural Kent.

As a concession to George Augustus, he was to be allowed to WRITE—for a time. But if the Writing proved un-remunerative within a reasonable period—such period to be determined by Isabel and the Other High Contracting Powers—he was to "practise" with more assiduity—and profit.

Failing which, George Augustus would hear about it, and

Isabel would apply for a maintenance order for herself and child.

Signed, sealed, and delivered over a quart bottle of East Kent Pale Ale.

Poor old George Augustus! the shadows of the prison were rapidly closing round *him*, though he didn't know it. He had a hell of a time with dear Mamma when he went home with his tail between his legs and without Isabel, and announced that they had determined to take a cottage in rural Kent and— WRITE. At the word "write," dear Mamma sniffed:

"And who, pray, will pay your washing-bills?"

In a spirit of loving-kindness and forbearance, George Augustus ignored this taunt, which was just as well, since he could think of nothing to say in reply.

Well, dear Papa came to the rescue again. He gave George Augustus as much of the furniture as he dared, and another gift of £50 he hadn't got. And Bulburry got George Augustus orders for an article on The Friends of Lorenzo the Magnificent, and another article on My Wanderings in Florence. Bulburry also advised George Augustus to write a book, either a history of The Decline and Fall of the Florentine Republic, or a novel on the un-hackneyed topic of Savonarola. In addition, Bulburry gave him an introduction to one of those enterprising young publishers who are always arising in London to witch the world with noble publishing, and then, after two or three years, always disappear in the bankruptcy court, leaving behind a sad trail of unpaid bills and disappointed authors and wrecked reputations.

So George Augustus set up in rural Kent as a WRITER, in a pleasant little cottage which Isabel had found for them.

(I do wish you could have seen the "artistic" ties George Augustus wore when he was a WRITER; they would have given you that big feeling.)

But—let us be just—George Augustus really worked—three hours a day, like all the great authors—at writing. He produced articles and he produced stories and he began the Decline and Fall of the Florentine Republic and the most blood-curdling novel about Savonarola, beginning: "One stormy night in

December 14—, two black-cloaked figures might have been
observed traversing the Piazza della Signoria in Florence on
their way from Or San Michele to the private residence of
Lorenzo the Magnificent, now known as the Palazzo Strozzi."

Poor George Augustus! Take it for all in all, we shall look
upon many like him again. He had a lot to learn. He had to
learn that the only books which have the least importance are
those which are made from direct contact with life, which are
built out of a man's guts. He had to learn that every age pul-
lulates with imitators of the authors who have done this, and
created a fashion—which in time and for a time kills them and
their influence.

But still, for a year or so he had his cottage in rural Kent
and was a Writer. He dreamed his dream, though it was a
pretty silly and castrated dream. If he hadn't married Isabel
and gotten her with child, he might have made quite a reason-
ably good literary hack. But, oh! those hostages given to Fortune! *** ***** *** *****, and your life will look after itself.

As for Isabel, she was happy for the first, and perhaps the last,
time in her life. She adored her cottage in rural Kent. What did
it matter that George Augustus wasted his time Writing? He
still had about £170 and earned a few guineas a month by articles and stories. But for her the thrill was having a real home
of her own. She furnished the cottage herself, partly with the
heavy mahogany 1850 stuff George Augustus had brought
from Sheffield, partly with her own atrocious taste and bamboo. George urged her to furnish "artistically," and the resultant chaos of huge, solid, stodgy, curly mahogany and flimsy
bamboo, palms, cauliflower chintzes, and framed photographs
would have rendered the late Mr. Oscar Wilde plaintive in less
than fifty seconds. Never mind; Isabel was happy. She had her
home and she had George Augustus under her eye and thumb,
and she had her baby—whom she adored with all the selfishness of a pure woman—and, best of all, she did NOT have dear
Mamma pestering and sneering and praying at her through
every hour of the day and at every turn. Dear Isabel, how
happy she was in her hum-ble little ho-o-ome! Put it to your-

self, now. Suppose you had been one of an innumerable family, enduring all the abominable discomforts and lack of privacy in that elementary Soviet System. And suppose you had then been uncomfortably impregnated and most painfully delivered, and then bullied and pried into and domineered over and tortured by dear Mamma: wouldn't you be glad to have a home of your own, however humble, and however flimsily based on sandy foundations of WRITING and arty ties? Of course you would. So Isabel looked after the baby, *tant bien que mal*, and cooked abominable meals, and was swindled by the tradesmen, and ran up bills which frightened her, and let young George catch croup and nearly die, and didn't interrupt George Augustus's wooing of the Muse more than half a dozen times a morning and—was happy.

But in all our little arrangements on this satellite of the Sun, we are apt to forget—among a multitude of other things—two important facts. We are the inhabitants of a planet who keep alive only by a daily consumption of the material products of that planet; we are members of a crude collective organisation which distributes these essential products in accordance with certain bizarre rules painfully evolved from chaos by primitive brains. George Augustus certainly forgot these two facts—if he had ever recognised them. A man, a woman, and a brat cannot live for ever on £170 and a few odd guineas a month. They couldn't do it even in the eighteen-nineties, even with extraordinary economy. And Isabel was not economical. Neither, for that matter, was George Augustus. He was mean, but he liked to be pretty comfortable, and his notions of the pretty comfortable were a bit extravagant. Torn between his respect for the Right Hnble. the Lord Tennyson's well-known predilection for port and Mr. Algernon Charles Swinburne's less notorious but undisguised preference for brandy neat, George Augustus finally became original, and fell back on his favourite claret. But, even in the 'nineties, claret was not cheap; and three dozen a month rather eat into an income of four to six guineas. And then Isabel was inexperienced. In housekeeping inexperience costs money! So a time arrived when the £170 was nearly at zero, and the few guineas a month became fewer instead of more numerous. Then George, young George, developed some infant malady; Isabel lost her head, and insisted on a doctor; the doctor, like all the English middle classes, thought a Writer was a harmless fool with money, to be bled ruthlessly, called far more often than was necessary, and sent in a much bigger bill than he would have dared send a stockbroker or a millionaire. Then George Augustus had the influenza and thought he was going to die. And after that Isabel was stricken with hæmorrhoids in her secret parts, and had to be treated. Consequently, the bank balance of a few guineas was turned into a deficit of a good many pounds; and the affable Bank Manager rapidly became strangely unaffable when his polite references to the overdraft remained unsatisfied with the manna of a few cheques.

It became obvious to Isabel—and would long ago have become obvious to almost any one but George Augustus—that Luv and WRITING in a cottage were hopelessly bankrupt.

Well, dear Papa pungled once more—with a pound a week; and Pa Hartly weighed in with a weekly five shillings. But that was misery, and Isabel was determined that, since she had married George Augustus for his "riches," "rich" he should be or perish in the act of trying to acquire riches. So she brought into play all the feminine arsenal, reinforced with a few useful underhand punches and jabs in the moral kidneys, learned from dear Mamma. George Augustus tried to keep high above these material and degrading necessities, but, as I said, Isabel finally Archied him down. When they could no longer get credit even for meat or bread, George Augustus capitulated, and agreed to "practise" once more. He wanted to go back to Sheffield and be pretty comfortable again, under the talons of dear Mamma. But Isabel was—quite rightly—adamant. She refused to return to Sheffield. George Augustus had got her on false pretences, *i.e.* that he was "rich." He was not rich. He was, in fact, damn poor. But he had taken on the responsibility of supporting a woman, and he had got that woman with child. He had no business to be pretty comfortable any longer under the wings of dear Mamma. His business was to get rich as quickly as possible; at any rate, to provide for his dependants.

Inexorable logic, against which I can find no argument even in sophistry.

So they went to a middling-sized, dreary coast town just then in the process of "development" (Bulburry's suggestion), and George Augustus put up another brass plaque. With no results. But then, just as the situation was getting desperate, dear Papa died. He did not leave his children a fortune, but he did leave them £250 each—and strangely enough he actually had the money. Dear Mamma was left in rather "straitened circumstances," but she had enough to be unreservedly disagreeable to the end of her days.

That £250—and the Oscar Wilde case—just saved the situation. The £250 gave them enough to live on for a year. The Oscar Wilde case scared George Augustus thoroughly out of æstheticism and writing. What! They were hanging men and women for wearing of the green? Then George Augustus would wear red. After "The Sentence," George Augustus, like most of England, decided that art and literature were niminypiminy, if not greenery-yallery. I don't say he burned his books and arty ties, but he put them out of sight with remarkable alacrity. The Great Voice of the English People had spoken in no Uncertain Tones, and George Augustus was not deaf to the Message. How could he be, with Isabel pouring it into one ear by word of mouth, and dear Mamma—unexpected but welcome ally—into the other by letter? A nation of Mariners and Sportsmen naturally excel in the twin arts of leaving a sinking ship and kicking a man when he is down. Three months after The Sentence you would never have suspected that George Augustus had ever dreamed of Writing. His clothes were of exemplary Philistinism—indeed, the height of his starched collars and the plainness of his ties had an almost Judas touch in their unæsthetic ugliness. Urged on by Isabel he became a Freemason, an Oddfellow, an Elk, a Heart of Oak, a Buffalo, a Druid, and God knows how many other mysterious things. He himself abandoned Florence, forgot even the blameless Savonarola, and prayed for Guidance. They attended the "best Church" twice on every Sunday.

Slowly at first, then more and more rapidly, George Augustus increased his practice; and the lust of earning money came upon him. They ceased to live in one room behind the office, and took a small but highly respectable house in the residential quarter of the town. Two years later they took a country cottage in a very high-class resort, Martin's Point. Two years after that they bought a large country-house at Pamber, and another smaller house just outside the "quaint old" town of Hamborough. George Augustus began to buy and to build houses. Isabel, whose jointure had been less than nothing when she married, now began to complain because her allowance was "only £1200 a year." In short, they prospered, and prospered greatly—for a time.

They had another child, and another, and another, and another. A man and a woman who can do nothing else can always have children, and, if they are legally married and are able to support their progeny, there seems no end to the amount of begetting they may do and the laurel crowns of virtue to which they are thereby entitled. Isabel put her vitality into child-bearing, boosting George Augustus to profitable action, thrusting herself ever onward and upward financially and socially, buying and furnishing houses, quarrelling with her friends, acquiring sheiks, malforming her children's minds, capriciously interfering with their education, swanking to the Hartlys with her money, patronising the now aged and less venomous dear Mamma, and other lofty and inspiring activities. Was she happy? What a question! We are not placed here by a benevolent Providence to be happy, but to make ourselves unpleasant to our neighbours and to impose the least amiable portions of our personalities on as many people as possible. Was George Augustus happy? Which I parry with—did he deserve to be happy? He made money, anyway, which is more than you and I can do. He dropped claret for whisky, and the æsthetes for the "English Classics," all those "noble" authors who have "stood the test of time," and thereby become so very dull that one prefers to go to the cinema, which has not stood any such test. He had a brougham, in which he drove daily to his office. He became a Worshipful Grand Master, and possessed any amount of funny little medals and coloured leather *caches-sexe*, which are apparently worn in the Mysteries of the Freemasons. He framed his certificates as a Solicitor, a Buffalo, a Druid, and all the other queer things, and hung them in various places to surprise and awe the inexperienced. He had a great many bills. For about ten years he was so prosperous that he was able to give up attending Church on Sundays.

4

George, the younger, liked Hamborough best, perhaps, Martin's Point next, Pamber hardly at all, and he detested Dullborough, the town which contained his father's offices and the minor public school which he attended.

The mind of a very young child is not very interesting. It has imagination and wonder, but too unregulated, too bizarre, too "quaint," too credulous. Does it matter very much that George babbled o' white lobsters, stirred up frogs in a bucket, thought that the word "mist" meant sunset, and was easily persuaded that a sort of milk pudding he detested had been made from an ostrich's egg? Of course, a good deal of adult imagination consists in people's persuading themselves that they can see white lobsters, just as their poetry consists in persuading themselves that the milk pudding *did* come out of the ostrich's egg. The child at least is honest, which is something. But on the whole the young child-mind is boring.

The intellect wakes earlier than the feelings, curiosity before the passions. The child asks the scientist's Why? before he asks the poet's How? George read little primers on Botany and Geology and the Story of the Stars, and collected butterflies, and wanted to do chemistry, and hated Greek. And then one evening the world changed. It was at Martin's Point. All one night the South-West wind had streamed over the empty downs, sweeping up in a crescendo of sound to a shrill ecstasy of speed, sinking into abrupt sobs of dying vigour, while underneath steadily, unyieldingly, streamed and roared the major volume of the storm. The windows rattled. Rain pelted on the panes, oozed and bubbled through the joints of the woodwork. The sea, dimly visible at dusk, rolled furiously—tossing the long breakers on the rocks, and made a tumult of white horses in the Channel. Even the largest ships took shelter. In the irregular harmony of that storm George went to sleep in his narrow, lonely child's bed, and who knows what Genius, what Puck, what elfin Spirit of Beauty came riding on the storm from the South, and shed the juice of what magic herb on his closed eyes? All next day the gale blew with ever-diminishing violence. It was a half-holiday, and no games on account of the wet. After lunch, George went to his room, and sank absorbed in his books, his butterflies, his moths, his fossils. He was aroused by a sudden glare of yellow sunlight. The storm had blown itself out. The last clouds, broken in lurid, ragged-edged fragments, were sailing gently over a soft blue sky. Soon even they were gone. George opened the window and leaned out. The heavy, dank smell of wet earth-mould came up to him with its stifling hyacinth-like quality; the rain-drenched privet was almost over-sweet; the young poplar leaves twinkled and trembled in the last gusts, shaking down rapid chains of diamonds. But it was all fresh—fresh with the clarity of air which follows a great gale, with the scentless purity of young leaves, the drenched grasses of the empty downs. The sun moved majestically and imperceptibly downwards in a widening pool of gold, which faded, as the great ball vanished, into pure, clear, hard green and blue. One, two, a dozen blackbirds and linnets and thrushes were singing; and as the light faded they dwindled to one blackbird tune of exquisite melancholy and purity.

Beauty is in us, not outside us. We recognise our own beauty in the patterns of the infinite flux. Light, form, movement, glitter, scent, sound, suddenly apprehended as givers of delight, as interpreters of the inner vitality, not as the customary aspect of things. A boy, caught for the first time in a kind of ecstasy, brooding on the mystery of beauty.

A penetrating voice came up the stairs:

"Georgie! Georgie! Come out of that stuffy room at once! I want you to get me something from Gilpin's."

What perverse instinct tells them when to strike? How do

they learn to break the crystal mood so unerringly? Why do they hate the mystery so much?

Long before he was fifteen George was living a double life—one life for school and home, another for himself. Consummate dissimulation of youth, fighting for the inner vitality and the mystery. How amusingly, but rather tragically, he fooled them! How innocent-seemingly he played the fine, healthy, barbarian schoolboy, even to the slang and the hateful games! Be ye soft as doves and cunning as serpents. He's such a *real* boy, you know—viz. not an idea in his head, no suspicion of the mystery. "Rippin' game of rugger to-day, Mother, I scored two tries." Upstairs was that volume of Keats, artfully abstracted from the shelves.

A double row of huge old poplars beside the narrow brook swayed and danced in the gales, rustled in the late spring breeze, stood spirelike heavy in July sunlight—a stock-in-trade of spires without churches left mysteriously behind by some mediæval architect. Chestnut trees hung over the walks built on the old town walls. In late May after rain the sweet musty scent filled the lungs and nostrils, and sheets of white and pink petals hid the asphalt. In summer the tiled roofs of the old town were soft deep orange and red, speckled with lemon-coloured lichens. In winter the snow drifted down the streets and formed a tessellated pattern of white and black in the cobbled marketplace. The sound of footsteps echoed in the deserted streets. The clock bells from the Norman tower, with its curious bulbous Dutch cupola, rang so leisurely, marking a fabulous Time.

Said the gardener:

"It's a rum thing, Master George, them rabbits don't drink, and they makes water; and the chickens don't make water, but they drinks it."

Insoluble problem, capricious decrees of Providence.

Confirmation classes.

"You'll have to go and see old Squish."

"What's he say to you?"

"Oh, he gives you a lot of jaw, and asks you if you know any smut."

In the School Chapel. Full-dress Preparation Class for Confirmation. The Head in academic hood and surplice entered the pulpit. Whispers sank to intimidated silence, dramatically prolonged by the hawk-faced man silently bullying the rows of immature eyes. Then in slow, deliberate, impressive tones:

"Within ten years one half of you boys will be DEAD!"

Moral: prepare to meet thy God, and avoid smut.

But did he know, that blind prophet?

Was he inspired, that stately hypocrite?

Like a moral vulture he leaned over and tortured his palpitating prey. Motionless in body, they writhed within, as he painted dramatically the penalties of Vice and Sin; drew pictures of Hell. But did he know? Did he know the hell they were going to within ten years, did he know *how* soon most of their names would be on the Chapel wall? How he must have enjoyed composing that inscription to those "who went forth unfalteringly, and proudly laid down their lives for King and Country"!

One part of the mystery was called SMUT. If you were smutty you went mad and had to go into a lunatic asylum. Or you "contracted a loathsome disease" and your nose fell off.

The pomps and vanities of this wicked world, and all the sinful lusts of the flesh. So it was wicked, like being smutty, to feel happy when you looked at things and read Keats? Perhaps you went mad that way too and your eyes fell out?

"That's what makes them lay eggs," said the little girl, swinging her long golden hair and laughing, as the cock leaped on a hen.

O dreadful, O wicked little girl, you're talking smut to me. You'll go mad, I shall go mad, our noses will drop off. Oh, please don't talk like that, please, please!

From fornication and all other deadly sins . . . What is fornication? Have I committed fornication? Is that the holy word for smut? Why don't they tell me what it means? Why is it the foulest thing a decent man can commit? When that thing happened in the night it must have been fornication; I shall go mad and my nose will drop off.

Hymn number . . . A few more years shall roll.

How wicked I must be!

Are there two religions? A few more years shall roll, in ten years half of you boys will be dead, Smut, nose dropping off, fornication and all other deadly sins. Oh, wash me in Thy Precious Blood, and take my sins away. Blood, Smut.

And then the other—a draught of vintage that has been cooled a long age in the deep-delved earth, tasting of Flora and the country green, dance and Provençal song, and sun-burned mirth? Listening to the sound of the wind as you fell asleep; watching the blue butterflies and the Small Coppers hovering and settling on the great scented lavender bush; taking off your clothes and letting your body slide into a cool, deep, clear rock-pool, while the grey kittiwakes clamoured round the sun-white cliffs and the scent of seaweeds and salt water filled you; watching the sun go down and trying to write something of what it made you feel, like Keats; getting up very early in the morning and riding out along the white empty lanes on your bicycle; wanting to be alone and think about things and feeling strange and happy and ecstatic—was that another religion? Or was that all Smut and Sin? Best not speak of it, best keep it all hidden. I can't help it if it is Smut and Sin. Is *Romeo and Juliet* smut? It's in the same book where you do parsing and analysis out of *King John*. Seize on the white wonder of dear Juliet's hand and steal immortal blessing from her lips. . . .

But more than words about things were things themselves. You looked and looked at them, and then you wanted to put down what they looked like, rearrange them in patterns. In the drawing-class they made you look at a dirty whitish cube, cylinder, and cone, and you drew and re-drew hard outlines which weren't there. But for yourself you wanted to get the colours of things and how they faded into each other and how they formed themselves—or did you form them?—into exciting patterns. It was so much more fun to paint things than even to read what Keats and Shakespeare thought about them. George spent all his pocket-money on paints and drawing-pencils and sketch-books and oil-sketching paper and water-colour blocks. For a long time he hadn't much to look at, even in reproductions. He had Cruikshank and Quiz illustrations which he didn't much care for; and a reproduction of a Bouguereau which he hated; and two Rossetti pictures which he rather liked; and a catalogue of the Tate Collection which gave him photographs of a great many horrible Watts and Frank Dicksees. Best of all, he liked an album of coloured reproductions of Turner's water-colours. Then, one spring, George Augustus took him to Paris for a few days. They did an "educative" visit to the Louvre, and George simply leaped at the Italians and became very Pre-Raphaelite and adored the Primitives. He was quite feverish for weeks after he got back, unable to talk of anything else. Isabel was worried about him: it was so *unboyish*, so—well, really, quite *unhealthy*, all this silly craze for pictures, and spending hours and hours crouching over paint-blocks, instead of being in the fresh air. So much nicer for the boy to be manly. Wasn't he old enough to have a gun licence and learn to kill things?

So George had a gun licence, and went out shooting every morning in the autumn. He killed several plovers and a wood-pigeon. Then one frosty November morning he fired into a flock of plovers, killed one, and wounded another, which fell down on the crisp grass with such a wail of despair. "If you wing a bird, pick it up and wring its neck," he had been told. He picked up the struggling, heaving little mass of feathers, and with infinite repugnance and shut eyes tried to wring its neck. The bird struggled and squawked. George wrung harder and convulsively—and the whole head came off in his hand. The shock was unspeakable. He left the wretched body, and hurried home shuddering. Never again, never, never again would he kill things. He oiled his gun dutifully, as he had been told to do, put it away, and never touched it again. At nights he was haunted by the plover's wail and by the ghastly sight of the headless, bleeding bird's body. In the daytime he thought of them. He could forget them when he went out and sketched the calm trees and fields, or tried to design in his tranquil room. He plunged more deeply into painting than ever, and thus ended one of the many attempts to "make a man" of George Winterbourne.

The business of "making a man" of him was pursued at School, but with little more success, even with the aid of compulsion.

"The type of boy we aim at turning out," the Head used to say to impressed parents, "is a thoroughly manly fellow. We prepare for the Universities, of course, but our pride is in our excellent Sports Record. There is an O.T.C., organised by Sergeant-Major Brown (who served throughout the South African War) and officered by the masters who have been trained in the Militia. Every boy must undergo six months' training, and is then competent to take up arms for his Country in an emergency."

The parents murmured polite approval, though rather tender mothers hoped the discipline was not too strict and "the guns not too heavy for young arms." The Head was contemptuously and urbanely reassuring. On such occasions he invariably quoted those stirring and indeed immortal lines of Rudyard Kipling which end up, "You'll be a man, my son." It is *so* important to know how to kill. Indeed, unless you know how to kill you cannot possibly be a Man, still less a Gentleman.

"The O.T.C. will parade in the Gymnasium for drill and instruction at twelve. Those who are excused will take Geography under Mr. Hobbs in Room 14."

George hated the idea of the O.T.C.—he didn't quite know why, but he somehow didn't want to learn to kill and be a thoroughly manly fellow. Also, he resented being ordered about. Why should one be ordered about by thoroughly manly fellows whom one hates and despises? But then, as a very worthy and thoroughly manly fellow (who spent the War years in the Intelligence Department of the War Office, censoring letters) said of George many years later: "What Winterbourne needs is discipline, *Discipline*. He is far too self-willed and independent. The Army will make a Man of him." Alas! it made a corpse of him. But then, as we all know, there is no price too high to pay for the privilege of being made a thoroughly manly fellow.

So George, feeling immeasurably guilty, but immeasurably repelled, sneaked into the Geography class, instead of parading like a thoroughly manly fellow in embryo. In ten minutes a virtuous-looking but rather pimply prefect appeared:

"Captain James's compliments, sir, and is Winterbourne here?"

As George was walked over to the Gymnasium by the innocent-looking, rather pimply, but thoroughly manly prefect, the latter said:

"Why couldn't you do what you're told, you filthy little sneak, instead of having to be ignominiously *fetched*?"

George made no answer. He just went hard and obstinate, hate-obstinate, inside. He was so clumsy and so bored—in spite of infinite manly bullyings—that the O.T.C. was very glad indeed to send him back to the Geography class after a few drills. He just went hate-obstinate, and obeyed with sullen, hate-obstinate docility. He didn't disobey, but he didn't really obey, not with anything inside him. He was just passive, and they could do nothing with him.

He wrote a great many impositions that term and lost a number of his precious half-holidays, the hours when he could sketch and paint and think about things. But they didn't get at the inside vitality. It retreated behind another wall or two, threw up more sullen, hate-obstinate walls, but it was there all right. It might be all Smut and Sin; but if it was, well, Smutty and Sinful he would be. Only, he wouldn't say "turd" and "talk smut" with the others, and he kicked out fiercely when any of the innocent-looking, rather pimply prefects tried to put their arms round him or make him a "case." He just wouldn't have it. He was more than hate-obstinate then, and blazed into fearful white rages, which left him trembling for hours, unable even to hold a pen. Consequently, the prefects reported that Winterbourne had "gone smutty" and was injuring his health, and he was "interviewed" by his House Master and the Head—but he baffled them with the hate-obstinate silence, and the inner exultation he felt in being Sinful and Smutty in his own way, along with Keats and Turner and Shakespeare.

The prefects gave him a good many "prefects' lickings" on various pretexts, but they never made him cry, even, let alone break down the wall between his inner aliveness and their thorough manliness.

He got a very bad report that term, and no remove. For which he was duly lectured and reprimanded. As the bullying urbane Head reproved, did he know that the sullen, rather hard-faced boy in front of him was not listening, was silently reciting to himself the Ode to a Nightingale, as a kind of inner Declaration of Independence? "Magic casements"—that was when you opened the window wide at sunset to listen to the birds, or at night-time to look at the stars, or first thing in the morning to smell the fresh sunlight and watch the leaves glittering.

"If you go on like this, Winterbourne, you will disgrace yourself, your parents, your House, and your School. You take little or no interest in the School life, and your Games record is abominable. Your set-captain tells me that you have cut Games ten times this term, and your Form Master reports that you have over a thousand lines of impositions yet to work off. Your conduct with regard to the O.T.C. was contemptible and unmanly to a degree we have never experienced in *this* School. I am also told that you are ruining your health with secret abominable practices against which I warned you—unavailingly, I fear—at the time I endeavoured to prepare you for Confirmation and Holy Communion. I notice that you have only once taken Communion since your Confirmation, although more than six months have passed. What you do when you cut Games and go running off to your home, I do not know. It cannot be anything good." (Magic casements opening on the foam.) "It would pain me to have to ask your parents to remove you from the School, but we want no wasters and sneaks here. Most, indeed all, your fellow-boys are fine manly fellows; and you have the excellent example of your House Prefects before you. Why can you not imitate them? What nonsense have you got into your head? Speak out, and tell me plainly. Have you entangled yourself in any way?"

No answer.

"What do you do in your spare time?"

No answer.

"Your obstinate silence gives me the right to suspect the worst. *What* you do I can imagine, but prefer not to mention. Now, for the last time, will you speak out honourably and manfully, and tell me what it is you do that makes you neglect your work and Games and makes you conspicuous in the School for sullen and obstinate behaviour?"

No answer.

"Very well. You will receive twelve strokes from the birch. Bend over."

George's face quivered, but he had not shed a tear or made a sound as he turned silently to go.

"Stop. Kneel down at that chair, and we will pray together that this lesson may be of service to you, and that you may conquer your evil habits. Let us together pray GOD that He will have mercy upon you, and make you into a really manly fellow."

They prayed.

Or rather, the Head prayed, and George remained silent. He did not even say "Amen."

After that the School gave him up and let him drift. He was supposed to be dull-minded as well as obstinate and unmanly, and was allowed to vegetate vaguely about the Lower Fifth. Maybe he picked up more even of the little they had to teach than they suspected. But as the silent, rather white-faced, rather worried-looking boy went mechanically through the day's routine, hung about in corridors, moved from classroom to classroom, he was busy enough inside, building up a life of his own. George went at George Augustus's books with the energy of a fierce physical hunger. He once showed me a list in an old notebook of the books he had read before he was sixteen. Among other things, he had raced through most of the poets from Chaucer onwards. It was not the amount that he read which mattered, but the way in which he read. Having no single person to talk to openly, no one to whom he could reveal himself, no one from whom he could learn what he wanted to

know, he was perforce thrust back upon books. The English
poets and the foreign painters were his only real friends. They
were his interpreters of the mystery, the defenders of the inner
vitality which he was fighting unconsciously to save. Naturally, the School was against him. They set out to produce "a
type of thoroughly manly fellow," a "type" which unhesitat-
ingly accepted the prejudices, the "code" put before it, docilely
conformed to a set of rules. George dumbly claimed to think
for himself, above all to *be* himself. The "others" were good
enough fellows, no doubt, but they really had no selves to *be*.
They hadn't the flame. The things which to George were the
very *cor cordium* of life meant nothing to them, simply passed
them by. They wanted to be approved and be healthy barbarians, cultivating a little smut on the sly, and finally dropping
into some convenient post in life where the "thoroughly manly
fellow" was appreciated—mostly, one must admit, minor and
unpleasant and not very remunerative posts in unhealthy colonies. The Empire's backbone. George, though he didn't realise
it then, wasn't going to be a bit of any damned Empire's backbone, still less part of its kicked backside. He didn't mind
going to hell, and disgracing himself and his parents and his
House and The School, if only he could go to hell in his own
way. That's what they couldn't stand—the obstinate passive
refusal to accept their prejudices, to conform to their minor-
gentry, kicked-backside-of-the-Empire code. They worried
him, they bullied him, they frightened him with cock-and-bull
yarns about Smut and noses dropping off; but they didn't get
him. I wish he hadn't been worried and bullied to death by
those two women. I wish he hadn't stood up to that machine-
gun just one week before the Torture ended. After he had
fought the swine (*i.e.* the British ones) so gallantly for so many
years. If only he had hung on a little longer, and come back,
and done what he wanted to do! He could have done it, he
could have "got there"; and then even "The School" would
have fawned on him. Bloody fool! Couldn't he see that we
have only one duty—to hang on, and smash the swine?

Once, only once, he nearly gave himself away to The School.
At the end of the examinations, as a sort of afterthought, there

as an English Essay. One of the subjects was: What do you want to do in Life? George's enthusiasm got the better of his caution, and he wrote a crude, enthusiastic, schoolboyish rhapsody, laying down an immense programme of life, from travel to astronomy, with the beloved Painting as the end and crown of all. Needless to say, he did not get the Prize or even any honourable mention. But, to his amazement, on the last day of term, as they went to evening Chapel, the Head strolled up, put an arm round his shoulders, and pointing to the planet Venus said:

"Do you know what that star is, my boy?"

"No, sir."

"That is Sirius, a gigantic sun, many millions of miles distant from us."

"Yes, sir."

And then the conversation languished. The Head removed his arm, and they entered the Chapel. The last hymn was "Onward, Christian Soldiers," because ten of the senior boys were going to Sandhurst.

George did not join actively in the service.

The summer holidays were the only part of the year when he was really happy.

The country inland from Martin's Point is rather barren. But, like all the non-industrialised parts of England, it has a character, very shy like a little silvery-grey old lady, which acts gently but in the end rather strongly on the mind. It was the edge of one of the long chalk downs of England, with salt marshes to left and right, and fertile clay land far behind—too far for George to reach even on a bicycle. In detail it seemed colourless and commonplace. From the crest of one of the high ridges, it had a kind of silvery-grey, very old quality, with its great, bare, treeless fields making faint chequer-patterns on the long, gentle slopes, with always a fringe of silvery-grey sea in the far distance. The chalk was ridged in long parallels, like the swell of some gigantic ocean arrested in rock. The ridges became more abrupt and violent near the coast, and ended in a long, irregular wall of silvery-grey chalk, poised like a huge wave of rock-foam for ever motionless and for ever silent,

while for ever at its base lapped the petty waves of the mobile
and whispering sea. The sheep-and-wind-nipped turf of the
downs grew dwarf bee-orchis, blue-purple bugloss, tall ragged
knapweed, and frail harebells. In the valleys were tall thistles
and foxgloves. Certain nooks were curiously rich with wild-
flowers mixed with deep rich-red clover and marguerite-
daisies. In the summer these little flowery patches—so precious
and conspicuous in the surrounding barrenness—were a
flicker of butterfly wings: the creamy Marbled Whites, electric
blue of the Chalkhill Blue, sky-blue of the Common and Holly
Blue, rich tawny of the Fritillaries, metallic gleam of the Coppers, cool drab of the Meadow Browns. The Peacock, the Red
Admiral, the Painted Lady, the Tortoiseshell wheeled over the
nettles and thistles, poised on the flowers, fanning their rich
mottled wings. In a certain field in August you could find
Clouded Yellows rapidly moving in little curves and irregular
dashes of flight over swaying red-purple clover, which seemed
to drift like a sea as the wind ran over it.

Yet with all this colour the "feel" of the land was silvery-
grey. The thorn-bushes and the rare trees were bent at an angle
under the pressure of the South-West gales. The inland hamlets and farms huddled down in the hollows behind a protect-
ing wall of elms. They were humble, unpretentious, but
authentic, like the lives of the shepherds and ploughmen who
lived in them. The three to ten miles which separated them
from the pretentious suburbanity of Martin's Point might have
been three hundred, so unmoved, so untouched were they by
its golf and its idleness and tea-party scandals and even its
increasing number of "cars." In hollows, too, crouched its low,
flint-built Norman churches, so unpretentious, for all the rich-
ness of dog-toothed porches and Byzantine-looking tympa-
nums and conventionalised satiric heads sneering and gaping
and grimacing from the string-courses. Hard, satiric people
those Norman conquerors must have been—you can see the
hard, satiric effigies of some of their descendants in the Temple Church. They must have crushed the Saxon shepherds and
swineherds under their steel gauntlets, smiling in a hard,
satiric way. And even their piety was hard and satiric, if you
can judge from the little flinty, satiric churches they scattered

over the land. They then must have pushed on westward to richer lands, abandoning those barren downs and scanty fields to the descendants of the oppressed Saxon. So the land seemed old; but the hard, satiric quality of the Normans only remained in odd nooks of their churches—all the rest had grown gentle and silvery-grey, like a rather sweet and gentle silvery-grey old lady.

All this George struggled to express with his drawing-and-paint-blocks. He tried to absorb—and to some extent did absorb—the peculiar quality of the country. He attempted it all: from the twenty-mile sweeps of undulating Down fringed by the grey-silver sea, to the church doors and little patient photographic, semi-scientific painting of the flowers and butterflies. From the point of view of a painter, he was always too literal, too topographical, too minutely interested in detail. He saw the poetry of the land but didn't express it in form and colour. The old English landscape school of 1770–1840 died long before Turner's body reached St. Paul's and his money went into the pockets of the greedy English lawyers instead of to the painters for whom he intended it. The impulse expired in painstaking topography and sentimental prettiness. There wasn't the vitality, the capacity to struggle on, which you find in the best work of painters like Friesz, Vlaminck, and even Utrillo, who can find a new sort of poetry in tossing trees or a white farmhouse or a *bistro* in the Paris suburbs. George, even at fifteen, knew what he wanted to say in paint, but couldn't say it. He could appreciate it in others, but he hadn't got the power of expression in him.

Hitherto George had been quite alone in his blind instinctive struggle—the fight against the effort to force him into a mould, the eager searching out for life and more life which would respond to the spark of life within. Now he began to find unexpected allies; discovered at first almost with suspicion, then with immense happiness, that he was not quite alone, that there were others who valued what he valued. He discovered men's friendship and the touch of girls' lips and hands.

First came Mr. Barnaby Slush, at that time a "most famous
novelist," who had hit the morbid-cretinish British taste with a
sensational, crude-Christian moral novel which sold millions
of copies in a year and is now forgotten, except that it probably lies embalmed somewhere in the Tauchnitz collection, that
mausoleum of unreadable works. Mr. Slush was a bit of a
boozer and highly delighted with his notoriety. Still, he did
occasionally look around him; he was not wholly blinkered
with prejudice and unheeding blankness like most of the
middle-class inhabitants of Martin's Point. He noticed George,
laughed at some of the pert but acute school-boyish remarks
George made and for which he was invariably squelched, was
"interested" in his passion for painting and the persistence he
gave to it.

"There's something in that boy of yours, Mrs. Winterbourne. He's got a mind. He'll do something in the world."

"Oh, do you think so, Mr. Slush?"—Isabel, half-flattered,
half-bristling with horror and rage at the thought that George
might "have a mind"—"he's just a healthy, happy schoolboy,
and only thinks of pleasing his Mummie."

"Umph," said Mr. Slush. "Well, I'd like to do something for
him. There's more in him than you think. *I* believe there's an
artist in him."

"If I thought that," exclaimed Isabel viciously, "I'd flog him
till all such nonsense was flogged out of him."

Mr. Slush saw he was doing George more harm than good
by this well-meant effort, and was discreetly silent. However,
he gave George one or two books, and tried to talk to him on
the side. But George was still too suspicious of all grown-ups,
particularly those who came and drank whisky in the evening
with George Augustus and Isabel. Besides, poor, flabby, drink-
sodden, kindly Mr. Slush rather repelled his hard, intolerant
youthfulness; and they got nowhere in particular. Still, Mr.
Slush was important to the extent that he prepared George to
give some confidence to others. He broke down the first outer
wall built by George against the world. The way in which Isabel got rid of Mr. Slush, whose possible influence on George
she instinctively suspected, was rather amusing. George Augustus and Mr. Slush went to a Freemasons' dinner together. Now

that Freemasonry had served its purpose, Isabel was intensely jealous of its mysteries—poor mysteries!—which George Augustus honourably refused to reveal to her, and she hated those periodical dinners with a bitter hatred. That night there arose one of the most terrific thunderstorms which had ever been known in that part of the country. For six hours forked and sheet lightning leaped and stabbed at earth and sea from three sides of the horizon; crash after crash of thunder broke over Martin's Point and rumbled terrifically against the cliffs, while desperate drenching sheets of rain beat madly on roofs and windows and gushed wetly down the steep roads. It was impossible for the men to get home. They remained—drinking a good deal—at the hotel until nearly four, and then drove home sleepily and merrily. Isabel put on her tragedy-queen air, sat up all night, and greeted George Augustus with horrid invective.

"Think of poor Mrs. Slush out there in that lonely farm, and me and the children crouching here in terror, while you men were guzzling, and besotting yourselves with whisky" . . . etcetera, etcetera.

Poor George Augustus attempted a feeble defence—it was swept away. Mr. Slush innocently walked over next day to see how things were after the storm, was insulted, and driven from the house in amazed indignation. He "put" Isabel a little vindictively "in his next novel," but, as she said and said truly, he never "darkened their doors" again.

In one way George loved the grey sea and barrenness, in another way he hated them. To get away to the lush inland country was a release, an ecstasy, the more precious in that it happened so rarely. When he was a small child, a maid-servant took him "down home" to the hop-picking. Confused and fantastic memories of it remained with him. He never forgot the penetrating sunlight, the long dusty ride in the horse-bus, the sensation of hot-sharp-scented shadow under the tall vines, the joy of the great rustling heaps falling downward as the foreman cut the strings, the tenderness of the rough women hoppickers, the taste of the smoky picnic tea and heavy soggy cake (so delicious!) they gave him. Later—in the fourteen-sixteen

years—it was a joy to visit the Hambles. They were retired professional people, who lived in a remote country-house among
lush meadows and rich woods. Mr. Hamble was a large, freckly
man who collected insects, and was a skilled botanist; and thus
charmed that side of George. But the real delight was the lush
countryside—and Priscilla. Priscilla was the Hambles' daughter, almost exactly George's age, and between those two was a
curious, intense, childish passion. She was very golden and
pretty—much too pretty, for it made her self-conscious and flirta-
tious. But the passion between those two children was a genuine thing.

For quite three years George was under the influence of his
passion for Priscilla, never really forgot her, always in a dim,
dumb, subconscious way felt the frustration. Like all passions
it was something fugitive, the product of a phase, but it ought
not to have been frustrated. It was a pity they were so often
separated, because that meant infinite letter-writing and so
made him always tend to too much idealising and intellectual-
ising in love affairs. But when they were together it was pure
happiness. Priscilla was a very demure and charming little
mistress. They played all sorts of games with other children,
and went fishing in the brook, picked flowers in the rich water-
meadows, hunted bird-nests along the hedges. All these things,
great fun in themselves, were so much more fun because Priscilla was there, because they held hands and kissed, and felt
very serious, like real lovers. Sometimes he dared to touch her
childish breasts. And the feeling of friendliness from the clasp
of Priscilla's hands, the pleasure of her short childish kisses
and sweet breath, the delicate texture of her warm childish-
swelling breasts, never quite left him; and to remember Priscilla was like remembering a fragrant English garden. Like
an English garden, she was a little old-fashioned and self-
consciously comely, but she was so spring-like and golden. She
was immensely important to George. She was something he
could love unreservedly, even if it was only with the mawkish
love of adolescence. But far more than that temporary service,
she gave him the capacity to love women, saved him from the
latent homosexuality which lurks in so many Englishmen and

makes them for ever dissatisfied with their women. She revealed to him—all unconsciously—the subtle inexhaustible joys of the tender companionate woman's body. Even then he felt the delicious contrast between his male nervous-muscled hands and her tender swelling breasts, opening flowers to be held so delicately and affectionately. And from her too he learned that the most satisfactory loves are those which do not last too long, those which are never made thorny with hate, and drift gently into the past, leaving behind only a fragrance—not a sting—of regret. His memories of Priscilla were few, but all roses. . . .

You see, they cannot really kill the spark if it is there, not with all their bullyings and codes and prejudices and thorough manliness. For, of course, they are not manly at all, they are merely puppets, the products of the system—if it may be dignified by that word. The truly manly ones are those who have the spark, and refuse to let it be extinguished; those who know that the true values are the vital values, not the £. s. d. and falling-into-a-good-post and the kicked-backside-of-the-Empire values. George had already found a sort of ally in poor Mr. Slush, and an exquisite child-passion in Priscilla. But he needed men too, and was lucky enough to find them. How can one estimate what he owed to Dudley Pollak and to Donald and Tom Conington?

Dudley Pollak was a mysterious bird. He was a married man in the late fifties, who had been to Cambridge, made the Grand Tour, lived in Paris, Berlin, and Italy, known numbers of fairly eminent people, owned a large country-house, appeared to have means, possessed very beautiful furniture and all sorts of *objets d'art*, and was a cultivated man—in most of which respects he differed exceedingly from the inhabitants of Martin's Point. Now what do you suppose was the reason why Pollak and Mrs. Pollak let their large house furnished, and spent several years in a small cottage in a rather dreary village street a couple of miles from Martin's Point? George never knew, and nobody else ever knew. The fantastic and scandalous

theories evolved by Martin's Point to explain this mystery
were amusing evidence of the vulgar stupidity of those who
formed them, and have no other interest. The Pollaks themselves said that they had grown tired of their large house and
that Mrs. Pollak was weary of managing servants. So simple is
the truth that this very likely was the real explanation. At any
rate, there they lived together in their cottage, crowded with
furniture and books; cooking their own meals, very often—
they were both excellent cooks—and waited on by a couple of
servants who "lived out." Now, although Pollak was forty
years older than George, he was in a sense the boy's first real
friend. The Pollaks had no children of their own, which may
go to explain this odd but deep friendship.

Pollak was a much wilier bird than poor old Slush. He sized
Isabel up very quickly and accurately, and just politely refused
to let her quarrel with him, and just as politely refused to
receive her. But he was so obviously a gentleman, so obviously
a man of means, that no reasonable objection could be made
when he proposed to George Augustus that "Georgie" should
come to tea once a week and learn chess. Martin's Point was a
very chessy place; it was somehow a mark of respectability
there. Before this, George had gone to play chess with a very
elderly gentleman, who put so much of the few brains he had
into that game that he had none left for the preposterous
poems he composed, or indeed anything else. So every Wednesday George went to tea with the Pollaks.

They always began, most honourably and scrupulously,
with a game of chess; and then they had tea; and then they
talked. Although George never suspected it until years afterwards, Pollak was subtly educating him, at the same time that
he tried to give him the kind of sympathy he needed. Pollak
had many volumes of Anderson's photographs, which he let
George turn over while he talked negligently but shrewdly
about Italian architecture, styles of painters, della Robbia
work; and Mrs. Pollak occasionally threw in some little anec-
dote about travel. By the example of his own rather fastidious
manners he corrected schoolboy uncouthnesses. He somehow
got George riding lessons, for in Pollak's days horse-riding

was an indispensable accomplishment. Pollak always worked
on the boy by suggestion and example, never by exhortation
or patronage. He always assumed that George knew what he
negligently but accurately told him. The manner in which he
made George learn French was characteristic of his methods.
One afternoon Pollak told a number of amusing stories about
his young days in Paris, while George was looking through a
volume of autograph letters of Napoleon, Talleyrand, and
other Frenchmen—which, of course, he could not read. Next
week, when George arrived he found Pollak reading.

"Hullo, Georgie, how are you? Just listen to this lovely thing
I've been reading, and tell me what you think of it."

And Pollak read, in the rather chanting voice he adopted in
reading poetry, André Chénier's "L'épi naissant mûrit, de la
faux respecté." George had to confess shamefacedly that he
hadn't understood. Pollak handed him the book, one of those
charming large-type Didot volumes; but André Chénier was
too much for George's public-school French.

"Oh, I *do* wish I could read it properly," said George. "How
did you learn French?"

"I suppose I learned it in Paris. ' 'Tis pleasing to be schooled
in a strange tongue by female eyes and lips,' you know. But
you could learn very soon if you really tried."

"But how? I've done French at school for ages, and I simply
can't read it, though I've often tried."

"What you learn at school is only to handle the tools—
you've got to learn to use them for yourself. You take *Les Trois
Mousquetaires*, read straight through a few pages, marking
the words you don't know, look them up, make lists of them,
and try to remember them. Don't linger over them too much,
but try and get interested in the story."

"But I've read *The Three Musketeers* in English."

"Well, try *Vingt Ans Après*. You can have my copy and
mark it."

"No, there's a paper-backed one at home. I'll use that."

In a fortnight George had skipped through the first volume
of *Vingt Ans Après*. In a month he could read simple French
prose easily. Three months later he was able to read *La Jeune*

Captive aloud to Pollak, who afterwards turned the talk on to Ronsard, and opened up yet another vista.

The Coningtons were much younger men, the elder a young barrister. They also talked to George about books and pictures, in which their taste was more modern if less sure than Pollak's urbane Second Empire culture. But with them George learned companionship, the fun of infinite, everlasting arguments about "life" and ideas, the fun of making *mots* and laughing freely. The Coningtons were both great walkers. George of course had the middle-class idea that five miles was the limit of human capacity for walking. Like Pollak, the Coningtons treated him as if he were a man, assumed also that he could do what they were showing him now to do. So when Donald Conington came down for a week-end, he assumed that George would want to walk. That day's walk had such an effect upon George that he could even remember the date, 2nd of June. It was one of those soft, cloudless days that do sometimes happen in England, even in June. They set out from Hamborough soon after breakfast and struck inland, going at a steady, even pace, talking and laughing. Donald was in excellent form, cheery and amusing, happy to be out of harness for a few hours. Four miles brought them beyond the limits of George's own wanderings, and after a couple of hours' tramp they suddenly came out on the crest of the last chalk ridge and looked over a wide, fertile plain of woodland and tilth and hop-fields, all shimmering in the warm sunlight. The curious hooked noses of oast-houses sniffed over the tops of soft round elm-clumps. They could see three church spires and a dozen hamlets. The only sound came from the larks high overhead.

"God!" exclaimed Donald in his slightly theatrical way, "what a fair prospect!"

A fair prospect indeed, and an unforgettable moment when one comes for the first time to the crest of a hill and looks over an unknown country shimmering in the sun, with the white coiling English lanes inviting exploration. Donald set off down the hill, singing lustily: "O mistress mine, where are you roaming?" George followed a little hesitatingly. His legs were already rather tired, it was long past eleven—how would they get back in time for lunch, and what would be said if they were late? He mentioned his fears timidly to Donald.

"What! Tired? Why, good God, man, we've only just started! We'll push on another four miles to Crockton, and have lunch in a pub. I told them we shouldn't be in until after tea."

The rest of the day passed for George in a kind of golden glory of fatigue and exultation. His legs ached bitterly—although they only walked about fifteen miles all told—but he was ashamed to confess his tiredness to Donald, who seemed as fresh at the end of the day as when he started. George came home with confused and happy memories—the long talk and the friendly silences, the sun's heat, a deer-park and Georgian red-brick mansion they stopped to look at, the thatched pub at Crockton where he ate bread and cheese and pickles and drank his first beer, the elaborately carved Norman church at Crockton. They sat for half an hour after lunch in the churchyard, while Donald smoked a pipe. A Red Admiral settled on a grey flat tombstone, speckled with crinkly orange and flat grey-green lichens. They talked with would-be profundity about how Plato had likened the Soul—Psyche—to a butterfly, and about death, and how one couldn't possibly accept theology or the idea of personal immortality. But they were cheerful about it—the only sensible time to discuss these agonising problems is after a pleasant meal accompanied with strong drink; and they felt so well and cheery and animal-insouciant in the warm sunlight, they didn't really believe they would ever die. In that they showed considerable wisdom; for you will remember that the wise Montaigne spent the first half of his life preparing for death, and the latter part in arguing that it is much wiser never to think about dying at all—time enough to think of *that* when it comes along.

For Donald that was just a pleasant day, which very soon took its place among the vague mists of half-memory. For George it was all extraordinarily important. For the first time he felt and understood companionship between men—the frank, unsuspicious exchange of goodwill and talk, the spontaneous collaboration of two natures. That was really the most important gain. But he also discovered the real meaning of travel. It sounds absurd to speak of a fifteen-mile walk as "travel." But you may go thousands of miles by train and boat between one international hotel and another, and not have the sensation of travelling at all. Travel means the consciousness of adventure and exploration, the sense of covering the miles, the ability to seize indefatigably upon every new or familiar source of delight. Hence the horror of *tourism*, which is a conventionalising, a codification, of adventure and exploration—which is absurd. Adventure is allowing the unexpected to happen to you. Exploration is experiencing what you have not experienced before. How can there be any adventure, any exploration, if you let somebody else—above all, a travel bureau—arrange everything before-hand? It isn't seeing new and beautiful things which matters, it's seeing them for yourself. And if you want the sensation of covering the miles, go on foot. Three hundred miles on foot in three weeks will give you infinitely more sense of travel, show you infinitely more surprising and beautiful experiences, than thirty thousand miles of mechanical transport.

George did not rest until he went on a real exploration walk. He did this with Tom Conington, Donald's younger brother—and that walk also was unforgettable, though they were rained upon daily and subsisted almost entirely upon eggs and bacon, which seems to be the only food heard of in English country pubs. They took the train to Corfe Castle, and spent a day in walking over to Swanage through the half-moor, half-marsh country, with its heather and gorse and nodding white cotton-grasses. Then they went along the coast to Kimmeridge and Preston and Lulworth and Lyme Regis, sleeping in cottages and small pubs. From Lyme Regis they turned inland, and went by way of Honiton, Collumpton, Tavistock, to Dulverton and Porlock, along the north Devon coast to Bideford, and back to South Molton, where they had to take the train, since they had spent their money and had only enough to pay their fares home. The whole walk lasted less than a fortnight, but it seemed like two months. They had such a good time, jawing away as they walked, singing out of tune, finding their way on maps, getting wet through and drying themselves by taproom fires, talking to every one, farmer or labourer, who would talk to them, reading and smoking over a pint of beer after supper. And always that sense of adventure, of exploration, which urged them on every morning, even through mist and rain, and made fatigue and bad inns and muddy roads all rather fun and an experience.

One gropes very much through all these "influences" and "scenes" and fragmentary events in trying to form a picture of George in those years. For example, I found the date of the Crockton walk and a few disjointed notes about it on the back of a rough sketch of Crockton church porch. And the itinerary of the walk with Tom Conington, with a few comments, I found in the back of a volume of selected English essays, which George presumably took with him on the walk. The heart of another is indeed a dark forest, and, however much I let my imagination work over these fragments of his life, I find it hard to imagine him at that time, still harder to imagine what was going on in his mind. I imagine that he more or less adjusted himself to the public-school and home hostility; that, as time passed and he began to make friends, he felt more confidence and happiness. Like most sensitive people he was subject to moods, affected by the weather and the season of the year. He could pass very rapidly from a mood of exuberant gaiety almost to despair. A chance remark—as I myself found—was enough to effect that unfortunate change. He had a habit always of implying more or less than he said, of assuming that others would always jump with the implied, not with the expressed, thought. Similarly, he always expected the same sort of subtle obliquity of expression in others, and very seldom took remarks at their face value. He could never be convinced or convince himself that there were not implications under the most commonplace remark. I suppose he had very early developed his habit of irony as a protection and as a method of being scornful with seeming innocence. He never got rid of it.

But for a time he was very happy. At home there was a kind of truce—ominous, had he only known—and he was left much to

himself. Priscilla awoke and satisfied the need for contact with
the feminine, fed the awakening sensuality. Then, when Priscilla somehow drifted away, there was another, much slighter,
more commonplace affair with a girl named Maisie. She was a
slightly coarse, dark type, a little older than George and much
more developed. They used to meet after dark in the steep lanes
of Martin's Point, and kiss each other. George was a little
scared by the way she gobbled his mouth and pressed herself
against him; and then felt self-reproachful, thinking of Priscilla
and her delicate, English-garden fragrance. One night, Maisie
drew them along a different walk to a deserted part of the
down, where a clump of thick pines made a close shadow over
coarse grass. They had to climb up a steep hill-side.

"Oh, I'm tired," said Maisie; "let's sit down."

She lay down on the grass, and George lay beside her. He
leaned over her and felt the low warm mounds of her breasts
through his thin summer shirt.

"The touch of your mouth is beautiful," said George. "Honey
and milk is under her tongue."

She lay passive and let him kiss her for a few minutes, and then
sat up abruptly.

"I must go home."

"Oh, but why? We were so happy here, and it's still early."

"Yes, but I promised mother I'd be home early to-night."

George walked back to the door of Maisie's house, and wondered why her good-night kiss was so un-tender, so perfunctory.

A few nights later George went out—on the pretext of
"mothing"—in the hope of finding Maisie. As he came silently
round a corner, he saw about twenty yards ahead, in the dusk,
Maisie walking away from him with a young man of about
twenty. His arm was round her waist, and her head was resting on his shoulder as she used to rest it on George's.

When a great liner came round the Foreland, you ran to the
telescope to see whether it was a P. & O., a Red Star, or a
Hamburg–Amerika. You soon got to recognise the majestic,
four-funnelled *Deutschland* as she moved rapidly up or down
the Channel. The yellow-funnelled boats for Ostend, the

white-funnelled boats for Calais and Boulogne, were daily
events, hardly to be noted—and yet how they seemed to lure
one to that unknown life across the narrow seas! On clear
days you could see the faint shining of the cliffs of France. On
foggy nights the prolonged anapæst of the Foreland Lightship
foghorn answered the hoarse spondees of the passing ships,
groping their way up Channel. Even on the most rainy or most
moonlit night the flash of the lighthouse made dabs of yellow
light on the walls of George's bedroom. There were no night-
ingales at Martin's Point, but morning and evening thrushes
and blackbirds.

Hamborough was so different, lying off the chalk downs on
the edge of the salt marshes, the desolate, silent, unresponsive
salt marshes, so gorgeous at sunset. The tidal river ran turbid
and level with its banks, or deep between walls of sinister
mud. Little flocks of fleetwinged grey-white birds—called
"oxey-birds"—flickered rapidly away in front of you on sickle-
moon wings. A brown-sailed barge, far inland, seemed to be
gliding overland through the flat, green-brown marsh land.
Behind, far across the flat, desolate ex-sea-bottom ran the old
coastline, and on a bluff stood the solid ruins of a Roman fort.
"Pe-e-e-wit," said the plunging plovers, "pee-e-ee-wit." No
other sound. The white clouds, dappled English clouds, moved
so silently over the cool blue English skies; such faint blue,
even on what the English call a "hot" day.

You went to the marshes by way of the Barbican, the Barbican through which the old English kings and knights had rid-
den with their men-at-arms, when they made one of their
innumerable descents on more civilised France. There stood the
mediæval Barbican, on the verge of the commonplace little
money-grubbing town, like a stranded vestige from some geo-
logical past. What was the Barbican to early twentieth-century
Hamborough? An obstacle to the new motor road, whose abo-
lition was always being discussed in the Town Council, and
whose destruction was only postponed because the thickness
of the walls made it too expensive. On the other side you
walked out into flat, fertile country, past almshouses and the
hoary stone-mullioned Elizabethan Grammar School, over the

level crossing, to Saxon Friedasburg, where tradition said a
temple to Freya had once stood. How silver-grey the distant
sea-fringe, how silver-grey the lines of rippling poplars! How
warmly golden—like Priscilla—the wheat-fields under the late
August afternoon sunshine!

These are the gods, the gods who must endure for ever, or
as long as man endures, the gods whom the perverse, blood-
lustful, torturing Oriental myths cannot kill. Poseidon, the sea-
god, who rules his grey and white steeds, so gentle and playful
in his rare moods of tranquillity, so savage and destructive in
his rage. With a clutch of his hand he crumples the wooden
beams or steel plates of the wave-wanderers, with a thrust of
his elbow he hurls them to destruction on the hidden sandbank
or the ruthless sharp-toothed rocks. Selene, the moon-goddess,
who flies so swiftly through the breaking clouds of the departing storm, or hangs so motionless-white, so womanly-waiting,
in the cobalt night-sky among her attendant stars. Phœbus,
who scorns these silvery-grey northern lands, but whose golden
light is so welcome when it comes. Demeter, who ripens the
wheat and plumps the juicy fruit and sets cordial bitterness in
the hop and trails ragged flower and red hip and haw along the
hedges. And then the lesser humbler gods—must there not be
gods of sunrise and twilight, of bird-singing and midnight
silence, of ploughing and harvesting, of the shorn fields and the
young green springing grass, gods of lazy cattle and the uneasily bleating flocks and of the wild creatures—(hedgehogs and
squirrels and rabbits, and their enemies the weasels)—tenuous
Ariel demi-gods of the trembling poplars and the many-
coloured flowers and the speckled fluttering butterflies? In
ever-increasing numbers the motor-cars clattered and ham-
mered along the dusty roads; the devils of golf leaped on the
acres and made them desolate; sport and journalism and gentility made barren men's lives. The gods shrank away, hid shyly in
forgotten nooks, lurked unsuspected behind bramble and
thorn. Where were their worshippers? Where were their altars?
Rattle of the motors, black smoke of the railways. One—
perhaps only one—worshipper was left them. One alone saw
the fleet limbs glancing through the tree-trunks, saw the bright

faun-eyes peering anxiously from behind the bushes. Hama-
dryads, fauns, do not fly from me! I am not one of "them," one
of the perverse life-torturers. I know you are there; come to me,
and talk with me! Stay with me, stay with me!

Then the blow fell.

5

"What can have happened? What can have happened? O my
God, what can have happened?"

Isabel paced up and down the room, uttering this and kin-
dred exclamations to nobody in particular, while an outwardly
calm, inwardly very much perturbed George silently echoed
the question. George Augustus had gone to London on his
usual weekly trip, and as usual George had met the six o'clock
train. No George Augustus. He met the seven-ten, the eight-
fifty, and the eleven-five, the last train: and still no George
Augustus. No telegram, no message. A feeling of impending
calamity hung over the house that night, and there was not
much sleep for Isabel and George. Next morning a long ram-
bling letter, emotional and vague, arrived from George Augustus. The gist was that he was ruined, and in flight from his
creditors.

It was a bitter enough pill for George, bitterer still for Isabel. She had schemed and boosted George Augustus for years,
she thought they were well off and getting better off. And she
had taken pride in it as her own work. She had George Augustus so much under her thumb that whatever he did was through
her influence. But the very perfection of her system was its
ruin. He was so afraid of her that he dared not confess when a
speculation went wrong. To keep up the standard of expense
he began to mortgage; to redeem the situation he plunged
deeper into speculation and neglected his practice. Rumours
began to get about. Then suddenly he was taken with panic,
and fled. Later investigation showed that his affairs were not
so compromised as he had imagined; but the sudden mad flight

ruined everything. In a day the Winterbournes dropped from
comparative affluence to comparative poverty.

The effect on George was really rather disastrous. After the
almost sordid distress of his early adolescence, he had succeeded in saving the spark, had built up a life for himself, had
created a positive happiness. But all that rested, in fact, on the
family money. The distrust of himself and others which had
gradually disappeared, the sense of suspicion and frustration,
came flooding back with renewed bitterness. And the whole
calamity was aggravated by circumstances of peculiar and
unnecessary suffering, which made distrust and bitterness not
unjustifiable. Demented apparently by that madness which
afflicts those whom the gods wish to destroy, George Augustus had "had a little talk" on the subject of a career with the
boy not three months before, when he must have known he
was hopelessly involved.

"Now, Georgie, you have only a few months longer, and
you will be leaving school. You must think of a career in life.
Have you thought about it?"

"Yes, father."

"That's right. And what career do you want to take up?"

"I want to be a painter."

"I rather expected you'd say that. But you must remember
that you can hardly expect to make money by painting. Even if
you have the talent, which I'm sure you have, it takes many
years to establish a reputation, and still more years before you
can hope to make an adequate income."

"Yes, I know that. But I'm convinced that if I had a small
income and could do what I wanted, I should be far happier
than if I made a great deal of money doing what I hated."

"Well, my boy, I'm really rather glad that you don't take the
purely money point of view. But think it over. If you take your
examinations and qualify, there is a regularly established practice in which you can take your place as my partner and, in
due course, as my successor. Think it over for a few months.
And if you finally decide to take the course you mention, I
dare say I can allow you two or three hundred a year, which
will be four hundred when I die."

Now all this was very fatherly and kindly and sensible. In an outburst of quite genuine affection and gratitude George protested first of all that he could not bear to think of his father's dying and that it was odious to think of profiting by his death.

"But," he added, "I am quite determined to be a painter in spite of everything. If you can help me as you say, it will all be perfect."

Nothing more was said on the subject, but in the following weeks George drew and painted hard, went twice to London to look at the galleries and get materials, and thought he was making progress. But what strange weakness permitted George Augustus to yield to the cruelty of raising these hopes which he must have known would be speedily wrecked? The thought of this was constantly in George's mind, as he moved about silently, rather scared, in the morning hours following the receipt of the letter. It was a problem he never solved, but the incident did not increase his trust in the world or himself.

Other incidents confirmed this mood. Both Isabel and George Augustus rather pushed George forward to take the brunt of the calamity. Isabel's first suggestion to George was that he should go as a grocer's errand-boy at three shillings a week, a proposition which George indignantly and properly rejected. Whereupon she called him a parasite and graceless spendthrift. Probably the suggestion was only hysteria, but it hit hard and rankled. Then, it was George do this, and George do that. It was George who had to interview insolent tradesmen and creditors, and plead for further credit and "time." It was George who recovered £90 in gold which had been stolen by the office boy, and was refunded. It was George who was sent to persuade his father to come back and face out the storm. It was George who was made to go and collect rents from suspicious and uneasy tenants. It was George who had to see solicitors and try to get a grasp of the situation. They even accepted his offer of the few pounds (birthday gifts saved up) which he had in the Post Office Savings Bank. Rather a shock for a boy not seventeen, who had been living an *exalté* inner life, and who had been led to suppose that his material future was assured. It is not wholly surprising that he was very

unhappy, a bit resentful, and that his mistrust became permanent, his modesty diffidence.

Things went on in this joyless way for about a year. "Disgrace" was avoided, but it was obvious that the Winterbourne
opulence was gone, and George Augustus had lost his nerve. It
was from this period that the beginnings of his subsequent
conversion dated. In defeat he returned to the beliefs of childhood, but some latent unrecognised hostility to the influence
of dear Mamma finally led him to the form of Christianity
most opposed to hers. As for George, he brooded a great deal
and oscillated between moods of hope and exultation and
moods of profound depression. They moved nearer to London, and he tried, with very little success, to sell some of his
paintings. They were too ambitious and too youthful, with no
commercial value. He was all the time uneasily conscious that
he ought to "get out" and that his family were anxious for
him to "do something." Kind friends wrote proposing the
most dreary and humiliating jobs they could think of. Even
Priscilla—a bitter blow—thought that "George should do
something *at once*, and in a few years might be earning two
pounds a week as a clerk." Then George made the acquaintance of a journalist, a very uneducated but extremely kindly
and good-natured man. Thomas had some sort of sub-editorship
in Fleet Street, and generously offered to allow George to do
some minor reporting for him, an offer which was jumped at.
George did his first job—which was passed—and returned
home, naturally very late, in a glow of virtuous exultation,
thinking how he would surprise his parents next morning with
the news, like a good little boy in a story-book. The surprise,
however, was his. He was met at the door by an angry Isabel,
who, without awaiting his explanation, demanded to know
what he meant by coming home at that hour, and accused him
of "going with a vile woman." George was too disgusted to
make any reply, and went to bed. Next morning there was a
glorious row, in which Isabel played the part of a broken-
hearted mother and George Augustus came out very strong
as a *père noble* of the Surrey melodrama brand. George was

upset, but his contempt kept him cool. George Augustus was perorating:

"If you continue in this way you will break your mother's heart!"

It was so ludicrous—poor old George Augustus!—that George couldn't help laughing. George Augustus raised his hand in a noble gesture of paternal malediction:

"Leave this house! And do not return to it until you have learned to apologise for your behaviour."

"You mean it?"

"I solemnly mean it."

"Right."

George went straight upstairs and packed his few clothes in a suit-case, asked if he might have the volume of Keats, and left in half an hour—with elevenpence in his pocket, humming:

"Now of my threescore years and ten, twenty will not come again."

So that was that.

END OF PART I

PART II

I

Bank pass-books and private account-books are revealing documents, strangely neglected by biographers. One of the most useful things to know about any hero is the extent of his income, whether earned or unearned, whether crescendo or diminuendo. Complicated *états d'âme* are the luxury of leisured opulence. Those who have to earn their living must accept Appearances as Reality, and have little time for metaphysical woes and passions. I once thought of beginning this section with an accurate facsimile of George's private account, and pass-books. But that would be *vérisme*. It is enough to say that his unearned income was nil, and his earned income small but crescendo. Like most people who are too high-spirited to work for stated hours at a weekly wage, he drifted into journalism, which may be briefly but accurately defined as the most degrading form of that most degrading vice, mental prostitution. Its resemblance to the less reprehensible form is striking. Only the more fashionable cocottes of the dual trade make a reasonable income. The similarity between the conditions of the two parallel prostitutions becomes still more remarkable when you reflect that on the physical side you pretend to be a milliner, or a masseuse, or a clergyman's daughter, or a lady of quality, or even a lady journalist in need of a little aid for which you are prepared to make suitable acknowledgment; and on the mental side you pretend to be a poet, or an expert in something, or a lady of quality, or a duke. Both require suppleness in a supreme degree, and in both the fatal handicaps are honesty, modesty, and independence.

All of which George discovered very rapidly, and acted

accordingly. But his powers of simulation were inadequate, and consequently he failed at all times to conceal the fact that he possessed some vitality and beliefs, and held to them. This, of course, for a long time prevented his obtaining work from any but crank periodicals, of which London before the war possessed about three, which believed in allowing contributors to say what they thought. Needless to say, they have since perished; and London journalism is now one compact sun of sweetness and light. If this, or indeed anything, much mattered, one might be tempted to deplore it.

In the course of his *naïf* peregrinations George became temporarily acquainted with numerous personages, whom he classified as morons, abject morons, and queer-Dicks. The abject morons were those editors and journalists who sincerely believed in the imbecilities they perpetrated, virtuous apprentices gone to the devil, honest boot-blacks out of a job. The morons were those who knew better but pretended not to, and who by long dabbling in pitch had become pitchy. The queer-Dicks were more or less honest cranks, or at least possessed so much vanity and obstinacy that they seemed honest. After a few vague and awkward struggles, George found himself limited to the queer-Dicks. Of these there were three, whom for convenience sake I shall label Shobbe, Bobbe, and Tubbe. Mr. or Herr Shobbe ran a literary review, one of those "advanced" reviews beloved by the English, which move rapidly forward with a crab-like motion. Herr Shobbe was a very great man. Comrade Bobbe ran a Socialist weekly which was subsidised by a demented eugenist and a vegetarian Theosophist. Since Marxian economics, eugenics, pure food, and theosophy did not wholly fill its columns, the organ of the intellectual and wage-weary worker permitted regular comments on art and literature. And since none of the directors of the journal knew anything whatever about these subjects, they occasionally and by accident allowed them to be treated by some one with ideas and enthusiasm. Comrade Bobbe was a very great man. As for Mr. Waldo Tubbe, who hailed (why "hailed"?) from the Middle Western districts of the United States, he was an exceedingly ardent and patriotic British Tory, standing for Royalism in Art, Authority in Politics, and Classicism in Religion.

Unfortunately, there was no dormant peerage in the family; otherwise he would certainly have spent all his modest patrimony in endeavouring to become Lord Tubbe. Since he was an unshakeable Anglo-Catholic, there were no hopes of a Papal Countship; and Tory Governments are proverbially shabby in their treatment of even the most distinguished among their intellectual supporters. Consequently, all Mr. Waldo Tubbe could do in that line was to hint at his aristocratic English ancestry, to use his (possibly authentic) coat-of-arms on his cutlery, stationery, toilet articles, and book-plates, and know only the "best" people. How George ever got to know him is a mystery; still more how he came to write for a periodical which once advertised that its list of subscribers included four dukes, three marquesses and eleven earls. The only explanation is that Mr. Tubbe's Americanised Toryism was a bit more lively than the native brand, or that he leaned so very far to the extreme Right that without knowing it he sometimes tumbled into the verge of the extreme Left. But, in any case, Mr. Waldo Tubbe was also a very great man.

Upon the charity of these three gentlemen our hero chiefly but not extravagantly subsisted, skating indeed upon very thin ice in his relations with them, and expending treasures of diplomacy and dissimulation which might have been employed in the service of his Country. It subsequently transpired (why "transpired"?) that his Country did not want his brains, but his blood.

Sunday in London. In the City, nuts, bolts, infinite curious pieces of odd metal, embedded in the black shiny roads, frozen rivers of ink, may be examined without danger. The peace of commerce which passes all desolation. Puritan fervour relapsed to negative depression. Gigantic wings of Ennui folded irresistibly over millions. Vast trails of automobiles hopelessly hooting to escape. Epic melancholy of deserted side-streets where the rhythmic beat of a horse's hoofs is an adagio of despair. Horrors of Gunnersbury. The spleen of the railway line between Turnham Green and Hammersmith, the villainous sordidness of Raynes Park, the ennui which always vibrates with the waiting train at Gloucester Road station, emerge triumphant when

the Lord is at rest and possess the streets. The rain is one melancholy, and the sun another. The supreme insult of pealing
bells morning and evening. Dearly beloved brethren, miserable
sinners, stand up, stand up for Jesus. Who will deliver us, who
will deliver us from the Christians? O Lord Jesus, come quickly,
and get it over!

It was a merry Sunday evening of merry England in the month
of March 1912. After a long day of unremitting but not very
remunerative toil, George had gone to call on his friend, Mr.
Frank Upjohn. The word "friend" is here, as nearly always,
inexact, if by friend is meant one who feels for another a disinterested affection unaccompanied by sexual desire. (Friendship accompanied by sexual desire is love, the phœnix or unicorn
of passions.) In the case of George and Mr. Upjohn there was
at least a truce to the instinctive hostility and grudging which
human beings almost invariably feel for one another. Ties of
mutual self-interest bound them. George made jokes and Mr.
Upjohn laughed at them: and vice versa. Mr. Upjohn desired
to make George a disciple, and George was not averse from
making use of Mr. Upjohn. Mutual admiration, implied if not
expressed and perhaps not wholly insincere, enabled them to
form a small protective nucleus against the oceanic indifference of mankind, and thus feel superior to it. They ate together,
and even lent each other small sums of money without security.
The word "friend" is therefore justified à peu près.

   Needless to say, Mr. Upjohn was a very great man. He was a
Painter. Since he was destitute of any intrinsic and spontaneous
originality, he strove much to be original, and invented a new
school of painting every season. He first created a sensation
with his daring and brilliant "****** ** * ********** *******,"
which was denounced in no unmeasured terms by the Press,
**** ****** *** *** ****** ** ****** ****** *** ***
********** ********** ** *** ****. "The Blessed Damozel in
Hell" passed almost unnoticed, when fortunately the model
most unjustly obtained an affiliation order against Mr. Upjohn
and thus drew attention to a neglected masterpiece, which was
immediately bought by a man who had made a fortune in
******** ****** *****. Mr. Upjohn then became aware of the

existence of modern French art. One season he painted in gorgeous Pointilliste blobs, the next in monotone Fauviste smears, then in calamitous Futuriste accidents of form and colour. At this moment he was just about to launch the Suprematist movement in painting, to which he hoped to convert George, or at any rate to get him to write an article about it. Suprematist painting, which has now unfortunately gone out of fashion, was, as its name implies, the supreme point of modern art. Mr. Upjohn produced two pictures in illustration (the word is perhaps inaccurate) of his theories. One was a beautiful scarlet whorl on a background of the purest flake white. The other at first sight appeared to be a brood of bulbous yellow chickens, with thick elongated necks, aimlessly scattered over a grey-green meadow; but on closer inspection the chickens turned out to be conventionalised phalluses. The first was called Decomposition-Cosmos, and the second Op. 49, Piano.

Mr. Upjohn turned on both electric lights in his studio for George to study these interesting productions, at which our friend gazed with a feeling of baffled perplexity and the agonised certainty that he would have to say something about them, and that what he would say would inevitably be wrong. Fortunately, Mr. Upjohn was extremely vain and highly nervous. He stood behind George, coughing and jerking himself about agitatedly.

"What I mean to say is," he said, puncturing his discourse with coughs, "there you've got it."

"Yes, yes, of course."

"What I mean is, you've got precise expression of precise emotion."

"Just what I was going to say."

"You see, when you've got that, what I mean is, you've got something."

"Why, of course!"

"You see, what I mean to say is, if you get two or three intelligent people to *see* the thing, then you've got it. I mean you won't get those damned block-headed sons of bitches like Quijasso and Cæsar Frank to see it, I mean, it simply smashes them, you see."

"Did you expect them to?"

"You see, what you've got is complete originality *and* The Tradition. One doesn't worry about the hacks, you see, but what I mean to say, one does *mildly* suppose Quijasso had a few gleams of intelligence, but what I mean is they won't *take* anything new."

"I get the originality, of course, but I admit I don't quite see the traditional side of the movement."

Mr. Upjohn sighed pettishly and waved his head from side to side in commiserating contempt.

"Of course, you *wouldn't*. What intelligence you have was ruined by your lack of education, and your native obtuseness makes you instinctively prefer the academic. I mean, can't you SEE that the proportions of Decomposition-Cosmos are exactly those of the Canopic vase in the Filangieri Museum at Naples?"

"How could I see that," said George, rather annoyed, "since I've never been to Naples?"

"That's what I mean to say," exlaimed Mr. Upjohn triumphantly, "you simply have no education *what-so-ever*!"

"Well, but what about the other?" said George, desiring to be placable; "is that in the Canopic vase tradition?"

"Christ-in-petticoats, NO! I thought even you'd see *that*. What I mean is, can't you *see* it?"

"They might be free adaptations of Greek vase painting?" said George tentatively, hoping to soothe this excitable and irritated genius. Mr. Upjohn flung his palette knife on the floor.

"You're *too* stupid, George. What I mean is, the proportion and placing and colour-values are exactly in the best tradition of American–Indian blankets, and what I mean is, when you've got that, well, I mean, you've got something!"

"Of course, of course, it *was* stupid of me not to see. Forgive me, I've been working at hack articles all day, and my mind's a bit muzzy."

"I mildly supposed so!"

And Mr. Upjohn, with spasmodic movements, jerked the two easels round to the wall. There was a short pause in the conversation. Mr. Upjohn irritatedly cast himself at full length upon a sofa, and spasmodically ate candied apricots. He

placed them in his mouth with his forefinger and thumb, holding his elbow at an angle of ninety degrees to his body, with
his chin far extended, and bit them savagely in half. George
watched this impressive and barbaric spectacle with the interest of one who at last discovers the meaning of the mysterious
rite of Urim and Thummim. A timid effort at making conversation was repelled by Mr. Upjohn, with a gesture which
George interpreted as meaning that Mr. Upjohn required complete silence to digest and sweeten with candied apricots the
memory of George's treasonable obtuseness. Suddenly George
started, for Mr. Upjohn, after coughing once or twice, swung
himself from his couch with incredible swiftness, hawked vigorously, flung open a window with unnecessary violence and
spat voluminously into the street. He then turned and said
calmly:

"You'd better come along to fat Shobbe's."

George, who was young enough to enjoy going to miscella-
neous parties, gratefully acquiesced; and was still further gratified by being allowed to witness the strange and complex
ablutions performed by Mr. Upjohn from a wash-basin star-
tlingly concealed in a veneered mahogany tallboy.

Mr. Upjohn was evidently a very clean man, at least in those
portions of his body exposed to the public gaze. He washed
and rinsed his faced thoroughly, brushed his teeth until George
apprehended lest the bristles be worn to the bone, gargled and
spat freely. He soaped and pumiced his hands, which were
large, yellow, and slightly spatulate; and excavated his nails
with singular industry and pertinacity. He then sat down
before a folding table-mirror in three parts, which reflected
both profiles as well as full-face, and combed and brushed and
re-brushed and re-combed his coarse hay-like hair until it
crackled with induced electricity. When Mr. Upjohn judged
that hygiene and beauty-culture had received their full due, he
arrayed himself in a clean collar, a tie of remarkable lustre and
size, and a narrow-waisted rather long coat which, taken in
conjunction with the worn but elegant peg-top trousers he had
on, gave him a pleasantly rakehelly and Regency look. This
singular scene, which occupied the better part of an hour, was
conducted by Mr. Upjohn with great gravity, varied by the

emission of a singular and discordant chant or hum, and wild petulant oaths whenever any object of the toilet or of his apparel did not instantly present itself to his hand. Oddly enough, Mr. Upjohn was not a sodomist. He was a professedly ardent admirer of what our ignorant forefathers called the soft sex. Mr. Upjohn often asserted that after the immense toils of Suprematist painting nothing could rest him but the presence of several beautiful women. While gallantly and probably necessarily discreet as to his conquests, he was always prepared to talk about love, and to give subtle erotic advice, which led any man who had actually lain with a woman to suspect that Mr. Upjohn was at best a fumbler and probably still a virgin.

Mr. Upjohn then endued a very Regency thin grey overcoat, stuck a long ebony cane with no handle under his left armpit, tossed a soft grey hat rakishly on to his hair, and made for the door. George followed, half-impressed, half-amused by this childish swagger and self-conscious bounce.

In the street the Sabbath ennui of London emerged from its lair like a large, dull grey octopus, and shot stealthy feelers of depression at them. Mr. Upjohn, safe as Achilles in the Stygian dip of his conceit, strode along energetically with an inward feeling that he had gone one better on James McNeill Whistler. The boredom of Mr. Upjohn came from within, not from without. He was so absorbed in Mr. Upjohn that he rarely noticed what was going on about him.

George fought at the monster and plunged desperately into talk.

"What about this coal strike? Will it ruin the country as the papers say? Isn't it a foolish thing on both sides?"

This strike was George's first introduction to the reality of the "social problem" and the bitter class-hatred which smoulders in England and at times bursts into fierce crises of hatred, restrained only by that mingling of fear and "decency" which composes the servile character of the British working-man.

"Well, what I mean to say is," said Mr. Upjohn, who very rarely managed to say what he meant but always meant to say something original and startling, "it ain't our affair. But what I mean is, if the miners get more money it'll be all the better for us. They're more likely to buy our pictures than sons of bitches like Bond and Pittsquith."

George was a bit staggered at this. In the first place, he had been looking at the problem from a national, not a personal, point of view. And, in the second place, he knew just a little about working-men and their conditions. He could not see how five shillings a week more would convert the miners to collecting the Suprematist school of painting, or make them abandon their cultivated amusements of coursing, pigeon-flying, gambling, wife-beating, and drinking. But Mr. Upjohn delivered his *obiter dicta* with so much aplomb that a boy of twenty might be excused for failing to see their complete absurdity.

They were walking up Church Street, Kensington, that dismal communication trench which links the support line of Kensington High Street with the front line of Notting Hill Gate. How curious are cities, with their intricate trench systems and perpetual warfare, concealed but as deadly as the open warfare of armies! We live in trenches, with flat revetments of house-fronts as parapet and parados. The warfare goes on behind the housefronts—wives with husbands, children with parents, employers with employed, tradesmen with tradesmen, banker with lawyer, and the triumphal doctor rooting out life's casualties. Desperate warfare—for what? Money as the symbol of power; power as the symbol or affirmation of existence. Throbbing warfare of men's cities! As fierce and implacable and concealed as the desperate warfare of plants and the hidden carnage of animals. We walk up Church Street. Up the communication trench. We cannot see "over the top," have no vista of the immense no-man's-land of London's roofs. We cannot pierce through the house-fronts. What is going on behind those dingy, unpierceable house-fronts? What tortures, what contests, what incests, what cruelties, what sacrifice, what horror, what sordid emptiness? We cannot pierce through the pavement and Belgian blocks, see the subterranean veins of electric cables, the arteries of gas- and water-mains, the viscera of underground railways. We cannot feel the water filtering through London clay; do not perceive the relics of ruined Londons waiting for archæologists from the antipodes; do not see, far, far down, the fossiled bones of extinct animals and their coprolites. Here in Notting Hill the sabre-toothed tiger roared and savagely devoured its victims; the huge-horned deer darted in terror; wolves howled; the brown bear preyed; overhead by day screamed the eagles and by night flitted huge bats. Mysterious forest murmurs, abrupt yells and threatening growls, and the amorous hatred of female beasts, were vocal when the Channel was the Rhine's estuary.

"Time passes," said George; "what do we know of Time? Prehistoric beasts, like the ichthyosaurus and ***** ********, have laired and copulated and brought forth . . ."

A motor-bus roared by, like a fabulous noisy red ox with fiery eyes and a luminous interior, quenching his words.

"Eh?" said Mr. Upjohn. "*****!"

"Now, look at these simian bipeds," George pursued, pointing to an inoffensive pair of lovers and a suspicious cop, "more foul, more deadly, more incestuously blood-lustful . . ."

"You see, what I mean is, nothing matters to these people but our conversation. . . . Now, what I mean is, you get fat Shobbe to let you write an article on me and Suprematism."

"We should go to the Zoo more often, and watch the monkeys. The chimpanzee leaps with the dexterity of a politician. The Irish-looking ourang smokes his pipe as placidly as a Camden Town murderer. The purple-bottomed mandrils in heat will initiate you into love. And the perpetual chatter of the small monkeys—how like ourselves! What ecstatic clicking about nothing! Go to the ape, thou poet."

Mr. Upjohn laughed abruptly and spat with a raucous cough:

"An old idea, but what's it got to do with *le mouvement*? Still, what I mean is, I might do something with it. . . ."

Poor old George! He was a bloody fool. He never learned how fatally unwise it is to express any sort of an idea to a brother—still less to a sister—artist.

Mr. Upjohn discoursed on Suprematism and himself.

At Notting Hill Gate, George halted. The Sabbath ennui shot its tentacles at him, and enlaced his spirit, dragging him down into the whirlpool of wanhope. Why go on? Why affront the

veiled hostility of people? Why suffer those eyes to search and
those nimble unerring tongues to wound? Oh, wrap oneself in
solitude, like an armoured shroud, and bend over the dead
words of a dead language! A simian biped! O gods, gods! And
Plato talks of Beauty.

"Come along," shouted Mr. Upjohn, a few paces ahead,
"this way. Holland Park. Old Shobbe'll be waiting for me in
that mob. What I mean is, he knows I'm the only other intelligent person in London."

George still hesitated. He sank deeper in the maelstrom of
unintelligible and causeless despair. Why go on? The adoles-
cent love of death and suicide—corollary to youth's vitality
and vivid energy—swept over him in choking waves. To cease
upon the midnight with no pain. . . .

"I think I shan't come," he shouted after the retreating Mr.
Upjohn.

Mr. Upjohn hurried back and seized George's arm:

"What's the matter with you? The best way to get an article
out of Shobbe is to go and see him on his Sunday evenings.
Come on. We shall be late."

No Euripidean chorus uttered gnomic reflections on the
inevitable and irresistible power of Ananke, the Destiny which
is above the gods. No bright god warned him, no oracular
voice spoke to him. Conflict of freewill and destiny! But is
there a conflict? Whether we move or are still, whether we go
to the right or the left, hesitate or rush blindly forward, the
thread is inexorably spun. Ananke, Ananke.

George yielded reluctantly to the tug at his arm.

"All right, I'll come."

2

As they were shown into Mr. Shobbe's large studio they
encountered an indescribable babble of human voices, which
gave strange point to George's zoological remarks, since it
sounded as if all the macaws at the Zoo had got into the

monkey-house to argue with its inhabitants about theology.
Mr. Shobbe's studio (or "stew-joe," as his humbler Cockney
contributors called it) was already dim with cigarette smoke.
The excited and elevated babble of voices was due to the fact
that this was one of Mr. Shobbe's rare caviar and champagne
evenings, and not one of the ordinary beer and ham-sandwich
débâcles. George and Mr. Upjohn were still in the doorway,
hidden by the opening door, when a couple of champagne
corks popped. George noticed a look of horror and perplexity,
mingled with the satisfaction always produced by the prospect
of free alcohol, in Mr. Upjohn's countenance. George wondered vaguely why, and followed the ebullient swagger of Mr.
Upjohn into the large room. It was not until long afterwards
that he realised the cause of this rapid and subtle flash of horror in Mr. Upjohn. The champagne and caviar evenings were
reserved for the "better" contributors to, and the wealthier
guarantors of, Mr. Shobbe's periodical. Upjohn was County
and Cambridge, with a small income and prospects of a large
inheritance from a senile aunt—he was therefore one of the
"better" contributors. George, on the other hand, was merely
middle-class, talented, and penniless. Mr. Upjohn had thus
committed a social error of hair-raising enormity by bringing
George to the champagne reception under the false impression
that it was merely a beer "do" for the common mob.

With genial bonhomie Mr. Shobbe greeted in Mr. Upjohn
the potential inheritance from the senile aunt. Upon George he
turned a coldly languid blue eye, and for a moment lent him a
hand even limper, flabbier, and clammier than usual. George
noticed the difference, but ingenuously assumed that it was
because he was younger than Mr. Upjohn and incapable of
producing "****** *** ********** *******" or the doctrines
of Suprematism. But Mr. Upjohn, with more acute social
ambitions, was aware of his *gaffe*. He mumbled his apology,
which was almost lost in the surrounding babble:

"Brought 'm 'long discuss 'n article on Me 'n S'prematism."

Mr. Shobbe only half-heard, and nodded vaguely. The slight
awkwardness of the situation was ended by the appearance of
Mrs. Shobbe, who greeted them both; and they passed into the

room. George attributed the feeling of strain to his own shyness and aloofness. He was still *naïf* enough to suppose that people are welcomed for their own sake.

In justice to the distinguished gathering in Mr. Shobbe's studio (two "social" journalists were present) it must be said that the babble and the excitement were not wholly due to the champagne. Pre-war London was comparatively sober. Numbers of women did not even drink at all, and cocktails and communal copulation had not then been developed to their present state of intensity. Whether the art of scandal-mongering has suffered by this new social activity is hard to say, but as ever it remains the chief diversion of the British intelligentsia. Serious conversation is of course impossible, on account of the paper-pirates who are always hovering about to snatch up an idea. One definite improvement is that the *bon mot*, the *recherché* pun, the intentional witticism, are definitely discouraged. Indeed, one of the brightest of the post-war reputations was created by a young man who had the self-restraint to sit through forty-five literary parties without saying a word. This frightened everybody so much that when this modern lay Trappist departed you heard on all sides:

"Brilliant young man."

"Extraordinarily clever."

"I hear he's writing a book on metaphysics in the Stone Age."

"No, really?"

"They say he's the greatest living authority on pre-Columbian literature!"

"How quite too marvellous."

But in those distant pre-war days people strove to chatter themselves into notice through a chaos of witticisms. On this particular evening, however, witticisms were in the background, for an event had occurred to stagger this small cosmos of affectation into sincerity. With the exception of George (who was too young and unknown to matter) and a few women, almost everybody present had been connected with a publishing firm which had suddenly gone bankrupt. On Mr. Shobbe's recommendation some of his wealthier guarantors had put

money into the firm; the painters were "doing" illustrated editions or writing books on the Renaissance artists still popular
in those unenlightened days; and the writers had received con-
tracts for an almost unlimited number of works. Money had
been lavishly spent and some rather amusing things had been
begun. Then suddenly the publisher vanished with the lady typ-
ist-secretary and the remainder of the cash. Hence the excited
babble.

George stood, a little dazed, beside a small group of youngish men and women. A dark, rather sinister-looking young
man kept saying:

"Le crapule! Ah! le crapule!"

George wondered vaguely who was a crapule and why, and
half-listened to the conversation.

"He was paying me three hundred a year and . . ."

"My last novel did so well that he gave me a five years' con-
tract and an advance of . . ."

"Yes, and I was getting twenty per cent. . . ."

"Yes, but do let me tell you this. Shobbe says that the lawyers told him four thousand pounds of the money came from
the diocesan funds of . . ."

"Yes, I know. Shobbe told us."

"Le crapule!"

"What'll the archbishop say?"

"Oh, they'll smother that up."

"Yes, but look here—do shut up for a minute, Bessie—what
I want to know is, how do we stand? What about our copy-
rights? Shobbe told me the legal position is . . ."

"Hang the legal position. What do we get out of it?"

"Crapule!"

"Nothing, probably. *You* won't get much, anyhow. He hadn't
even published your book, and I was to get three hundred a
year and . . ."

"It isn't so much the money I mind as having my book off
the market when it was going so well—did you see the long
article on me in last week's . . ."

"Crapule!"

George glanced almost affectionately at the sinister-looking

young man. It struck him that the repeated "crapule" was
addressed as much to his present audience as to the unknown
perpetrator of these calamities. At that moment Mr. Upjohn
came along, and George took him aside.

"I say, Frank, what's all this talk about?"

"Dear Bertie has eloped with Olga and the cash."

"Dear Bertie? Oh, you mean . . . But the firm will go on,
won't it?"

"Go on the streets. You see, there isn't a cent left. What I
mean is, I shall have to find some one else to do my Suprematist book. What I mean to say is, Bertie had a glimmering of
intelligence . . ."

"Who's Olga?"

But at that moment a lady with two unmarried daughters
and private information about the senile aunt's fortune plunged
sweetly at Mr. Upjohn.

"Oh, Mr. Upjohn, how *nice* to see you again! How *are*
you?"

"Mildly surviving."

"You *never* came to my last at-home. Now you *must* come
and have dinner next week. Sir George was *so* much impressed
last week by what you said about the new school of painting
you have founded—what *is* the name? I'm so *stupid* about
remembering names."

Mr. Upjohn introduced them:

"Lady Carter—George Winterbourne. He's a painter—of
sorts."

Lady Carter took in George at a glance—shabby clothes,
old tie carelessly knotted, hair too long, abstracted gaze, poor,
too young anyway—and was politely insolent. After a few
words, she and Mr. Upjohn walked away. She pretended to be
amused by Mr. Upjohn's conversation.

George went over to the table and took a sandwich and a glass of
champagne. The ceaseless babble of petty talk about petty interests irritated and bored him. He felt isolated and hate-obstinate.
So this was Upjohn's "only intelligent group in London"! If this
is "intelligence," then let me be a fool, for God's sake. Better the

great octopus ennui outside than these jelly-fish tentacles sting-
ing with conceit, self-interest, and malice.

He went over to talk to Comrade-Editor Bobbe. Mr. Bobbe
was a sandy-haired, narrow-chested little man with spiteful
blue eyes and a malevolent class-hatred. He exercised his
malevolence with comparative impunity by trading upon his
working-class origin and his indigestion, of which he had been
dying for twenty years. Nobody of decent breeding could hit
Mr. Bobbe as he deserved, because his looks were a perpetual
reminder of his disease, and his behaviour and habits gave continual evidence of his origin. He was the Thersites of the day,
or rather that would have been the only excuse for him. Intellectually he was Rousseau's sedulous and somewhat lousy ape.
His conversation rasped. His vanity and class-consciousness
made him yearn for affairs with upper-class women, although
he was obviously a homosexual type. Admirable energy, a swift
and sometimes remarkable intuition into character, a good
memory and excellent faculty of imitation, a sharp tongue and
brutal frankness, gave him power. He was a little snipe, but a
dangerous one. Although biased and sometimes absurd, his
weekly political articles were by far the best of the day. He
might have been a real influence in the rapidly growing Socialist Party if he could have controlled his excessive malevolence,
curbed his hankering for aristocratic alcoves, and dismissed his
fatuous theories of the Unconscious which were a singular
mixture of misapprehended theosophy and ill-digested Freud.
George admired his feverish energy and talents, pitied him for
his ill-health and agonised sense of class inferiority, disliked his
malevolence, and ignored his theories.

"What are *you* doing here, Winterbourne? I shouldn't have
thought Shobbe would invite *you*. You haven't any money,
have you?"

"Upjohn brought me along."

"Upjohn-and-at-'em? What's he want of you?"

"An article on his new school of painting, I think."

Mr. Bobbe tittered, screwing up his eyes and nose in disgust, and flapping his right hand with a gesture of take-it-
away-it-stinks.

"Suprematist painting! Suprematist dung-bags! Suprematist conceit and empty-headed charlatanism! Did you see him toady to that Carter woman, *Lady* Carter? Puh!"

There was such vindictiveness in that "puh" that George was disconcerted. True, he himself suspected Mr. Upjohn was a bit of a charlatan, and knew he was odiously conceited; at the same time, there was something very kind-hearted and generous in poor Upjohn-and-at-'em, who had received that nickname for his furious onslaughts on any one who was established and successful, in alleged defence of any one who was struggling and neglected. Unfortunately, these vituperative efforts of poor Mr. Upjohn did no good to his friends and served only to bring himself advertisement—the advertisement of ridiculousness. But George felt he ought to say something in defence.

"Well, of course he's eccentric and sometimes offensive, but he's got a streak of curious genius and real generosity."

Mr. Bobbe snarled rather than tittered.

"He's an insignificant, toadying little cheese-worm. That's what he is, a toadying little *cheese-worm*. And you won't be much better, my lad, if you let yourself drift with these people. You'll go to pieces, you'll just go *com-plete-ly* to pieces. But humanity's rotten. It's all rotten. It stinks. It's worm-eaten. Look at those mingy fellows prancing round those women on the tips of their toes. Cold-hearted, **************, mingy sneaks! Look at the women, pining for a bit o' real warm-hearted man's love, and what do they get? Mingy cold-hearted ********! I know 'em, I know 'em. Curse the mingy lot of 'em. But it won't last long, it can't. The workers won't stand it. There'll be a revolution and a bloody one, and soon too. Mingy sons of spats and eye-glasses!"

George was amazed and embarrassed by this outburst. He did indeed feel repelled by most of the gathering, particularly by persons like Mr. Robert Jeames, the Poets' Friend, who made anthologies of all the worst authors, wore a monocle and spats, and lisped through a wet tooth. But after all Mr. Jeames was harmless and quite amiable. One might not agree with his taste; one might not feel attracted by him, or indeed by most of the people present. But there was certainly a wide difference between such a feeling and "mingy sneaks" and "cheese-worms." Moreover, George was a little offended by Mr. Bobbe's proletarian vocabulary, while he failed to see exactly why the sexual frigidity of a few men in dinner-jackets should cause the workers to rise in bloody revolution.

"I shouldn't think the workers care a hoot. If it's as you say, the women are more likely to join the suffragettes."

"Faugh!" said Mr. Bobbe, "puh! Suffragettes? Take them away. They smell. They're unclean. They're obscene. Women and votes! It's the last stage of decomposition of the mingy world. When the women start to get power, it's the end. It means the men are done for, mingy cold-hearted sneaks. Once let the women in, and nothing can save the world. Socialism, perhaps, and a genuine out-reaching of the inward unconscious Male-life to the dark Womb-life in Woman. But no, they're not worthy of it. Let 'em go. You'll see, my lad, you'll see. Within five years there'll be a . . ."

"Oh, Mr. Bobbe," said Mrs. Shobbe's voice, and a timid little greyish lady, all in grey and silver, appeared, gentle and fluttering beside them, like a large gentle grey moth. "Oh, Mr. Bobbe, do forgive me for interrupting your *interesting* conversation. Lady Carter is *so* anxious to meet you and admires you so much. I'm sure you'll like her and her two daughters—such *beautiful* girls."

George watched Mr. Bobbe as he bowed servilely to Lady Carter and entered into an animated conversation with that living rung in the social ladder. He watched the scene for several minutes, and was just thinking of leaving when Mr. Waldo Tubbe came near him.

"Well, Winterbourne," he remarked in his neat, mincing English, "you appeared sunk in thought. What was the precise object of your contemplation?"

"Bobbe was inveighing against Upjohn for toadying to Lady Carter, and then as soon as Mrs. Shobbe came and asked him to be introduced, he rushed off and you can see him there sitting at Lady Carter's feet with clasped hands."

Mr. Tubbe looked unnecessarily grave.

"O-oh," he said, with a very genteel roll to the 'o,' and an air

of suggesting unutterable things. This was a very great asset to
Mr. Tubbe in social intercourse. He found that an interrogative
silence on his part forced other people to talk, and made them
slightly ill at ease, so that they betrayed what they did not
always wish to express. He would then gravely remark "Oe-oh"
or "In-deed?" or "Really?" with a deportmental air which was
highly impressive and somehow slightly reproving. It was
reported that Mr. Tubbe spent hours practising in private the
exact intonation of his "Oe-ohs," "Reallys," and "Indeeds." He
had certainly brought them to a high pitch of gentility and suppressed significance. Mr. Tubbe drank a good deal—gin mostly;
but it must be said for him that the drunker he got, the more
genteel and darkly significant he became.

There was a pause after Mr. Tubbe's "Oe-oh." His interrogative silence did its work. George plunged into talk, saying
the first thing which came into his head.

"I came along with Upjohn, after seeing his new pictures."

"In-deed?"

"He would like me to write an article on them, but it's very
difficult. Honestly, I don't understand them and think they're
rather nonsense; don't you?"

"Oe-oh."

"Have you seen them?"

"Noe-o."

Say something, blast you!

Another long pause.

"Well, my dear Winterbourne, I am very happy to have had
some conversation with you. Come in and see me soon, quite
soon. Will you excuse me? I must ask Lord Congreve a question. Good-bye. *Good*-bye!"

George observed the greeting between Mr. Waldo Tubbe and
Lord Congreve.

"Hullo, Waldo!"

"My *dear* Bernard! . . ."

Mr. Tubbe shook hands with an air of restrained but very considerable emotion. He treated Lord Congreve with a kind of dignified familiarity, rather like Phélypeaux playing billiards with

Louis Quatorze. Mr. Shobbe, who was the third party to this interesting reunion, behaved more easily, with a *puissance-à-puissance* geniality. George could not hear what they were saying, and did not want to. He was watching Mrs. Shobbe, who was talking gently with two younger women on a couch in one corner of the studio. Poor Mrs. Shobbe, of whom one always thought as a soft, kind grey moth, for ever fluttering with kindly intent and for ever fluttering wrong. She had that sweet exasperating gentleness and refined incompetence which marked so many women of the wealthier class whose youth was blighted by Ruskin and Morris. Her portrait had been painted by Burne-Jones—there it was on the wall, over-sweet, over-wistful, stylised to look like one of his Arthurian damosels. And there she was grey and moth-like, the sweetness gone insipid, the wistfulness become empty and regretful. Had she ever looked like that portrait? No one would have known it was she, unless they had been told.

Poor Mrs. Shobbe! In turns one pitied, almost loved, despised, and was exasperated by her. Such crushed insipidity. And yet such a gallant effort to do "what is right." But she somehow disgusted one with refinement and trying to do what is right, and made one yearn sympathetically towards a hard-swearing, hard-working, hard-drinking motor mechanic. Her life must have been very unhappy. Her well-off Victorian parents (wholesale wine trade, retired) had given her a good education of travel and accomplishments, and had systematically and gently crushed her. It was chiefly the mother, of course, that abominable mother-daughter "love" which is compact of bullying, jealousy, parasitism, and baffled sexuality. With what ghastly pertinacity does a disappointed wife "take it out" on her daughter! Not consciously, of course; but it is the unconscious cruelty and oppression of human beings which seem the most dreadful. To escape, she had married Shobbe.

Nothing can be more fatal for a girl than to marry an artist of any kind. Have affairs with them, my dears, if you like. They can teach you a great deal about life, human nature, and sex, because they are directly interested in these matters, whereas other men are cluttered with prejudices, ideals, and literary reminiscences. But do not marry them, unless you have a writing of divorcement in the pocket of your night-gown. If you are poor, life will be horrid even though there are no children; and if you have children, it will be hell. If you have money, you may be quite sure that it is not you but your money which has been espoused. Every poor artist and intellectual is looking for a woman to keep him. So you look out too. Of course, not only are there no delicious marriages, there are not even any good ones—Rochefoucauld was such an optimist. And in any case marriage is a primitive institution bound to succumb before the joint attack of contraceptives and the economic independence of women. Remember, artists are not seeking tranquillity and legitimate posterity, but experience and an income. So look out!

Poor Mrs. Shobbe did not look out; she had never been allowed to do anything so unmaidenly. She became the means whereby Mr. Shobbe avoided the dismal but common fate of working for a living. He snubbed her, he patronised her, he neglected her, he was unfaithful to her, but hung on to her like a sloth to a tree-branch—she had three thousand a year, most of which he spent. As for Shobbe, he was a plump and talented snob of German origin. His aquiline nose was the one piece of evidence, apart from his bad manners, which supported his claim to aristocratic birth. Before the Great War he was always talking about his year's service in an aristocratic German regiment, or beginning a sentence, "When I was last with the Kaiser," or talking voluble German whenever there was an audience, or saying "Of course, you English. . . ." After the war he discovered that he was and always had been a patriotic English gentleman. Be it said to his credit, he "rolled up" himself and did not only "give" a few cousins. But then, there was Mrs. Shobbe to get away from on a legitimate excuse—how many patriotic English gentlemen in the war armies were rather avoiding their wives than seeking their country's enemies? Shobbe was an excellent example of the artist's amazing selfishness and vanity. After the comfort of his own person he really cared for nothing but his prose style and literary reputation. He was also an amazing and very amusing liar—a sort of literary Falstaff. As for his affairs with women—my God! Yet, after all, were they really so lurid? Probably they were grossly exaggerated because Shobbe had talent, and everybody was jealous of it. . . .

George suddenly became aware that Mrs. Shobbe was beckoning to him from the couch. Some of the noisier guests had departed—probably to drink more freely—and a wide-opened window had carried away much of the tobacco smoke. George emerged from his reverie and went quickly over to her.

"You know Mrs. Lamberton, don't you, Mr. Winterbourne? And this is Miss Paston, Elizabeth Paston."

How-do-you-do's.

"And, oh, Mr. Winterbourne, will you get us some iced lemonade, please? We're all dying of thirst in this smoky room."

George brought the drinks, and sat down in a chair facing the women. They chatted aimlessly. Soon Mrs. Shobbe went away. She saw a lonely old maid in the opposite corner of the room, and felt it "right" to talk to her. Mrs. Lamberton sighed.

"Why does one come to these intellectual agapes? An expense of spirit in a waste of time."

"Now, Frances!" said Elizabeth, with her hard, nervous little laugh, "you know you'd hate it if you weren't asked."

"Besides, it's one place where you're sure not to meet your husband," said George.

"Oh, but then I *never* see him. Only last week I had to ask the servants where Mr. Lamberton was. I didn't know whether he was still alive or only preoccupied with a new conquest."

"And was he?"

"What?"

"Alive. I didn't know he ever had been."

They laughed, though the paltry jest was near the truth.

"And yet," George pursued, with the ruthless clumsiness of youth, "you must have liked him once. Why? Why do women like men? And on what singular principle do they choose their husbands? Instinct? Self-interest?"

Neither answered. Women do not like these questions, especially from young men whose duty it is to be dazzled by charms they cannot analyse. Of course, the questions were impertinent;

but if a young man is not impertinent, what on earth is the use of him?

The women lit cigarettes. George looked at Elizabeth Paston. A slender figure in red silk: black, glossy hair drawn back from a high, intellectual forehead; large, very intelligent dark eyes; a rather pale, rather Egyptian-looking face with prominent cheek-bones, slightly sunken cheeks, and full red lips; a nervous manner. She was one of those "near" virgins so common in the countries of sexual prohibition. Her hands were slender, the line from her ear to her chin exquisitely beautiful, her breasts too flat. She smoked cigarettes too rapidly, and had a way of sitting with a look of abstraction in a pose which showed off the lovely line of her throat and jaw. Her teeth were a little irregular. The delicate ear was like a frail pink shell under the dark sea-fronds of her hair. Her calves and ankles, such important indications of female character and temperament, were hidden under the long skirts of those days; but the bared arms and wrists were slender and a little sensual as they lay along her clothed thighs. George was greatly attracted. Apparently she also liked him, and Mrs. Lamberton noticed it with that swift, rather devilish intuition of women. She rose to leave.

"Oh, Frances, don't go yet!" exclaimed Elizabeth. "I only came to see you, and you were so surrounded by men I have scarcely seen you."

"Yes, don't go."

"I must. You don't know the duties awaiting a careful wife and good mother."

She slipped away, leaving them alone.

"Isn't she a dear?" said Elizabeth.

"Something very lovely and precious. Even when she talks nonsense in that slightly affected way she seems to be saying something valuable."

"Do you think she is beautiful?"

"Beautiful? Yes, in a way, but she isn't one of those horrid regular beauties. You notice her at once in a room, but you'd never see her on the walls of the Academy. It isn't her beauty so much as her personality, and that you feel more by intuition than by observation. And yet the effect is beauty."

"Are you very much in love with her?"

"Why, aren't you? Isn't every one?"

"In love with her?"

George was silent. He was not sure whether the question was *naïf* or very much the reverse. Elizabeth changed the conversation.

"What do you 'do'?"

"Oh, I'm a painter, and I write hack articles for Shobbe and such people to earn a living."

"But don't you sell your pictures?"

"I try to; but you see, people in England aren't much interested in modern art, not as they are on the Continent or even in America. They want the same old thing done over again and done with more sugar. One thing about the British bourgeois— he doesn't know anything about pictures, but very stoutly stands for what he likes, and what he likes is anything except art. The newest historians say that the Anglo-Saxons come from the same race as the Vandals, and I can well believe it."

"Surely there are some up-to-date collectors in England."

"Why, yes, of course, probably as many as anywhere else, but too many of them collect pictures as an investment and so only take what the dealers advise them to buy; others are afraid to touch English art, which has gone soggy with Pre-Raphaelitism and touched imbecility with the anecdotal picture. There are people with taste and enthusiasms, but they're nearly all poor. It's much the same in Paris. The new painters there are having a terrific struggle, but they'll win. The young are with them. And then in Paris it's rather chic to know the latest movements and to defend the rebel artists against the ordinary mass ignorance and hostility. Here they're still terrified by the fate of Oscar, and it's chic to be a sporting imbecile. The English think it's virile to have no sensibilities."

"Are you English or American?"

"English, of course. Should I care about them if I were not? In a way, of course, it doesn't really matter. The nationalist epoch of painting is over—it's now an international language centred in Paris and understood from Petersburg to New York. What the English think doesn't matter."

George was excited and talking volubly. Elizabeth encouraged him. Females know instinctively or by bitter experience that males like to tell them things. It is so very curious that we talk of vanity as if it were almost exclusively feminine, whereas both sexes are equally vain. Perhaps males are vainer. Women are sometimes plainly revolted by really inane compliments, while there is no flattery too gross for a male. There simply isn't. And not one of us is free from it. However much you may be on your guard, however much you may think you dislike it, you will find yourself instinctively angling for female flattery—and getting it. Oh yes, you'll get it, just as long as that subtle female instinct warns them there is potency in your loins. . . .

"Mother of the race of Aeneas, voluptuous delight of gods and men, sacred Aphrodite"—how does it go? But the poet is right. She, the sacred one, the imperious reproductive instinct, with all Her wiles and charms, is indeed the ruler over all living things, in the waters, in the air, on land. Over us Her sway is complete, for it is not seasonal but permanent. (Who was the lady who said that if the animals don't make love all the time the reason is that they are *bêtes*?) Priests, with all weapons from circumcision to prudery, have warred with Her; legislators have laid down rules for Her; well-meaning persons have tried to domesticate Her. Useless! "At thy coming, goddess," the celibate hides his shaved crown and sneaks to a brothel, the clerk in holy orders enters into holy matrimony, the lawyer visits the little shopgirl he "helps," domestic peace is shaken alive with adulteries. For man is an ambulatory digestive tube which wants to keep alive, and Death waits for him. Descartes was a fool in these matters, like so many philosophers. "I think, therefore I am." Idiot! I am because others loved; I love that others may be. Hunger and Death are the realities, and between those great chasms flits a little Life. The enemy of Death is not Thought, not Apollo with gold shafts of light, useless against the Foe of gods and men, as you see him in the prologue to *Alkestis*. It is She, the Cyprian, who triumphs, womanlike, with her wiles. Generations She yields Him, the Devourer,

as His prey, and unwearyingly raises up new races of men and
women.

It is She who plumps the flat white belly and then, treacherous
and cruel to Her instrument once Her purpose is achieved,
with intolerable anguish tears forth from shaking mother-flesh
the feeble fruit of Man. All the thoughts and emotions and
desires of adult men and women circle about Her, and Her
enemies are but Death's friends. You may elude Her with
asceticism, you may thwart Her purpose (who shall write a
new myth of the rubber-tree, Death's subtle gift?), but if you
love Life you must love Her, and if you puritanically say She is
not, you are both a fool and Death's servant. If you hate Life,
if you think the suffering outweighs the pleasure, if you think
it the supreme crime to transmit life, then you must indeed
dread Her as the author of the supreme evil—Life.

Elizabeth and George talked and found each other delightful.
They thought it was their interest in art and ideas. Delightful
error! All the arts of mankind are the Cyprian's handmaids,
and even the chaste and tweeded spectre Sport has unwittingly
been made Her pander—for with no grudging hand does the
Goddess scatter Her gifts, smiling upon the amorous play of
children and not disdaining even those who desire their own
sex. She is beneficent and knows there are only too many ready
to propagate, and is not anxious to create too many victims
for Hunger, and therefore patronises even the heretics of
Sparta and Lesbos. . . .

We should turn churches into temples to Venus, and set up a
statue to Havelock Ellis, the moral Hercules who has partially
succeeded in cleansing the Augean stable of the white man's
mind. . . .

Under the benign influence of the Cyprian they talked, they
went on talking. They had drifted on to the topics of Christ
and Christianity, that interminable *pons asinorum* of youthful
discussions.

"But I think Christ is wonderful," Elizabeth was saying

with an air of having discovered something, "because he completely ignored social values and considered people only for
what they really were in themselves. It is so strange to think of
his being made the pretext for the world's most elaborate system of priestcraft when the whole of his life and teaching is a
protest against it. And then I like his going about with fisher-
men and prostitutes."

"The bohemian Christ? But have you noticed what a Pro-
teus he is? Everybody interprets the historical Jesus to please
himself. He is a whole mythology in himself. If you really try
to discover the historical Jesus, you find you keep stripping
away veil after veil, and then just as you think you are coming
to the real figure you find there's nothing there. But, I grant
you, Christ is a very sympathetic figure. What I cannot endure
is Christianity and the harm it has done Europe. I detest its
system of values, its persecution, its hatred of life (it worships
a tortured and expiring god), its cult of self-sacrifice and sexual aberrations like sadism, masochism, and chastity. . . ."

Elizabeth laughed, a little shocked.

"Oh, oh! Now you are exaggerating!"

"Not at all. I think I could prove what I say, at the expense
of some time and boring you. Consider the lives of Saints like
Catherine of Siena, Sebastian and all the infinite martyrs; look
at their representation in art; and then ask yourself what
instincts are really satisfied by the cult of these personalities
and images."

"That sounds like good Protestant prejudice."

"There are lots of things I detest in Protestantism—its smug-
ness and aridity, for instance—but I like its honesty. And we
owe it a great deal. It was because of the political inconveniences resulting from a multitude of sects that Holland and
England reintroduced religious tolerance, which had disappeared with the triumph of the Christians. Of course, the tolerance is not complete, because the Christians are still persecutors
at heart and have a thousand ways of vexing and maligning
those who disagree with them or are merely indifferent. Hence
the extraordinary defensive puritanism of English rationalists.
But something has been achieved. After all, during many centuries I should have been arrested, tortured, and probably

murdered for what I have just said to you, and you would have thought me a carbonised monster. Now any alleged truth or moral proposition or belief which has to be enforced by torture or defended by sophistry stands self-condemned."

Was ever woman in this manner wooed? But George had mounted one of his hobby-horses and was careering away through a dust of words. Elizabeth, with practical instinct, stopped him.

"Where do you live?"

"In Greek Street. I've got a large room there, big enough to paint in. Where do you live?"

"In Hampstead. It's rather horrid and the place is full of old maids. But anything is better than being at home. I don't mind my father, but my mother makes me so nervous when I'm at home that I feel I shall just die if I have to be any longer with her."

"I'm glad you hate your parents, at least one of them. It's so important to recognise these antipathies, which are after all perfectly natural. Most animals hate their mature young. I remember I used to watch the young robins exterminating their fathers, and think how right it was. But it ought to be the mothers. Men sometimes leave each other alone."

"Oh, it's partly due to the awful domestic-den family life. They can't really help it, poor dears. The den was forced on them, and they had to live in it."

"Not really. They must have wanted it. It's all part of people's amazing cowardice, their panic terror of life. It's a device of governments, an official cheat." George was off again. "All states are founded on the obligation of a man to provide for the child he begets and the woman who produces it. The State wants children, wants more and more 'citizens' for various reasons. The State exploits the love of a man for a woman and his tenderness towards her children—even she may not know whether they are his or not. And so she's taught to say: 'Be careful, step warily, don't offend any one, remember your first duty is to provide for me and the children, you mustn't let us starve, oh, do be careful,' with the result that the poor man very soon becomes a member of the infinite army of respectable season-ticket holders. . . ."

"Oh! Oh!" Elizabeth laughed again. "Why are you so full of moral indignation?"

"I'm not. Only, I live a great deal alone. I'm always thinking about things and rarely have a chance of speaking about them. Most of my brilliant acquaintances, like Upjohn, have so much to say about themselves that I never seem to get a chance of discussing anything else. And my non-brilliant acquaintances are simply shocked and reproving. They think I'm utterly damned because I read Baudelaire, for instance. Have you noticed the British middle-class superstition that anything they can label 'Gallic' must necessarily be libidinous and depraved? I get tired of telling them that the beauty of Baudelaire's verse is infinitely more spiritual and 'uplifting'—to use their damned cant—than all the confounded nonconformist-baptist-cum Salvation Army . . ."

But the end of George's denunciation was never uttered, for at that moment they were interrupted by the gentle Mrs. Shobbe.

"Excuse me for interrupting you, Mr. Winterbourne. Elizabeth dear, do you know how late it is? I'm afraid you'll miss the last bus, and you know I promised your dear mother I would look after you. . . ."

Both George and Elizabeth saw with surprise and some embarrassment that the studio was nearly empty. Almost every one else had gone and they hadn't noticed it, absorbed in their delightful exploration of each other. Of course, in these cases it isn't what is said that matters, but all that remains unsaid. The talk is mere "parade," a rustling out of the peacock's tail, a kind of antennæ delicately fumbling. Lovers are like mirrors—each gazes rapturously at himself reflected in the other. How delicious the first flashes of recognition!

Elizabeth jumped nervously to her feet, almost upsetting a small table.

"Oh my! I'd no idea it was so late. I must go. Good-bye, Mr.——, Mr.——"

"Winterbourne," said George. "But if you're going to Hampstead, let me take you back as far as Tottenham Court Road and put you on the Hampstead bus. It's not out of my way at all."

"Yes, do, Elizabeth. I feel so nervous at your being alone in London at night like this. Whatever should we do if anything happened to you?"

"Why, what's likely to happen?" said George contemptuously, ever ready to defend the cause of female emancipation; "she's got sense enough not to let herself be run over, and if any one tries to rape her she can yell for a policeman."

"Such a violent and rude young man," Mrs. Shobbe lamented as they went for Elizabeth's things. "But they're all like that now. They seem to have *no* respect for *anything*, not even the purity of womanhood. I don't know if I ought to let him take you home, Elizabeth."

"Oh, that's all right; besides, I rather like him. He's quite amusing. I shall ask him to come and have tea with me at my studio."

"*Elizabeth!*"

But Elizabeth was already at the door, where George was waiting. All the guests had departed except Mr. Upjohn and Mr. Waldo Tubbe. A last whiff of their conversation reached George's ears:

"You see, what I mean is, you take Suprematism, what I mean is, you see, there you've got something . . ."

And like the toll of Big Ben over the sleeping city came Mr. Tubbe's last, deep-breathed, significant, deportmental:

"Oe-oh."

3

This banal party and banal conversation with Elizabeth were of capital importance in George's life. The party, with its revelations of character and general tedium, confirmed George in his growing dislike for the intellectual banditti. Self-interest, though universal, is less tolerable in those who are supposed to be above it—there is, of course, no reason why a good artist should not be successful; but when one considers the intrigues now necessary for success, there is a natural prejudice in favour of those who do not elbow in the throng. Vanity is none the less odious even when there is some reason for it, though why any one should feel vain of publishing books and exhibiting pictures is a mystery, when you reflect that two thousand novels a year are published in England alone and that tens of thousands of canvases are showed annually in Paris. Gossip and scandal are none the less scandal and gossip even when witty and when the victims are more or less conspicuous in the small world which receives, or haughtily disdains to receive, Press-cuttings. George felt it rather unimportant to know which talented lady was "with" which famous gentleman. His interest was comparatively so languid that he forgot most of the scandal he was told ten minutes after he heard it, and rarely bothered to repeat what little he remembered. Somehow people are frightfully offended if you say "Does it matter?" when they tell you with sparkling eyes that somebody you know has run away with the mistress of Snooks, the painter, or that Pocock, the eminent impressario, has just celebrated the birth of his twenty-fifth illegitimate child. Does it matter, indeed! Why this fascinated delight in the private lives of the great? They're just as sordid as everybody else's.

The artist, anyway, is not nearly so important as he thinks himself. It's all poppycock and swagger for Baudelaire to say that a man can live three days without food but not a day without poetry. It may have been true of Baudelaire; it certainly isn't true of the world in general. In any nation only a comparatively small minority are interested in the arts, and most of those merely want to be amused. If all the artists and writers of a nation were suddenly obliterated by some plague of Egypt, some legitimately vengeful angel, most people would be totally unaware that they had suffered any loss, unless the newspapers made a fuss about it. But let the journeymen bakers go on strike for a fortnight. . . . If I were a millionaire it would amuse me to go about giving high-minded artists five hundred pounds a year to shut up. The suggestion is not copyright.

Our young friend was, of course, filled with numerous high-falutin delusions about the supreme importance of art and the dazzling supremacy of artists over the rest of mankind. But he had two fairly sound ideas. One was that the artist should do his job, like any one else, as well as he could, without making too much fuss about it; the other was that knowledge of the arts and practice of any art are chiefly important for sharpening the intelligence and perceptions, extending one's experience and intensifying life. These objects are not furthered by scandal, preposterous vanity, and arrivism. He was therefore perfectly right in feeling a certain amount of contempt for Mr. Shobbe's guests. The life of Rousseau the Douanier is infinitely more respectable than that of a fashionable portrait-painter, touting socially for orders.

Elizabeth and George continued their conversation on the bus from Holland Park to Tottenham Court Road. Like most bright young things they abounded in their own sense. As George said, it was perfectly obvious that they were an immense improvement on their predecessors, that they knew exactly how to avoid the lamentable errors and absurdities of former generations, and that they were going to have most interesting and delightful lives. Anybody who has not felt these pleasing delusions at the age of twenty must, I fear, be ranged in George's category of abject morons. Youth is so much more valuable than experience; it is also far more intelligent. Few things are more astounding and touching than the kindly tolerance of the young for their imbecile elders. For, have no doubts about it, even the greatest minds degenerate annually, and the finest moral character is repulsive at forty. Think of the fire and flash and inspiring genius of young General Bonaparte and the stupid degeneracy of the Emperor who had to retreat ignominiously from Moscow. A nation which relies on the alleged wisdom of sexagenarians is irrevocably degenerate. Attila was only thirty when he sacked sexagenarian Rome—at least, he ought to have been.

Elizabeth and George were very young, and hence, on *a priori* grounds, extremely intelligent. Probably the highest intensity of life ever reached by man or woman is in the early stages of their first real love affair, particularly if it is not thwarted by insane social and religious prejudices inherited from the timid and envious aged, and not contaminated by marriage.

They emerged from the stuffy, smoke-heavy room into the broad avenue, and walked towards Notting Hill tube station.

A warm south-westerly wind was blowing, moisture-laden, the kindly courier of Spring. Gone was the raw, acrid damp of Winter, and they imagined they could taste in the air the faint, salt flavour of southern seas and the earthy English acres.

"We shall have rain to-morrow," said George, instinctively looking up at the cloudy sky invisible beyond the glare of street lamps. "It is Spring at last. The crocuses will be nearly over. I must go and look at the flowers at Hampton Court. Will you come?"

"I'd love to, but isn't Hampton Court full of trippers?"

"Not if you go at the right time. I have walked there in the early morning as solitary as ever King Charles when the Privy Garden was really private. I should rather like to live in King William's summer-house."

"I like wilder and more primitive country, the Downs and those great round empty Exmoor hills. And I like the clear rough waves dashing against the rocks in Cornwall."

"I don't know Cornwall, but I love the Downs above Storrington, and I've walked over Exmoor twice. But now I'm rather in revolt against mere country— 'Nature,' as they used to call it. Nature-worship is a sort of Narcissus-worship, holding up Nature's mirror to ourselves. And how abominably selfish these Nature-worshippers are! Why! they want a whole landscape to themselves, and they complain bitterly when farm-labourers want modern grocery stores and w.c.s. Whole communities apparently are to live in static ignorance and picturesque decay in order to gratify their false ideas of what is beautiful."

"Of course, I hate the Simple-Lifers too. There was a set of them near the place at the seaside where we went for the holidays as children . . ."

"Oh! Have you got brothers and sisters?"

"A sister and two brothers. Why, haven't you?"

"Yes, I believe so, but I never think about it. Relatives are awful—they contribute absolutely nothing to your interest in life, and think that gives them a perpetual right to interfere in your affairs. And they have the monstrous impudence to pretend that you ought to love them. 'Blood is thicker than water,' they say sententiously. So it may be, but I don't want to dabble in thick blood. I hate proverbs—don't you? I've always noticed that anything absurd or tyrannical or fatuous can always be supported by a proverb—the collective stupidity of the ages. But, I say, I'm so sorry I interrupted you. I go on talking and talking, and don't give you a chance to say a word."

"Oh, I like it. I think your ideas are amusing."

"Not amusing, merely common sense. But you mustn't let me talk all the time. You see, I find most people rather oppress my spirits, and keep me from saying what I really think. So as a rule I'm silent, but when I find a sympathetic victim—well, you've already had a bitter experience of how I chatter nineteen to the dozen. There I'm off again! Now tell me what you were going to say about the Simple-Lifers."

"The Simple-Lifers? Oh, yes, I remember. Well, there was a set of people down there who had fled from the horrors of the mechanical age—you know, the usual art-y sort, Ruskin-cum-William Morris . . ."

"Handlooms, vegetable diet, long embroidered frocks, with home-spun tweed trousers from the Hebrides? I know them. 'News from Nowhere' people. What a gospel to lead nowhither!"

"Yes. Well, they were to lead the simple life, work with their hands part of the time, and do arts and crafts and write the rest of the time. They were also to show the world an example of perfect community life. They used to make the farm-girls dance round a Maypole—the boys wouldn't come, they stood in the lane and jeered."

"And what happened?"

"Well, those who hadn't private incomes got very hard up, and were always borrowing money off the two or three members who had money. The arts and crafts didn't sell, and the toiling on the land had very meagre results. Then they got themselves somehow into two or three cliques, always running down the people in the other cliques, talking scandal about them, and saying they were ruining everything by their selfish behaviour. Then the wife of one of the rich members ran away with one of the men, and the other rich members were so scandalised that they went away too, and the whole community broke up. The village was very glad when they went. The farmers and gentry were furious because they talked Socialism and the ideal State to the labourers. And all the labourers' wives were furious because the Simple-Life women tried to brighten up their lives and make them furnish their cottages 'artistically.' . . ."

They had missed two buses outside the tube station in their excited chatter. A third came along. George grabbed Elizabeth's arm:

"Come on, here's our bus. Let's go on top."

The bus-top was empty except for a couple spooning on a back seat. George and Elizabeth a little haughtily went to the very front.

"Other people's love-affairs are very tedious," said George sententiously.

"Oh, very."

"Rather primitive and humiliating."

"Why humiliating?"

"Oh, because . . ."

"Fares, please!"

The conductor lurched skilfully against the front of the bus as it made a cow-like leap forward. George raked in his pocket for the pennies.

"Let me pay my share."

Elizabeth produced a sixpence.

"Oh no, please. Look, let me take you back to Hampstead, and you can pay from Tottenham Court Road."

"All right."

The conductor and the fare-paying had interrupted the rhythm of their communication. They were silent. The bus ran noisily along the wave-furrowed, shiny, tarred street, with the dark mystery of Kensington Gardens to the right and the equally mysterious boarding-houses of Bayswater to the left. Near the street-lamps the grass behind the railing was a vivid artificial green, as if some one had splashed down a bucketful of bright paint. Like savages in some primitive dance, the ancient trees swayed slowly, irregularly, and mysteriously in the strong wind. A red apocalyptic glow from the lights of Oxford Street stained luridly and uneasily the low rolling clouds before them. The grey monster Ennui of Sunday-in-London had vanished. George took his hat off and let the wind rumple his hair. Their young cheeks were fresh with driving moist wind.

"Don't you really like the Pre-Raphaelites?" asked Elizabeth, as the bus slowed down near Lancaster Gate.

"I used to. About three years ago I was quite cracked about Rossetti and Burne-Jones and Morris. Now I simply hate them. I can still read Browning and Swinburne—Browning for his sense of life, Swinburne for his intoxicating rhetoric. But after spending three months in Paris I got frightfully excited about modern painting. Do you know Apollinaire?"

"No, who's he?"

"Oh, he's a Polish Jew who has written some quite good poems and does amusing word-pictures he calls Calligrammes. He lives by writing and editing obscene books, and he's the great defender of the new painters like Picasso and Braque and Léger and Picabia."

"The Cubists?"

"Yes."

"I've only heard of them. I never saw any of their work. I thought they were just 'wild men' and *fumistes*?"

"You wait ten years, and see then if you dare to say that Picasso is a *fumiste*! But haven't you been to Paris?"

"Yes, I was there last year, in September."

"We must have been there together. How curious! I wish I'd seen you."

"Oh, it was very dull. I was with father and mother, and everybody we met kept talking about the coming war with Germany. A friend of father's in the Admiralty told him in confidence that it was absolutely certain to happen."

"What nonsense!" said George explosively, "what absolute nonsense! Haven't you read Norman Angell's *Great Illusion*? He shows quite conclusively that war does nearly as much damage to the victor as the conquered. And he also says that the structure of modern international commerce and finance is so delicate and widespread that a war couldn't possibly last more than a few weeks without coming to an end automatically, because all the nations would be ruined. I'll lend you the book if you like."

".I don't know anything about such things, but father's friend said the Government were very worried about the position."

"I can't believe it. What! A war between European nations in the twentieth century? It's quite unthinkable. We're far too civilised. It's over forty years since the Franco-Prussian War . . ."

"But there's been a Russo-Japanese War and the Balkan Wars . . ."

"Well, yes, but they're different. I can't believe any of the big European nations would start a war with another. Of course, there are Chauvins and Junkers and Jingoes, but who cares a hang about them? The people don't want war."

"Of course, I don't know, but I heard Admiral Partington telling father that the navy is bigger, newer, and more efficient than it's ever been. And he said the German army is huge and most efficient, and the French are so frightened they've made the period of conscription three years. And he said, look out when the Kiel Canal is opened."

"Good Lord, you surely don't believe what stodgy old Admirals say, do you? It's their job to frighten people with war scares so that they can go on getting money out of the country and building their ridiculous Dreadnoughts. I met a coast-guard officer last summer, who got drunk and said he'd sealed orders as to what to do in case of war. I told him I thought that seal would not be broken until the angels in the Apocalypse arrived."

"And what did he say to that?"

"He just shook his head, and ordered another whisky."

"Well, it doesn't concern us. It's not our business."

"No, thank God, it doesn't and can't concern us."

They were in Oxford Street, rolling past the shuttered shop-fronts. A good many people were on the pavements, but the street was comparatively empty of vehicles, empty and sonorous. As they ran down past Selfridge's, the curved line of lights in the centre of the street looked like an uncoiled necklace of luminous, glittering beads. At Oxford Circus they gazed down the old Regent Street with its long lines of *café-au-lait* Regency houses, broken only at the Quadrant by the new Piccadilly Hotel.

"Isn't that like us?" said George. "We have an attempt at town-planning, and, dull as Nash is, at any rate his design is simple and dignified, and then we go and ruin the Quadrant with a horrid would-be modern hotel."

"But I thought you believed in modernity in art."

"So I do, but I don't believe in mucking up the art of the past if it can be avoided. Besides, I don't call these pastiches of Renaissance palaces modern architecture. The only people who have got a live modern architecture are the Americans, and they don't know it."

"Those awful skyscrapers!"

"They're awful in one way, but they're original. I saw some photographs of New York from the harbour recently, and I thought it the most beautiful city in the world, a sort of gigantic and stupendous Venice. I'd like to go there—wouldn't you?"

"No; I'd like to go to Paris and live in the real students' quarter, and to Italy and Spain."

The bus stopped at the end of Tottenham Court Road. They got down, and crossed the street to wait for the Hampstead bus.

"Look here," said Elizabeth: "why do you bother to come all the way out to Hampstead? I'm perfectly used to going about alone. I shall be all right."

"Of course, you would be. But I'd like to come most awfully. I hope I shall see a good deal of you, and we haven't arranged where and when to meet again."

"But there won't be a bus back."

"Oh, I shall walk. I like walking. And it'll be an antidote to the fug and idiotic talk at Shobbe's. Here's the bus. Come on."

They clambered on to the top of the bus, and again got the front seat. Elizabeth took off her right-hand glove to pay the fare, and after the conductor had gone George gently and rather timidly put his hand on hers. She did not withdraw it. Having established this delicious and dangerous contact, they sat silent for a while. The firm, cool male hand gently espoused her slim, glove-warmed fingers. In them both was the exaltation of the

Cyprian, potential desire recognised only as a heightening of vitality. The first step along the primrose path—how delightful! But whither does it lead? To what everlasting bonfires of servitude or ashy wastes of indifference? Neither of them thought of the future. Why should they? The young at least have the sense to live only in the present moment.

Preceded by the silver dove-drawn chariot of the Paphian, the heavy bus lumbered northward. Sweet is the smile of Cypris, but ironic and a little terrifying, enigmatic as the fixed smile of the Veian Apollo.

Like all imaginative and sensitive men, George was not what is called an enterprising lover. He had too much male modesty, the inherent *pudor* which is so much stronger and more genuine than the induced modesty of women, that coquettish flight of the nymph who casts a rosy apple at her pursuer to encourage him to continue. Odd, but perhaps in the nature of things, that those men who have most contempt for women are generally the most successful with them. There must be a vast amount of latent masochism in women, ranging from the primitive delight in being knocked down, to the subtle enjoyment of complex jealousies. How ghastly—if you think about it—their passion for soldiers! To breed babes by him who has slain men—puh! there's too much spilt blood in the world; one sickens at it. Give me some civet. . . .

Once more they fell into talk—eager, excited, more intimate talk. They were calling each other "George" and "Elizabeth" before they reached the stately homes of Camden Town. By the time they passed Mornington Crescent they had admitted that they liked each other "frightfully" and would see a good deal of each other. In their excitement they talked rather incoherently, jumping from one topic to another in their eagerness to say something of all that seemed to clamour for expression, recklessly wasting their emotional energy. Their laughter had the ring of pure happiness. George slipped his arm through Elizabeth's and held her fingers more amorously. Their natures expanded in a sudden delicious efflorescence; great coloured plumes of flowers seemed to sway and nod above their heads.

They were enclosed in a nimbler air, the clear oxygen of desire, so light, so compact, so resistant to the grey monster Ennui of Sunday-in-London.

"Isn't it strange!" George exclaimed, with that fatuity peculiar to lovers; "I only met you this evening and yet I feel as if I had known you all my life!"

"So do I!"

He gratefully squeezed her fingers in silence, caught in a sudden panic of bashfulness, unable to pursue further.

"Do let's meet often. We can go to the galleries and Queen's Hall and Hampton and Oxshott. I can get you tickets for the new picture shows. Do you know the Allied Artists?"

"Yes, I belong."

"Do you? Why ever didn't you tell me you are a painter too?"

"Oh, I'm such a bad painter; besides, you didn't ask me."

"*Touché*! How self-absorbed one is! I apologise."

"You must come and have tea at my studio and look at my—what I call my pictures. But you mustn't be too critical. When can you come?"

"Any time. To-morrow if you like."

Elizabeth laughed.

"Oh! Oh! You are impatient. Can you come on Friday?"

"So long? It seems ages away!"

"Well, Thursday, then."

"All right; what time?"

"About four."

Elizabeth was probably not acquainted with Stendhal's ingenious theory of crystallisation, but she acted instinctively in accordance with it. Three days and four nights made exactly the right period. To-morrow was too soon, the crystals would be in process of formation. A week would be rather too long, they would be tending to disintegrate. . . . Infinite subtlety of females! One must admit they need it.

George accompanied Elizabeth to the boarding-house where she lived and took the address of her studio. She held out her hand, after putting the latch-key in the Yale lock.

"Till Thursday, then, good-night."

"Good-night."

He held her hand a moment, and then awkwardly and tim-idly kissed it. In her turn she felt a sudden panic, opened the door swiftly, and disappeared inside, with a last hasty "Good-night, good-night!"

George stood for several moments irresolutely on the step. He was desolated, thinking he had offended her.

Inside Elizabeth was murmuring silently to herself! "He kissed my hand, he kissed my hand! I've a lover, a lover!"

The sudden panic and flight were a masterpiece of erotic strategy—they left that feeling of uncertainty, of mingled hope and fear, so valuable to the production of a powerful crystal-lisation.

George walked back to Greek Street, enclosing in himself a small chaos of emotions and thoughts. He went by way of Fitzjohn's Avenue and St. John's Wood. The infinite debate in a lover's mind—did she or didn't she, would she or wouldn't she?—moved in those curious arabesques where a mind continually wanders away from a main stem of thought, and perpetually comes back to it. Upjohn's ridiculous conceit, Shobbe's party, never go to that sort of thing again, Bobbe's acrid offensiveness, how delicate that line from her ear to her throat, I should like to paint her, now, in that article to-morrow I must try to show clearly and definitely what the new painters are attempting, I wonder if she was really offended when I kissed her hand, but I must think about that arti-cle, let me see, begin with an explanation of non-representational, yes, that's it, I must get a new tie for Thursday, this one's worn out. . . . And thus, with merciless iteration.

Under a gas-lamp near Marlborough Road Station he stopped and tried to write his first poem, and was surprised to find how difficult it was and what nonsense he wrote. A policeman came out of a side-street, and looked a little suspiciously at him. George moved on. A little later he began to sing "Bid me to live," interrupted himself half-way through to make a note for a study in analysis of form. He walked rapidly and absorbedly, unconscious of his physical fatigue. Just before he crossed Oxford Street, he stopped and clapped his hands together. My God! I was a fool to kiss her hand the first time I met her, she'll think I do that to every girl and won't want to speak to me again. Oh well, it's done. I wish I could kiss her mouth. I must remember to tell her on Thursday about that show at the Leicester Gallery. . . .

He lay awake long that night, unable to sleep for very love of living. So much to see, so much to experience, so much to achieve, so much to be and do! How wonderful to do things with Elizabeth! It would be fun to go to New York, of course, but perhaps one ought to see the Old World first? She said something about Paris and Spain. We might go together. Cursed money difficulty. Never mind, if one wants to do a thing hard enough, one always manages to do it. I suppose I'm in love with her? It would be divine to kiss her and touch her breasts and . . . Of course, one mustn't have a baby, that would be too ghastly. I must find out. I wish we could go to Paris, the trees will be leafing in the Luxembourg. . . .

In the night-silence, water dripped with insistent melody in some hidden tank. From outside came the shrill distant notes of train whistles, rather silvery and exquisite, bringing the yearning for travel, "the horns of elf-land faintly blowing." Where had he read that? Oh, of course, Stevenson. Funny how the Coningtons thought Stevenson a good author. . . .

Good-night, Elizabeth, good-night, sweet, sweet Elizabeth, good-night, good-night.

4

Before our eyes we have the regrettable examples of George Augustus and Isabel, Ma and Pa Hartly, dear Mamma and dear Papa—eponyms of sexual infelicity.

Are we more intelligent than our ancestors? What a question for the British Press or for those three musketeers of publicity cheap and silly, of tattered debates on torn topics—Shaw,

Chesterton, and Belloc! Shaw, yes, the puritan Beaumarchais— *un coup de chapeau*; but the others! To the goddess Ennui sung by Pope, the groans of the Britons. Who will deliver us from the R.C. bores?

The problem may be stated thus:

Let X equal the ménage dear Mamma-dear Papa, or a typical couple of the 'seventies and 'eighties;

And let Y equal the ménage George Augustus and Isabel, or a typical couple of the 'nineties and 'noughts;

And further, let Z equal Elizabeth and George, or a typical bright young pair of the Georgian or European War epoch;

Then, it remains to be proved whether Z is equal to, or greater than, or less than X and/or Y.

A pretty theorem, not to be solved mathematically—too many unknown quantities involved.

I am naturally prejudiced in favour of Z, because I belong to their generation, but what do *les jeunes*, the sole competent authority, think? For, after all—let us be perfectly frank—dear Papa expired peacefully in his bed; George Augustus was unhappily but accidentally slain in the performance of his religious duties; whereas George, if you accept my interpretation of the facts, virtually committed suicide at the age of twenty-six.

But then dear Papa and George Augustus did not have to fight the European War. . . .

The problem, you see, is almost insoluble, no doubt because it is wrongly stated. Let us examine it in different terms.

Without going back to Horace's egg, may we not assume that he and she have lived well who have lived with felicity?

This not only involves the problem of the *summum bonum* or sovereign good, so much debated by the ancient philosophers, but the awful difficulty of knowing who is to decide whether another person has lived with felicity. Is there such a thing as a happy life? And, if there is, would it be the most desirable life? Would you like to be Claudian's old man of Verona? Or Mr. John D. Rockefeller? Or Mr. Michael Arlen? Or any other type of unabridged felicity?

There are, of course, lots of things and people who will

eagerly or dogmatically tell you exactly what you have to do to be happy. There is, for instance, the collective wisdom of the ages, as embodied in our religions, philosophies, laws, and social customs. What a mess! What a junk-shop of dusty relics! And in any case, "the collective wisdom of the ages" is merely one of the innumerable devices of government by which the Anglo-Saxon peoples are humbugged into thinking themselves free, enlightened, and happy.

But let us abandon these abstruse and arid speculations. . . . The point is, did George and Elizabeth (consider them for the moment, please, rather as types than individuals) come better prepared to the erotic life than their predecessors, were they more intelligent about it, did they make a bigger mess of things? Does the free play of the passions and intelligence make for more erotic happiness than the taboo system? Liberty versus Restraint. Wise Promiscuity versus Monogamy. (This is becoming a Norman Haire tract.)

* * * * * * * *

* * * * * * * *

Mother of the race of Aeneas, voluptuous delight of gods and men, sacred Aphrodite, who from the recesses of Thy divine abode lookest in pity upon the sorrowing generations of men and women, and sheddest upon us rose-petals of subtle and recurrent pleasure and the delicious gift of Sleep, do Thou, Goddess, be ever with us, and neglect not the felicity of Thy worshippers! Do Thou, alone beautiful, daughter of the Gods, drench us with loveliness!

From which to the lives of Pa and Ma Hartly *et al.* is indeed a staggeringly long step. . . .

I hold a brief for the war generation. J'aurais pu mourir; rien ne m'eût été plus facile. J'ai encore à écrire ce que nous avons fait. . . . (Bonaparte à Fontainebleau—admirez l'érudition de l'auteur.)

Yet why should we mourn, O Zeus, and why should we laugh? Why weep, why mock? What is a generation of men that we should mourn for it? As leaves, as leaves, says the poet, spring, bourgeon, and fall the generations of Man—No! but as rats in the rolling ship of the Earth as she plunged through the roar of the stars to the inevitable doom. And like rats we pullulate, and like rats we scramble for greasy prey, and like rats we fight and murder our kin. . . . And—O gigantic mirth!—the voice of the Thomiste is heard!

Peace be to you, O lovers, peace unto Juliet's grave!

At the time of which I am writing—the three or four years preceding 1914—young men and women were just as much interested in sexual matters as they are now, or were at any other time. They were in revolt against the family or domestic-den ethic, that "ordained for the procreation of children" attitude whereby the State turns its adult members into a true proletariat, mere producers of *proles*. And they were almost as much in revolt against Tennysonian and Pre-Raphaelite "idealism," which made love a sort of hand-holding in the Hesperides. But, let it be remembered, Freudianism (as distinct from Freud, that great man whom every one talks about and nobody reads) had scarcely begun to penetrate. All things were not interpreted in terms of sexual symbolism: and if one had the misfortune to slip on a banana-peel in the street, he was not immediately told that this implied repressed desire to undergo the initiatory mutilating rite of the Mohammedans. They thought they were rediscovering the importance of the physical in love; they hoped they were not neglecting the essential tenderness, and the mythopœic faculty of lovers which is the source of much beauty.

Late in April, George and Elizabeth went to Hampton Court. They met at Waterloo about nine, went by train to Teddington, and walked through Bushy Park. Each had brought a frugal lunch, half because of poverty, half from some Pythagorean delusion about austerity in diet.

They walked on the grass through the long elm naves.

"How blue the sky is!" said Elizabeth, throwing back her head and breathing the soft air.

"Yes, and look how the elms make long Gothic arches!"

"Yes, and do look at the young leaves, so shrill, so virginal a green!"

"Yes, and yet you can still see the beautiful tree skeleton—youth and age!"

"Yes, and the chestnut blossom will be out soon!"

"Yes, and the young grass is—Oh, Elizabeth, look, look! The deer! There's two young ones."

"Where? Where are they? I can't see them. I *want* to see them!"

"There they are! Look, look, running across to the right."

"Oh yes! How funny the little ones are! But how graceful! How old are they?"

"Only a few days, I should think. Why are they so beautiful and young babies so hideous?"

"I don't know. They're always supposed to look like their fathers, aren't they?"

"*Touché*—but I should think that would make the mothers hate them, and they love the little beasts."

"Not always. A friend of mine had a baby last year, and she didn't want it when it was coming, but kept thinking she would love it when it came. And when she saw it, she simply loathed it, and they had to take it away. But she simply *made* herself look after it. She says it's ruined her life and she doesn't find it a bit interesting, but now she's fond of it and couldn't bear it to die."

"Perhaps she didn't love her husband."

"Oh yes, she does. She simply dotes on him."

"Well, maybe it wasn't his child."

"Oh! Oh!" Elizabeth slightly shocked. "It *was* his child. But one reason why she didn't like it was because it separated them."

"How long had they been married when the child was born?"

"Oh, I don't know—less than a year."

"Idiotic!" said George, banging the end of his walking-stick on the ground; "ab-so-lute-ly idiotic! Why the devil did they go and have a child bang off like that? Of course, she's unhappy and they're 'separated.' Serves 'em right."

"But could they help it? I mean—well, you know—it just happens, doesn't it?"

"Good Lord, Elizabeth, what a prehistoric notion! Of course it doesn't 'just happen.' There are several ways . . ."

"It seems a bit revolting!"

"Not a bit! You may feel so because you've had mushy ideas about maidenly modesty and such twaddle instilled into you. That's all part of the taboo. Now, I think the really civilised thing is *not* to let such things happen to us like animals, but to control them. It's all most frightfully important, and perhaps the one really important problem for our generation to solve."

"But you surely don't think everybody should give up having children?"

"Why, of course not! I do say so sometimes when I feel discouraged and disgusted with the poor scarecrows of humanity we are now. Fewer and better babies. Isn't it insane that we exercise over animals the control they haven't got themselves, and yet resolutely refuse even to discuss it about human beings? How can you have a fine race if you breed insensately like white mice?"

"Well, but, George dear, you can't interfere with other people's lives like that!"

"I didn't say one should. But I believe that if people have the necessary knowledge and we get rid of the taboo, they will for their own sakes come to breed more eugenically. Of course, it's an intimate and private matter—no need for Sir Thomas More's insane regulations and naked exhibitions before modest matrons and discreet old gentlemen. It's not for the old to interfere with the lusts of youth! Damn the old! But here's another point. Like most intelligent women and a few men, you're indignant at the way women have been treated in the past and at the wicked mediæval laws of this country. You want women to be free to live more interesting lives. So do I. Any man who isn't an abject moron would rather see women becoming more intelligent and magnanimous instead of having them kept ignorant and timid and repressed, and meekly acquiescent, and therefore sly and catty and wanting to get their own back. But you won't achieve that with Suffrage. Of course, let women have votes if they want them. But who the devil wants a vote? I'd gladly give you mine if I had one. But the point is this—when women, all women, know how to control their bodies, they'll have an enormous power. They'll be able to choose when and how they'll have a child and what man they want as its father. Over-population causes wars as much as commercial greed and diplomatic deceit and imbecile patriotism. Talk about the miners' strike! What I want to see is a universal strike of women. They could bring all the governments of the world to their knees in a year. Like the Lysistrata, you know, but not a failure this time."

"Oh, George, you are amusing with your fancies! You make me laugh!"

"Laugh away! But I'm serious. Of course, it isn't possible to have such a concerted action all over the world. For one thing, it wouldn't be politic to announce it, because the unscrupulous governments will always go to any extent of force and fraud to sustain their infamous régimes. . . ."

They had crossed the road outside Bushy Park and entered the palace gates. Between the wall which backs the Long Border, the Tudor side of the palace, and another long high wall, is the Wilderness, or old English garden, composed on the grandiose scale advocated by Bacon. It is both a garden and a "wilderness," in the sense that it is planted with innumerable bulbs (which are thinned and renewed from time to time), but otherwise allowed to run wild. George and Elizabeth stopped with that sudden ecstasy of delight felt by the sensitive young—a few of them—at the sight of loveliness. Great secular trees, better protected than those in the outer Park, held up vast fans of glittering green-and-gold foliage which trembled in the light wind and formed moving patterns on the tender blue sky. The lilacs had just unfolded their pale hearts, showing the slim stalk of closed buds which would break open later in a foam of white and blue blossoms. Underfoot was the stouter green of wild plants, spread out like an evening sky of verdure for the thick-clustered constellations of flowers. There shone the soft, slim yellow trumpet of the wild daffodil; the daffodil which has a pointed ruff of white petals to display its gold head; and the more opulent double daffodil which, compared with the other two, is like an ostentatious merchant between Florizel and Perdita. There were the many-headed jonquils, creamy and thick-scented; the starry narcissus, so alert on its long, slender, stiff stem, so sharp-eyed, so unlike a languid youth gazing into a pool; the hyacinth-blue frail squilla almost lost in the lush herbs; and the hyacinth, blue and white and red, with its firm, thick-set stem and innumerable bells curling back their open points. Among them stood tulips—the red, like thin blown bubbles of dark wine; the yellow, more cup-like, more sensually open to the soft furry entry of the eager bees; the large parti-coloured gold and red, noble and sombre like the royal banner of Spain.

English spring flowers! What an answer to our ridiculous "cosmic woe," how salutary, what a soft reproach to bitter-ness and avarice and despair, what balm to hurt minds! The lovely bulb-flowers, loveliest of the year, so unpretentious, so cordial, so unconscious, so free from the striving after origi-nality of the gardener's tamed pets! The spring flowers of the English woods, so surprising under those bleak skies, and the flowers the English love so much and tend so skilfully in the cleanly wantonness of their gardens, as surprisingly beautiful as the poets of that bleak race! When the inevitable "fuit Ilium" resounds mournfully over London among the appalling crash of huge bombs and the foul reek of deadly gases while the planes roar overhead, will the conqueror think regretfully and tenderly of the flowers and the poets? . . .

When George, on one of our walks, told me the gist of this conversation with Elizabeth, I was at once more amused and more interested than I allowed him to see. There are certain aspects of people's bodies, certain things they say and do, which not only determine one's attitude towards them but seem to explain them. And more, in some cases they seem to reveal an epoch. Every one has experience of attraction or repulsion caused by another's body. For instance, there was once a poet whose work I admired; but the first time I met him he tried to hold a girl's hand. I didn't mind *that*—au contraire.

What I minded was the awful spectacle of his large, ugly, raw-red hand, with knotty fingers and gnawed mourning nails, trying to enclose the washed and chubby hand of my little friend. . . . I could never read his poems again without thinking of that Mr. Hyde-like hand, the Barrymore film hand of Mr. Hyde.

Now, I had a reason for dwelling at some length on these preliminary conversations of George and Elizabeth, with George much in the foreground. They seem to explain a great deal, at least to me. They reveal him and at the same time "throw more light" (as the learned say) on the state of mind of a generation of young men who mostly perished in their twenties. As a rule, George was very silent. Like most people who think at all, he had very little of the small change of conversation and disliked aimless babbling. But when he was with somebody he liked, he talked. My God, how much he talked! He was passionately interested in ideas, passionately interested in his own reactions to the appearances of things, comparatively little interested in the lives of other people except in a general and abstract way. He noticed in a flash the girl at a party who looked like a Botticelli (people still admired Botticelli in those days, and girls lived up to it), but he would never see, for example, the look on the face of the rather plain woman whom one guessed to be in love with the handsome host uxoriously devoted to his new wife. Consequently his talk was all ideas and impressions. He had an almost indecent love of ideas. If you threw George a new idea he caught it with a skilled and grateful snap, like a seal at the Zoo catching a fish jerked at it by the keeper.

Of course, it is very natural that young men and women should be interested in ideas which are new to them though probably stale enough to those a bit older. But the young War Generation seem to me to have been abnormally swayed by ideas of grandiose "social reform." England swarmed with Social Reformers. I don't pretend to know why. Perhaps it was due to the political idealism of Ruskin and Morris, aided by the infinitely more sensible work of the Fabians. Everybody was the architect of a New Jerusalem, and a rummy assortment of plans they provided. This passion has now reached the disinterested and noble-minded trade unionist and to some extent even the agricultural labourer. Consequently, you may now hear, at Hyde Park Corner or in pubs or third-class carriages, beautifully garbled versions of the highbrow talk of about twenty years ago. You thus have the encouraging and delightful spectacle of a proletariat eagerly expecting a millennium, impossible at any time, but particularly impossible after a catastrophe which has plunged the intellectuals into Spenglerian pessimism and hurled the weaker or more cynical into the ironic bosom of Mother Church. . . .

George was pretty much affected by this Social Reform bunk. He was always looking at things from "the point of view of the Country," and far more frequently from "the point of view of humanity." This may have been a result of his Public School, kicked-backside-of-the-Empire training. I know he resisted it with commendable contempt and fury, but where so much pitch was flying about he could scarcely avoid some of it. Perhaps the young are always like that, although one does not seem to notice it. As I pointed out to George years afterwards, he was quite right to discuss the matter frankly and openly with Elizabeth before they proceeded further, but all this bunk about eugenics and women's rights and preventing wars by birth-control would have discouraged any girl who had not fully made up her mind already that she wanted him. It was appallingly bad strategy as seduction—though, *en passant*, let it be noted that "seduction" is one of those primitive notions which could only inhabit the degenerate minds of lawyers and social uplifters, since in nine cases out of ten the "seducer," if any, is the woman. I thought that George ought to have imparted a little elementary information, and have pointed out that in the present state of human affairs it is not quite right for people to have a child without being legally married because it's so hard on the child, although in some cases it should be done deliberately as a protest against a foolish prejudice. He ought then to have explained how it may spoil a sexual relationship to have a child too soon and unthinkingly. And he should then have demonstrated by example and precept that love is an art, and a very difficult art, and one most dismally and disastrously neglected, especially by "well-bred" Englishmen. It sounds incredible, but it is true, that there are thousands of such men, perfectly decent, humane persons, who despise a woman if they think, or know that she experiences any sexual pleasure. And then they wonder vaguely why women are shrewish and discontented. . . .

All this will sound very elementary to some people and very reprehensible to others. I am simply trying to explain these people. Of course, there is always the superior person who veils puritanism by saying: "I'm so bored with all this talk about sex. Why can't people go to bed with the person they want to, and stop talking about it?" Well, why shouldn't we talk about what interests us, and what, after all, is extremely important to adult life and happiness? Maybe we can learn something from the adulteries of others. It seems to me that the error of the Elizabeth and George generation was that they were far too absolute, too general, too dogmatic in their "ideas" about sex. They *would* let the Social Reform bunk distort their view. They had seen in their own homes the dreadful unhappiness and suffering caused by Victorian, and indeed Edwardian, ignorance and domestic dennery and swarming infants and they reacted violently against it. So far, good. But they failed to see that in the way they went about it they were merely setting up another tyranny—the tyranny of free love. Why shouldn't people be monogamous if they want to be? Maybe it suits them. Don't be dragooned into it, of course, but don't be frightened out of it if you're made that way. There are certain elementary precepts which always hold good—for instance, Balzac's "Never begin marriage with a rape"; but this is a wholly personal and very complex and delicate relation which people must work out for themselves. All one asks is that they shall not be interfered with by law and busybodies. It is an interesting comment on the sadism latent in communities that the cruelty and misery of the Victorian home are legally protected and held up as shining examples of behaviour, whereas any attempt to make people a little more natural and happy and tolerant is supposed to be wicked. How men

destroy their own happiness! How they hate happiness and
pleasure! Think of the insane delusion of female chastity
which holds that any woman who has "had" more than one
man is "impure," whereas in fact many women soon come to
dislike profoundly their first lover, and most are only really
happy and satisfied with a fourth or sixth or tenth.

Alas! "with human nature what it is," the love-lives of most
people will always alternate between brief periods of happiness and long periods of suffering. The "sexual problem" will
only be solved with the millennium which produces a perfect
humanity. Until then we can only look on and sigh at the
ruined lives; and reflect that men and women might be to each
other the great consolation, while in fact they do little but torment each other. . . .

I do not pity Elizabeth and George. They were very happy that
day—and on other days—and to be quite happy even for one
day is sufficient sanction for the misfortune of existence.

They went from the Wilderness into the large garden and
walked slowly beside the Long Border, where the gardeners
were busily potting out spring flowers. The crocuses were
almost over, and the large motor lawn-mower was smoothly
humming over the delicate green turf of the great lawns. They
looked at the trimmed yews and wondered if they had been
planted by Cardinal Wolsey. They criticised, somewhat
adversely, the lead statue of the three Graces, and, walking
under the trees by the canals, noticed the cold green lily-leaves
just beginning to unfold under water. They stood at the end of
the Long Border and for a long time in silence watched the
swirl and eddy of the Thames, the house-boats being freshly
painted for the season, the exquisite swaying fronds of the
young willows. In the Privy Garden, on the raised walk and
under the lime-tree avenue where the great clumps of crocuses
lay sprawled and dying and overgrown at the foot of each tree,
they talked of King Charles, and fought over the age-old contest of King and Parliament. Elizabeth was romantically for
the handsome, melancholy King; George, Whiggish and all for
political freedom, though gravely disapproving of Puritan

vandalism. They went through the Fountain Court and the beautiful Tudor Courts, and walked along the river, and sat under a tree to eat their lunch. They talked and argued and laughed and made plans and reformed the world and felt important (God knows why!) and held hands and kissed when they thought no one was looking. . . . And yes, they were very happy.

Dear Lovers! If it were not for you, how dreary the world would be! Never shall a pair of you pass me without a kindly discreet glance and a murmured wish, "Be happy." How my heart warmed to an old French poet as we walked slowly on the Boulevard, and the lovers in the soft evening air passed us by, hand so close in hand, bodies so amorously near, eyes so sparkling and alive! Now and then, in the intoxicating air of the spring and the tolerant kindliness of the Parisians, a pair would feel so exuberant and so enthusiastic and so moved with each other's perfections, that they would have to stop and exchange a long kiss, perfunctorily hidden by a quite inadequate tree-trunk. Nobody interrupted them, nobody scowled, no policeman arrested them for indecency. And the old poet paused, and laid his hand on my arm, and said: "Mon ami, I grow old! I am nearly sixty. And sometimes as I pass along the streets and see these warm young people I find myself thinking: 'How impudique! Why is this permitted? Why do they intrude their passions on me?' And then I remember that I too was young, and I too passed eagerly and happily with one or other of my young mistresses whom I thought so beautiful, each of whom I loved with so immortal a love! And I look at the lovers passing and I say to myself: 'Allez-y, mes enfants, allez-y, soyez heureux!'"

Dear Lovers! Let us never forget that you are the sweetness of the bitter world.

And Elizabeth and George lingered through the sunny hours; and before the afternoon became too chill—for April is cold in England—they went back slowly through the long glades of the Park, they too hand in hand like the lovers on the Boulevard, they too with bodies amorously near, they too with eyes sparkling and alive, they too pausing to join their lips when the loveliness of life and the ecstasy of loving drew them together in a kiss.

They were so happy they did not know they were tired.

5

It is fascinating to observe how people organise and disorganise their lives, fascinating to see how an impulse of vitality sends them off on a certain line, how they wobble, err, suffer, recover themselves. What is the most banal street, the most tedious place you know? Think how fascinating if only you knew the real lives of those tedious people!

There are two centres or poles of activity in every adult life—the economic and the sexual. Hunger and Death, the enemies. Your whole adult life depends on how you deal with the two primitive foes, Hunger and Death. Never mind how much the conditions of collective human life seem to have altered them, they are there; you can never really get away from Hunger and Death, from the need to eat and the will to live again.

Thus, two problems are created—the economic and the sexual. There is no cut-and-dried solution of either. Existence is tolerable—I will not say "happy," though I believe in happiness—to the extent that as an individual you are successful in solving these two problems. Certain traditional solutions are presented to us all in youth, and the swiftness with which we see their foolishness is an almost unerring test of intelligence. When we have seen through them, a new and delicate problem presents itself—we have to create our own happiness underneath or in despite of the Laws (or rules for collective life) and at the same time preserve intact the sense of Justice, or that which is due to each.

The primitive, the proletarian, the common man and woman solution is merely one of *quantity*. Get all the grub and copulation you want and more than you want, and *ipso facto* you will be happy. Put money in thy purse. Excellent Iago, what a fool you are! Noble Caliban, what a silly beast! Savages, the heroes of Homer, and workingmen gorge on the flesh of beeves. To sack a town and rape all the women was the sexual ideal of centuries of civilised savages. To do the same thing with money sneakingly, instead of with the sword openly, is the actual ideal of Dr. Frank Crane's world-famous business men. The judgment of the wiser world is upon them all. Let them join the megatherium and the wild ass.

Then you have the Rudyard Kipling or British Public School solution. Not so far removed from the other as you might think, for it is a harnessing of the same primitive instincts to the service of a group—the nation—instead of to the service of the individual. Whatever is done for the Empire is right. Not Truth and Justice, but British Truth and British Justice. Odious profanation! You are the servant of the Empire; never mind whether you are rich or poor, do what the Empire tells you, and so long as the Empire is rich and powerful you ought to be happy. Woman? A rag, a bone, and a hank of hair. Get rid of the sexual problem by teaching men to despise women, either by open scorn or by putting them on the pedestal of chastity. Of course, they're valuable as possessions. Oh, quite! There can be no world peace because the man who has the most money gets the best woman, as the German Kaiser said at the gathering of the nations. As if the nations were a set of Kiplingesque characters bidding against each other for an expensive tart! How despicable, how odious!

No, each of us has to work out the problems for himself, and, I repeat, on the correct solution of both depends happiness in life. I do not pretend to be able to teach what is your solution. I think I know what is mine; but that is not necessarily yours. But I am quite sure that the quantitative and the British Public School solutions are wrong. . . .

The struggle with Hunger, or the economic problem, leads to situations of astonishing "human interest," as Balzac recognised. But we are not much concerned with it here. It was highly important in the case of Isabel: very little in the case of Elizabeth and George. They were content with very little, which they obtained quite easily—Elizabeth from her parents, George by various odd jobs which occupied only a comparatively small part of his time. Each wanted to avoid the slavery of working eight hours a day at a stated wage, for someone else, though both were willing to work sixteen hours a day on their own, at what they wanted to do. Neither had the slightest ambition to dominate others through wealth. Of course, you may say they solved the economic problem by dodging it. However, as far as they are concerned as individuals, that *was* a solution.

But this "dodging solution" (if you like to call it such) involved the sexual problem too. It was quite obvious that George was incapable of supporting a woman and children on his perfunctorily performed jobs, while his painting was rather a liability than an asset. On the other hand, it was equally obvious that Elizabeth was not rich enough to afford the luxury of an artist husband and a family. It therefore followed that they could not afford children; and since they didn't want them, this was a misfortune they contemplated with calm. But, since they didn't want children, it followed that there was no need to get married. Why get married, except for the sake of the unfortunate little bastard?

All of which they talked out very fully before they ever lay together. You may say, of course, that this is very wicked and "unnatural," that if every one acted in this way the human race would soon come to a full stop. I shall not make the obvious retort of "a good job, too," but merely say that I observe no danger of under-population in Europe. Since the population of England is about three times the amount which the land of England can feed, I am inclined to think that George and Elizabeth should be regarded as a national hero and heroine in this respect. . . .

If you are as quick-witted as you ought to be, you will already have noticed one big difference between the George–Elizabeth ménage (I don't mean the legal irregularity, which is of no importance) and the ménages of George Augustus–Isabel, Dear Mamma–dear Papa, Ma-and-Pa Hartly. "They talked it out very fully before they ever lay together." You get the point? They used their intelligence, they actually used their intelligence, *before* embarking on a joint sexual experience. That's the great break in the generations. Trying to use some intelligence in life, instead of blindly following instincts and the collective imbecility of the ages as embodied in social and legal codes. Isabel "married for money" and got what she deserved, viz. bankruptcy. But she had been obliquely taught that it was a girl's duty to use men's sexual passion as a means of acquiring property. Whoring within the law. The Trade Union of married women. George Augustus was greatly attracted by Isabel and wanted to lie with her. Why not? My God! why not? But he had never thought about the problems. He didn't want children; Isabel didn't want children. Not really. But they had been taught that if a man and woman wanted to lie together it was horribly wicked to do so unless they were "married." The parson, the public ceremonies, and the signatures made "sacred" what was otherwise inexpressibly wrong and sinful. But in the code on which George Augustus and Isabel were reared, "marriage" meant "a dear little baby" nine months after the wedding bells. All right for those who go into it with open eyes. Perfect. Charming. I'll be godfather every ten months. *J'adore les enfants*. But all wrong, all so rottenly wrong, if you go into it like a couple of ninnies, mess up your sexual life, disappoint the man, disgust the woman, and produce an infant you can't look after properly. . . .

Which is precisely what George Augustus and Isabel did, and what their parents did before them. . . .

Now, the marriage of Moliére's time was jolly sensible so far as it went. You, Eraste, love Lisette? Good. You, Lisette, love Eraste? Admirable. You wish to crown your flame? Most natural and delightful. But you know that means infants? Perfect. How much money have you got, Eraste? Nothing? Ah! . . . But your father approves? Will give ten thousand crowns if Lisette's father will give another five thousand? Delicious. *Quite* a different situation. Your father approves, Lisette? Yes? Quick, a notary. Bless you, my children!

That was blunt, bluff common-sense. I'm sorry for Lisette, but not for Lisette's children.

The only trouble was that Lisette and Eraste were not very happy sexually—hence the *amants* of Lisette and the *amies* of Eraste. So you dropped into promiscuity, and Eraste didn't know if Lisette's later brats were his; and Lisette didn't know how many dear little bastards Eraste was scattering about the world. All of which made for nastiness, cantankerousness, and hypocrisy.

The simple process of dissociating sex life from the philo-progenitive instinct was performed by the War Generation— at least on the grand scale, for isolated practitioners had long existed. The march of Science (how delightful clichés are!) had brought certain engines within the reach of all; and sensible people profited by them. The old alternative of burning or marrying disappeared. And the following, far better, proposi-tion arose. It was perfectly possible for man or woman to live a satisfactory sex life without having children. Hence, by the scientific process of trial and error, it became possible for each to seek the really satisfactory lover; while those who were philoprogenitively inclined might marry (*en attendant mieux*) for the sake of the children. Thus there was a return to the wise promiscuity of the Ancients (if the Ancients ever did any-thing so sensible, which I greatly doubt), which was a great advance on humbug, domestic tyranny, furtive promiscuity, and whoring. One definite result, which we see to-day, is an undeniable decline in the number of whores—the first time this has occurred since the Edict of Milan.

Unfortunately the pre-war "engines" were rather crude and not wholly reliable. . . .

George and Elizabeth, then, were either extremely sensible or disgustingly immoral—I don't mind what your judgment is, I am recording facts. I don't, however, attempt to disguise my own prejudice, which is that intelligence makes for a far better life than "Luv" and "God," those euphuisms for stupidity and ignorance. In a manner of speaking they were pioneers. At any rate, they thought they were, which is all that matters here. They really thought they had worked out a more sensible, more intelligent, more humane relationship between the sexes. But there were certain rather important little snags they over-looked. Like most bright young things, they were very cock-sure of themselves, a good bit too cocksure. And then, while one doesn't at all deny that they were pretty bright, and on the right track, their knowledge was unhappily theoretical, chiefly derived from George's reading and meditations. It's a confoundedly dangerous thing for two virgins to take on the job of initiating each other into a complicated art they only know theoretically. Dangerous, in that high hopes may be dashed, rather lovely emotions sadly frustrated, and a beautiful relationship spoiled. There are dangers in meeting the undeniably right person too soon in life. Two handsome young married people, obviously deeply in love—what a charming spectacle, how delightful! . . . Wait! You wait! Not very long, either. . . .

You haven't forgotten Fanny and the young man from Cambridge. . . .

Well, Elizabeth and George worked out their scheme, and for a considerable time it all worked admirably. But for the war and the upset of every one's mind and life and character, it might have weathered the small storms of Fanny and the young man—and perhaps other Fannies and other young men—and still have gone on working. Elizabeth abandoned her Hampstead boarding-house and found a large room, which did as a studio, in Bloomsbury. She wrote her parents in Manchester that she did this for the sake of economy and to be nearer her "work"—whatever that might mean. The economy consisted in the fact that when she spent the night with George at his "studio" she was obviously not wearing out her own bed-clothes. Elizabeth's mother paid her a surprise visit. Most luckily George had gone away for the week-end, and Elizabeth was "discovered" calmly painting by herself. She behaved with the admirable dissimulation which comes so naturally to women, swiftly whipped away one or two objects (such as a tobacco pipe and pouch, *The Psychology of Sex* inscribed "To darling Elizabeth from George") which might have betrayed a certain intimacy with a male, and sent George a long warning telegram. Mrs. Paston stayed three days. Of course, she suspected "something." Elizabeth looked about ten times prettier, was much more smartly dressed, talked differently, used all sorts of new phrases, and was obviously very happy, so happy that even three days of her mother failed to depress her completely. Elizabeth treated her char-lady with reasonable humanity, so when Mrs. Paston severely cross-examined her in secret about Elizabeth, the char-lady just went beautifully stupid and stood by Elizabeth nobly. "Oh no, ma'am, I never seen nothin' wrong." "Oh yes, ma'am, Miss Elizabeth's such a nice young lady." "I'm only here of mornings, ma'am." So Mrs. Paston, baffled but somewhat suspicious—what right had Elizabeth to look so well and happy and pretty away from her dear parents?—had to return home and present a blank report.

So that alarm died down.

Elizabeth became inordinately proud of being no longer a virgin. You might have thought she was the only devirginated young woman in London. But, like King Midas, she burned to share her secret, to make somebody else envious. So one week when George had run over to Paris about some pictures, she invited Fanny to tea, and after a tremendous amount of preparation confessed the lovely secret. Partly to Elizabeth's disappointment and partly to her relief, Fanny took the news as something very ordinary.

"I'm really surprised you waited so long, my dear."

"But you're nearly as old as I am!"

"Oh, but, darling, didn't you *know*? I've had two or three affairs. Only, I didn't say anything to *you*. I thought you'd be shocked."

"Shocked?" Elizabeth laughed scornfully, though she *was* a bit surprised. "Why on earth should *I* be shocked? *I* think people should be free to have all the love affairs they want."

"Do tell me who he is!"

Elizabeth blushed slightly and hesitated.

"No, I won't tell you now, but you'll meet him soon."

"But, Elizabeth, I hope you're careful? You won't go and have a baby?"

Elizabeth laughed scornfully again.

"Have a baby? Of course not! Why ever do you think I'm so silly? George and I talked it—"

"Oh! His name's 'George,' is it?"

"Yes. Did I let that out? Yes, George Winterbourne. Well, we talked it all out, and we've got a perfectly good arrangement.

George says we're too young to have children, so why get married; and anyway we're too poor. If we want children later on, we can always *get* married. I said I wouldn't tie myself down with *any* man—I don't want anybody else's name. I told George that if I wanted other lovers I should have them, and if he wanted any one else he was to have her. But, of course, when there's a relationship as firmly established as ours, one doesn't *want* any one else."

Fanny smiled.

As a matter of fact, Elizabeth had not said anything of the sort, when George drew up his Triumphal Scheme of the Perfect Sex Relationship. She had been rather timid and uncertain at first. But George's discourses and the books on physiology and psychology and sex which he made her read, and her own exultation at being no longer a virgin, had sent her spinning in the other direction. She had, in a few months, far out-distanced George in "freedom." Her argument was rational and quite defensible; indeed, it was a corollary to George's own views, though he hadn't seen it. Because you were very fond of one person, she argued, that was no reason why you shouldn't be attracted by others. Monogamy was established to tyrannise women and to make sure offspring were "legitimate" and to provide for them and the mother. But where women are free and there is no offspring, what on earth is the good of an artificial and forced fidelity? Directly one has to *promise* fidelity, directly an effort of will is made to "remain faithful," a false position is set up. The effort of keeping such a promise is the surest assurance that it will be broken sooner or later. On the other hand, while you are in love with someone, well, you're in love, and you either don't want any one else, or if you do, you're probably only too happy to get back speedily to the person you do really care for.

There was logic, and a good deal of sense, in this, George had to admit. But he also had to admit to himself that he didn't altogether like the idea of Elizabeth "going with" somebody else. Nor, for that matter, would Elizabeth have liked George "going with" another girl. But she deceived herself unknowingly. At that time she was very much under the influence of a Swedish book she had read, a book devoted to the Future of the Race. This was the work of an earnest-minded virgin of fifty who laid it down as an indisputable axiom that there must be complete frankness between the sexes. "The old notion of sexual fidelity must go," declared this enthusiastic writer, "and only from the golden sun-bath of divinely nude freedom can rise the glorious new race," etc., etc. Elizabeth didn't know the authoress was an old maid, and she was annoyed with George for making fun of the "golden sun-bath of divinely nude freedom."

"But, Elizabeth," George had said, when she propounded this argument, "of course I believe that people should be free, and it's disgusting for them to stay together when they don't any longer love each other. But suppose I happened to want someone else, just a sort of whim, and went on loving you, wouldn't it be better if I said nothing about it? And the same with you?"

"And tell each other lies? Why, George, you yourself have said time and again that there can be no genuine relationship which involves deceit. The very essence and beauty and joy of our relation depend upon its being honest and frank and accepting facts."

"Why, yes, but . . ."

"Look at the lives of our parents, look at all the sneaking adulteries going on at this very moment in every suburb of London. Don't you see—why, you *must* see—that what's wrong about adultery is not the sexual part of it at all, but the plotting and sneaking and dissimulation and lies and pretence. . . ."

"That's true," said George slowly and reflectively; "that's true. But—suppose I told you that when I was last in Paris I spent the nights with Georgina Harris?"

"Did you?"

"No, of course not. But, you see . . ."

"What would it have mattered if you had? My Swedish woman you make fun of is very sound about that. She says that two people should spend a few days or more away from each other every few weeks, and that it may be a very good thing for them to have other sexual experience. It prevents any feeling of sameness and satiety, and often brings two people together more closely than ever, if only they're frank about it."

"I wonder," said George, "I wonder. Is there any one you're interested in, Elizabeth?"

"Of course not. You're really rather unintelligent about this, George. You know perfectly well I love you passionately and shall never love any one else so much. But there mustn't be any lying and dissimulation, and no artificial fidelity. If you want to go off for a night or a week-end or a week with some charming girl or woman, you must go. And if I want to do the same with a man, I must. Don't you see that by thwarting a mere *béguin* you may turn it into something more serious, whereas by enjoying it you get rid of it? Probably, as my Swedish woman says, one is so much disappointed that a single night is more than enough, and one returns to one's love eagerly, cured of wandering fancies for the next six months."

"Yes, I dare say there's something in that. It seems sound. And yet if the original relationship is so secure and if the other affair is so slight and unimportant and merely physical, it seems unnecessary to hurt one's love by speaking about it. I don't tell you every day what I had for lunch. Besides, even if one spends only one night with another person, that implies at least a one-night's preference, which might hurt."

"Which might hurt!" Elizabeth mocked. "George, you're being positively old-fashioned. Why, when you go to Paris, isn't that a preference? And when I go to Fanny's cottage in the country for a week-end, isn't that a preference? How do you know we're not Sapphic friends?"

"I'm jolly sure you're not! You're neither of you in the least bit Lesbian types. Besides, you'd have told me."

"You see! You know quite well I'd have told you."

"Yes, but going to Paris or the country for a few days isn't the same sort of 'preference.'"

The argument tailed off in a futile attempt to define "preference." Ultimately Elizabeth carried her point. It was definitely established that "nothing could break" a relationship such as theirs; but that "love itself must have rest," and therefore there was wisdom in occasional short separations; that so far from breaking up such a relationship, occasional "slight affairs" elsewhere would only strengthen and stimulate it. George allowed himself to be convinced. The snag here lay in the fact that he had definitely sensed the possible danger of arousing jealousy; whereas Elizabeth, confident in herself and the theories of her Swedish old maid, scorned the idea that so base a passion could even enter *their* relation.

About two months after this, George and Elizabeth were cheerfully dining in a small Soho restaurant when Fanny came in with a young man, the "young man from Cambridge," Reggie Burnside.

"Oh, look!" exclaimed Elizabeth, "there's Fanny and a friend with her. Fanny! Fanny!" signalling across the room. Fanny came across.

"This is George Winterbourne. You've often heard of Fanny, George. I say, Fanny, do come and have dinner with us."

"Yes, do."

"But I've got Reggie Burnside with me."

"Well, bring him along too."

The young man was introduced, and they sat down at the table. In most respects Fanny was curiously different from Elizabeth; each was not so much the antithesis as the complement to the other. Fanny was just a little taller than Elizabeth (George disliked short women); and where Elizabeth was dark and Egyptian-looking and pale, Fanny was golden and English (not chocolate-box English) and most delicate white and red. She was a bit like Priscilla, George thought, but with the soft gold of Priscilla made hard and glittering, like an exquisite metallic flower. There was something both gem-like and flower-like in Fanny. Perhaps that was due to her eyes. With other women you are conscious almost immediately of all sorts of beauties and defects, but with Fanny you are instantaneously absorbed by the eyes. When you thought about her afterwards, you just saw a mental image of those extraordinary blue eyes, disassociated from the rest of her, like an Edgar Poe vision. But, unlike so many vivid blue eyes, they were gemlike rather than flower-like; they were not soft or stupid or sentimental or languid, but clear, alert, and rather hard. You may see exactly their shade of colour in the deeper parts of Lake Garda on a sunny day. Yet the quality was not aqueous, but vitreous. Venetian glass, perhaps? No, that is too opaque.

It is very hard to say what was the quality which made them so remarkable. Men looked at them once and fell helplessly in love, one might say almost noisily in love—Fanny didn't mind, it was obviously her *métier* to have men fall in love with her. Perhaps Fanny's eyes were simply made a symbol in the imagination of that mysterious sexual attraction which radiated from her, or perhaps they conformed to some unwritten but instinctively recognised canon of the perfect eye, the Platonic "idea" of eyes. . . .

With Elizabeth you saw not the eyes alone, but the whole head. You would have liked to keep Fanny's eyes, magnificently set in gold, in an open jewel-casket, to look at when you doubted whether any beauty remained in the dull world. But with Elizabeth you wanted the whole head, it was so much like one of those small stone heads of Egyptian princesses in the Louvre. So very Egyptian. The full, delicately-moulded lips, the high cheek-bones, the slightly oblique eye-sockets, the magnificent line from ear to chin, the upward sweep of the wide brow, the straight black hair. Oddly enough, on analysis Elizabeth's eyes proved to be quite as beautiful as Fanny's, but somehow less ostentatiously lovely. They were deeper and softer, and, which is rare in dark eyes, intelligent. Fanny's blue eyes were intelligent enough, but they hadn't quite the subtle depths of Elizabeth's, they hadn't the same reserve.

Elizabeth lived very much in and on herself; Fanny was a whole-hearted extravert. Where Elizabeth hesitated, mused, suffered, Fanny acted, came a cropper, picked herself up gaily and started off again with just the same zest for experience. She was more smartly dressed than Elizabeth. Of course, Elizabeth was always quite charming and attractive, but you guessed that she had other things to think about beside clothes. Fanny loved clothes, and, with no more money than Elizabeth, contrived to look stunningly fashionable where Elizabeth merely looked O.K. Oddly enough, Fanny was not devoured by the Scylla of clothes, the monster of millinery which is never satiate with its female victims. Her energy saved her from that. She and Elizabeth were both restlessly energetic; but whereas Elizabeth's energy went into dreaming and arguing and trying to paint, Fanny's went into all sorts of activities with all sorts of persons. She did not "do" anything, having sense enough to see that in most young women "art" is merely a kind of safety-valve for sex. Fanny, I'm glad to say, did not need a safety-valve for her sex; the steam-pressure was kept regulated and the engine worked perfectly, thank you very much. She was emotionally and mentally far less complicated than Elizabeth, less profound; therefore to her the new sexual régime, where perfect freedom has happily taken the place of service, presented fewer possible snags. I've said, of course, that Fanny sometimes came a cropper; she did, but she hadn't Elizabeth's capacity for suffering, Elizabeth's desolate despair when her silk purse turned out to be a sow's ear—which every one else had known long before.

Perhaps the remarkable quality of Elizabeth's mind and character is best showed by the fact that she never said or implied anything mean or nasty about Fanny's clothes. . . .

Reggie Burnside was a rich young man engaged in some mysterious "research work" at Cambridge, something connected with the structure of the atom, and highly impressive because the nature of his work could only be explained in elaborate mathematical symbols. He wore spectacles, talked in a high intellectual voice with the peculiar intonation and blurred syllables favoured by some members of that great centre of learning, and appeared exceedingly weary. Even Fanny's impetuous dash never galvanised him into a spontaneous action or a natural remark. He also was extremely modern, and was devoted to Fanny. He always was at hand when nothing better presented itself—the permanent second string to the fiddle, or, as Fanny put it, one of her *fautes*, adding *sotto voce*, my *faute-de-mieux*.

The talk at first was the usual highbrow chatter of the period— Flecker and Brooke and Mr. Russell, referred to as "Bertie" in a casual way by Fanny and Reggie, to the mystification of George. This is one of the charming traits of the English intelligentsia. Every one they don't know is an outsider, and they love to keep the outsider outside by a gently condescending patronage. A most effective method is to talk nonchalantly about well-known people by their Christian names:

"Have you read Johnny's last book?"

"No-oh. Not yet. The last one was a dreadful bore. Is this any better?"

"No-oh, I don't think so. Tommy dislikes it profoundly. Says it reminds him of sports on the village green."

"How *amusing*!"

"Oh, Tommy can be quite *amusing* at times. I was with him and Bernard the other day, and Bernard said . . ."

And if the outsider is silly enough to bite, and to say timidly or bluntly, "Who's Johnny?" the answer comes swift and sweet:

"O-oh! Don't you *know* . . . !"

And then the dazzled outsider is condescendingly informed who "Johnny" is, and, especially if a mere American or Continental, is crushed to learn that "Johnny" is Johnny Walker or some other enormously brilliant light in the firmament of British culture. . . .

George got sick of hearing about "Bertie" without being told who the devil Bertie was, and began to talk about Ezra Pound, Jules Romains, and Modigliani. But he soon learned by sweet implication that such people might be all very well in their way, but after all, well, you know what I mean, Cambridge *is* Cambridge. . . . So George shut up and said nothing. Then Reggie began to talk to Elizabeth about Alpine climbing, the sport of Dons—and a very appropriate one too, if you think about it. And Fanny talked to George.

Now Fanny was quite a subtil little beast of the field, and saw that George was a bit sulky, and guessed why. Vapourish airs were indifferent to her. She had been brought up among such people, and unconsciously adopted their tone when speaking to them. But when she was among other sorts of people she just as unconsciously dropped the vapourish airs and let her natural self respond to theirs. She had a foot, one might almost say a leg, in several social worlds; and got on perfectly well in any of them. There was a sort of physical indifference in Fanny which at first sight looked like mere hardness, and wasn't. In fact, she wasn't nearly as hard as Elizabeth, who could be quite Stonehengey at times. And then suddenly crumble. But Fanny's physical indifference carried her through a lot; one felt that her morning bath had something Lethean about it, and washed away the memory of last night's lover along with his touch.

So Fanny began to talk to George quite naturally and gaily. He was suspicious, and gave her three verbal bangs in quick succession. She took them with unflinching good-humour, and went on talking and trying to find out what he was interested in. George pretty soon melted to her gaiety—or perhaps it was the gem-like eyes. He looked at them, and wondered what it felt like to possess natural organs which were such superb *objets d'art*. They must, he reflected, cause her a good deal of annoyance. Every man who met her would feel called upon to inform her that she had wonderful eyes, as if he had made an astounding discovery, hitherto unrevealed by any one. George decided that it would be well *not* to comment upon Fanny's eyes at a first meeting.

Reggie had failed to interest Elizabeth in Alpine climbing, and switched off to "*amusing*" anecdotes, which were more successful. Under the mild influence of a little wine and a sympathetic listener Reggie shed some of his worst mannerisms and became almost human. He liked Elizabeth. She might not be wholly "*amusing*," but she was "*refreshing*." (She was a good listener.) And when the talk once again became general, George began to think that Reggie was not such a bad fellow after all; there was a sort of "niceness" about him, the genuine English pride and good-nature under a screen of affection.

They sat over coffee and cigarettes until the fidgeting of the waiter and "Madame's" little games with the electric switches warned them that their money and absence would now be more welcome than their company. It was well after ten—too late for the cinema. They walked down Shaftesbury Avenue, George with Reggie, and Elizabeth with Fanny.

"I like your George," said Fanny.

"Do you? I'm so glad."

"He's a bit *farouche*, but I like the way he enthuses about what interests him. It's not put on."

"I think Reggie's rather nice."

"Oh! Reggie . . ." and Fanny waved her hand with a little shrug.

"But he *is* nice, Fanny. You know you like him."

"Yes, he's all right. I'm not wild about him. You can have him, if you want."

"Oh! Oh!" Elizabeth laughed; "wait till I ask you!"

They separated at Piccadilly Circus. Fanny and Reggie went off somewhere in a taxi. Coming down Shaftesbury Avenue, George had noticed that it was a clear night with a full moon, and insisted on going to the Embankment to see the moonlight on the Thames. They turned into the Haymarket.

"What do you think of Fanny?" asked Elizabeth.

"I think she has most marvellous eyes."

"Yes, that's what every one says."

"I was trying to be original! But she's a nice girl, too. At first, when she and Burnside began talking, I thought she was hopelessly infected by his sort of affectation."

"Why! Don't you like him? I thought he was charming."

"Charming? I shouldn't say that. I think he's not a bad sort of fellow really, but you know how exasperating I find the Cambridge bleat. Ah'd much raver lis'n to a muckin' Cawkn'y, swop me bob, I would."

"But you know he's a very important young scientist, and supposed to be doing marvellous research work."

"Do you know what it is?"

"No. Fanny couldn't tell me. She said you had to be a specialist yourself to understand what he's doing."

"Well, I must say I'm a bit suspicious of these mysterious 'specialists,' who can't even tell you plainly what they're doing. I think Boileau's right—what's accurately conceived can be clearly expressed. When Science begins to talk the language of mystic Theology and superstition, I begin to suspect it vehemently. Besides, only the feeble sections of any aristocracy take on vapourish airs and affected ways of talk. Well-bred people haven't any affectations. And men with really fine minds haven't any intellectual vanity."

"Oh, but Reggie isn't vain. He didn't even mention his work to me. And he told such *amusing* stories."

"That's just another form of insolence—they assume you're too ignorant and stupid to understand their great and im-

portant labours, so they never condescend even to mention
them, but tell 'amusing stories,' as I see you've already learned
to call Common-Room gossip."

Elizabeth was silent, ominously silent. She was more used to
the Cambridge manner than George was, and thought he
fussed too much about it. Besides, she had been really attracted
by Reggie. She thought George was making a jealous scene.
There she did him a wrong; it never occurred to George that
Elizabeth might fall in love with Reggie. (Oddly enough, it
never *does* occur to a husband or a lover *in esse* to suspect his
probable coadjutor—until it is too late. He suspects plenty of
wrong people, but rarely the right one. The Cyprian undoubtedly has artful ways.) As a matter of fact, George had not the
slightest feeling of jealousy. He was merely saying what he felt,
as he would have done about any other chance acquaintance.
He respected Elizabeth's silence. It was one of their numerous
pacts—to respect each other's silence. So they walked mutely
down Whitehall, while George thought vaguely about Fanny
and his next day's work, and cocked his head up to try to see
the moon, and watched the occasional buses bounding along
like rapid barges in the empty light-filled river of Belgian
blocks; and Elizabeth brooded over the supposed revelation of
a hitherto unsuspected tendency to silly jealousy in George.
But just as they approached the Abbey, George slipped his arm
through hers so naturally, affectionately, and unsuspiciously
that Elizabeth's ill-humour vanished, and in two minutes they
were chattering as volubly as ever.

They walked along the Embankment from Westminster
Bridge towards the City. A serene sky hung over London,
transposed to an astonishing blue by the complementary yellow of the brilliant street lights. A few trams and taxis were
still moving on the Embankment, but after the ceaseless roar
of day traffic the air seemed almost silent. At times they could
hear the lap and gurgle of the swift river water, as the strong
flood tide ran inland, bearing a faint flavour of salt. The river
was beautifully silver in the soft, steady moonlight which
wavered into multitudes of ripples as soon as it touched the
broken surface of the Thames. Blocks of moored barges stood
black and immovable in the silver flood. The Southern bank

was dark, low, and motionless, except for the luminous announcements of the blessings of Lipton's Tea and the *Daily Mail*. The Scotchman in coloured moving lights pledged the bonny Highlands in countless sparkling glasses of electric whisky. Hungerford Railway bridge seemed filled with the red eyes of immense dragons, whose vast bulk lay coiled somewhere invisibly on either bank. Occasionally a red eye would wink green, a brightly-lit train would crawl cautiously and heavily over the vibrating bridge. The lighted windows of the Cecil and the Savoy aroused no envy in them. Nor did they pine to inspect the records of a great people lying behind the darkened and silent façade of Somerset House.

Opposite the quiet Temple Garden they paused by the parapet and looked up and down that magnificent sweep of river, with its amazing mixture of dignified beauty and almost incredible sordidness. They stood for some time, talking in quiet tones, comparing the Thames with the Seine, and wondering what dreamlike city would have arisen by those noble curves if London had been inhabited by a race of artists. Elizabeth wanted to set Florence or Oxford on either side of the Thames between Westminster and St. Paul's. George agreed that that would be lovely, but thought the buildings would be dwarfed by the width of the river, the long bridges, and the length of façade. And they finally agreed that with all its sordidness and hugger-mugger and strange contrast of palaces abutting on slums, the Embankment had a beauty of its own which they would not exchange even for the dream-city of a race of artists.

Midnight boomed with majestic, policeman-like slowness from Big Ben; and as the last deep vibrations faded from the air, the great city seemed to be gliding into sleep and silence. They lingered a little longer, and then turned to go.

Then, for the first time they noticed what they knew would be there but had forgotten in their absorbed delight in the silvery water and moon-washed outlines of the city—that on every bench sat crouched or huddled one or more miserable, ragged human beings. In front of them ran the mystically lovely river; behind them the dark masses of the Temple rose solidly and sternly defensive of Law and Order behind the spear-front of its tall sharp-pointed iron fence. And there they crouched and huddled in rags and hunger and misery, free-born members of the greatest Empire the earth has yet seen, citizens of Her who so proudly claimed to be the wealthiest of cities, the exchange and mart of the whole world.

George gave what change he had in his pockets to a noseless syphilitic hag, and Elizabeth emptied her purse into the hand of a shivering child which had to be awakened to receive the gift, and cowered as if it thought it was going to be struck.

Ignoring the hag's hoarse "Thank yer kindly, Sir, Gord bless yer, Lidy," they fled clutching each other's hands. They did not speak until they said good-night outside Elizabeth's door.

6

During 1913 life ran on very pleasantly and happily for George and Elizabeth. As in the cases of the fortunate nations without a history, there appears to be very little to record about this year. I make no doubt that it was the happiest in George's life. He was, as they say, "getting on," and had less need to worry about money. In the spring they went to Dorsetshire and stayed at an inn. Elizabeth did a certain amount of painting, but apart from a few sketches George did not attempt land-scape, especially the picturesque landscape—he wanted his painting to be urban, contemporary, and hard. They walked a good deal over Worbarrow Down and the rather desolate heath land round about. On more than one occasion they traversed the very same piece of land where George was afterwards in camp with me, a coincidence which seemed to make a great impression upon him. Certain aspects of a familiar landscape always call up the same train of thought; and as people are never weary of telling us what particularly strikes them, so George rarely failed to convey this piece of stale news to me as we walked out of camp by what had once been the rough cart-track he and Elizabeth had followed in less desolate days. He seemed to think it remarkable that he should be so miserable in exactly the same place where he had once been so happy. As I pointed out, that showed great ignorance of the ironic temper of the gods, who are very fond of such genial contrasts. They delight to lay a corpse in a marriage bed, and to strike down a great nation in the fullest flush of its pride and power. One might think that happiness was "hubris," the excess which calls down the vengeance of Fate.

They returned to London for a few weeks, and then went to Paris. Elizabeth adored Paris, and wanted to live there permanently; but George was against it. He had got some bug about the best art being "autochthonous," and declared that an artist ought to live in his own country. But the real reason was that Parisian life seemed so pleasant and the town so full of artists more gifted and more advanced than himself, that he found it almost impossible to work there. It was easier to feel important in the comparative desert of London. So they returned to London; and in the autumn George had his first "show," which was not altogether such a failure as he had expected.

When autumn turned to winter, and the yellow leaves of the plane-trees drifted down into heaps in the London squares, lying miserably sodden under the rain, the everlasting London drizzle, Elizabeth got very restless. She wanted to get away, anywhere under blue skies and sun. Her throat and lungs were rather sensitive, and when the weather turned foggy she nearly choked in the heavy, soot-laden, stifling air. They talked about going to Italy or Spain, but George knew only too well that he could not afford it. He might indeed get assurances from various impresarios he frequented that "work could go on as usual," but he knew only too well that a month's absence would mean a decline and that after three months he would be practically forgotten and dropped. It's a dangerous thing to have a national reputation for honesty—people get to trading upon it and seem to think it absolves them from individual obligations. So George, after forming various vague plans for a delightful winter in Sicily or the island of Majorca, had to admit to Elizabeth that he simply dared not go. He begged her to go alone, or to find some friend to go with her. But Elizabeth flatly refused to go without him. So they stayed in London, and worked and coughed together. Perhaps it might have been better to take the risk, for as things turned out George never saw either Spain or Italy, which he had wanted so much to see.

Fanny came to London for a week in November, before going South for the winter; and they saw her nearly every day. Fanny and George were by this time on a footing of pretty friendly familiarity. That is to say, they always kissed each other on meeting and parting—after Fanny had kissed Elizabeth—and held hands in taxis whether Elizabeth was there or not. Elizabeth didn't object at all. Not only because of her theory of freedom. She was at that time rather deeply involved in some theory of "erogenous zones" in women, and men's reaction to them. And she had got it firmly into her mind that Fanny was "sexually antipathetic" to George, because he had one day innocently and casually remarked that he thought Fanny rather flat-chested. Elizabeth leaped on this—it confirmed her theory so nicely. George had known Fanny for over a year and "nothing had happened" between them, and therefore it was plain that Fanny's "erogenous zones" awoke no response in him.

"Most peculiar," said Elizabeth, when she discussed the matter with a demure-looking but mighty ironical Fanny. "*I* should have thought you'd be the very type of woman to attract him. But he only talks about your 'marvellous eyes,' and they aren't erogenous zones at all. That means he only likes you as a human being. . . ."

So Elizabeth took no notice when Fanny kissed George; or when she said: "George darling, do go and get some cigarettes for me," and George departed with alacrity; or when George called Fanny "My love" or "Fanny darling." People throw these endearments about so liberally nowadays, how on earth is one to know? And, in fact, all this went on for a long time, and nothing did "happen." George was quite devoted to Elizabeth, and then they were away when Fanny was in London, and Fanny was away when they were in London. Both George and Fanny begged Elizabeth to "go South" with Fanny, but Elizabeth wouldn't. She was very loyal, and wouldn't take a holiday George couldn't share. But by this time Fanny had become fond of George, very fond indeed. She was weary of Reggie, who was sometimes so absorbed in atoms that he neglected his functions as Fanny's *faute-de-mieux.* She thought it might be an excellent plan if she and Elizabeth swopped riders, so to speak. Not that she wanted to "take George away" from his mistress. Oh! not at all. Fanny didn't want him as a *permanence*—Elizabeth was welcome to that. But she felt he might do excellently as a *locum tenens*, while Elizabeth was widening her experience with Reggie. So there was an unusual warmth in her farewell kiss to George, who had gone down to see her off at Victoria, and a lingeringly soft pressure of her hand, and a particularly inviting look in her beautiful eyes.

"Good-bye, darling!" and she leaned from the window and to his surprise kissed him again on the lips. "Of course, I'll write—often. And mind you write to me. I shall be back in March at latest."

Fanny did write—occasionally to Elizabeth, once or twice to them both, frequently to George. Her letters to George were much longer and more amusing than the others. George showed some of them to Elizabeth and forgot to show others. He replied punctually and affectionately.

Just before Christmas, Reggie Burnside passed through London on his way to Mürren. He dropped into Elizabeth's studio for tea, and finding her alone asked her to marry him, in a casual, offhand way, rather as he might have suggested their going to Rumpelmayer's instead of having tea in the studio. Elizabeth was surprised, flattered, and fluttered. They had quite a long discussion. Elizabeth was amazed that Reggie should want to marry, and above all to marry her. If she hadn't been so flattered, she would have been offended at any one's thinking she would do such a thing. She had almost the "thank-you-I'm-not-that-sort-of-girl" sniffiness about it.

"Is this a new brand of joke, Reggie?"

"Good God, no! I'm perfectly serious."

"But why in heaven's name do you want to *marry*?"

"It's more convenient, you know, addressing letters and meeting people and all that."

"But why want to marry *me*?"

"Because I'm in love with you."

Elizabeth pondered a little over this.

"Well," she said slowly, "I don't believe I'm in love with you.

I'm sure I'm not. I like you most awfully, but I'm not in love with you, I'm in love with George."

"Oh, George!" Reggie waved a contemptuous hand. "What's the good of your wasting your time with a man like that, Elizabeth? He won't do anything. He doesn't know anybody worth mentioning, except ourselves, and nobody at Cambridge thinks anything of his painting."

Elizabeth was on the defensive immediately.

"Don't talk nonsense, Reggie! George is a dear, and I won't have you say things like that about him. And as if anybody cares a hang what mouldy young Cambridge thinks about a painter!"

Reggie changed his tack.

"All right, if you don't want to marry me, don't. But, look here. You oughtn't to spend the winter in London with that cough and your chest. I'll give up Mürren if you'll come for a month with me to some small place on the Riviera. We can easily find a place where there aren't any English."

This was a far more gratifying and dangerous proposal to Elizabeth than matrimony. She was heartily sick of London fog and cold and drizzle and mire and soot and messy open fires which fill the room with dust but don't warm it. More than once she had regretted not having gone away with Fanny. Moreover, a "month's affair" with Reggie would perfectly well fit into the arrangement with George, whereas they hadn't thought of and hadn't discussed the possibility of either marrying someone else. Elizabeth hesitated, but she had a feeling that it would be rather mean to leave George suddenly alone in London and go off on her own with Reggie, if only for a month. She certainly was extraordinarily fond of George.

"No, Reggie, I can't come this time. Go to Mürren, and when you come back, perhaps . . . well, we'll see."

Elizabeth made toast and tea, and they sat on a large low divan in front of the fire. The dingy light soon faded from the soiled sky; but they sat on in the firelight, holding hands.

She let Reggie kiss her as much as he wanted, but for the time being resisted any further encroachments.

Elizabeth's resistance, at that precise moment, to the advances of Mr. Reginald Burnside seems to me a striking example of

George's infelicity. I mean that I see a direct link between it and the sudden inexplicable standing up of a man in khaki before a murderous machine-gun fire, not long after dawn, on the morning of the 4th of November 1918. . . . Not that I wish melodramatically "to set the brand of Cain" upon Elizabeth or upon Fanny or upon both jointly. Far from it. *They* didn't make the war. *They* didn't give George the jumps. And after all there is a doubt, almost a mystery, involved in George's death. Did he really commit suicide? I don't know. I've only got circumstantial evidence and my own hunch about it, a sort of intuition, a something haunting in my memory of the man, an Orestes-like feeling of some inexpiated guilt. Who is to say whether a man can really commit suicide on a battlefield? Desperate recklessness and looking for trouble may be the very means of his escaping the death which finds the prudent coward crouching in a shell-hole. And suppose he did deliberately get himself killed, ought we, ought I, to attach any blame to Elizabeth and Fanny? I don't think so. There were plenty of other things to disgust him with life. And even supposing that he realised the war was ending, realised that in his state of mind he simply could not face the problem of his relation with those two women, still I think them utterly blameless. The mess was as much his fault as theirs. It was really quite an easy mess to clear up. What made it impossible was George's shattered nerves, and for that they were not to blame. Oh, not in the least. Perhaps I'm as much to blame as anybody. I ought to have done something to get George sent out of the line. I think I might have gone to the Brigadier and have told him in private what I knew about George's state of mind—or perhaps to his Colonel. But I didn't go. At that time I was not *persona grata* with those in authority, for I happened to sympathise then with the young Russian Revolution, and had foolishly argued hotly about it. So perhaps my effort would have been wasted. And anyhow it was a very difficult and ticklish thing to do, and I was tired, very, very tired. . . .

At any rate, just about a fortnight after Reggie went to Mürren, the abominable winter climate of London gave Elizabeth some sort of a chill inside and upset her interior economy. Within four or five days she became quite demented. She insisted that she was with child, and insisted that the only solution was for George to marry her—at once. Perhaps the afternoon with Reggie had somehow inserted the idea of marriage into her "subconscious." At all events, her extraordinary energy was suddenly concentrated upon attaining a state which she had hitherto utterly scorned. It was a silly thing to do, but one really cannot blame her. Men are oddly callous about these mysterious female maladies and demoniacal possessions. They get peevish and pathetic enough if something goes wrong with their own livers, but they are strangely unsympathetic about the profounder derangements of their yoke-fellows in iniquity. Perhaps they might feel a little more humane if they too had a sort of twenty-eight-day clock inside them, always a nuisance, often liable to go wrong and set up irregular blood-pressure and an intolerable poisoning of the brain. George ought to have hiked her off to a gynecologist at once. Instead of which, he behaved as stupidly as any George Augustus would have done under the circumstances. He did nothing but grasp and stare at Elizabeth's whirling tantrums, and worry, and offer exasperating comfort, and propose remedies and measures which, as Elizabeth told him, with a stamp of her foot, were impossible, impossible, *impossible*. Of course, by the Triumphal Scheme for the Perfect Sex Relation, it was duly enacted that under such circumstances there was nothing to do but marry the girl. But elementary prudence would suggest that it might be sensible to make certain the circumstances *had* arisen, a precaution which they entirely overlooked in the mental disarray caused by Elizabeth's regrettable dementia.

The change wrought in Elizabeth's outlook in a few days was amazing. If she hadn't felt so tragically about it, she would have been ludicrous in her mental manœuvres. The whole Triumphal Scheme was scrapped almost instantaneously, and by a rapid and masterly series of evolutions her whole army of arguments was withdrawn from the outpost line of Complete Sexual Freedom, and fell back upon the Hindenburg line of Safety First, Female Honour, and Legal Marriage. It was, of course, ridiculous for them to marry at all, either of them. They weren't the marrying sort. They were adventurers in life, not good citizens. Neither of them was the kind of person who exults in life insurance and buying a house on the hirepurchase system and mowing the lawn on Saturday afternoon and taking the "kiddies" (odious word) to the seaside. Neither of them looked forward to the "Old Age Will Come" summit of felicity, with an elderly and imbecilely contented-looking George sitting beside a placid and motherly white-haired Elizabeth in the garden of a dear little home, contemplating together with smug beatitude the document from the insurance company guaranteeing a safe ten pounds a week for the remainder of their joint lives. I am glad to say that George and Elizabeth would have shuddered at any such prospect. But Elizabeth insisted upon marriage, and married they duly were, despite the feeble protests of Elizabeth's family and the masterly denunciations of Isabel, already recorded.

In all outward respects the legal marriage made no difference whatever to their lives and relationship. Elizabeth retained her studio, and George his. They met no more frequently and on exactly the same terms of affectionate sensuality, into which their first exultant passion had long ago evolved. One of the terms of the Triumphal Scheme emphatically laid down the axiom that it was most undesirable and dangerous for two lovers to inhabit the same flat or small house. If they were rich enough to live in separate wings of a large house, all well and good; but if not, then they should live no nearer than neighbouring streets. The essence of freedom is the disposal of one's own time in one's own way, and how can two people do that if they are living on top of each other? Moreover, a daily absence of several hours is quite indispensable to the avoidance of the domestic-den atmosphere. It is far better for two lovers to be happy together for three or four hours a day than to be indifferent or miserable for twenty-four. The joint marriage-bed, Elizabeth used to state impressively, is destructive of all self-respect and sexual charm, and blunts the finer edges of sensibility. . . .

Soon after the legal formalities were irrevocably accomplished and Elizabeth's social anxieties somewhat calmed, it occurred to her that she ought to consult a doctor, in order to learn how to behave during these months of "expecting," as the modest working-class matron calls it. So she got the address of a "modern" physician, who was supposed to have

all the latest and most enlightened methods of dealing with
pregnancy and its distresses. To Elizabeth's amazement she
found she was not pregnant at all! With the not unnatural suspicion that most doctors are more or less charlatans imposing
on the ignorance of the public, she refused to believe him until
he told her flatly that in her present condition she might wait
till doomsday for the appearance of an infant, but that if she
neglected her present slight disorder it might become serious
and permanent. She then condescended to accept his diagnosis
and advice. George had accompanied her, and was sitting in
the specialist's waiting-room. A serious, concentrated, rather
pi-jaw Elizabeth had left him to enter the consulting-room,
and George fidgeted over the imbecilities of *Punch*, wondering
how on earth they would deal with the problem of an infant,
and feeling that he would probably have to take a job and "set-
tle down" into the horrible morass of domestic life. To his
amazement, as the consulting-room door opened, he heard
Elizabeth laugh with her old merry gaiety which was so attractive, and caught the words:

"Well, if it's twins, doctor, you shall be godfather."

To which the doctor replied with a laugh George thought
rather ribald and heartless under the circumstances. Elizabeth
rushed into the room exclaiming:

"It's all right, darling, a false alarm. I'm no more pregnant
than you are."

George, who was wool-gathering, might have remained
indefinitely perplexed, if the doctor had not taken him aside
and told him briefly the situation, adding that for a little time
it would be well if Elizabeth refrained from sexual relations.

"How long do you advise?" asked George.

"Oh, let her follow the treatment prescribed for about a
month, and then let me examine her again. I've no doubt whatever that she'll be perfectly all right again. As a matter of fact,
she couldn't have a child without a slight operation. Only, in
the future she must avoid chills. She ought not to spend the
winter in England."

George wrote out a cheque for three guineas (which Elizabeth insisted on repaying afterwards), and they celebrated the
event with a dinner.

"Let us drink," said George, "to this happy occasion when we have NOT committed the unforgivable sin of thrusting an unwanted existence upon one more unfortunate human being."

But perhaps the most amazing circumstance in this peculiar episode was the speed with which Elizabeth once more evacuated the old familiar Hindenburg line, and reoccupied the most advanced positions of Sexual Freedom. But, of course, she did so with a difference. Though she wouldn't admit it even to herself, and though George tried not to see it, in her case the Triumphal Scheme had broken down badly under its first stern test. Directly that test had come, she had fallen back in panic on the old cut-and-dried solution; she hadn't had the courage to go through with it. In a way one could excuse her by saying that the interior trouble had temporarily deranged her brain, that she wasn't really responsible for her actions. But that's only a quibble—the fact remains that she did fly in a panic to social safety and the registrar. And then the legal tie introduced a subtle difference in their relation. You may say, of course, that it needn't; that since they continued to live in exactly the same way and to profess exactly the same attitude towards each other and "freedom," it made no difference whether they were legally married or not. But it did. And it does. You can see that perfectly well if you watch people. Somehow the mere fact of marriage introduces the sense of possession, and hence jealousy. Lovers, of course, may be and frequently are just as possessive and quite as jealous. But there is a difference. As a rule lovers are not first occupants, so to speak; and they are generally willing to grant each other more liberty and to "forgive." But you will see married people who have become totally indifferent to each other rise in a fury of possessiveness and jealousy when they happen to find out that the wife or husband, as the case may be, is in love with someone else. This indeed may be only another aspect of that peculiar vindictiveness bred by marriage. And another curious modification of their relationship arose. When Elizabeth reoccupied the Sexual Freedom line, without knowing it she did so for herself alone, and not for George. If George liked to accept the subsequent Elizabeth-Reggie affair, in accordance with the provisions of the Triumphal Scheme, all well and good; that was his look-out. But when it came to Elizabeth's accepting the Fanny-George affair in the same spirit, that was a very different matter. Elizabeth now felt somehow responsible for George, and feeling responsible translated itself into keeping possession of. . . .

However, three months after the false alarm Elizabeth seemed more "advanced" and full of "freedom" than ever. Her position as a married woman enabled her to talk with greater liberty on all sorts of topics which are now discussed in every nursery but at that time were considered highly improper and not to be named before Citizens of the Empire. She got hold of a book on the woes of the Uranians, and was deeply affected by it. She wanted to start a crusade on their behalf, and was greatly disappointed by the coolness with which George met her enthusiasm.

"It is ridiculous," said Elizabeth, "that these unfortunate people should be persecuted by obsolete laws derived from the prejudices of the Jewish prophets and mediæval ignorance."

"Of course it is, but what can one do about it? Persecution-mania has always existed. It's a very curious coincidence that the vulgar English word for one sort of intermediate sexual type originally meant a heretic. But there's nothing to be done."

"I think something ought to be done."

"Well, I think it's too soon to do anything. You've got to allow time for knowledge to percolate into rock-like heads, and for ignorance and superstitions to be dispelled. Let's get the ordinary relations of men and women on to a decent basis first, and then it'll be time to think about the heretics in love."

"But, George darling, these people are hunted and exiled and despised for something which is not their 'fault' at all, some difference in their physiological or psychological structure. There probably isn't any such thing as a perfectly 'normal' sexual type. Simply because we're 'normal,' why should we hate and despise these people?"

"I know, I know. Theoretically, I agree with you absolutely. But it's no good my mind trying to defend what my instincts and feelings reject. Frankly, I don't like homosexuals. I respect their freedom, of course, but I don't like them. As a matter of fact, I don't know any, at least so far as I am aware. No doubt some of our friends are homosexual; but as I'm not personally interested in it, I never notice it."

"Yes, but because you don't notice it doesn't mean that it doesn't exist. Don't be narrow-minded, George. There are probably tens of thousands of people living miserable lives . . ."

"Oh, I know all about that! But you can't break down the inherited prejudices of ages in five minutes. I personally don't object to such people doing as they want. There's no tort to person or property. But my advice to them would be to keep jolly quiet about it, and not try to make themselves martyrs, and flaunt themselves publicly."

"Oh, oh!" Elizabeth laughed; "Grandpa George forgathering with the Victorians!"

"All right, but I'm not going to say what I don't feel. In this matter you must look upon me as a neutral."

"Well, I think you ought to look into it more carefully and sympathetically, and get Bobbe to let you write some articles on it."

"Thanks very much. You ask him to do it himself; it's far more likely to attract *him*. If I wrote such articles I should immediately be suspect. It's a damned dangerous thing to do in England; in most cases the suspicion is far too likely to be true!"

And they left it at that.

All this time the war was drawing steadily nearer. Probably it had become certain since 1911, though most people were taken quite unawares. Why did it happen? Who was responsible? Questions which have been interminably debated already and will furnish exultant historians with controversial material for generations to come. Already one foresees the creation of Chairs in the History of the First World War, to be set up in whatever civilised countries remain in existence after the next one. But for us the debate is vain, as vain as the pathetic and reiterated enquiry, "*Where* did I catch this horrible cold?" If any body or bodies engineered this catastrophe they must have been gratified by its shattering success. Few lives indeed in the

belligerent countries remained unaffected by it, and in most
cases the effect was unpleasant. Adult lives were cut sharply
into three sections—pre-war, war, and post-war. It is curious—perhaps not so curious—but many people will tell you
that whole areas of their pre-war lives have become obliterated
from their memories. Pre-war seems like pre-history. What did
we do, how did we feel, what were we living for in those
incredibly distant years? One feels as if the period 1900–14
has to be treated archæologically, painfully recreated by
experts from slight vestiges. Those who were still children at
the Armistice, who were so to speak born into the war, can
hardly understand the feeling of tranquil security which
existed, the almost smug optimism of our lives. Especially in
England, for the French retained uncomfortable memories of
1870; but still, even in France life seemed established and
secure. Since Waterloo, England had engaged in no great war.
There were frontier and colonial skirmishes, and the reputation of the country for military organisation and efficiency
was immensely strengthened in the world's eyes by the conduct of the Crimean and Boer Wars. But there had been nothing on a really big scale. The Franco-Prussian War was just
one of those unfortunate occurrences one must expect from
backward Continental nations, and the huge struggle of the
War of Secession was observed through the wrong end of the
telescope. In some quarters, indeed, that war had been considered as a peculiar mercy of God to His Chosen People, enabling
the British Merchant Marine to re-establish an indisputable
primacy at the expense of a regrettable upstart among nations.

Talleyrand used to say that those who had not known
Europe before 1789 had never known the real pleasure of living. No one would dare to substitute 1914 for 1789 in that
sentence. But such a wholesale shattering of values had certainly not occurred since 1789. God knows how many governments and rulers crashed down in the earthquake, and those
which remain are agitatedly trying to preserve their existence
by the time-honoured methods of repression and persecution.
And yet 1914 was greeted as a great release, a purgation from
the vices supposed to be engendered by peace! My God! Three
days of glory engender more vices and misery than all the

alleged corruptors of humanity could achieve in a millennium. *Les jeunes* would be amazed if they read the nauseous poppy-cock which was written in 1914–15 in England, and doubtless in all the belligerent countries, except France, where practically nothing was printed at all. (However, the French have made up handsomely for the loss since then.) "Our splendid troops" were to come home—oh, very soon—purged and ennobled by slaughter and lice, and were to beget a race of even nobler fellows to go and do likewise. We were to have a real revival in religion, for people's thoughts were now turned from frivolities to great and serious themes. We were to have a new and greater literature—hence the alleged vogue for "war poets," which resulted in the parents of the slain being asked to put up fifty pounds for the publication (which probably cost fifteen) of poor little verses which should never have passed the home circle. We were to have . . . but really I lack courage to continue. Let those who are curious in human imbecility consult the newspaper-files of those days. . . .

But we are still lingering in the golden calm of the last few months preceding August 1914.

Fanny had followed Elizabeth's amazing evolutions with considerable surprise and that feeling of "something not displeasing" with which we contemplate the misfortunes of our best friends. She chiefly felt rather sorry for George. . . .

"You have a vendetta of the dead against the living." Yes, it is true, I have a vendetta, an unappeased longing for vengeance. Yes, a vendetta. Not a personal vendetta. What am I? O God, nothing, less than nothing, a husk, a leaving, a half-chewed morsel on the plate, a reject. But an impersonal vendetta, an unappeased conscience crying in the wilderness, a river of tears in the desert. What right have I to live? Is it five million, is it ten million, is it twenty million? What does the exact count matter? There they are, and we are responsible. Tortures of hell, we are responsible! When I meet an unmaimed man of my generation, I want to shout at him: "How did you escape? How did you dodge it? What dirty trick did you play? Why are you not dead, trickster?" It is dreadful to have outlived your

life, to have shirked your fate, to have overspent your welcome. There is nobody upon earth who cares whether I live or
die, and I am glad of it, so glad of it. To be alone, icily alone.
You, the war dead, I think you died in vain, I think you died
for nothing, for a blast of wind, a blather, a humbug, a newspaper stunt, a politician's ramp. But at least you died. You did
not reject the sharp, sweet shock of bullets, the sudden smash
of the shell-burst, the insinuating agony of poison gas. You got
rid of it all. You chose the better part. "They went down like a
lot o' Charlie Chaplins," said the little ginger-hair sergeant of
the Durhams. Like a lot of Charlie Chaplins. Marvellous met-
aphor! Can't you see them staggering on splayed-out feet and
waving ineffective hands as they went down before the accurate machine-gun fire of the Durhams sergeant? A splendid
little hero—he got the Military Medal for it. Like a lot of
Charlie Chaplins. Marvellous! But why weren't we one of
them? What right have we to live? And the women? Oh, don't
let's talk about the women. They were splendid, wonderful.
Such devotion, such devotion! How they comforted the troops!
Oh, wonderful, beyond all praise! They got the vote for it, you
know. Oh, wonderful! Steel-true and blade-straight. Yes,
indeed, wonderful, wonderful! What ever should we have
done without them? White feathers, and all that, you know.
Oh, the women were marvellous. You can always rely upon
the women to come up to scratch, you know. Yes, indeed.
What would the Country be without them? So splendid, such
an example.

On Sundays the Union Jack flies over the cemetery at Etaples. It's not so big as it was in the old wooden-cross days,
but it's still quite large. Acres and acres. Yes, acres and acres.
And it's too late to get one's little lot in the acres. Too late, too
late. . . .

Yes, Fanny was sorry for George, and showed it with practical
feminine sympathy. In the late spring Elizabeth "had" to go
and spend a fortnight with her parents in the north. Mrs. Paston—who never failed in any of her duties, and took jolly good
care to let you know it—was accustomed to write every week
to Elizabeth. This weekly letter was supposed to be a nice,

chatty, affectionate record of the little home circle and friends, something to keep Elizabeth in touch with their purer lives (of pure boredom) and preserve her from the decadents and degenerates she frequented in London. In fact the letter was almost invariably a perfidious and insinuating effort to make Elizabeth uncomfortable and to discourage her with her own life. Under the endearing words of conventional family affection lurked a curious resentment and hatred. If Mrs. Paston could think of anything likely to worry Elizabeth she never failed to convey it, in the strain of "Isn't it a pity, dear! . . ." Sometimes Elizabeth answered these letters, sometimes she did not. Recently, they had been filled with discouraging hints about the state of Mr. Paston's health. "Your dear father" could not shake off his "bronchitis" (*i.e.* a cold in the head), he was very "languid" (*i.e.* bored, the golf-links were under water), he "scarcely ever went out" (he hardly ever had done, except to play golf), he was "getting so frail and white-haired, poor darling daddy" (he'd been grey for fifteen years and still ate four hearty meals daily), he "seemed to be failing fast"—a pure piece of mythology. Elizabeth was rather fond of her father, and began to get alarmed, although she was more or less aware of her mother's strategy. But it is the misfortune of youth never really to credit the aged with their full meed of perfidy and dislike. She felt she ought to go and see her father for herself—it would be awful if he suddenly died without her seeing him. She told George she was going.

"All right, of course, if you want to. I'll take you to the station. When are you going?"

"I wish you'd come with me, George. Father and mother would like to see you, and they'd appreciate it so much."

"Now look here, Elizabeth, don't let's have any humbug here. I don't ask you to meet my parents and I don't see why I should have to stay with yours. I think your mother's quite awful, one of those nagging martyr women who're always taking on unnecessary jobs and worries, and then grumbling about how much they have to do and how little they're appreciated. Your father's all right. He's a decent sort, with a human respect for other people. But after I've feigned an interest I don't feel in golf and we've shaken our heads over the wickedness of Liberal Governments, we've really nothing left to say to each other."

"But it's so much easier for me if you'd come too."

"No, it wouldn't. We'd be shown off as the happy married pair to your mother's friends, and our sufferings would be dreadful. Besides, it'll be easier for you to adjust yourself temporarily to their prejudices if you don't have the sensation of a satirical me watching you."

So Elizabeth went by herself, and George remained alone in London. He always missed Elizabeth frightfully when she went away, but instead of going out and amusing himself he stayed in and tried to pass the time by over-working. By the evening of the fifth day he was thoroughly fed up. He decided to go out and ring up various friends in turn, until he found someone to have dinner with him. He had just finished washing and was putting on a clean collar, when someone knocked at the door of his studio.

"Half a minute," shouted George; "I'm dressing. Who is it?"

The door opened, and in came Fanny, wearing a charming new dress and a gay wide-brimmed hat with a large feather in it.

"Why, Fanny! How good to see you, and how lovely you look!"

They kissed affectionately. Fanny sat down on the bed.

"I've come to be taken out to dinner. If you think you're doing anything else, you're mistaken. You'll have to ring up and say you can't come."

"As a matter of fact, I was on the point of going out to find somebody to dine with me, so your coming is a god-send."

"How's Elizabeth?"

"She's all right. I got a letter from her this morning. She's with her parents, you know."

"Yes, I know. How long'll she be away?"

"Another ten days. Poor darling, she sounds awfully bored already."

"And what are you doing?"

"Oh, fighting the lone hand here. Do you want to see the picture I'm finishing?"

And George dragged round an easel with a large canvas on it, into the light.

"But it's good, George! It's got great qualities of energy and design."

"You don't think it's too hard and angular?"

"No, not a bit. It's excellent. By far the best thing you've done."

And Fanny jumped up from the bed, put her arm round George, and kissed him again. For the first time her lips were not cool, shut and sisterly, but warm and open and delicious— the lips of an accomplice. The sudden flicker of warm desire awoke in George's flesh, and he felt his heart leap and the blood flush to his face. He held her to him, and pressed eager firm lips to her soft yielding mouth. For a few seconds she seemed to resist, and made as if to thrust him from her. He held her more closely, and suddenly her stiffened body yielded delicately, moulded itself to his, her head moved slowly back- wards with closed eyes. ******* *** ***** ****** ** *** **** ** **** ** *** *** ********* ****** ** * ****** *********. George gently laid his hand on her left breast, and felt the rapid beating of her heart. She softly drew away her lips and looked at him.

"Fanny! Fanny!"

Her gem-like eyes, now all flower-like, looked at him.

"Fanny! Most dear Fanny! I must have loved you a long time without knowing it."

Fanny spoke slowly, still watching him:

"You're such a nice man, George, and yet such a boy."

"And you are divine and inexpressibly lovely and thrilling and adorable. . . ."

They kissed again, and stood there embraced until George felt dizzy with the blood beating in his brain. He pulled her gently towards the bed, and they lay down, clothed, in each other's arms. George's hand moved tenderly and delicately over her uncorseted girl body, so warm and firm and fragile under the thin, cool silk dress. The incoherent words of lovers gave place to silence, and they lay trembling in each other's arms, almost like frightened children comforting each other.

Fanny sighed, and opened her eyes.

"What time is it?"

George fumbled for his watch.

"Nearly half-past eight!"

"Heavens! We shall be too late for dinner if we don't hurry."

George went to get his coat, and returned to find Fanny unconcernedly drawing her silk stockings tight and trim.

"Where can we go that's near?"

"There's a new place just started in Frith Street—we can go there."

George watched her as she smoothed her mussed hair and absorbedly fitted on the large hat before the mirror. He was still trembling a little, and noticed how steady her hands were. Only a few minutes before they had been so close, all the barriers down, each existence melted in the other. That had been perfect, complete happiness. "Had been." Already the current of ordinary life was sweeping them apart again. Oh, not very far really, still within hailing distance. But very far, compared with that wonderful nearness. Such an ecstasy could not last. But why not? Perhaps one of the many bitter jests of the gods— to show us for an hour what happiness might be if we were gods. None can possess another, none can be possessed. Is it possible to give, is it possible to take? Does one existence really melt into another for a few minutes, or does it only seem to? What is she thinking now? Her mind is as remote from mine as if she had slipped into another dimension. Romantically we ask too much. It is much that she is lovely and finds me desirable. Let us not ask too much. Enjoyment is enough. Yet how fragile even that is! It is as if one tried to carry a small flickering light in a thin glass vessel through a tumultous, hostile crowd. How earnest is the world to suppress the delight of lovers! How bitterly wrong all that is!

They went down into the warm, airless street, where the lamps were already lighted. Dirty children still played noisily and screamed on the side-walks. An Italian woman slip-slopped past them in felt slippers, carrying a jug of beer. Soho smelled frowzy and stale. Fanny noticed this.

"Why do you and Elizabeth live in this horrid district? It must be awfully unhealthy, especially for Elizabeth."

"Oh, one gets used to it. Hampstead's too far out, Kensington's too dear, Chelsea's both dear and ungetatable. When I'm in town I like to be in the middle of it. Suburbs are beastly. We all suffer from the English "home" system of building—one hut, one family. And from our peculiar desire to be in a town and the country simultaneously, we don't seem able to live the purely urban life of the Latins. But London's too big and frowzy."

They dined in the small restaurant, which had been "decorated" with rather feeble pictures by young artists, to give it that Latin Quarter air. It was somehow ineffectual. A bit amateurish. However, they didn't care about that. Since they were comparatively old friends, they did not suffer the haunting and disagreeable uneasiness and strangeness which fall between those who suddenly become lovers. The spontaneity of their passion absorbed any possible feeling of remorse. They talked quietly, but without any strain and effort. Fanny gave some amusing descriptions of the odd freaks among the British "colonies" on the Riviera. Why is it that one sees such curious and freakish specimens of one's countrymen abroad, types one never sees at home? Do the foreign surroundings bring out the freakishness, or were such people destined to emigration by their very oddity? . . . But there could be no doubt—Fanny and George were on a new footing with each other. There was a new and delicious intimacy between them. Strange that a few kisses and caresses should make such a difference.

As they were leaving the restaurant, Fanny was hailed by some friends at a table near the door.

"Hullo, Fanny! How are you? I say, why don't you come along with us? We're all going to Marshall's chambers at ten. There'll be lots of people there. It ought to be amusing."

"No, I want to see that new film at the Shaftesbury."

"But you can see that any time."

"No, this is the last week, and I'm going to Dieppe tomorrow for a week."

"Oh, all right. Sorry you won't come. Look us up when you get back. Good-bye, good-bye."

They got into a taxi, and Fanny gave the address of her flat.

"Did you really mean that you are going to Dieppe tomorrow?" asked George a little wistfully.

Fanny squeezed his arm, and kissed him briefly and skilfully as the taxi lurched them together.

"Of course not, goose! We're going to be together, unless

you piously decide not to. But it's useful to have an alibi. People are still fussy about one's 'reputation,' you know."

"But suppose we meet them, or someone else who knows you?"

"I shall say I changed my mind, or that I got bored and came straight back."

Fanny's flat was small, but pleasantly clean and modern. After the picturesque but rather dingy antiquity of his large eighteenth-century panelled room, George found it delightful to be in bright-painted, clean rooms with a white-tiled bathroom. Among Fanny's many remarkable efficiencies was the genius of discovering excellent flats at a fabulously cheap rental, furnishing them charmingly for about five pounds, and running them perfectly without the slightest fuss. She generally shifted her quarters about every six months, and invariably for the better. How pleasant is efficiency in others, especially when you are rather inefficient yourself! I wouldn't exactly say that George was inefficient, but the details of material life rather bored him. When you had so much else to do and so little time to do it in, he thought it rather a waste of life to be too pernickety about one's surroundings and fixings. However, he decided then and there that he and Elizabeth would have to get out of Soho. It was too disgustingly frowzy.

Fanny was a marvellous lover. Or, at least George thought so. It was not only that she was golden and supple and lithe, where Elizabeth was dark and rather stiff and virginal, but she really cared about love-making. It was her art. It was for her neither a painful duty nor a degrading necessity nor a series of disappointing experiments, but a delightful art which gave full expression to her vitality, energy, and efficiency. Like all great artists, she was entirely disinterested—art for art's sake. She chose her lovers with great care, and rather preferred them to be poor, to avoid any suspicion of commercialism or arrivism. She knew she had the genius of touch, and was unwilling that it should be wasted. If she hadn't been a great lover, she might have been a good sculptor. But like all artists she was exacting, and had her vanity. She would not waste her talents. If a subject was not profoundly responsive and appreciative, she put him aside at the earliest possible moment. No clumsy, inhibited Englishman for her! No, thank you. Perhaps that is why she spent so much of her time abroad.

But this particular Englishman was not inhibited or ineradicably clumsy. Crude perhaps, rather lacking in style and finish, but capable of rapid progress under expert guidance. Fanny, with the artist's unerring glance, had long ago perceived that there were considerable possibilities in George. He had natural aptitudes and, what is far more important, the sense of delicate artistry which finds its highest satisfaction in bestowing delight. He was neither a bull nor a turkey gobbler. Fanny was satisfied; she had not made a mistake. . . .

For the remaining days of Elizabeth's absence George did no work whatever. And a very good thing, too, for he needed a holiday. He stayed at Fanny's flat. They made picnic meals in the flat, or ate out at places where they were pretty certain not to meet friends—City stock-brokers' taverns, or curious pubs with sawdust and spittoons on the floors, where you sat on stools at the bar and had a cut from the joint and two veg. with beer. They went to "low" music-halls and saw all the primitive films of the day—Charlie's were the only good ones—and for a lark went to see what the inside of the Abbey looked like, a place no Londoner ever visits. They agreed that it looked like the atelier of an incredibly bad academic sculptor installed in an overcrowded but rather beautiful Gothic barn. Fanny rather hated Gothic architecture—she said all those points and squiggles gave her the creeps; but George said that if you wanted to see the real spirit of mediæval sculpture you ought to look underneath the seats of the canons' stalls. But they didn't quarrel about that. They were far too happy.

Nothing more was said about Elizabeth, until the day before she returned.

"You'll meet her, of course?" said Fanny.

"Of course."

"Well, give her my love."

"I suppose I ought to tell her about us," said George, reflectively.

Fanny saw the danger in a flash. Her "freedom" was of a different kind from Elizabeth's rather theoretical and idealising kind. Fanny's was light-hearted and practical; moreover, she had observed human beings and knew her Elizabeth far better than George did. She also knew her George. If George told Elizabeth, she knew quite well there would be a bust-up, that Elizabeth's theories would be abandoned as speedily as on the former occasion. But she knew it was useless to reveal the truth to George. On the other hand, she didn't want to lose him and didn't want to "take him away" from Elizabeth—not until much later when Elizabeth started the struggle. Fanny knew that George had to be managed within the limits of masculine stupidity.

"Oh, tell her if you like. But I shouldn't discuss it with her, if I were you. She must have long ago felt subconsciously the attraction between us, and you can see by her attitude that she accepts it. I don't see the need for all this talk and re-hashing of what's a private and personal matter between two people. We're so hypnotised by words, that we think nothing exists until we have talked about it. How can you interpret all these deep feelings and sensations in words? It's because words don't suffice that we need touch. Tell Elizabeth by loving her better."

"Then you really think she knows?"

Fanny was a little annoyed. Why couldn't he *see*, why couldn't he take a hint?

"If she's as acute and experienced as she tells us, she ought to have seen the possibility long ago. No doubt, if she's said nothing about it to you, the reason is that she just doesn't want to discuss it. If she accepts, that's enough."

"But she always believes that two people should be perfectly open and frank with each other about their other affairs."

"Does she? Well, I advise you to say nothing until she asks you."

"All right, darling, if you think so."

George duly met Elizabeth at Euston. She was delighted to be back in London, away from the stuffiness of family and the solemn boredom of middle-class existence. She leaned out the window of the taxi and sniffed the air.

"How lovely to smell dirty old London mud again! It means I'm free, free, free again!"

"Was it very awful?"

"Oh, awful, interminable."

"I'm so glad you're back."

"It's wonderful. And lovely to be with you again! How well you look, George!—quite handsome and Italian!"

"That's because you haven't seen me for a fortnight."

"How's Fanny?"

"Oh, very well. Sent her love to you."

"Dear old beastly, ugly Tottenham Court Road!" said Elizabeth with her nose out the window again.

"By the way, it was awfully frowsty in Soho while you were away. Don't you think we might move to somewhere more modern?"

"What, to a suburb? Why, George! you know you hate suburbs, and always said you liked to live in the middle of London."

"Yes, I know. But we might find something at Chelsea."

"But we couldn't possibly afford two places at Chelsea rents."

"Well, why not share a fairly large one?"

"What, and live in the same flat? George!"

"Oh, all right, if you don't want to, but Fanny thinks Soho is unhealthy for you."

"Well, we'll see."

Whether, as the Swedish old maid hinted in her book, it was the stimulus of another affair, or whether George was anxious to display the artistries of Fanny, or whether it was merely remorse, Elizabeth found George peculiarly charming and ardent.

She attributed this to the happy effect of a brief absence.

7

In a few weeks they duly moved to Chelsea. Fanny found them an excellent apartment, with two large rooms, a kitchen, and a modern bathroom, for less than the combined rental of their two ramshackle rooms in Soho. Elizabeth developed an unexpected talent for "home-making," and fussed a good deal over the installation in spite of George's light satire. But they were both only too happy to get away from the frowstiness of Soho to a clean modern flat.

This was in June 1914. They did not go away when the hot weather arrived, intending to stay the summer in London and go to Paris for September and October. Elizabeth spent a good deal of her spare time with Reggie Burnside, and George was absorbed in his painting. He wanted to get enough good canvases for a small show in Paris in the autumn.

One day towards the end of July he left his painting early, to meet Reggie and Elizabeth for lunch somewhere near Piccadilly. It was a benign day, with fine white fleecy clouds suspended in a blue sky, and a light wind ruffling the darkened foliage of summer trees. Even the King's Road looked pleasant. George noticed, and afterwards remembered vividly, because these were the last really tranquil moments of his life, how the policeman's gloves made a clear blotch of white against a plane-tree as he regulated the traffic. A little band of sparrows were squabbling and twittering noisily in the lilacs of one of the gardens. The heat was reflected, not unpleasantly, from the warm white flag-stones of the sidewalk.

As he waited for the No. 19 bus, George did what he very rarely did—bought a newspaper. He always said it was a waste of life to read newspapers—if something really important happened, people would tell you about it soon enough. He didn't know why he bought a paper that morning. He had been working hard for two or three weeks without seeing any one but Elizabeth, and perhaps thought he would see what was going on in the world. Perhaps it was only to see if there was any new film.

George clambered to the top of the bus, with the paper under his arm, and paid his fare. He then glanced casually at the headlines and read: "Serious Situation in the Balkans, Austro-Hungarian Ultimatum to Servia, Servian Appeal to Russia, Position of Germany and France." George looked up vaguely at the other people on the bus. There were four men and two women; each of the men was intently reading the same special early edition of the evening paper. He read the despatches eagerly and carefully, and grasped the seriousness of the

situation at once. The Austrian Empire was on the verge of war
with Serbia (Servia it was then called, until the country became
one of our plucky little allies); Russia threatened to support
Serbia; the Triple Alliance would bring in Germany and Italy
on the side of Austria; France would be bound to support Russia under the Treaty of Alliance, and the Entente Cordiale
might involve England. There was a chance of a European War,
the biggest conflict since the defeat of Napoleon. The event he
had always declared to be impossible—a war between the
"civilised" nations—was threatened, was at hand. He refused
to believe it. Germany didn't want war, France would be mad
to want it, England couldn't want it. The "Powers" would
intervene. What was Sir Edward Grey doing? Oh, suggesting a
conference. . . . The man on the seat opposite George leaned
towards him, tapping the newspaper with his hand:

"What do you say to that, sir?"

"I think it looks confoundedly serious."

"Chance of a war, eh?"

"I sincerely hope not. The newspapers always exaggerate,
you know. It would be an appalling catastrophe."

"Oh, liven things up a bit. We're getting stale, too much
peace. Need a bit of blood-letting."

"I don't think it'll come to that. I . . ."

"It's got to come sooner or later. Them Germans, you know.
They'd never be able to face our Navy."

"Well, let's hope it won't be necessary."

"Ah, I dunno. Shouldn't mind 'avin' a go at the Germans
myself, and I reckon you wouldn't either."

"Oh, I'm a neutral," said George, laughing; "don't count
on me."

"Umph!" said the man, as he got up to leave the bus, casting
a suspicious look at this foreign-looking and unpatriotic person. "Yes, that's it, a foreigner, a bloody foreigner. Umph!
What's he doing in England, I'd like to know? Umph!"

George was back in the newspaper, unaware of the turmoil
he had excited in that elderly but patriotic bosom.

"I say," exclaimed George, as soon as he met Elizabeth and
Reggie, "have you two seen the newspaper to-day?"

"Why?" said Elizabeth; "what's in it? Something about you?"

"No, there's a war threatened in the Balkans, and it may apparently involve every one else."

Reggie sneered.

"Oh, piffle! How absurd you are, George, to believe a news-paper sensation! Why, we were talking about it last night in the Common Room, and every one agreed that the conflict would have to be localised and that Grey would probably make a statement in a day or two. It'll all blow over."

Elizabeth had grabbed the newspaper, and was trying to find her way through the unfamiliar mazes of sensational rhetoric.

"So you don't think it'll come to anything?" said George, hanging up his hat, and sitting down at the restaurant table.

"Of course not!" said Reggie contemptuously.

"What do you think, Elizabeth?"

"I don't know," she said looking up bewildered from the paper; "I can't understand this curious language. Are all news-papers written like that?"

"Mostly," said George; "but I'm glad you think it's only a scare, Reggie. I admit I was startled when I read those head-lines. That's what comes of living absorbed in one's own life, and neglecting the fountain-heads of truth."

All the same, he was not quite reassured, and on the way home left an order with a local newsagent for the delivery of a daily paper until further notice. He hoped the next morning's news would be better. It wasn't. Neither was the next day's. Then came the news that Russia was mobilising, and that the Grand Fleet had sailed from Spithead "on manœuvres," but under sealed orders. George remembered the coast-guard officer who got drunk and let slip that he had sealed orders in case of war. Perhaps the man would be opening those orders in a few days, perhaps he had already opened them. He tried to paint, and couldn't; picked up a book, and found himself thinking: Aus-tria, Russia, Germany, France, England perhaps—good God, it's impossible, impossible! He fidgeted about, and then went into Elizabeth's room. She was delicately painting a large blue bowl of variegated summer flowers. The room was very quiet. One of the windows was opened on to a large communal garden surrounded by the backs of houses. A wasp came in through the striped orange-and-black curtain and buzzed towards a bunch of grapes on a large Spanish plate.

"What is it, George?"

The room was so peaceful, so secure, Elizabeth so unperturbed and as usual, that George felt half-surprised at his own agitation.

"I'm worried about this war situation."

"Really, George! What *is* the good of getting into such a fuss? You know Reggie told you there was nothing in it, and he hears all the latest news at Cambridge."

"Yes, darling, but it isn't a matter of Cambridge now, but of Europe. The Tsar and the Kaiser won't consult the Dons before launching a war."

Elizabeth, rather annoyed, went on painting.

"Well," she said through the brush between her teeth, "I can't help it. Anyway, it won't concern us."

It won't concern us! George stood irresolute a moment.

"I think I'll go out and see what's the latest news."

"Yes, do. I'm dining with Reggie to-night."

"All right."

George spent the first few days of August wandering about London, taking buses, and buying innumerable editions of newspapers. London seemed perfectly calm and as usual, and yet there was something feverish about it. Perhaps it was George's own feverishness exteriorised; perhaps it was the unwonted number of special editions, with shouting newsboys in unusual places handing out copies as fast as they could to little groups of impatient people. His memories of those days were confused, and he couldn't remember the chronological order of events. Two or three scenes stood out vividly in his mind—all the rest became a blur, the outlines obliterated by more dreadful scenes.

He remembered dining with Elizabeth and some other friends in a private suite of the Berkeley as the guests of a wealthy American. The talk kept running on the possibility of war, and

the positions of England and America. George still clung to the
great illusion that wars between the highly industrialised countries were impossible. He elaborated this view to the American
man, who agreed, and said that Wall Street and Threadneedle
Street between them could stop the universe.

"If there *is* a war," said George, "it will be a sort of impersonal, natural calamity, like a plague or an earthquake.
But I think that in their own interests all the governments will
combine to avert it, or at least limit it to Austria and Servia."

"But don't you think the Germans are spoiling for a war?"
said another Englishman.

"I don't know, I simply don't know. What does any of us
know? The governments don't tell us what they're doing or
planning. We're completely in the dark. We can make surmises,
but we don't *know*."

"It's probably got to come sooner or later. The world's too
small to hold an expanding Germany and a non-contracting
British Empire."

"The irresistible force and the immovable mass. . . . But it's
not a question of England and Germany, but of Austria and
Servia."

"Oh, the murder of the Archduke's just a pretext—probably
arranged beforehand."

"But by which side? I can't see the situation as a stage scene,
with villains on one side and noble-minded fellows on the
other. If the Archduke's murder was the result of an intrigue,
as you suggest, it was a damned despicable one. Now, either
the various governments are all despicable intriguers ready to
stoop to any crime and duplicity to attain their ends, in which
case we shall certainly have a war, if they want it; or they're
more or less decent and human men like ourselves, in which
case they'll do anything to avert it. We can do nothing. We're
impotent. They've got the power and the information. We
haven't. . . ."

The white-gloved, immaculate Austrian waiters were silently
handing and removing plates. George noticed one of them, a
young man with close-cropped golden hair and a sensitive face.
Probably a student from Vienna or Prague, a poor man who
had chosen waiting as a means of earning his living while

studying English. They both were about the same age and height. George suddenly realised that he and the waiter were potential enemies! How absurd, how utterly absurd! . . .

After dinner they sat about and smoked. George took his chair over to the open window and looked down on the lights and movement of Piccadilly. The noise of the traffic was lulled by the height to a long continuous rumble. The placards of the evening papers along the railings beside the Ritz were sensational and bellicose. The party dropped the subject of a possible great war; after deciding that there wouldn't be one, there couldn't. George, who had great faith in Mr. Bobbe's political acumen, glanced through his last article, and took great comfort from the fact that Bobbe said there wasn't going to be a war. It was all a scare, a stock-market ramp. . . . At that moment three or four people came in, more or less together, though they were in separate parties. One of them was a youngish man in immaculate evening dress. As he shook hands with his host, George heard him say rather excitedly:

"I've just been dining with Tommy Parkinson of the Foreign Office. He had to leave early and go back to Downing Street. It seems there are Cabinet meetings all the time. Tommy was frightfully depressed and pessimistic about the situation."

"What did he say?" asked three or four eager voices.

"He wouldn't commit himself at all. He was simply very gloomy and *distrait*, and wouldn't say anything definite."

"Why didn't you ask him whether Germany is mobilising?"

"I did, but he wouldn't tell me anything."

"Oh, well, perhaps he only has a liver."

Among the other guests was a tall, very erect, rather sunburned man of about forty, who had taken no part in the conversation. He was sitting on a couch in silence beside a woman younger than himself—his wife—who was also silent. George heard him introduced to another man as Colonel Thomas. After a few minutes George went over and spoke to him.

"My name's Winterbourne. You're Colonel Thomas, aren't you?"

"Yes."

"What do you think of the situation we've all been discussing so intelligently?"

"I don't think anything. A soldier mustn't have political 'views,' you know."

"Well, but do you think the Germans are mobilising?"

"I don't know. I believe they are. But that doesn't necessarily mean war. They may be mobilising for manœuvres. We're mobilised for manœuvres on Salisbury Plain."

"Mobilised! The British Army mobilised!"

"Only for manœuvres, you know."

"Are you mobilised too?"

"Yes, I leave to-morrow morning."

"Good God!"

"Oh, it's only manœuvres. They always happen at this time of the year."

Another day—it must have been the Sunday before the 4th of August—George went down to Trafalgar Square to attend a Socialist peace meeting. The space round the Nelson Column was so crowded that he could not get near enough to hear the speakers, who were standing on the plinth above the heads of the crowd. An eager-faced man with white hair and an aristocratic voice made a speech, directed at mob prejudices. He apparently took the view that the threatened war was the work of Imperial Russia. George caught repeatedly the words "knout," "Cossacks," and the phrase "the eagles of war are spreadin' their wings." Some of the listeners at a rival war meeting started an attack on the peace party. There was a scuffle, which was very soon dispersed by mounted police. The crowd surged away from Trafalgar Square. George found himself carried towards the Admiralty Arch and up the Mall. He thought he might as well go back that way, and try to get a bus at Victoria. But opposite Buckingham Palace the road was blocked by a huge crowd, which was continually reinforced from all three roads. The Palace Gates were shut, with a cordon of police in front of them. The red-coated Guardsmen in their furry busbies stood at ease in front of the sentry-boxes.

"We want King George! We want King George!" chanted the mob.

"We want King George!"

After several minutes a window was opened on to the centre

balcony, and the King appeared. He was greeted by an immense ragged cheer, and acknowledged it by raising his hand to his forehead. The crowd began another chant:

"We want War! We want War! We want WAR!"

More cheering. The King made no gesture of approval or disapproval.

"Speech!" shouted the mob, "Speech! WE WANT WAR!"

The King saluted again, and disappeared. A roar of mingled cheering and disappointment came from the crowd. There were several of the inevitable humorous optimists to cry:

"Are we down-hearted?"

"No-ooo!"

"Is Germany?"

"Yuss!"

"Do we care for the Germans?"

"No-oooo!"

There could be no doubt about the feelings of that small section of the English population. . . .

Even then George still clung to hopes of peace, bought only the more pacific Radical papers, and believed that Sir Edward Grey would "do something." Touching faith of the English in the omnipotence of their rulers! After all, Sir Edward was not God Almighty, but merely a harassed Secretary of State for Foreign Affairs in a difficult position, with a divided Cabinet behind him. What on earth could the man have done? Possibly a frank statement in July that if France or Belgium were attacked, England would "come in"? People say so now, but then it might have looked like a gesture of provocation. . . . Who are we to pass judgments? And the nations cannot altogether pose as the victims of their rulers. It is certain that the mobs in the capitals were howling for war. It is certain that the largest popular demonstrations in favour of peace occurred in Germany. . . .

When the news came that France had mobilised, and that the Germans had crossed the Belgian frontier, George abandoned all hope immediately. He knew that one of the cardinal points of British policy is never to allow Antwerp to rest in the possession of a Great Power. The principle is as old as the reign of Queen Elizabeth or older. Who was it said, "Antwerp is a pistol pointed at England's head"? All Europe was in arms, and England would join. The impossible had happened. They were in for three months of carnage and horrors. Yes, three months. It couldn't last longer. Probably less. Oh, much less. There would be an immense financial collapse, and the governments would have to cease fighting. Why, Bank rate was ten per cent. already. He jumped on a bus at Hyde Park Corner and sat just inside the entrance.

"What's the news?" said the conductor.

"Very serious: the French have mobilised."

"What abaht us?"

"We've done nothing yet. But it looks inevitable."

"Wy, we ain't declared war, 'ave we?"

"No, not yet."

"Well, there's still 'opes, then. I reckon we'd best mind ah own business, and keep aht of it."

Mind our own business! How quickly that unselfish sentiment was crystallised in the national slogan: Business As Usual!

The long, unendurable nightmare had begun. And the reign of Cant, Delusion, and Delirium. I have shown, with a certain amount of excusable ferocity, how devilishly and perniciously the old régime of Cant affected people's sexual lives, and hence the whole of their lives and characters and those of their children. The subsequent reaction was, at least in its origin, healthy and right. There simply *had* to be a better attitude, the facts had to be faced. And nobody with any courage will allow himself to be frightened out of saying so, either by the hush-hush partisans of the old régime or the doing-what-grandpa-did-and-let's-pretend-it's-all-lovely, or by the fact that numerous congenital idiots have prattled and babbled and slobbered about "sex" until the very word is an exacerbation. But the sexual life *is* important. It is in so many cases the dominant or the next to dominant factor in people's lives. We can't write about their lives without bringing it in; so for God's sake let's do so honestly and openly, in accordance with what we believe to be the facts, or else give up pretending that we are writing about life. No more Cant. And I mean free-love Cant just as much as orange-blossoms and pealing church bells Cant. . . .

If you're going to argue that Cant is necessary (the old political excuse), then for Heaven's sake let's chuck up the game and hand in our checks. But it isn't necessary. It can only be necessary when deceit is necessary, when people have to be influenced to act against their right instincts and true interests. If you want to judge a man, a cause, a nation, ask: Do they Cant? If the War had been an honest affair for any participant, it would not have needed this preposterous bolstering up of Cant. The only honest people—if they existed—were those who said: "This is foul brutality, but we respect and admire brutality, and admit we are brutes; in fact, we are proud of being brutes." All right, then we know. "War is hell." It is, General Sherman, it is, a bloody, brutal hell. Thanks for your honesty. You, at least, were an honourable murderer.

It was the régime of Cant *before* the War which made the Cant *during* the War so damnably possible and easy. On our coming of age the Victorians generously handed us a charming little cheque for fifty guineas—fifty-one months of hell, and the results. Charming people, weren't they? Virtuous and far-sighted. But it wasn't their fault? They didn't make the War? It was Prussia, and Prussian militarism? Right you are, right ho! Who made Prussia a great power and subsidised Frederick the Second to do it, thereby snatching an empire from France? England. Who backed up Prussia against Austria, and Bismarck against Napoleon III? England. And whose Cant governed England in the nineteenth century? But never mind this domestic squabble of mine—put it that I mean the "Victorians" of all nations.

One human brain cannot hold, one memory retain, one pen portray the limitless Cant, Delusion, and Delirium let loose on the world during those four years. It surpasses the most fantastic imagination. It was incredible—and I suppose that was why it was believed. It was the supreme and tragic climax of Victorian Cant, for after all the Victorians were still in full blast in 1914, and had pretty much the control of everything.

Did they appeal to us honestly, and say: "We have made a colossal and tragic error, we have involved you and all of us in a huge war; it's too late to stop it; you must come and help us, and we promise to take the first opportunity of making peace and making it thoroughly"? They did not. They said they didn't want to lose us, but they thought WE ought to go; they said our King and Country needed us; they said they'd kiss us when we came home (*merci!* effect of the Entente Cordiale?); they said one of the most civilised races in the world were "Huns"; they invented Cadaver factories; they asserted that a race of men notorious during generations for their kindliness were habitual baby-butchers, rapers of women, crucifiers of prisoners; they said the "Huns" were sneaks and cowards and skedaddlers, but failed to explain why it took fifty-one months to beat their hopelessly outnumbered armies; they said they were fighting for the Liberty of the World, and everywhere there is less liberty; they said they would Never sheathe the Sword until etcetera, and this sort of criminal rant was called Pisgah-Heights of Patriotism. . . . They said . . . But why continue? Why go on? It is desolating, desolating. And then they dare wonder why the young are cynical and despairing and angry and chaotic! And they still have adherents, who still dare to go on preaching to *us*! Quick! A shrine to the goddesses Cant and Impudence. . . .

I don't know if George was aware of all this, because we never discussed it. There were numbers of things you prudently didn't discuss in those days; you never knew who might be listening and "report." I myself was twice arrested, as a civilian, for wearing a cloak and looking foreign, and for laughing in the street; I was under acute suspicion for weeks in one battalion because I had a copy of Heine's poems and admitted that I had been abroad; in another I was suspected of not being myself, God knows why. That was nothing compared with the persecution endured by D. H. Lawrence, probably the greatest living English novelist, and a man of whom—in spite of his failings—England should be proud.

I do know that George suffered profoundly from the first day of the War until his death at the end of it. He must have realised the awfulness of the Cant and degradation, for he occasionally talked about the yahoos of the world having got loose and seized control, and, by Jove! he was right. I shan't attempt to describe the sinister degradation of English life in the last two years of the War: for one thing, I was mostly out of England; and for another, Lawrence has done it once and for all in the chapter called "The Nightmare" in his book *Kangaroo*.

In George's case, the suffering which was common to all decent men and women was increased and complicated and rendered more torturing by his personal problems, which somehow became related to the War. You must remember that he did not believe in the alleged causes for which the War was fought. He looked upon the War as a ghastly calamity, or a more ghastly crime. They might talk about their idealism, but it wasn't convincing. There wasn't the *élan*, the conviction, the burning idealism which carried the ragged untrained armies of the First French Republic so dramatically to Victory over the hostile coalitions of the Kings. There was always the suspicion of dupery and humbug. Therefore, he could not take part in the War with any enthusiasm or conviction. On the other hand, he saw the intolerable egotism of setting up oneself as a notable exception or courting a facile martyrdom of *rouspetance*. Going meant one more little brand in the conflagration; staying out meant that some other, probably physically weaker, brand was substituted. His conscience was troubled before he was in the Army, and equally troubled afterwards. The only consolation he felt was in the fact that you certainly had a worse and a more dangerous time in the line than out of it.

As a matter of fact, I never really "got" George's position. He hated talking about the subject, and he had thought about it and worried about it so much that he was quite muddle-headed. It seemed to involve the whole universe, and his attempts to express his point of view would wander off into discussions about the Greek city-states or the principles of Machiavelli. He was frankly incoherent, which meant a considerable inner conflict. From the very beginning of the War he

had got into the habit of worrying, and this developed with
alarming rapidity. He worried about the War, about his own
attitude to it, about his relations with Elizabeth and Fanny,
about his military duties, about everything. Now, "worry" is
not "caused" by an event; it is a state which seizes upon any
event to "worry" over. It is a form of neurasthenia, which may
be induced in a perfectly healthy mind by shock and strain.
And for months and months he just worried and drifted.

When Elizabeth decided, somewhere towards the end of
1914, that the time had come when the principles of Freedom
must be put into practice in the case of herself and Reggie, and
duly informed George, he acquiesced at once. Perhaps he was
so sick at heart that he was indifferent; perhaps he was only
loyally carrying out the agreement. What surprised me was
that he did not take that opportunity of telling her about
Fanny. But he was apparently quite convinced that she knew.
It was there for an additional shock when he found out that
she didn't know, and a still greater shock to see how she
behaved. He suffered an obnubilation of the intellect in dealing with women. He idealised them too much. When I told
him with a certain amount of bitterness that Fanny was probably a trollop who talked "freedom" as an excuse, and that
Elizabeth was probably a conventional-minded woman who
talked "freedom" as in the former generation she would have
talked Ruskin and Morris politico-æstheticism, he simply got
angry. He said I was a fool. He said the War had induced in
me a peculiar resentment against women—which was probably true. He said I did not understand either Elizabeth or
Fanny—how could I possibly understand two people I had
never seen and have the cheek to try to explain them to *him*,
who knew them so well? He said I was far too downright,
over-simplified, and *tranchant* in my judgments, and that I
didn't—probably couldn't—understand the finer complexities
of people's psychology. He said a great deal more, which I have
forgotten. But we came as near to a quarrel as two lonely men
could, when they knew they had no other companion. This
was in the Officers' Training Camp in 1917, when George was
already in a peculiar and exacerbated state of nerves. After

that, I made no effort at any sort of ruthless directness, but just allowed him to go on talking. There was nothing else to do. He was living in a sort of double nightmare—the nightmare of the War and the nightmare of his own life. Each seemed inextricably interwoven. His personal life became intolerable because of the War, and the War became intolerable because of his own life. The strain imposed on him—or which he imposed on himself—must have been terrific. A sort of pride kept him silent. Once when it was my turn to act as commander of the other cadets, I was taking them in company drill. George was right-hand man in the front rank of No. I Platoon, and I glanced at him to see that he was keeping direction properly. I was startled by the expression on his face—so hard, so fixed, so despairing, so defiantly agonised. At mess—we ate at tables in sixes—he hardly ever spoke except to utter some banality in an effort to be amiable, or some veiled sarcasm which sped harmlessly over the heads of those for whom it was intended. He sneered a little too openly at the coarse, obscene talk about tarts and square-pushing, and was too obviously revolted by water-closet wit. However, he wasn't openly disliked. The others just thought him a rum bloke, and left him pretty much alone.

Probably what had distressed him most was the row between Elizabeth and Fanny. With the whole world collapsing about him, it seemed quite logical that the Triumphal Scheme for the Perfect Sex Relation should collapse too. He did not feel the peevish disgust of the reforming idealist who makes a failure. But in the general disintegration of all things he had clung very closely to those two women; too closely, of course. But they had acquired a sort of mythical and symbolical meaning for him. They resented and deplored the War, but they were admirably detached from it. For George they represented what hope of humanity he had left; in them alone civilisation seemed to survive. All the rest was blood and brutality and persecution and humbug. In them alone the thread of life remained continuous. They were two small havens of civilised existence, and alone gave him any hope for the future. They had escaped the vindictive destructiveness which so horribly possessed the

spirits of all right-thinking people. Of course, they were persecuted; that was inevitable. But they remained detached, and
alive. Unfortunately, they did not quite realise the strain under
which he was living, and did not perceive the widening gulf
which was separating the men of that generation from the
women. How could they? The friends of a person with cancer
haven't got cancer. They sympathise, but they aren't in the
horrid category of the doomed. Even before the Elizabeth-
Fanny row he was subtly drifting apart from them against his
will, against his desperate efforts to remain at one with them.
Over the men of that generation hung a doom which was
admirably if somewhat ruthlessly expressed by a British Staff
Officer in an address to subalterns in France: "You are the
War generation. You were born to fight this War, and it's got
to be won—we're determined you shall win it. So far as you
are concerned as individuals, it doesn't matter a tinker's damn
whether you are killed or not. Most probably you will be
killed, most of you. So make up your minds to it."

That extension of the Kiplingesque or kicked-backside-of-
the-Empire principle was something for which George was not
prepared. He resented it, resented it bitterly, but the doom was
on him as on all the young men. When "we" had determined
that they should be killed, it was impious to demur.

After the row, the gap widened, and when once George had
entered the army it became complete. He still clung desperately to Elizabeth and Fanny, of course. He wrote long letters
to them trying to explain himself, and they replied sympathetically. They were the only persons he wanted to see when on
leave, and they met him sympathetically. But it was useless.
They were gesticulating across an abyss. The women were still
human beings; he was merely a unit, a murder-robot, a wisp of
cannon-fodder. And he knew it. They didn't. But they felt the
difference, felt it as a degradation in him, a sort of failure.
Elizabeth and Fanny occasionally met after the row, and made
acid-sweet remarks to each other. But on one point they were
in agreement—George had degenerated terribly since joining
the army, and there was no knowing to what preposterous
depths of Tommydom he might fall.

"It's quite useless," said Elizabeth; "he's done for. He'll never be able to recover. So we may as well accept it. What was rare and beautiful in him is as much dead now as if he were lying under the ground in France."

And Fanny agreed. . . .

END OF PART II

PART III

I

The draft, under orders to proceed overseas on Active Service without delay, paraded again, in full marching order, at three-thirty.

Number two in the front rank was 31819, Private Winterbourne, G.

They had been "sized" that morning, so each man knew his number and place. They fell in rapidly, without talking, and stood easy, waiting for the officers, on the bleak gravelled parade-ground inside the bleak isolated citadel. Their view was rectangularly cut short either by the damp grey masonry of the fortress walls or by the dirty yellow brick frontals of the barracks built under the ramparts.

They numbered one hundred and twenty, and had been under orders to proceed overseas for more than a week, during which period they had been forbidden to leave the citadel under threat of court-martial. All sentry duties were performed by troops not in the draft, and five rounds of ball ammunition were issued to each sentry. These exceptional measures were the result of nervousness on the part of the Colonel, who had been censured for what was not his fault—two men had deserted on the eve of the departure of the last draft, and two others had to be substituted at the last moment. "Does the old mucker think we're going to run away?" was the comment of the draft, wounded in their pride, when they accidentally found this out.

A stiff, coldish wind was blowing soiled-looking ragged clouds and occasional gusts of chilly rain over a greyish winter sky. The men fidgeted in the ranks, some bending forward to ease the strain of straps, some throwing their packs a fraction higher with a jerk of their shoulders and loins; one or two had taken the regulation step forward and were adjusting their puttees or the fold in their trouser legs. Winterbourne stood with his weight on his right leg, holding the projecting barrel of his obsolete drill rifle loosely in his right hand; his head was bent slightly forward as he gazed at the gravel expressionlessly.

The draft had been parading for various purposes all through the day, when they thought they would be free to idle and write letters. The canteen had been put out of bounds to prevent a possible drunken departure. The parades had included two kit inspections and several visits to the Quartermaster's stores to draw new winter clothing and other objects for use overseas. Consequently, in their mood of restrained excitement, they had become rather irritated and impatient. The fidgeting increased under the reproving gaze of the N.C.O.'s and the rather boiled-looking glare of the Regimental Sergeant-Major, a military pedant of exacting standards; nothing, however, was said, since movement is permitted at the "stand easy."

The mood of the draft was not improved by a sudden flurry of cold rain which swept across the parade-ground in a long moaning gust, at the moment when three or four officers came out of their Mess.

"Draft!" came the R.S.M.'s warning bellow.

The hundred and twenty hands slipped automatically down the rifles, and the men stood silent and motionless, looking to the front, and trying not to sway when the pressure of the rising gale suddenly increased or suddenly relaxed.

"Stand still there! Stand *steady*!"

There was a slight bulge in the front of each of the short service-jackets, where two field dressings in a water-proof case and a phial of iodine had been thrust into the pocket provided for them, inside the right-hand flap.

"Draft!—Draft! 'Tenshun!"

Two hundred and forty heels met smartly in one collective snap at the same time that the rifles were sharply brought to the sides. The draft stood to attention, gazing fixedly to the front. A man unconsciously turned his head slightly in trying to catch a glimpse of the approaching officers out of the corner of his eye.

"Stand still, that man! Look to your front, can't you?"

Silence, except for the moaning-wind and the crunch of gravel under the officers' boots. The Colonel and the Adjutant wore spurs, which jingled very slightly. The Colonel acknowledged the R.S.M.'s salute and his "All present and c'rect, sir."

"Rear rank—one pace step back—March!"

One—two. The hundred and twenty legs moved mechanically like one man's.

"Rear rank—stand-at—Ease!"

The Colonel inspected the front rank, and took a long time, fussing over various details. A man with cold fingers dropped his rifle.

"Ser'ant 'Icks, take that man's name and number, and forward the charge with his Crime Sheet!"

"Very good, sir."

The front rank stood at ease while the Colonel inspected the rear rank less minutely. It was beginning to get dark, and he had to make a speech. He stood about thirty yards in front of the draft with the other officers behind him. The youthful Adjutant held his riding-crop against his right thigh like a field-marshal's baton. The Colonel, an eccentric but harmless half-wit who had been returned with thanks from France early in his first campaign, was speaking:

"N.C.O.'s and Men of the 8th Upshires! Er—you are—er—proceeding overseas on Active Service. Er. Er. I—er—trust you will do your—er—duty. We have wasted—er—spared no pains to make you efficient. Remember to keep yourselves smart and clean and—er—walk about in a soldierly way. You must always—er—maintain the honour of the Regiment which—er—er—which stands high in the records of the British Army. I— . . . "

A very faint murmur of "Muckin' old fool," "Silly old mucker," " 'Struth!" came from the draft, too faint to reach the officers' ears, but the alert R.S.M. caught it, though without distinguishing the words, and cut short the Colonel's peroration with his stentorian:

"Stand still, there! Stand *steady*! Take their names, Ser'ant 'Icks!"

A short pause, and the R.S.M. shouted:

"P'rade again at four-fifteen outside the Armoury, in clean

fatigue, to hand in rifles. Mind they're properly clean and pulled-through. An' no talking as you walk off p'rade."

The Adjutant had been talking to the Colonel, and saluted as his superior departed. He walked over to the R.S.M.

"All right, Sergeant-Major, you and the other N.C.O.'s not in the draft may fall out. I'll dismiss the men."

"Very good, sir."

The Adjutant walked over to the draft and stood with his right hand on his hip. He spoke slowly but without hesitation:

"Stand at ease. Stand easy. You can wash out what the R.S.M. just said. Leave your rifles in the racks, but try to leave 'em clean or I shall get strafed. . . . I'm afraid we've chased you about a bit under the new intensive scheme of training, but it's all in the day's work, you know. I'm sorry we're not going out as a unit, but battalions are being broken up everywhere for drafts. When you get out, don't forget to look after your feet—you get court-martialled for trench feet nowadays—and don't be in a hurry to shove your heads over the top! I'm due to follow you myself soon, so I expect we'll all be in the next push. Good-bye. And the very best of luck to you all."

"Good-bye, sir. Thank you, sir. Same to you, sir. Good-bye, sir."

"Good-bye. Draft, 'shun. Slope arms. Dis-miss."

Simultaneously their hands tapped the rifle-butts in salute, as they turned right.

The draft confusedly moved over the darkened ground to the barrack-room, chattering excitedly:

"What's the next thing?"

"P'rade at eight-thirty to move off at nine."

"Who said so?"

"It's in B'ttalion orders."

"Silly ole mucker old Brandon is, give me the fair pip he did with 'is 'walk about soldierly'—yes! up to yer arse in mud."

"Bloody old ***."

"Yes, but the Adjutant was all right."

"Oh, 'e's a gentleman, 'e is."

"Makes all the difference when they've bin in the ranks theirselves."

"Wonder what it'll be like in the line?"

"Wait till y' get there and see."

"I reckon we'll be there this time to-morrow night."

"Shut up, Larkin, and don't get the wind up."

"I ain't got the wind up."

"I say, Corporal, Corp'ral! What time do we p'rade to-night?"

"Ask the Ord'ly Sergeant."

"Tea's up, boys. Come on!"

They fell in again at eight-thirty. The night was very dark, with a cold, damp, gusty wind from the west. All the N.C.O.'s were on parade, carrying lighted hurricane lanterns which moved and flitted and stood still in the darkness like will-o'-th'-wisps. The draft were in full marching order, without rifles and side-arms, wearing their greatcoats. Their excitement occasionally broke through the military restraint and rose from a whisper to a loud hum, which would cringe abruptly under the R.S.M.'s "Stop talking, there!" It took a long time to read the roll-call by the flicker of the lantern. At the sound of his name each man clicked his heels, "Here, sir."

"31819, Winterbourne, G."

"Here, sir."

"That's the lot, Ser'ant-Major, isn't it?"

"That's the lot, sir."

"Move off in five minutes."

"Very good, sir."

The draft stirred restlessly in the darkness. Winterbourne looked to his left and noticed how the line of shadowy figures disappeared into the night—he might have been at one end of a line stretching to infinity for all he could see.

"Draft! Draft! 'Tenshun! Move to the right in column of fours—form fours! Form two deep! Form fours! Right! By the right—Quick march!"

They found themselves immediately behind the regimental band, which struck up one of the Mark III. marches supplied to Army musicians. The draft knew it well—"How can I draw rations—if I'm not the ord'ly man?" They marched over the familiar parade-ground, out through the postern, over the swaying drawbridge, where the sentry presented arms.

"By the left. March at—ease. March easy."

The band had ceased playing. They were descending the long, winding hill road to the village and the station. As they went along they were joined by civilians, mostly girls, who were waiting in ones and twos. The girls called to their men in the ranks, and they, emboldened by excitement and this momentous change in their lives, dared to answer back. March discipline relaxed, and the draft was already marching raggedly as it passed the first houses of the village. After the dense blackness of the hillside, the light from the few gas-lamps was dazzling.

The band struck up again. Although it was past ten, the whole village was awake and in the street to watch them go by. The loud brass music reverberated from the house fronts. The draft were amazed to find themselves for a moment the centre of public interest; for so long they had learned to consider themselves fatally insignificant and subordinate. Voices came from all sides: " 'Ullo, Bert! Good-bye, 'Arry! Hullo, Tom! Good-bye, Jack!" Winterbourne, in the front rank, looked behind; he noticed that some of the girls had broken into the ranks and were marching with their men, clinging to their arms. They appeared to be enjoying themselves greatly. An exceedingly ragged company surged excitedly through the village, intoxicated by the sounding brass and the cheers and other attentions of the inhabitants.

The civilians were not allowed on the station platform. As the draft marched through the open gate, with a picket of military police on either hand, there was another chorus of "Good-bye, Bert! Good-bye, 'Arry! Good-bye, Tom! Good-bye, Jack! Good luck. Come 'ome soon. Good-bye. Good luck. Good-bye."

They piled into the waiting troop-train, which was to pick up other drafts on the way. Twelve to a carriage. Winterbourne managed to get the window-seat next the platform. The Adjutant came up.

"Winterbourne! Winterbourne!"

"Sir?"

"Oh, there you are. Looking for you. The R.T.O. says you go to Waterloo, and then proceed to Folkestone, he thinks."

"Thanks very much, sir. It's so much less tedious when you know what you're doing and why and where you're going."

"You ought to have a commission. You'll easily get one in France."

"Yes, but you know why I wanted to stay in the ranks, sir."

"Yes, I know, but men like you are needed as officers. The casualties among officers are terrifically high."

"All right, I'll think about it, sir."

"Well, good-bye, old man, the very best of luck to you."

"Thank you. And to you."

They shook hands, to the impressed horror of the N.C.O.'s.

The crowd had gathered outside the railings by the fore part of the train, where they were not masked by the station buildings. The band were drawn up in front of them, on the platform. The train gave a warning whistle. The band struck up the Regimental March, and then "Auld Lang Syne," as the train slowly steamed out of the station; they played their instruments with one hand, and ludicrously waved the other hand to the draft crowded in the moving windows. A long wavering cheer went up. The red faces of the soldiers on the platform were all turned slightly upwards, and their mouths were open. Their right arms were raised above their heads. In a blare of band music, cheering, and shouting, the cheering draft drew out of the station.

"Good-bye, Bert. Good-bye, Harry. Good-bye, Tom. Good-bye, Jack. Good-bye."

The last person Winterbourne saw was the little Colonel, standing at the extreme end of the platform under a gaslamp, standing very erect, standing rather tense and emotional, standing with his right hand raised to his cap, standing to salute his men proceeding on Active Service.

He wasn't a bad little man; he believed intensely in his Army.

2

In fifteen minutes the excited chatter over fags dwindled to the monotony of an ordinary railway journey. The men were tired, for it was already long after Last Post. They began to drowse. One man in the far corner from Winterbourne was already asleep. The racks were full of overcoats and equipment. Under the Anti-Aircraft Regulations the curtains of the train windows were closely drawn.

Winterbourne felt entirely unsleepy. He ceased talking to the man beside him, and drifted into a reverie. His mind slid backwards and forwards from one theme of thought to another. Already he found it difficult to read or to think consecutively. He had reached the first expressionless stage of the war soldier, which is followed by the period of acute strain; and that in turn gives place to the second expressionless stage—which is pretty hopeless.

The real test was beginning. Like everybody who had not been there, he was almost entirely ignorant of life in the trenches. Newspapers, illustrated periodicals, almost useless. He had heard a lot of tales from returned wounded soldiers. But many of them either blathered or were quite inarticulate. Here and there a revealing detail or memory. "And all the time I was delirious after I was wounded, I kep' seein' them aeryplanes goin' round and round and then makin' a dive at me." And the little Cockney: " 'Struth! I got me tunic and me trowses all 'ung up in Fritz's wire, an' I couldn't get orf. Got me pockets full o' bombs, I 'ad, as well as them stick-bombs in paniers. One of the paniers was 'ung up too, an' I ses to myself, I ses, 'If you drop them muckin' bombs, Bert, you'll blow yer muckin' 'ead orf.' And there was old Fritz's machine-gun bullets whizzin' by, *zip, zip*. I could see 'em cuttin' the wire—and me cursin' and blindin'. Blimey! I wasn't arf afraid. But I got me muckin' blighty, anyway."

Where did he meet that amusing little Cockney? Ah, yes, in the depot the day after he joined. There had been several soldiers just out of the hospital in the barrack-room, all swopping yarns. Winterbourne's mind reverted to himself and the past dreary months. He had been unfortunate in the N.C.O.'s of his training battalion—old regulars, who had been bullied and driven in their time, and thought they'd escape being sent out to France by zealously bullying and driving the new drafts. No doubt they were paying off some of the old Army grudge against civilian contempt for the mercenary soldier. They particularly hated any educated or well-bred man in the ranks, and delighted to impose painful or humiliating tasks on him. George remembered the man who "took particulars" of his religion.

"What are yer? C. of E., Methodist, R.C.?"

"I haven't any official religion. You'd better put me down as a rationalist."

"Garn! What's a muckin' rationalist? Yer in the Army now."

"Well, I haven't got one."

"Bloody well find one, then. Yer'll want suthin' over yer muckin' grave in France, won't yer? An' yer'll bloody well be in it in six months. No religion! Strike me muckin' pink!"

An amiable hero. In his zeal for religion he got Winterbourne sent on all the dirtiest and longest Sunday fatigues, until in self-defence he had to put himself down Church of England. There was, of course, no religious compulsion in the Army; that was why Church Parade was a parade.

Winterbourne smiled as he thought of the ludicrous scene. It had been none the less painful. His gorge rose at the memory of the filth he had tried to remove from the Officers' Mess Kitchen—filth which had been left there untouched by fifty less scrupulous "fatigues." The kitchen was inspected every day.

He looked at his hands in the concentrated light of the railway carriage. They were coarsened and chapped, ingrained with dirt impossible to remove with ice-cold water. He thought of the delicate hands of Fanny and Elizabeth's slender fingers.

On parade the officers never swore at the men, the N.C.O.'s rarely, whatever they might do off parade. It was an offence under King's Regs. The Physical Training Instructors were, however, an exception. They sometimes displayed an uncouth humour in their objurgations. There were time-honoured pleasantries, such as "Yer may break yer muckin' mother's 'eart, but yer won't break mine!" There was the Bayonet

Instructor, a singularly rough diamond from Whitechapel, who in mimic bayonet-fighting at the stuffed bags loved to give the command:

"At 'is stummick an' goolies—Point!"

This gentleman, offended at the awkward posture of a rather plump recruit doing the "double knee bend," had apostrophised the unfortunate man:

" 'Ere, you, Frost. ***'* *** *** **** **** * ******' *******, *** *** **** * ****** ***** ***** ***'* ****' *******?"

Winterbourne smiled again to himself. The road to glory was undoubtedly devious in our fair island story.

From Reveille at five-thirty until Lights Out they had been driven and harassed and bullied for weeks to the strain of: "Look to yer front, there!" " 'Old yer 'eads *up*, can't yer? all them tanners was picked up on first p'rade." "Smith, yer got them straps crossed wrong—if yer do it again, I'll crime yer." And over the voices of the various sergeant-instructors shouting to their squads, boomed the R.S.M.'s inevitable "Stand still, there! Stand *steady*." Just like the South Foreland light-ship in a fog. The fatigue of continual over-exercise and of the physical and mental strain was severe to men fresh from sedentary lives, or stiff from the plough and the workshop. For the first weeks especially they were sore all over, and sank into heavy, unrefreshing sleep at night. Winterbourne bore it better than most. His long walks and love for swimming had kept him supple. He could not raise weights like the draymen or dig like the navvies, but he could out-march and out-run them all, learn every new movement in half the time, dismount a Lewis gun while they were wondering which way the handle came off, score four bulls out of five, and saw immediately why you made head-cover first when digging in. But he too felt the fatigue. He remembered one perfectly awful day. They had been drilled and marched and drilled and inspected from dawn to evening of a baking autumn day; then at seven there had been three hours of night operations. At twelve they were all awakened by a false Fire Alarm, and had to turn out in trousers and boots. Winterbourne had taken over his shoulder the arm of a man who was too exhausted to run unassisted on to the parade-ground. The N.C.O.'s yelped them on like sheep-dogs.

It was not the physical fatigue Winterbourne minded, though he hated the inevitable physical degradation—the coarse, heavy clothes, too thick for summer; the hobnailed boots; the plank bed; horribly cooked food. But he accepted and got used to them. He suffered mentally; suffered from the shock of the abrupt change from surroundings where the things of the mind chiefly were valued, to surroundings where they were ignorantly despised. He had nobody to talk to. He suffered from the communal life of thirty men in one large hut, which meant that there was never a moment's solitude. He suffered because he brooded over Elizabeth and Fanny, over the widening gulf he knew was dividing him from them, and suffered abominably as month after month of the war dragged on with its interminable holocausts and immeasurable degradation of mankind. The world of men seemed dropping to pieces, madly cast down by men in a delirium of homicide and destructiveness. The very apparatus of killing revolted him, took on a sort of sinister deadness. There was something in the very look of his rifle and equipment which filled him with depression. And then, in the imagination, he was already facing the existence for which this was but a preparation, already confronting the agony of his own death. Horrific tales—alas! only too true—were told of companies and battalions wiped out in a few instants. N.C.O. after N.C.O., as Winterbourne got to know them better, assured him that they were the only men—or almost the only men—left alive from their platoons or companies. And it was the truth. The proportion of casualties was undoubtedly high in infantry units. It was, perhaps, selfish of Winterbourne to worry about his own extinction when so many better men had already been obliterated. He felt rather ashamed and apologetic about it himself. But it is human to recoil from a violent death, even at twenty-two or three. . . .

The train began to slow down at a large junction, and he returned to his present surroundings with a start. The other men were asleep. Well, all the training and presenting arms and saluting by numbers were over and in the past. They were

on Active Service. It was an immense relief. Now henceforth
he would be facing dread realities, not Regular Army pedants
and bullies. As Winterbourne once remarked, one of the horrors of the War was not fighting the Germans, but living under
the British.

After picking up more drafts, the train went on, grinding its
way heavily through the silent darkness. The men were all
asleep. He noticed the carriage was getting stuffy and head-
achey with foul air. Someone had shut the windows and
ventilators while he was day-dreaming. That was the old
bother—whether in huts or barracks, they *would* try to sleep
in foul air. He softly slipped the window open a couple of
inches—better already. Wonder why they like a fug? Mental
and moral fug, too. Poor devils! All brought up to touch their
hats to the gentry, do what they're told, and work. Sort of hel-
ots. Yet they're decent enough, got character, but no intelligence. That's the real war, the only war worth fighting, the
battle of the intelligence against inertia and stupidity and . . .
Still, the intelligence is not always defeated; we've got here
somehow. Yes! and look where we are!
    His mind half-sleepily ran off along a familiar track. What's
really the cause of wars, of this War? Oh, you can't say one
cause; there are many. The Socialists are silly fanatics when
they say it's the wicked capitalists. I don't believe the capitalists
wanted a war—they stand to lose too much in the disturbance.
And I don't believe the wretched governments really wanted
it—they were shoved on by great forces they're too timid and
too unintelligent to control. It's the superstition of more babies
and more bread, more bread and more babies. Of course, all
wars haven't been mere population wars. 'Course not—Greek
city-states, mediæval Italian republics, wars of petty jealousy;
naval wars for commercial advantages—Pisa, Genoa, Venice,
Holland, England; the sport of kings, eighteenth-century diversion of the aristocracy; wars of fanaticism, Moslems, the Cru-
sades; emigration wars like the irruption of the barbarians. . . .
There may be commercial motives behind this War, jolly short-
sighted ones—they've already lost more than they can possibly
gain. No, this is fundamentally a population War—bread and

babies, babies and bread. It's all oddly mixed up with the sexual problem we were battling with so brightly when this little packet of trouble was dumped on us by our virtuous forebears. It's the babies-and-bread superstition. You encourage, you force people to have babies, lots of babies, millions of babies. As they grow up, you've got to feed 'em. You need bread. We all live from the land. England, and the rest of the world after it, went crazy with the Industrial Revolution—thought you could eat steel and railways. You can't. The world of men is an inverted pyramid based on the bowed shoulders of the ploughman—or the steel tractor—on the land. It's the hunger-and-death business again. "Increase and multiply." Damned imbecility of applying to over-populated and huge nations the sexual taboos forced on a little crowd of unhygienic Semitic nomads by sheer force of circumstance. Think of their infantile death-rate! Breed like rabbits or vanish. Doesn't apply to us. We're a sacrifice to over-breeding. Too many people in Europe. A damn sight too many babies. The people could be made to see, are beginning to see it—but the hurray-for-our-dear-Fatherland people, and the priests and the fanatics and the timid and the conservative, won't see it. Go on, breed, you beauties—breed in column of fours, in battalions, brigades, divisions, army corps. Wait till the population of England is five hundred million and we're all packed like herrings in a tub. Lovely. Wonderful. England über alles! But there comes a time when there isn't enough bread for the growing babies. Colonise. Why? Either grow more food or produce more things to exchange for food. England's got huge colonies. Germany very small ones. The Germans breed like tadpoles. The British breed like rather slower tadpoles. What are you going to do with them? Kill 'em off in a war? Kind. Humane. Kill 'em off, and grab land and commercial advantages from the defeated nation? Right. And what next? Oh, go on breeding. Must be a great and populous nation. And the defeated nation? Suppose they start breeding harder than ever? Oh, have another war, go on having 'em, get the habit. Europe's decennial picnic of corpses. . . .

Yes, but why so sentimental? Why all this fuss over a few million men killed and maimed? Thousands of people die weekly and somebody's run over in London every day. Does that argument take you in? Well, the answer is that they're not *murdered*. And your "thousands who die weekly" are the old and the diseased; here it's the young and the strong and the healthy, the physical pick of the race. All men, too, and no women. That'll set up a pretty nice resentment between the sexes—more sodomy and lesbianism. Loud cheers—we're winning. Yes, but, going back to murder—people are murdered all the time; look at Chicago. Look at Chicago! We're always patting ourselves on the back and looking smugly at wicked Chicago. When there's a shoot-up between gangs, do you approve of it, do you give the winning side medals for their gallantry, do you tell 'em to go to it and you'll kiss them when they come back, do you march 'em by with a brass band and tell 'em what fine fellows they are? Do you take the gunman as the high ideal of humanity? I know all about military grandeur and devotion to duty—I'm a soljer meself, marm. Thanks for all you've done for us, marm. If violence and butchery are the natural state of man, then let's have no more of your humbug. Violence and butchery beget violence and butchery. Isn't that the theme of the great Greek tragedies of blood? Blood will have blood. All right, now we know. It doesn't matter whether murder is individual or collective, whether committed on behalf of one man or a gang or a state. It's murder. When you approve of murder you violate the right instincts of every human being. And a million murders egged on, lauded, exulted over, will raise a legion of Eumenides about your ears. The survivors will pay bitterly for it all their lives. Never mind, you'll go on? More babies, soon make up the losses? Have another merry old war soon, sooner the better. . . .

O my son Absalom, my son, my son Absalom! Thank God I have no son, O Absalom, my son, my son!

Winterbourne nodded uneasily asleep. He started awake as the train slowed down at London Bridge and not at Waterloo. Where am I? Railway station. Oh, of course, on a draft going out to France. . . .

The draft were turned out at London Bridge, and collected

in two ranks on the platform, yawning, stretching, and adjusting their equipment. The draft-conducting officer, a mild, brown-eyed young man on home service after being wounded, explained that they had nearly three hours to wait. Would they like to go to a Soldiers' Canteen and get some food?

"Yes, sir!"

They marched through the empty, muddy streets. It was about midnight. Some one began to sing one of the inevitable marching songs. The officer turned round:

"Whistle, but don't sing. People asleep."

They began to whistle "Where are the lads of the village to-night?"

Winterbourne found himself crossing the Thames, and looked once more at the familiar townscape. He noticed that the street-lamps had been dimmed further since he had left London, and that the once brilliantly-lighted capital now lay cowering in darkness. The dome of St. Paul's was just faintly visible to an eye which knew exactly where to look for it. The man next to Winterbourne was a Worcestershire ploughman who had never been to London and was most anxious to see St. Paul's. Winterbourne tried hard to show him where it was, but failed. The ploughman never did see St. Paul's—he was killed two months later.

Curious to march through this unfamiliar London—everything the same, but everything so different. The dimmed street-lights, the carefully blinded windows, the rather neglected streets, the comparative absence of traffic, the air of being closed down indefinitely, all gave him an uneasy feeling. It was as if a doom hung over the great city, as if it had passed its meridian of power and splendour, and was sinking back, back into the darkened past, back into the clay hills and marshes on which it stands. That New Zealander sketching the ruins from a broken pile of London Bridge seemed several centuries nearer.

"Where are the lads of the village to-night?
Where are the lads we knew?
In Piccadilly or Leicester Square?
No, not there! No, not there!
They're taking a trip on the Continong. . . ."

The foolish words ran in Winterbourne's brain as the men whistled the tune with exasperating pertinacity. It was curious to be so near to Fanny and Elizabeth. He wondered vaguely what they were doing.

"No, not there! No, not there!"

He had sent Elizabeth a telegram from a station on the way up, but probably it had not reached her.

They crowded into the Canteen, and ate sandwiches and eggs and bacon, and drank ginger-beer. It was too late for beer. Our temperate troops didn't need beer at that hour of the night.

About 2 A.M. they marched back to the station. To Winterbourne's surprise and delight, Elizabeth and Fanny were there. Elizabeth had received his telegram although it was after hours. She had rung up Fanny, and they had gone to Waterloo together, only to find that the train with the Upshires draft was not there. Fanny had used her charms upon a susceptible R.T.O., and he had told them where to go, so there they were. All this Elizabeth poured out in a rapid, nervous, jerky way. While Fanny just clutched Winterbourne's left hand and pressed it hard, saying nothing. They had about ten minutes before the train left. The draft-conducting officer noticed that Winterbourne was speaking to two women, "obviously ladies," and came up.

"Get in anywhere you like, Winterbourne, only don't miss the train."

"Very good, sir, thank you," and saluted smartly.

"D'you always have to do that?" asked Elizabeth with a little giggle.

"Yes, it's the custom. They seem to attach great importance to it."

"How absurd!"

"Why absurd?" said Fanny, feeling that Winterbourne was somehow hurt by the contempt in her voice. "It's only a convention."

The whole train was filled with different drafts of soldiers who had been ordered into the carriages. Only Winterbourne and the two girls were left on the platform, except for the

R.T.O. and one or two other officers. As often happens in railway partings, they seemed embarrassed, with nothing to say
to each other. Winterbourne simply felt dull and uneasy, tongue-
tied. He was saying farewell, perhaps for the last time, to the
only two human beings he had really loved, and found he had
nothing to say. He just felt dull and uneasy, dully remote from
them. He noticed they were both wearing new hats he hadn't
seen, and that skirts were being worn much shorter. He wished
the train would go. Interminable waiting. What was Elizabeth
saying? He interrupted her:

"Is that the new fashion?"

"What?"

"Shorter skirts."

"Why, yes, of course, and not so very new. Where have your
eyes been?"

"Oh, there were only village women where I've been. I
haven't seen a properly dressed woman since my firing leave."

Tactless! He had spent those few days with Fanny. Dear
Fanny! A good sort. She had thought it an awful lark to go on
a week-end with a Tommy. She was dreadfully sick of the Staff.
Still, it was inconvenient that the only decent hotels and restau-
rants were out of bounds to Tommies. Fanny felt quite demo-
cratic about it. Elizabeth hadn't cared. She lived with a kind of
inner intensity which kept her from noticing such things.

They were silent for seconds which dragged like minutes.
Then they all began to say something together, interrupted
themselves. "Sorry, I didn't mean to interrupt." "What were
you going to say?" "Oh, nothing, I forget." And then relapsed
into silence again.

Winterbourne found he was slightly intimidated by the presence of these two well-dressed ladies. What on earth were they
doing at two o'clock in the morning, talking to a Tommy? He
tried to hide his dirty hands.

Damn the train! Won't it ever go? He felt uncomfortably hot
in his greatcoat and began to unbutton it. The engine whistled.

"All aboard!" shouted the R.T.O.

Winterbourne hastily kissed Fanny and then Elizabeth.

"Good-bye, good-bye; don't forget to write. We'll send you
parcels."

"Thanks, ever so. Good-bye."

He made for the compartment where a door had been left open for him, but found it full. The luggage-van, piled with the men's rations, was next door. Winterbourne jumped in.

"You'll have to stand!" exclaimed Fanny.

"Why, no. There's plenty of room on the floor."

The train moved.

"Good-bye."

Winterbourne waved his hand. He felt no particular emotion, merely an intensifying of the general depressingness of things. He watched them receding, as they waved their hands. Beautiful girls, both of them, and so smartly dressed.

"Be happy!" he shouted as a valediction, in a sudden gust of disinterested affection for them. And then lost sight of them.

Fanny and Elizabeth were both crying.

"What did he shout?" asked Elizabeth through her sobs.

" 'Be happy!' "

"How curious of him! And how like him! Oh, I know I shall never see him again!"

Fanny tried to comfort her. But Elizabeth somehow felt it was all Fanny's fault.

Winterbourne sat on his pack in the joggling van for about ten minutes. It was almost dark. The guard was trying to read a newspaper by the light of a dim oil-lamp. The soldiers who had to see that the rations weren't stolen were already lying on the floor. Winterbourne buttoned up his coat, turned up the collar, arranged a woollen scarf on his pack to make a pillow, and lay down on the dirty floor beside them. In five minutes he was asleep.

3

It was not nearly dawn when they reached Folkestone. The drafts from various units were now amalgamated, but still remained under their own officers. They were marched through the dull little town and bivouacked in a row of large empty houses, probably evacuated boarding-houses, fitted up with the usual inconveniences of small English hotels. They washed and had some breakfast. All rather dismal.

At seven they were marched to the quay, and then marched back. The officer had mistaken the word "eleven" for "seven." So they had to wait again. It was their first introduction to the curious fact that much of the War consisted in waiting about and in undoing things which somebody had ordered in error or through mistaken zeal. The men, sitting on their packs in the empty room, were eagerly and vainly discussing their immediate future—which Base Camp would they go to, which unit would they be drafted to, what part of the line? Winterbourne went over to the uncurtained window and looked out. Drifting heavy clouds, a moderately rough, dirty-looking sea. The Esplanade was practically deserted. The shelters looked dilapidated; most of the glass in them was smashed. The unused gas-lamps looked somehow desolate on their rusting standards. Another wounded town—dying, perhaps. Depression, monotony, boredom. He looked at his wrist-watch. Still more than two hours to wait. Now that the inevitable had occurred, he was very impatient to get into the front line. The only interest he had left was a consuming curiosity to see what the War was really like.

Curse this hanging about! He drummed his fingers on the window-pane. The men in the room went on talking, aimlessly, foolishly, talking to no purpose. Winterbourne wondered at his own lack of emotion. All his past life seemed a dream, all his vital interests had become utterly indifferent, his ambitions were dissolved, his old friends seemed incredibly remote and unimportant; even Fanny and Elizabeth were unsubstantial, graceful ghosts. Depression, monotony, boredom—but a peculiar sort, a strained, worried, exasperated sort. For God's sake get a move on. It'll never end, so for the love of Mike let's get it over. Let's catch our little packet. We know our numbers are up, so let's get them quickly.

One of the men was whistling:

"What's the use of worry-ing?"

What indeed? But can you help it? You, cheery idiot, are worrying just as much as any one else. Villiers' torture by hope. If you were *quite* certain that your number was up, you'd have at least the tranquillity of resignation. But you're not quite certain. Even in the infantry men come back. With a really healthy wound you might be out of the line for six or nine months. That was called "getting a blighty one," if you were lucky enough to get sent back to England—"Blighty." The men were discussing blighties. Which was the most convenient blighty? Arm or leg? Most agreed that if you lost your left hand or a foot, you were damned lucky—you were out of the bloody War for good and you got a pension and a wound-gratuity. Winterbourne stood with his back to them, looking out of the window; the ghosts of past summer visitors thronged the Esplanade. Left hand or a foot. Live a cripple. No, not that, not that, my God! Come back whole, or not at all. But how those men love life, how blindly they cling to their poor existences! You wouldn't think they'd much to live for. No beautiful and smartly-dressed Fannies and Elizabeths. Oh, they have their "tarts," they've all got a girl's "photo" in their pay-books—and what girls! Tarts for Tommies. Cream tarts for Tommies.

He turned away abruptly from the window and sat down to clean his buttons. Always keep yourself clean and smart, and walk about in a soldierly way. . . .

His mood changed and his spirits rose as they marched down to the docks. Only twelve hours had passed since they left, and yet it seemed a tremendously long time. Winterbourne realised that the monotony, the imbecile restrictions, the incredible nagging of military pedants, had been crushing him into a condition of utter stupidity. He regretted deeply that he had been kept in England so long. At least you were doing something real in France, and there was movement. . . .

Troops were pouring along the quay, and mounting the gangways on to three black-painted troopships. Winterbourne recognised the ships as old friends—they were pre-war Channel packet-boats transformed. Huge notices were displayed on the quays: "No. 1 Ship, 33rd Div., 19th Div., 42nd Div., 118th

Brigade." An officer with a megaphone shouted: "Leave Men to the Right, Drafts to the Left." Another megaphone shouted: "First Army Men, Number 1 Ship." "Third and Fourth Armies, Number 3 Ship." "Captain Swanson, 11th Seaforth Highlanders, report to R.T.O.'s office immediately." It was rather stirring—animated and efficient as well as bustling.

The draft went on board, and were shepherded to one end of the upper deck. The whole ship was swarming with leave men returning to France. Winterbourne gazed at them fascinatedly—these were the real war soldiers, fragments of the first half-million volunteers, the men who had believed in the War and wanted to fight. They made a kind of epitome of the whole army. Every arm of the service was represented—Field Artillery, Heavies, dismounted Cavalry, Gunners, Sappers, R.E. Sigs., Army Service Corps, Army Medical Corps, and infantry everywhere. He recognised some of the infantry badges, the bursting grenade of the Northumberland Fusiliers, the tiger of the Leicesters, the Middlesex, the Bedfords, Seaforth Highlanders, Notts and Jocks, the Buffs. He was immediately struck by their motley and picturesque appearance. He and the other draft troops were all spick-and-span—buttons bright, puttees minutely adjusted, boots polished, peaked cap stiffened with wire, pack mathematically squared, overcoat buttoned up to the throat. The leave men were dressed anyhow. Some had leather equipment, some webbing. They put their equipment together as it suited them, and none of it had been shined or polished for months. Some wore overcoats, some shaggy goatskin or rough sheepskin jackets. The skirts of some overcoats had been roughly hacked off with jack-knives—not to trail in the deep mud, Winterbourne guessed. The equipment which still weighed so heavily on the shoulders of the draft seemed to give the real soldiers no concern at all—they either wore it unconcernedly or chucked it carelessly on the deck with their rifles. Winterbourne was charmed. He noticed with amused scandal that the bolts and muzzles of their rifles were generally tightly bound with oiled rags. Winterbourne looked more carefully at their faces. They were lean and still curiously drawn although the men had been out of the line for a fortnight; the eyes had a peculiar look. They seemed strangely worn and mature, but filled with energy, a kind of slow, enduring energy. In comparison the fresh faces of the new drafts seemed babyish—rounded and rather feminine.

For the first time since the declaration of War, Winterbourne felt almost happy. These men were men. There was something intensely masculine about them, something very pure and immensely friendly and stimulating. They had been where no woman and no half-man had ever been, could endure to be. There was something timeless and remote about them, as if (so Winterbourne thought) they had been Roman legionaries or the men of Austerlitz or even the invaders of the Empire. They looked barbaric, but not brutal; determined, but not cruel. Under their grotesque wrappings their bodies looked lean and hard and tireless. They were Men. With a start Winterbourne realised that in two or three months, if he were not hit, he would be one of them, indistinguishable from them, whereas now, in the ridiculous jackanapes get-up of the peace-time sol-dier, he felt humiliated and ashamed beside them.

"By God!" he said to himself, "you're men, not boudoir rab-bits and lounge lizards. I don't care a damn what your cause is—it's almost certainly a foully rotten one. But I do know you're the first real men I've looked upon. I swear you're better than the women and the half-men, and by God! I swear I'll die with you rather than live in a world without you."

Winterbourne moved a short distance away from the draft and watched a small group of leave men. One, a Scotsman in the uniform of an English line regiment, was still wearing his full equipment. He was leaning on his rifle, talking to two other infantrymen, who were sitting on their packs. One of them, a Corporal with scandalously untrimmed hair and a dirty sheepskin jacket, was lighting a pipe.

"An' wha' y' think?" said the Scot in sharp-clipped speech: "when ah got hame, they wan'ed me ta gae and tak' tea wi' th' Meenister and then gie a speech at a Bazaar for Warr Worrkers."

"Ah!" said the Corporal, "did you tell 'em—puff—all about the wicked Huns—puff—and say that what we want in the came out of her cottage and began rheumatically and wearily to pump water. She did not even look at the passing troops—much too accustomed to them. The Cockney shouted to her:

" 'Ere we are! War'll soon be over now; keep yer pecker up, Ma!"

They spent the night under canvas at the Boulogne rest camp. From his tent Winterbourne had an excellent view of the Channel and the camp incinerator. His first duty on active service was picking up dirty paper and other rubbish, and dumping it in the incinerator. They were told nothing about their future; the Army theory being that your business is to obey orders, not to ask questions. Winterbourne fumed and fretted at the inaction. The other men speculated interminably as to where they were going.

The tents had wooden floors. The men drew a blanket and waterproof ground-sheet each, and slept twelve to a tent. It was a bit hard, but not impossible to sleep. Winterbourne lay awake for a long time, trying to get some order into his reflections. His attitude was plainly modified by that day's experience. Was there a contradiction in it? Did it imply that he now supported the War and the War partisans? On the contrary. He hated the War as much as ever, hated all the blather about it, profoundly distrusted the motives of the War partisans, and hated the Army. But he liked the soldiers, the War soldiers, not as soldiers but as men. He respected them. If the German soldiers were like the men he had seen on the boat that morning, then he liked and respected them too. He was with them. With them, yes, but against whom and what? He reflected. With them, because they were men with fine qualities, because they had endured great hardships and dangers with simplicity, because they had parried those hardships and dangers not by hating the men who were supposed to be their enemies, but by developing a comradeship among themselves. They had every excuse for turning into brutes, and they hadn't done it. True, they were degenerating in certain ways, they were getting coarse and rough and a bit animal, but with amazing simplicity and unpretentiousness they had retained and developed a certain essential humanity and manhood. With them, then, to

line is more tiled bathrooms and girls and not so many woollen mufflers and whizz-bangs?"

"Ah did not; ah said, 'Gie me over that bottle o' whisky, wumman, and haud y' whist.'"

"What Division are you, Jock?" said the other man.

"Thirrty-thirrd. We've bin spendin' a pleasant summer on th' Somme, and we're now winterrin' at the Health-resorrts o' Ypres."

"We're forty-first Division. Just on your left in the Salient. We came up there a month ago from Bullycourt."

"Bullycourt's a verry guid place to get away from. . . ."

Winterbourne could not listen any further—a zealous N.C.O. herded him back to the draft. He went unwillingly. He had been waiting eagerly for the men to get away from their time-honoured jests and speak of their real experiences. He was disappointed that these men talked in such a trivial and uninteresting way. He felt they ought to be saying important things in Shakespearean blank verse. Something adequate to their experience, to the intensity of manhood he instinctively felt in them and admired so humbly. But, of course, that was ridiculous of him. He felt that at once. Part of their impressiveness was this very triviality, their complete unconsciousness that there was anything extraordinary or striking about them. They would have been offended at the suggestion. They were ignorant of their own qualities. As Winterbourne himself rapidly merged with these men and became one of them, he lost entirely this first sharp impression of meeting a new, curious race of men, the masculine men. It was then the other people who became curious to him. He found that the real soldiers, the front-line troops, had no more delusions about the War than he had. They hadn't his feeling of protest and agony over it all, they hadn't tried to think it out. They went on with the business, hating it, because they had been told it had to be done and believed what they had been told. They wanted the War to end, they wanted to get away from it, and they had no feeling of hatred for their enemies on the other side of No Man's Land. In fact, they were almost sympathetic to them. They also were soldiers, men segregated from the world in this immense barbaric tumult. The fighting was so impersonal as a rule that it seemed rather a conflict with dreadful hostile forces of Nature than with other men. You did not see the men who fired the ceaseless hail of shells on you, nor the machine-gunners who swept away twenty men to death in one zip of their murderous bullets, nor the hands which projected trench-mortars that shook the earth with awful detonations, nor even the invisible sniper who picked you off mysteriously with the sudden impersonal "ping!" of his bullet. Even in the perpetual trench raids you only caught a glimpse of a few differently-shaped steel helmets a couple of traverses away; and either their bombs got you, or yours got them. Actual hand-to-hand fighting occurred, but it was comparatively rare. It was a war of missiles, murderous and soul-shaking explosives, not a war of hand-weapons. The sentry gazed at dawn over a desolate flat landscape, seamed with irregular trenches and infinitely pitted and scarred with shell-holes, thorny with wire, littered with debris. Five to ten thousand enemies were within range of his vision, and not one would be visible. For days on end he might strain his eyes, and not see one of them. He would hear them at night—clink of shovels and picks, the scream of a wounded man, even their coughing if there happened to be a cessation of artillery and machine-gun fire. But not see them. In the two hours following dawn in "quiet" sectors there was sometimes a kind of truce after the feverish work and perpetual firing during the night. After morning stand-down the front-line troops snatched a little sleep. At such a time the silence was eerie. Twenty thousand men within a mile, and not a sound. Or so it seemed. But that was by contrast. In fact, there was always some shelling going on—heavies firing on back areas—and generally in the distance the long rumble which meant a general engagement. . . .

The soldiers, then, were not vindictive. Nor, in general, were they long duped by the War talk. They laughed at the newspapers. Any new-comer who tried to be a bit highfalutin was at once snubbed with "Fer Christ's sake don't talk patriotic!" They went on with a sort of stubborn despair—why, they didn't quite know. The authorities obviously mistrusted them, and forbade them to read the pacific *Nation* while allowing

them to read the infamies of "**** ****." The mistrust was unnecessary. They went on in their stubborn despair, with their sentimental songs and cynical talk and perpetual grousing; and it's my belief that if they'd been asked to do so, they'd still be carrying on now. They weren't crushed by defeat or elated by victory—their stubborn despair had taken them far beyond that point. They carried on. People sneer at the War slang. I, myself, have heard intellectual "objectors" very witty at the expense of "carry on." So like carrion, you know. All right, let them sneer.

The troopships crossing the Channel were escorted by four plunging little black torpedo-boats. Submarines in the Channel. A merchant-ship had been sunk that morning. Winterbourne had thought he would be apprehensive—on the contrary, he found that he scarcely thought about it. Nobody bothered about a little risk like that. They made for Boulogne, and the soldiers cheered the torpedo-boats as they turned back from the harbour entrance.

In his inexperience Winterbourne had assumed that they would at once entrain for the front, and that he would spend that night in the trenches. He had forgotten the element of waiting, the deliberation necessary in moving vast masses of men about, which made the slow, ruthless movement of the huge war-machine so inexorable. You hung about, but inevitably you moved, your tiny little cog was brought into action. And this, too, was strangely impersonal, confirmed the feeling of fatalism. It seemed insane to think that you had any individual importance.

The docks at Boulogne were crowded with materials of war, and the whole place seemed English. Notices all in English, the Union Jack, British officers and troops everywhere, even British engines for the trains. The leave men were roughly formed into columns and marched off to entrain. Every one wanted to know where his Division was. The R.T.O.'s dealt with them swiftly and efficiently. The drafts were also formed into a column and marched up the hill to the rest camp. They were in good spirits, and the inevitable Cockney humorist was in action. As they went up the hill, a poor old Frenchwoman

the end, because of their manhood and humanity. With them, too, because that manhood and humanity existed in spite of the War and not because of it. They had saved something from a gigantic wreck, and what they had saved was immensely important—manhood and comradeship, their essential integrity as men, their essential brotherhood as men.

But what were they really against? who were their real enemies? He saw the answer with a flood of bitterness and clarity. Their enemies—the enemies of German and English alike—were the fools who had sent them to kill each other instead of help each other. Their enemies were the sneaks and the unscrupulous; the false ideals, the unintelligent ideas imposed on them, the humbug, the hypocrisy, the stupidity. If those men were typical, then there was nothing essentially wrong with common humanity, at least so far as the men were concerned. It was the leadership that was wrong—not the war leadership, but the peace leadership. The nations were governed by bunk and sacrificed to false ideals and stupid ideas. It was assumed that they *had* to be governed by bunk—but if they were never given anything else, how could you tell? De-bunk the World. Hopeless, hopeless. . . .

He sighed deeply, and turned in his blanket wrapping. One man was snoring. Another moaned in his sleep. Like corpses they lay there, human rejects chucked into a bell-tent on the hill above Boulogne. The pack made a hard pillow. Maybe he was all wrong, maybe it was "right" for men to be begotten only to murder each other in huge, senseless combats. He wondered if he were not getting a little insane through this persistent brooding over the murders, by striving so desperately and earnestly to find out why it had happened, by agonising over it all, by trying to think how it could be prevented from occurring again. After all, did it matter so much? Yes, did it matter? What were a few million human animals more or less? Why agonise about it? The most he could do was die. Well, die, then. But O God! O God! is that all? To be born against your will, to feel that life might in its brief passing be so lovely and so divine, and yet to have nothing but opposition and betrayal and hatred and death forced upon you! To be born for the slaughter like a calf or a pig! To be violently cast back into nothing—for what? My God! for what? Is there nothing but despair and death? Is life vain, beauty vain, love vain, hope vain, happiness vain? "The war to end wars!" Is any one so asinine as to believe that? A war to breed wars, rather. . . .

He sighed and turned again. It's all useless, useless, to flog one's brain and nerves over it all, useless to waste the night hours in silent agonies when he might lie in the oblivion of sleep. Or the better oblivion of death. After all, there were plenty of children, plenty of war babies—why should one agonise for their future, any more than the Victorians thought about ours? The children will grow up, the war babies will grow up. Maybe they'll have their war, maybe they won't. In any case they won't care a hang about us. Why should they? What do we care about the men of Albuera, except that the charge of the Fusiliers decorates a page of rhetorical prose? Four thousand dead—and the only permanent result a page of Napier's prose. We have Bairnsfather. . . .

He gave it up. Time after time he reverted to the whole gigantic tragedy, and time after time he gave it up. Two solutions. Just drift and let come what may; or get yourself killed in the line. And much any one would care whichever he did.

4

They paraded at nine next morning, were casually inspected by an officer they did not know, and told to stand by. At eleven they drew bully beef and biscuits, and were ordered to parade again in half an hour, ready to move off. Winterbourne's spirits rose. At last they were getting somewhere. He would be in the trenches that night, and take his chance with the rest. No more fiddle-faddle.

He was mistaken. They entrained at Boulogne in a train which crawled interminably, and they detrained at Calais. They were simply transferred to another base.

The Base Camp at Calais was desperately overcrowded. It was filled with new drafts sent over to make up the losses on the Somme, and new columns of men kept pouring in daily from England, faster than the overworked Staff could allot them to units. They were crowded into hastily erected bell-tents, twenty-two to a tent, which is closer than you can squeeze animals, and about as close as you can squeeze men. There was just room to lie down, and no more. Nothing to do after parade, except to moon about in the frosty darkness or lie down in one's little slice of space, or play crown-and-anchor and drink coffee-and-rum while the estaminets were open. The town of Calais was out of bounds, except to men with passes. And not many passes were granted.

The weather grew daily colder. The misery of the intermin-able waiting and the overcrowded tents and the lack of any-thing to do, was not thereby alleviated. Every morning huge greyish columns of men undulated over the sandy soil, and were drawn up in long lines. An officer on horseback shouted orders through a megaphone. Nothing much happened, and they raggedly undulated back again. Yet they drew nearer to the mysterious "line." They were given large jack-knives on lanyards. They were given gas-masks and steel helmets. They were given service rifles and bayonets.

The gas-masks were still the old flannel diving-bell variety soaked in chemicals. They had a sharp, acrid, inhuman taste, and if worn too long had been known to produce skin erup-tions. The drafts were given constant gas-drill, and had to pass five minutes in a gas-chamber containing a concentration of the old chlorine gas sufficient to kill in five seconds. One man in Winterbourne's lot lost his head and tried to tear off his mask. The instructor leapt at him, shouting curses through his own mask, and with the help of two of the men held him until the doors were opened. Winterbourne noticed that the gas had tarnished his bright brass buttons and the metal on his equipment. Their clothes reeked of the gas for a couple of hours.

They carefully cleaned the long steel bayonets, and exam-ined the short wood-enclosed rifles. Winterbourne's had a long groove cut by a bullet on the butt, and the bolt showed signs of considerable rust—obviously a rifle picked up on the battlefield and re-conditioned. Winterbourne wondered who was the man from whom he inherited it, and who would inherit it from him.

The days and nights grew colder and colder. Morning and evening rose and sank in blood-red mists, and at noon the sun was a cold, bloody smear in a misty sky. Ice formed on the dykes and the water-taps froze. It became more and more difficult to wash, and shaving and washing in the ice-cold water became an agony. Their skins chapped as the light north wind breathed sharper and sharper cold. There appeared to be no baths, and they could not remove their clothes at night. To sleep, they took off their boots, wrapped themselves in an overcoat and blanket, and shivered asleep, huddling together like sheep in a snowstorm. Most of them caught colds and began to cough; one man of the draft was taken to hospital with pleurisy.

And still day after day passed and they were not sent to their units. Monotony, depression, boredom. By four it was dark, and there was nothing to do until dawn. The canteens and estaminets were thronged. Winterbourne luckily discovered that the pickets could be bribed, and several evenings went into Calais to dine. He bought a couple of French books and tried to read—in vain. He found he was unable to concentrate his mind, and fell into a deeper depression. There were few parades, and he had plenty of time for brooding.

They passed Christmas Day at the Base. The English newspapers, which they easily obtained a day or two late, were filled with glowing accounts of the efforts and expense made to give the troops a real hearty Christmas dinner. The men had looked forward to this. They ate their meals in huts which were decorated with holly for the occasion. The Christmas dinner turned out to be stewed bully beef and about two square inches of cold Christmas pudding per man. The other men in Winterbourne's tent were furious. Their perpetual grumbling annoyed him, and he attacked them:

"Why fuss so much over a little charity? Why let them salve their consciences so easily? In any case, they probably meant well. Can't you see that drafts at the Base are nobody's children? The stuff's gone to the men in the line, who deserve it far more than we do. We haven't done anything yet. Or it's been embezzled. Anyway, what does it matter? You didn't join the Army for a bit of pudding and a Christmas cracker, did you?"

They were silent, unable to understand his contempt. Of course, he was unjust. They were simply grown children, angry at being defrauded of a promised treat. They could not understand his deeper rage. Any more than they could have understood his emotion each night when "Last Post" was blown. The bugler was an artist and produced the most wonderful effect of melancholy as he blew the call—which in the Army serves for sleep and death—over the immense silent camp. Forty thousand men lying down to sleep—and in six months how many would be alive? The bugler seemed to know it, and prolonged the shrill, melancholy notes—"last post! last post!"—with an extraordinary effect of pathos. "Last post! Last post!" Winterbourne listened for it each night. Sometimes the melancholy was almost soothing, sometimes it was intolerable. He wrote to Elizabeth and Fanny about the bugler, as well as about the leave men he had seen on the boat. They felt he was getting hopelessly sentimental.

"Un peu gaga?" Elizabeth suggested.

Fanny shrugged her shoulders.

Two days after Christmas their orders came. They were taking off their equipment after morning parade when the Orderly Corporal pushed his head through the tent flap:

"You've clicked!"

"What? How? What y' mean?" said several voices.

"Goin' up the line. Parade at one-thirty, ready to move off immediate. Over you go, an' the best of luck!"

"What part of the line?"

"Dunno; you'll find that when y' get there."

"What unit?"

"Dunno. Some o' you's clicked for a Pioneer Batt."

"What's that?"

"Muckin' well find out. Don't f'get I warned yer for p'rade." And he was off to the next tent. The men began talking excitedly, "wondering" this and "wondering" that, futilely as usual. Winterbourne walked away from the tent lines, and stood looking over the desolate winter landscape. Half a mile away the tent lines of another huge camp began. Army lorries lumbered along a flat, straight road in the distance. It was beginning to snow from a hard, grey sky. He wondered vaguely how you slept in the line when there was snow. His breath formed little clouds of vapour in the freezing air. He pulled his muffler closer round his neck, and stamped on the ground to warm his icy feet. He felt as if his faculties were slowly running down, as if his whole mental power were concentrated upon mere physical endurance, a dull keeping alive. Time, like a torture, seemed infinitely prolonged. It seemed years since he left England, years of discomfort and depression and boredom. If the mere "cushy" beginning were like that, how endure the months, perhaps years, of war to come?

He experienced a rapid fall of spirits to a depth of depression he had never before experienced. Hitherto, mere young vitality had buoyed him up, the *élan* of his former life had carried him along through the days. In spite of his rages and his worryings and the complications and boredoms, he had really remained hopeful. He had wanted to go on living, because he had always unconsciously believed that life was good. Now something within him was just beginning to give way, now for the first time the last faint hues of the lovely iris of youth faded, and in horror he faced the grey realities. He was surprised and a little alarmed at his own listlessness and despair. He felt like a sheet of paper dropping in jerks and waverings through grey air into an abyss.

The dinner bugle-call sounded. He turned mechanically and joined the men thronging towards the eating-huts. The snow was falling faster, and the men stamped their feet as they waited for the doors to open, cursing the cook's delay. There was the usual animal stampede for the best platefuls when the door opened. Winterbourne stood aside and let them struggle. The expressions on their faces were not pretty. He was practically the last in, and did not fare well. He ate the stewed bully, hunk of bread, and soap-like cheese with a sort of dog gratitude for the warmth, which was humiliating. He scarcely even resented the humiliation.

The train taking them to rail-head crawled interminably through a frozen landscape thinly sprinkled with snow. The light was beginning to wane. The skeleton outlines of dwarf trees, twisted by the wind, loomed faintly past the window. It was bitterly cold in the unwarmed third-class French carriage; one of the windows was smashed, and the bitter air and snow swept in. The men sat in silence, wrapped in their greatcoats and stamping their feet rhythmically on the floor in vain efforts to keep warm. Winterbourne was cold to the knees, and yet felt feverish. His cough had grown worse, and he realised he had a temperature. He felt dirtily uncomfortable, because he had not taken his clothes off for days. The water at the camp had all frozen, and it had been impossible to get a bath.

Darkness slowly intensified. Slowly, more slowly, the train crawled along. Winterbourne was in that section of the draft going to the Pioneer Battalion. He had asked the Sergeant what that meant:

"Oh, it's cushy, much better than the ordinary infantry."

"Why, what do they do?"

"Workin' parties in No Man's Land," said the Sergeant with a grin, "an' go over the top when there's a show."

The train slightly increased its speed as they passed through a large junction. Somebody said it was St. Omer, somebody else said St. Pol, someone else suggested Bethune. They did not know where they were, or where they were going. About two miles outside the junction the train came to a stop. Winterbourne peered into the thick darkness. Nothing. He leaned out the glassless window and heard only the hissing steam from the stationary train, saw only the faint glow of the furnace. Suddenly, far away in front and to the left, a quick flash of light pierced the blackness and Winterbourne heard a faint boom. The guns! He waited, straining eyes and ears, in the freezing darkness. Silence. Then again—flash. Boom. Flash. Boom. Very distant, very faint, but unmistakable. The guns. They must be getting near the line.

Once again the train started and crawled interminably once more. For about half an hour they passed through a series of deep cuttings. Then, from the right this time, came a much nearer and brighter flash, followed almost at once by a deep boom audible above the noise of the train. The other men heard it this time:

"The guns!"

The train crept on stealthily for another couple of minutes through the gloom. The men were all crowded round the window. Flash. Boom. Another two minutes. Flash. Boom.

Three-quarters of an hour later, they detrained at rail-head in complete darkness.

5

Winterbourne had an easy initiation into trench warfare. The cold was so intense that the troops on both sides were chiefly occupied in having pneumonia and trying to keep warm. He found himself in a quiet sector which had been fought over by the French in 1914 and had been the scene of a fierce and prolonged battle in 1915 after the British took over the sector. During 1916, when the main fighting shifted to the Somme, the sector had settled down to ordinary trench warfare. Trench raids had not then been much developed, but constant local attacks were made on battalion or brigade fronts. A little later the sector atoned for this calm.

To Winterbourne, as to so many others, the time element was of extreme importance during the war years. The hour-goddesses who had danced along so gaily before, and have fled from us since with such mocking swiftness, then paced by in a slow, monotonous file as if intolerably burdened. People at a distance thought of the fighting as heroic and exciting, in terms of cheering bayonet charges or little knots of determined men holding out to the last Lewis gun. That is rather like counting life by its champagne suppers and forgetting all the rest. The qualities needed were determination and endurance, inhuman endurance. It would be much more practical to fight modern wars with mechanical robots than with men. But then, men are cheaper, although in a long war the initial outlay on the robots might be compensated by the fact that the quality of the men deteriorates, while they cost more in upkeep. But that is a question for the War Departments. From the point of view of efficiency in war, the trouble is that men have feelings; to attain the perfect soldier, we must eliminate feelings. To the human robots of the last war, time seemed indefinitely and most unpleasantly prolonged. The dimension then measured as a "day" in its apparent duration approached what we now call a "month." And the long series of violent stalemates on the Western front made any decision seem impossible. In 1916 it looked as if no line could be broken, because so long as enough new troops were hurried to threatened points the attacker was bound to be held up; and the supplies of new troops seemed endless. It became a matter of which side could wear down the other's man-power and moral endurance. So there also was the interminable. The only alternatives seemed an indefinite prolongation of misery, or death or mutilation, or collapse of some sort. Even a wound was a doubtful blessing, a mere holiday, for wounded men had to be returned again and again to the line.

For the first six or eight "weeks" Winterbourne, like all his companions, was occupied in fighting the cold. The Pioneer Company to which he was attached were digging a sap out into No Man's Land and making trench-mortar emplacements just behind the front line. They worked on these most of the night, and slept during the day. But the ground was frozen so hard that progress was tediously slow.

The Company were billeted in the ruins of a village behind the reserve trenches, over a mile from the front line. The landscape was flat, almost treeless except for a few shell-blasted stumps, and covered with snow frozen hard. Every building in sight had been smashed, in many cases almost level with the ground. It was a mining country with great queer hills of slag and strange pit-head machinery in steel, reduced by shell-fire to huge masses of twisting rusting metal. They were in a salient, with the half-destroyed, evacuated town of M——— in the elbow-crook on the extreme right. The village churchyard was filled with graves of French soldiers; there were graves inside any of the houses which had no cellars, and graves flourished over the bare landscape. In all directions were crosses, little wooden crosses, in ones and twos and threes, emerging blackly from the frozen snow. Some were already askew; one just outside the ruined village had been snapped short by a shell-burst. The dead men's caps, mouldering and falling to pieces, were hooked on to the tops of the crosses—the German grey round cap, the French blue-and-red kepi, the English khaki. There were also two large British cemeteries in sight— rectangular plantations of wooden crosses. It was like living in the graveyard of the world—dead trees, dead houses, dead mines, dead villages, dead men. Only the long steel guns and the transport waggons seemed alive, There were no civilians, but one of the mines was still worked about a mile and a half further from the line.

Behind Winterbourne's billet were hidden two large howitzers. They fired with a reverberating crash which shook the ruined houses, and the diminishing scream of the departing shells was strangely melancholy in the frost-silent air. The Germans rarely returned the fire—they were saving their ammunition. Occasionally a shell screamed over and crashed sharply among the ruins; the huge detonation spouted up black earth or rattling bricks and tiles. Fragments of the burst shell-case hummed through the air.

But it was the cold that mattered. In his efforts to defend himself against it, Winterbourne, like the other men, was strangely and wonderfully garbed. Round his belly, next the skin, he wore a flannel belt. Over that a thick woollen vest, grey flannel shirt, knitted cardigan jacket, long woollen underpants and thick socks. Over that, service jacket, trousers, puttees, and boots; then a sheepskin coat, two mufflers round his neck, two pairs of woollen gloves and over them trench gloves. In addition came equipment—box respirator on the chest, steel helmet, rifle and bayonet. The only clothes he took off at night were his boots. With his legs wrapped in a greatcoat, his body in a grey blanket, a ground-sheet underneath, pack for pillow, and a dixie of hot tea-and-rum inside him, he just got warm enough to fall asleep when very tired.

Through the broken roof of his billet Winterbourne could see the frosty glitter of the stars and the white rime. In the morning, when he awoke, he found his breath frozen on the blanket. In the line his short moustache formed icicles. The boots beside him froze hard, and it was agony to struggle into them. The bread in his haversack froze greyly; and the taste of frozen bread is horrid. Little spikes of ice formed in the cheese. The tins of jam froze and had to be thawed before they could be eaten. The bully beef froze in the tins and came out like chunks of reddish ice. Washing was a torment. They had three tubs of water between about forty of them each day. With this they shaved and washed—about ten or fifteen to a tub. Since Winterbourne was a latecomer to the battalion, he had to wait until the others had finished. The water was cold and utterly filthy. He plunged his dirty hands into it with disgust, and shut his eyes when he washed his face. This humiliation, too, he accepted.

He always remembered his first night in the line. They paraded in the ruined village street about four o'clock. The air seemed crackling with frost, and the now familiar bloody smear of red sunset was dying away in the southwest. The men were muffled up to the ears, and looked grotesquely bulky in their sheep- or goat-skin coats, with the hump of box respirators on their chests. Most of them had sacking covers on their steel helmets to prevent reflection, and sacks tied round their legs for warmth. The muffled officer came shivering from his billet, as the men stamped their feet on the hard, frost-bound road. They drew picks and shovels from a dump, and filed silently through the ruined street behind the officer. Their bayonets were silhouetted against the cold sky. The man in front of Winterbourne turned abruptly left into a ruined house. Winterbourne followed, descended four rough steps, and found himself in a trench. A notice said:

> HINTON ALLEY
> ☛   To the Front Line.

To be out of the piercing cold wind in the shelter of walls of earth was an immediate relief. Overhead shone the beautiful ironic stars.

A field-gun behind them started to crash out shells. Winterbourne listened to the long-drawn wail as they sped away and finally crashed faintly in the distance. He followed the man ahead of him blindly. Word kept coming down: "Hole here, look out." "Wire overhead." "Mind your head—bridge." He passed the messages on, after tripping in the holes, catching his bayonet in the field telephone wires, and knocking his helmet on the low bridge. They passed the Reserve line, then the Support, with the motionless sentries on the fire-step, and the peculiar smell of burnt wood and foul air coming from the dug-outs. A minute later came the sharp message: "Stop talking—don't clink your shovels." They were now only a few hundred yards from the German front line. A few guns were firing in a desultory way. A shell crashed outside the parapet about five yards from Winterbourne's head. It was only a whizz-bang, but to his unpractised ears it sounded like a heavy. The shells came in fours—crump, crump, CRUMP, CRRUMP—the Boche was bracketing. Every minute or so came a sharp "ping!"—fixed rifles firing at a latrine or an unprotected piece of trench. The duck-boards were more broken. Winterbourne stumbled over an unexploded shell, then had to clamber over a heap of earth where the side of the trench had been smashed in, a few minutes earlier. The trench made another sharp turn, and he saw the bayonet and helmet of a sentry silhouetted against the sky. They were in the front line.

They turned sharp left. To their right were the fire-steps, with a sentry about every fifty yards. In between came traverses and dug-out entrances, with their rolled-up blanket gas-curtains. Winterbourne peered down them—there was a faint glow of light, a distant mutter of talk, and a heavy stench of wood smoke and foul air. The man in front stopped and turned to Winterbourne:

"Halt—password to-night's 'Lantern.'" Winterbourne halted, and passed the message on. They waited. He was standing almost immediately behind a sentry, and got on the fire-step beside the man to take his first look at No Man's Land.

" 'Oo are you?" asked the sentry in low tones.

"Pioneers."

"Got a bit o' candle to give us, chum?"

"Awfully sorry, chum, I haven't."

"Them muckin' R.E.'s gets 'em all."

"I've got a packet of chocolate, if you'd like it."

"Ah! Thanks, chum."

The sentry broke a bit of chocolate and began to munch.

"Muckin' cold up here, it is. Me feet's fair froze. Muckin' dreary, too. I can 'ear ole Fritz coughin' over there in 'is listenin' post—don't 'arf sound 'ollow. Listen."

Winterbourne listened, and heard a dull, hollow sound of coughing.

"Fritz's sentry," whispered the man. "Pore ole ******—needs some liquorice."

"Move on," came the word from the man in front. Winterbourne jumped down from the fire-step and passed on the word.

"Good-night, chum," said the sentry.

"Good-night, chum."

Winterbourne was put on the party digging the sap out into No Man's Land. The officer stopped him as he was entering the sap.

"You're one of the new draft, aren't you?"

"Yes, sir."

"Wait a minute."

"Very good, sir."

The other men filed into the sap. The officer spoke in low tones:

"You can take sentry for the first hour. Come along, and don't stand up."

The young crescent moon had risen and poured down cold, faint light. Every now and then a Verey light was fired from the German or English lines, brilliantly illuminating the desolate landscape of torn, irregular wire and jagged shell-holes. They climbed over the parapet and crawled over the broken ground past the end of the sap. The officer made for a shell-hole just inside the English wire, and Winterbourne followed him.

"Lie here," whispered the officer, "and keep a sharp lookout for German patrols. Fire if you see them and give the alarm. There's a patrol of our own out on the right, so make sure before you fire. There's a couple of bombs somewhere in the shell-hole. You'll be relieved in an hour."

"Very good, sir."

The officer crawled away, and Winterbourne remained alone in No Man's Land, about twenty-five yards in front of the British line. He could hear the soft, dull thuds of picks and shovels from the men working the sap, and a very faint murmur as they talked in whispers. A Verey light hissed up from the English lines, and he strained his eyes for the possible enemy patrol. In the brief light he saw nothing but the irregular masses of German wire, the broken line of their parapet, shell-holes and debris, and the large stump of a dead tree. Just as the bright magnesium turned in its luminous parabola, a hidden machine-gun, not thirty yards from Winterbourne, went off with a loud crackle of bullets like the engine of a motor-bicycle. He started, and nearly pulled the trigger of his rifle. Then silence. A British sentry coughed with a deep hacking sound; then from the distance came the hollow coughing of a German sentry. Eerie sounds in the pallid moonlight. "Ping!" went a sniper's rifle. It was horribly cold. Winterbourne was shivering, partly from cold, partly from excitement.

Interminable minutes passed. He grew colder and colder. Occasionally a few shells from one side or the other went wailing overhead and crashed somewhere in the back areas. About four hundred yards away to his left began a series of loud, shattering detonations. He strained his eyes, and could just see the flash of the explosion and the dark column of smoke and debris. These were German trench-mortars, the dreaded "minnies," although he did not know it.

Nothing different happened until about three-quarters of an hour had passed. Winterbourne got colder and colder, felt he had been out there at least three hours, and thought he must have been forgotten. He shivered with cold. Suddenly he thought he saw something move to his right, just outside the wire. He gazed intently, all tense and alert. Yes, a dark something was moving. It stopped, and seemed to vanish. Then near it another dark figure moved, and then a third. It was a patrol, making for the gap in the wire in front of Winterbourne. Were they Germans or British? He pointed his rifle towards them, got the bombs ready, and waited. They came nearer and nearer. Just before they got to the wire, Winterbourne challenged in a loud whisper:

"Halt, who are you?"

All three figures instantly disappeared.

"Halt, who are you?"

"Friend," came a low answer.

"Give the word or I fire."

"Lantern."

"All right."

One of the men crawled through the wire to Winterbourne, followed by the other two. They wore balaclava helmets, and carried revolvers.

"Are you the patrol?" whispered Winterbourne.

"Who the muckin' hell d'you think we are? Father Christmas? What are you doin' out here?"

"Pioneers digging a sap about fifteen yards behind."

"Are you Pioneers?"

"Yes."

"Got a bit o' candle, chum?"

"Sorry, I haven't; we don't get them issued."

The patrol crawled off, and Winterbourne heard an alarmed challenge from the men working in the sap, and the word "Lantern." A Verey light went up from the German lines just as the patrol were crawling over the parapet. A German sentry fired his rifle and a machine-gun started up. The patrol dropped hastily into the trench. The machine-gun bullets whistled cruelly past Winterbourne's head—zwiss, zwiss, zwiss. He crouched down in the hole. Zwiss, zwiss, zwiss. Then silence. He lifted his head, and continued to watch. For two or three minutes there was complete silence. The men in the sap seemed to have knocked off work, and made no sound. Winterbourne listened intently. No sound. It was the most ghostly, desolate, deathly silence he had ever experienced. He had never imagined that death could be so deathly. The feeling of annihilation, of the end of existence, of a dead planet of the dead arrested in a dead time and space, penetrated his flesh along with the cold. He shuddered. So frozen, so desolate, so dead a world—everything smashed and lying inertly broken. Then "crack—ping!" went a sniper's rifle, and a battery of field-guns opened out with salvoes about half a mile to his right. The machine-guns began again. The noise was a relief after that ghastly dead silence.

At last the N.C.O. came crawling out from the sap with another man to relieve him. A Verey light shot up from the German line in their direction, just as the two men reached him. All three crouched motionless, as the accurate German machine-gun fire swept the British trench parapet—zwiss, zwiss, zwiss, the flights of bullets went over them. Winterbourne saw a strand of wire just in front of him suddenly flip up in the air where a low bullet had struck it. Quite near enough—not six inches above his head.

They crawled back to the sap, and Winterbourne tumbled in. He found himself face to face with the platoon officer, Lieutenant Evans. Winterbourne was shivering uncontrollably; he felt utterly chilled. His whole body was numb, his hands stiff, his legs one ache of cold from the knees down. He realised the cogency of the Adjutant's farewell hint about looking after feet, and decided to drop his indifference to goose grease and neat's-foot oil.

"Cold?" asked the officer.

"It's bitterly cold out there, sir," said Winterbourne through chattering teeth.

"Here, take a drink of this," and Evans held out a small flask.

Winterbourne took the flask in his cold-shaken hand. It chinked roughly against his teeth as he took a gulp of the terrifically-potent Army rum. The strong liquor half-choked him, burned his throat, and made his eyes water. Almost immediately he felt the deadly chill beginning to lessen. But he still shivered.

"Good Lord, man, you're frozen," said Evans. "I thought it was colder than ever to-night. It's no weather for lying in No

Man's Land. Corporal, you'll have to change that sentry every half-hour—an hour's too long in this frost."

"Very good, sir."

"Have some more rum?" asked Evans.

"No, thanks, sir," replied Winterbourne; "I'm quite all right now. I can warm up with some digging."

"No; get your rifle and come with me."

Evans started off briskly down the trench to visit the other working parties. About a hundred yards from the sap he climbed out of the trench over the parados; Winterbourne scrambled after, more impeded by his chilled limbs, his rifle and heavier equipment. Evans gave him a hand up. They walked about another hundred yards over the top, and then reached the place where several parties were digging trench-mortar emplacements. The N.C.O. saw them coming and climbed out of one of the holes to meet them.

"Getting on all right, Sergeant?"

"Ground's very hard, sir."

"I know, but——"

Zwiss, zwiss, zwiss, zwiss came a rush of bullets, following the rapid tat-tat-tat-tat-tat-tat-tat of a machine-gun. The Sergeant ducked double. Evans remained calmly standing. Seeing his unconcern, Winterbourne also remained upright.

"I know the ground's hard," said Evans, "but those emplacements are urgently needed. Headquarters were at us again to-day about them. I'll see how you're getting on."

The Sergeant hastily scuttled into one of the deep emplacements, followed in a more leisurely way by the officer. Winterbourne remained standing on top, and listened to Evans as he urged the men to get a move on. Tat-tat-tat-tat-tat. Zwiss, zwiss, zwiss, very close this time. Winterbourne felt a slight creep in his spine; but since Evans had not moved before, he decided that the right thing was to stand still. Evans visited each of the four emplacements, and then made straight for the front line. He paused at the parados.

"We're pretty close to the Boche front line here. He's got a machine-gun post about a hundred and fifty yards over there."

Tat-tat-tat-tat-tat-tat. Zwiss, zwiss, zwiss.

"Look! Over there."

Winterbourne just caught a glimpse of the quick flashes.

"Damn!" said Evans, "I forgot to bring my prismatic compass to-night. We might have taken a bearing on them, and got the artillery to turf them out."

He jumped carelessly into the trench, and Winterbourne dutifully followed. About fifty yards further on, he stopped.

"I see from your pay-book that you're an artist in civil life."

"Yes, sir."

"Paint pictures, and draw?"

"Yes, sir."

"Why don't you apply for a draughtsman's job at Division? They need them."

"Well, sir, I don't particularly covet a hero's grave, but I feel very strongly I ought to take my chance in the line along with the rest."

"Ah! Of course. Are you a pretty good walker?"

"I used to go on walking tours in peace time, sir."

"Well, there's an order that every officer is to have a runner. Would you like the job of Platoon Runner? You'd have to accompany me, and you're supposed to take my last dying orders! You'd have to learn the lie of the trenches, so as to act as guide; take my orders to N.C.O.'s; know enough about what's going on to help them if I'm knocked out; and carry messages. It's perhaps a bit more dangerous than the ordinary work, and you may have to turn out at odd hours, but it'll get you off a certain amount of digging."

"I'd like it very much, sir."

"All right, I'll speak to the Major about it."

"It's very good of you, sir."

"Can you find your way back to the sap? It's about two hundred yards along this trench."

"I'm sure I can, sir."

"All right. Go back and report to the Corporal, and carry on."

"Very good, sir."

"You haven't forgotten the password?"

"No, sir—'Lantern.'"

About thirty yards along the trench, there was a rattle of equipment, and Winterbourne found a bayonet about two feet from his chest. It was a gas-sentry outside a Company H.Q. dug-out.

"Halt! Who are yer?"

"Lantern."

The sentry languidly lowered his rifle.

"Muckin' cold to-night, mate."

"Bloody cold."

"What are you—Bedfords or Essex?"

"No; Pioneers."

"Got a bit of candle to give us, mate? It's muckin' dark in them dug-outs."

"Very sorry, chum, I haven't."

Rather trying, this constant demand for candle-ends from the Pioneers, who were popularly supposed by the infantry to receive immense "issues" of candles. But without candles the dug-outs were merely black holes, even in the daytime, if they were any depth. They were deep in this front, since the line was a captured German trench reorganised. Hence the dug-outs faced the enemy, instead of being turned away from them.

"Oh, all right; good-night."

"Good-night."

Winterbourne returned to the sap, and did two more half-hour turns as sentry, and for the rest of the time picked, or shovelled the hard clods of earth into sandbags. The sandbags were then carried back to the front line and piled there to raise the parapet. It was a slow business. The sap itself was camouflaged to avoid observation. Winterbourne hadn't the slightest idea what its object was. He was very weary and sleepy when they finally knocked off work about nine in the morning. An eight-hour shift, exclusive of time taken in getting to and from the work. The men filed wearily along the trench, rifles slung on the left shoulder, picks and shovels carried on the right. Winterbourne stumbled along half-asleep with the cold and the fatigue of unaccustomed labour. He felt he didn't mind how dangerous it was—if it was dangerous—to be a runner, provided he got some change from the dreariness of digging, and filling and carrying sandbags.

After they passed the Support line, the hitherto silent men began to talk occasionally. At Reserve they got permission to smoke. Each grabbed in his pockets for a fag, and lighted it as he stumbled along the uneven duck-boards. After what seemed an endless journey to Winterbourne, they reached the four steps, climbed up, and emerged into the now familiar ruined street. It was silent and rather ghostly in the very pale light of the new moon. They dumped their picks and shovels, went to the cook to draw their ration of hot tea, which was served from a large black dixie and tasted unpleasantly of stew. They filed past the officer, who gave each of them a rum ration.

Winterbourne drank some of the tea in his billet, then took off his boots, wrapped himself up, and drank the rest. Some real warmth flushed into his chilled body. He was angry with himself for being so tired, after a cushy night on a cushy front. He wondered what Elizabeth and Fanny would say if they saw his animal gratitude for tea and rum. Fanny? Elizabeth? They had receded far from him; not so far as all the other people he knew, who had receded to several light years, but very far. "Elizabeth" and "Fanny" were now memories and names at the foot of sympathetic but rather remote letters. Drowsiness came rapidly upon him, and he fell asleep as he was thinking of the curious "zwiss, zwiss" made by machine-gun bullets passing overhead. He did not hear the two howitzers when they fired a dozen rounds before dawn.

6

Except for the episode with the officer, this specimen night may stand as a type of Winterbourne's life in the next eight or ten days. They went up the line at dusk; they were shot at, worked, and shivered with cold; went down the line, slept, tried to clean themselves, and paraded again. Four or five times they passed corpses being carried down the trenches as they went up. There was, of course, nothing to report on the Western front.

Then, just as the monotony was becoming almost as intolerable as drilling to the home-service R.S.M.'s "Stand still, there, stand *steady*!" they had a night off, and were transferred to the day-shift. But this was even more tedious. They paraded soon after dawn, and worked in Hinton Alley, about two hundred yards from the Front line. Their job was to hack up the frozen mud—which was about as malleable as marble—extricate the worn duck-boards, dig "sump-holes," and re-lay new duck-boards. A job which in moist weather might have occupied two men for half an hour, in that frost occupied four men all day.

A Lieutenant-General came along while Winterbourne was laboriously jarring his wrists, trying to hack up the marble-like mud.

"Well, and what are you doing, my man?"

"Replacing duck-boards, sir," said Winterbourne, bringing his pick smartly to his side, and standing to attention, toes at an angle of forty-five degrees.

"Well, get on with it, my man, get on with it."

Vive l'Empereur!

Diversions were few, but existed. There were, for instance, the rats. Winterbourne had been too much absorbed by other new experiences to pay much attention to them at first. And during the day they kept rather out of sight. One evening, just about sunset, as they were returning down Hinton Alley, there was a block in the trench. Winterbourne happened to be just at the corner of the Support line, with its damaged, revetted traverses, and piles of sandbags on the parapet. The Germans were sending up some rather fancy signal-rockets from their front line, and he was vaguely wondering what they meant, when a huge rat darted, or rather scrambled, impudently just past his head. Then he noticed that a legion of the fattest and longest rats he had ever seen were popping in and out the crevices between the sandbags. As far as he could see down the trench in the dusk, they were swarming over parapet and parados. Such well-fed rats! He shuddered, thinking of what they had probably fed upon.

In a very short time he had become perfectly accustomed to the very mild artillery fire, sniping, and machine-gunning. No casualties had occurred in his own company, and he began to think that the dangers of the War had been exaggerated, while

its physical discomforts and tedium had been greatly underes-
timated. The intense frost prevented his shaking off the heavy
cold he had caught at Calais, and at the same time had given
him a chill on the liver. The same thing had happened to half
the men in the company, whether newcomers or old stagers;
and all suffered from diarrhœa due to the cold. There was thus
the added diversion of frequent visits to the latrine. Those in
the line were primitive affairs of a couple of biscuit-boxes and
buckets, interesting from the fact that the Germans had fixed
rifles trained on most of them and might get you if you happened to stand up inopportunely. If you had any sense you
waited until the bullet ping-ed over, and then calmly walked
out; for lack of which elementary precaution somebody occasionally was popped off. The Pioneers' latrine, just behind
their billet, was a more elaborate six-seater (without separate
compartments) built over a deep trench and surrounded with
sacking on posts. One of the posts had been damaged by a
shell, and there were numerous rents in the sacking from shell
splinters. Here Winterbourne was forced to spend a larger
portion of his spare time than was pleasant in cold weather.
One day when he entered he found another occupant, an artilleryman. This person was carefully examining his grey flannel
shirt; and such portions of his body as were exposed to view
were covered with small bloody blotches. Some horrid skin
disease, Winterbourne surmised. He attended to his own
urgent private affairs.

"Still terribly cold," he ventured.

"Muckin' cold," said the artilleryman, continuing absorbedly the mysterious search in his shirt.

"Those are nasty skin eruptions you have."

"It's them muckin' chats. Billet's fair lousy with 'em."

Chats? Lousy? Ah, of course, the artilleryman was lousy. So
lousy that he had been bitten all over, and had scratched himself raw. Winterbourne felt uncomfortable. He detested the
idea of vermin.

"How d'you get them? Can't you get rid of them?"

"Get 'em? Everybody gets 'em. Ain't you chatty? And there
ain't no gettin' rid of 'em. The clothes they gives you at the

baths is as chatty as those you 'ands in. Where there's dug-out and billets, there's chats; and where there's chats, they cops yer."

Winterbourne departed from the lousy artilleryman with a new preoccupation in life—to remain one of the chatless as long as possible. It was not many weeks, however, before he too became resigned to the louse as an inevitable war comrade.

Like a good many recruits, when first in the line he was inclined to be foolhardy rather than timorous. When a shell exploded near the trench, he popped his head up to have a look at it; and listened to the machine-gun bullets swishing past with great interest. The older hands reproved him:

"Don't be so muckin' anxious to look at whizz-bangs. You'll get a damn sight too many pretty soon. And don't keep shovin' yer 'ead over the top. *We* don't care a muck if ole Fritz gets yer, but if he sees yer he might put his artillery on *us*."

Winterbourne rather haughtily decided they were timorous, an impression confirmed by the manner they instantly ducked and crouched when a shell came whistling towards them. So many shells exploded harmlessly that he wondered at their inefficiency. Late one afternoon the Germans began firing on Hinton Alley—little salvoes of four whizz-bangs at a time. The men went on with their work, but a little apprehensively. Winterbourne clambered partly up the side of the trench and watched the shells bursting—crump, Crump, CRUMP, CRUMP. The splinters hummed harmoniously through the air. Suddenly he heard a loud whizz, and zip-phut, a large piece of metal hurtled just past his head and half-buried itself in the hard chalk of the trench. More surprised than scared, he jumped down and levered the metal up with his pick. It was a brass nose-cap, still warm from the heat of the explosion. He held it in his hand, gazing with curiosity at the German lettering. The other men jeered and scolded him in a friendly way. He felt they exaggerated—his nerves were still so much fresher than theirs.

That night, just after he had got down into kip, the night

silence was abruptly broken by a discharge of artillery. Gun after gun, whose existence he had never suspected, opened out all round, and in half a minute fifty or sixty were in action. From the line came the long rattle of a dozen or more machine-guns, with the funny little pops of distant hand-grenades. He got up and went to the door. Ruins interrupted a direct view, but he saw the flashes of the guns, a sort of glow over a short part of the Front line, and Verey lights and rockets flying up continually. A Corporal came unconcernedly into the billet.

"What is it?" asked Winterbourne; "an attack?"

"Attack be jiggered. Identification raid, I reckon."

The German artillery had now opened up, and a shell dropped in the village street. Winterbourne retired to his earth floor. In about three-quarters of an hour the firing quieted down; only one German battery of five-nines kept dropping shells in and about the village. Winterbourne began to reflect that shell-fire in gross might be more deadly than the few odd retail discharges he had hitherto experienced.

Next morning, the Corporal's diagnosis proved correct. As they went up Hinton Alley soon after dawn, they met a British Tommy escorting six lugubrious personages in field grey, whose faces were almost concealed in large white bandages swathed all round their heads.

"Who are they?" he asked.

"Fritzes. Prisoners."

"I wonder why they are all wounded in the head."

"Koshed on the napper with trench clubs. I reckon they've got narsty 'eadaches, pore old barstards."

About a week after that, they had a day off, and were warned to parade at five p.m. to begin another night-shift. (Each platoon in turn did a week's day-shift and three weeks' night-work.) The Sergeant turned to Winterbourne:

"And you're to report at the Officers' Mess fifteen minutes before parade."

Winterbourne duly reported, wondering uneasily what breach of military discipline he had committed. He was met on the doorstep by Evans, who was just coming out, all muffled up.

"Ah, there you are, Winterbourne. Major Thorpe says you may act as my runner, so hereafter you'll parade here fifteen minutes earlier than the rest each night."

"Very good, sir."

All this time Winterbourne was rather wretchedly ill, and remained so for weeks. He had a permanent cough and cold, and was weakened by the prolonged diarrhœa. Every night he felt feverish, passing rapidly from a cold shivering to a high temperature. On the day after his arrival in the line, he had "gone sick" to get something to relieve his hard cough. Major Thorpe had chosen to consider this as an attempt to evade duty, and had promptly insulted him. Whereupon Winterbourne had decided that so long as he could stand he would never "go sick" again. So he carried on. The stretcher-bearer in his platoon had a clinical thermometer. One night, just before going up the line, Winterbourne got the man to take his temperature. It was 102.

"You didn't ought to go up the line like that, mate," said the man, with a sort of coarse kindness Winterbourne liked. "I'll tell the orfficer you ain't fit for service, an' make it all right with the M.O. to-morrer." Winterbourne laughed.

"That's decent of you, but I shan't go sick. I only wanted to see if I were imagining things."

"You're a bloody fool. You c'd get a cushy night in kip."

It was a relief, therefore, to act as Evans's runner. On the night when Evans was on duty Winterbourne did not carry a pick and shovel, and did no manual labour. He simply followed Evans about on his rounds, and carried messages to the N.C.O.'s for him. It was undoubtedly cushy. Almost an officer's job.

Winterbourne was brought into much closer intimacy with Evans, and had some opportunity to observe him. The officer was distinctly friendly, and they talked a good deal in the long hours of hanging about in the Front line. Evans brought sandwiches and a flask of rum with him, and invariably shared them with his runner—a kindness which touched Winterbourne profoundly. Usually about ten o'clock they sat on a fire-step under the frosty stars, and ate and talked. Occasionally a few shells would go whining overhead, or a burst of machine-gun fire would interrupt them. Their low voices sounded strangely muffled in the cold, dead silence.

Evans was the usual English public-school boy, amazingly ignorant, amazingly inhibited, and yet "decent" and good-humoured. He had a strength of character which enabled him to carry out what he had been taught was his duty to do. He accepted and obeyed every English middle-class prejudice and taboo. What the English middle classes thought and did was right, and what anybody else thought and did was wrong. He was contemptuous of all foreigners. He appeared to have read nothing but Kipling, Jeffery Farnol, Elinor Glyn, and the daily newspapers. He disapproved of Elinor Glyn, as too "advanced." He didn't care about Shakespeare, had never heard of the Russian Ballets, but liked to "see a good show." He thought *Chu Chin Chow* was the greatest play ever produced, and the Indian Love Lyrics the most beautiful songs in the world. He thought that Parisians lived by keeping brothels, and spent most of their time in them. He thought that all Chinamen took opium, then got drunk, and ravished white slaves abducted from England. He thought Americans were a sort of inferior Colonials, regrettably divorced from that finest of all institutions, the British Empire. He rather disapproved of "Society," which he considered "fast," but he held that Englishmen should never mention the fastness of Society, since it might "lower our prestige" in the eyes of "all these messy foreigners." He was ineradicably convinced of his superiority to the "lower classes," but where that superiority lay Winterbourne failed to discover. Evans was an "educated" pre-War public-school boy, which means that he remembered half a dozen Latin tags, could mumble a few ungrammatical phrases in French, knew a little of the history of England, and had a "correct" accent. He had been taught to respect all women as if they were his mother; would therefore have fallen an easy prey to the first tart who came along, and probably have married her. He was a good runner, had played at stand-off half for his school and won his colours at cricket. He could play fives, squash rackets, golf, tennis, water-polo, bridge, and vingt-et-un, which he called "pontoon." He disapproved of baccarat, roulette, and *petits chevaux*, but always went in for the Derby sweepstake. He could ride a horse, drive a motor-car, and regretted that he had been rejected by the Flying Corps.

He had no doubts whatever about the War. What England did must be right, and England had declared war on Germany. Therefore, Germany must be wrong. Evans propounded this somewhat primitive argument to Winterbourne with a condescending air, as if he were imparting some irrefutable piece of knowledge to a regrettably ignorant inferior. Of course, after ten minutes' conversation with Evans, Winterbourne saw the kind of man he was, and realised that he must continue to dissimulate with him as with every one else in the Army. However, he could not resist the temptation to bewilder him a little sometimes. It was quite impossible to do anything more. Evans possessed that British rhinoceros equipment of mingled ignorance, self-confidence, and complacency which is triple-armed against all the shafts of the mind. And yet Winterbourne could not help liking the man. He was exasperatingly stupid, but he was honest, he was kindly, he was conscientious, he could obey orders and command obedience in others, he took pains to look after his men. He could be implicitly relied upon to lead a hopeless attack and to maintain a desperate defence to the very end. There were thousands and tens of thousands like him.

Winterbourne noticed that when they were in the line at night, Evans made a point of walking over the top, instead of in the trenches, even when it was plainly far more inconvenient and slower to do so, on account of the wire and shell-holes and other obstacles. At the time, he paid little attention to this, thinking either that it was expected of an officer, or that Evans did it to encourage the men. Evans rather deliberately exposed himself, and always maintained complete calm. If the two men were exposed to shells or machine-gun fire, Evans walked more slowly, spoke more deliberately, seemed intentionally to linger. It was not until months afterwards that Winterbourne

suddenly realised from his own experience that Evans had
been reassuring, not his men, but himself. He had been deliberately trying to prove to himself that he did not mind being
under fire.

Any man who spent six months in the line (which almost
inevitably meant taking part in a big battle) and then claimed
that he had never felt fear, never received any shock to his
nerves, never had his heart thumping and his throat dry with
apprehension, was either superhuman, subnormal, or a liar. The
newest troops were nearly always the least affected. They were
not braver, they were merely fresher. There were very few—
were there any?—who could resist week after week, month after
month of the physical and mental strain. It is absurd to talk
about men being brave or cowards. There were greater or less
degrees of sensibility, more or less self-control. The longer the
strain on the finer sensibility, the greater the self-control needed.
But this continual neurosis steadily became worse and required
a greater effort of repression.

Winterbourne at this time was in the state when danger—
and that was slight in these first weeks—was almost entirely a
matter of curiosity, rather stimulating than otherwise. Evans,
on the other hand, had been in two big battles, had spent
eleven months in the line, and had reached the stage when conscious self-control was needed. When a shell exploded near
them, both men appeared equally unmoved. Winterbourne
was really so, because he was fresh, and had no months of war
neurosis to control. Evans only appeared so, because he was
awkwardly and with shame struggling to control a completely
subconscious reflex action of terror. He thought it was his
"fault," that he was "getting windy," and was desperately
ashamed in consequence. And that, of course, made him
worse. Winterbourne, on the other hand, was obviously a man
who would develop the neurosis rapidly. He had a far more
delicate sensibility. He had already reached a state of acute
"worry" over Fanny and Elizabeth and the War and his own
relation to it. And yet his pride would compel him to urge himself far beyond the point where another man would merely
have collapsed. He endured a triple strain—that of his per-

sonal life, that of exasperation with Army routine, and that of battle.

Perhaps it was through the implicit if unexpressed attitude of the women that Winterbourne also endured the strain of feeling a degradation to mind and body in the hardships he endured in common, after all, with millions of other men. It was a fact that his mind degenerated; slowly at first, then more and more rapidly. This could scarcely have been otherwise. Long hours of manual labour under strict discipline must inevitably degrade a man's intelligence. Winterbourne found that he was less and less able to enjoy subtleties of beauty and anything intellectually abstruse. He came to want common amusements in place of the intense joy he had felt in beauty and thought. He watched his mind degenerating with horror, wondering if one day it would suddenly crumble away like the body of Mr. Valdemar. He was bitterly humiliated to find that he could neither concentrate nor achieve as he had done in the past. The *élan* of his former life had carried him through a good many months of the Army; but after about two months in the line, he saw that intellectually he was slowly slipping backwards. Slipping backwards, too, in the years which should have been the most energetic and formative and creative of his whole life. He saw that even if he escaped the War he would be hopelessly handicapped in comparison with those who had not served and the new generation which would be on his heels. It was pretty bitter. He had been forced to smash through obstacles and to triumph over handicaps enough already. These lost War months, now mounting to years, were a knock-out blow from which he could not possibly recover.

And he felt a degradation, a humiliation, in the dirt, the lice, the communal life in holes and ruins, the innumerable deprivations and hardships. He suffered a feeling that his body had become worthless, condemned to a sort of kept tramp's standard of living, and ruthlessly treated as cannon-fodder. He suffered for other men too, that they should be condemned to this; but since it was the common fate of the men of his generation, he determined he must endure it. His face lost its fineness and took on the mask of "a red-faced Tommy," as he was politely told later by a genial American friend. His hands seemed permanently coarsened, his feet deformed by heavy army boots. His body, which had been unblemished when he joined, was already infested with lice, and his back began to break out in little boils—a thing which had never happened to him—either from impure drinking-water or because the clothes issued from the baths were infected.

No doubt it was the painter's sense of plastic beauty which made him feel this as something so humiliating and degrading. How else account for the feelings of shame and horror he felt at an occurrence which most men would have promptly forgotten? He had been in the line about a month, and his diarrhœa had got steadily worse. One night, when accompanying Evans on his rounds, Winterbourne felt a physical necessity, and asked permission to go to a latrine. They were about two hundred yards away, and before Winterbourne got there the contents of his bowels were irresistibly evacuated in spite of his desperate efforts to control them. It was one of the coldest nights of that long, bitter winter—the thermometer was below zero Fahrenheit. Winterbourne halted in horror and disgust with himself. What on earth was he to do? How return to Evans? He listened. It was one of the quietest nights he ever experienced in the line, hardly a shot fired. Nobody was coming along the trench. He rapidly undressed, shivering with cold, stripped off his under-pants, cleaned himself as well as he could, and hurled the soiled clothes into No Man's Land. He dressed again and rushed back to meet Evans, who asked him a little sharply why he had been so long about it. The discomfort passed; but the humiliation remained.

January slowly disappeared; they were half-way through February, and still the frost held. It was a dreary experience. Each day was practically the replica of that before and after—up the line, down the line, sleep, attempt to get a little clean in the morning, inspection parade, dinner, an hour or two to write letters, then parade again for the line. Towards the end of February, the welcome news came that they were going out of the line for four days' rest. On the last night before they went out, Evans and Winterbourne were watching the men working, when they heard a series of rapid, sharp explosions. They looked over and could see the dull red flashes of bombs or small trench-mortars bursting about three hundred yards away. Simultaneously they exclaimed:

"It's on our sap!"

Evans jumped into the trench and rushed toward the sap, followed by Winterbourne, who tore the bolt-cover from his rifle and stuffed it in his pocket as he ran. They could hear the "crash, crash, crash-crash, crash" of the small mortars, which abruptly ceased when they were about forty yards short. Verey lights were shooting up in all directions, and the British machine-guns were rattling away. Evans dashed round a traverse and went plump into two of his own men who were staggering away from the sap, half-dazed and silly with the shock of explosions.

"What's happened?"

They were incoherent, and Evans and Winterbourne rushed on to the sap. Dimming down his torch with his left hand, Evans peered in; and Winterbourne behind him saw two bodies splashed with blood. The head of one man was smashed into his steel helmet and lay a sticky mess of blood and hair half-severed from his body. The other man, the Corporal, was badly wounded, but still groaning. Obviously, one of the mortars had dropped plump in the sap. Another discharge came crashing on either side. Evans shoved his haversack under the Corporal's head, and shouted to make himself heard over the explosions:

"Get the stretcher-bearer, and send those windy ******* back here."

"What about the sentry?" bawled Winterbourne.

"I'll get him in. Off with you."

Evans began to unbutton the Corporal's tunic, to bind his wounds, as Winterbourne left. The man was bleeding badly. Three hundred yards to the stretcher-bearer and three hundred yards back. Winterbourne raced, knowing that a matter of seconds may save the life of a man with a severed artery. He was too late, however. The Corporal was dead when he and the stretcher-bearer rushed panting into the sap.

They got the sentry's body later.

7

Next day they marched back about four miles to another village, half-destroyed but still partly inhabited. For the first time in two months Winterbourne sheathed his bayonet. It seemed symbolical of the four days' rest they were promised. Four days! An immense respite. The men were cheery, and sang all the war songs as they marched off in platoons: "Where are the boys of the village to-night?" "There's a long, long trail a-winding." "I'm so happy, oh, so happy, don't you envy me?" "Pack up your troubles in your old kit-bag." "If you're going back to Blighty." "I want to go home." "Rolling home." But not "Tipperary." So far as Winterbourne knew, none of the troops in France ever sang "Tipperary."

He had not slept well, haunted by the vision of the dead man's smashed, bloody head, and the groaning Corporal. Evans looked a little pale. But they said nothing to each other. And after all, they were going on rest, four days' rest. Winterbourne tried to join in the singing. Major Thorpe trotted past them on his horse. They marched to attention, and ceremonially saluted. That also seemed peaceful.

In the village they were billeted in large barns. A thaw set in, so rapid that they started out on frozen ground and arrived in a village street deep in slushy mud. The nights were still cold, and old broken-down barns and earthen floors made chilly bedrooms. There seemed to be no water supply in the village, and they had to wash in thawing flood-pools, breaking the new thin ice with tingling fingers. But they went to the baths and changed their underclothes. The baths were in a shell-smashed brewery. Thirty or forty men stripped in one room and then went into another which had rows of iron pipes running across it, about eight feet from the ground. Small holes were punched in the pipes at intervals of about six feet.

A man stood under each hole, and then a little trickle of warm water began to fall on his head and body. They had about five minutes to soap themselves and get clean. Winterbourne went back there alone the next day. By judicious bribing he managed to get an officer's bath and a new set of underclothes. It was delicious to be clean and de-loused again.

The four days passed very quickly. They paraded in the morning, did a little drill, played football or ran in the afternoons, and went to the estaminets in the evening. Winterbourne treated his section to beer, and drank half a bottle of Barsac himself. The men, all beer and spirit drinkers, despised the finer flavour of French wines and called them "vinegar." After dark, they sneaked out and stole sandbags of "boulets"—coal-dust made into large pellets with tar—and burned them in a brazier to warm the chilly barn. Winterbourne protested against this thievery. But since the others went anyhow, and he benefited by the theft, he thought he might as well share the crime too. True, it was French Government property; and nobody minds stealing from governments. But still, he hated to be a thief. The men called it "scrounging." Under pressure of necessity, every man in the line became a more or less unscrupulous scrounger.

On the third night Winterbourne "clicked unlucky." He was on Gas and Fire Picket. They sat all night round the Company field kitchen and drank tea, while one man was always on guard. The tin hat and the fixed bayonet were unwelcome reminders that they were soon returning to the line. The men talked of their homes in England, wished the War would end, hoped anyway they'd get leave or a blighty soon, and envied the officers sleeping in beds. One man grumbled because there was no "red lamp" in the village. Winterbourne felt glad there wasn't. Not that he would have been tempted, for he was quite fiercely chaste unless in love, but he hated the thought of these men giving their lean, sinewy bodies to the miserable French whores in the war-area bawdy-houses.

"It's all right in Bethune," said the grumbler. "You can see 'em lining up outside the red lamps after dark under a Sergeant."

Winterbourne got up and walked out to the muddy road. The stars were faint and dim and lovely in the soft, misty night sky; there seemed to be a first quiver of Spring in the scentless pure air. O Andromeda, O Paphian!

At dawn the birds twittered and sang, a little hesitantly in the cold morning mist. The sun rose in a golden haze, behind rows of poplars, over the flat dark earth.

They went into the line again, three miles to the right of their former positions. Their billets were about a mile and a quarter behind the town of M——, right in the crook of the salient. They lived in cellars in a small mining village, badly smashed, and entirely evacuated of civilians. A long, treeless road led straight up to M—— and Hill 91, one of the most fought-over places in the line, seamed with trenches, pitted with shell-holes, honey-combed with galleries, eviscerated with huge mine-craters, blasted bare of all vegetation. At Hill 91 the German line turned sharply left and linked up with a long slag-hill, about five hundred yards from the Pioneers' billets. Consequently, although they were a long way from Hill 91, their billets were under observation and within machine-gun range, while the road to M—— was constantly shelled, and enfiladed by machine-guns. It was a rotten position, and would have been evacuated but for the "prestige" of keeping M——. A costly bit of prestige. It was estimated that venereal disease held continually a division of troops immobilised at Base Hospitals, to keep up the prestige of British purity: and another division must have been obliterated to retain that barren prestige of holding M——.

They arrived about eleven, and almost immediately Evans's servant came and told Winterbourne to report at the Officers' Mess cellar, in fighting order. Evans was waiting for him.

Hitherto the Company had been under strength, and officered by Major Thorpe and the two subalterns, Evans and Pemberton, who took duty alternately. While on rest, they had been made up to full strength, and were joined by three other subalterns, Franklin, Hume, and Thompson. They thus went up the line one hundred and twenty strong, with six officers, one of whom was supernumerary. Evans had been made a sort of unofficial second-in-command, while continuing to act as platoon officer. Since he was the most experienced of the subalterns, he was to overlook the new officers until they knew their jobs. He explained all this to Winterbourne as they went along.

"You must give me your word not to mention it to the other men, but there is almost certainly a show coming off on this front. Probably in about four weeks. You mustn't let the men know."

"Of course not, sir."

"We shall have twelve-hour shifts up here, I'm afraid. I've got to take three platoons up to Hill 91, over there, at five to-night; and I want to reconnoitre. We've got to repair and revet the front communication trenches, clear away some of our wire, and fill the gaps with knife-rests. We've also got to repair Southampton Row, the main communication trench to your left. Every time we go up we've got to take Mills bombs or trench-mortars or S.A.A. I think we're going to have a lively time. I rode out about ten miles yesterday and saw fifteen batteries of heavies and a lot of tanks camouflaged by the road. The officers said they were booked for this sector or a little south."

They were walking up the narrow, straight road to M——. About every minute a heavy shell—or a salvo of heavy shells—plonked into M——. There was a sudden spout of black smoke and debris, a heavy, sullen reverberating CLAANG as the loud detonation shook the twisted steel mining machinery and re-echoed from the chalky slopes of Hill 91. To their right was a long slag-hill, mangled with shell-holes. Evans pointed to it.

"The Boche front line runs just in front of that, about four hundred yards away. At some points our own front line is only twenty yards from theirs. It's a rummy and awkward position. Most of the transport for M——has to come up this road, and the poor devils are shelled and machine-gunned wickedly every night. All troops on foot have to use Southampton Row, the communication trench to your left. You see it's got fire-steps and a parapet—it's also a Reserve line which we have to man in case of necessity."

They got into the ruined streets of M——and were promptly lost. The town was blasted to about three feet of indistinguishable ruins. A wooden notice-board over a mass of broken

stones said: "CHURCH." Another further on said: "POST
OFFICE." Evans got his map, and they stood together trying to
make out the direct way to the section of trench they wanted.
ZWIIING, CRASH, CLAANG!—four heavy shells screamed
towards them and detonated with awful force within a hundred yards. The nearest swished over their heads and exploded
twenty yards away. Four great columns of black smoke leaped
up like miniature volcanoes; broken bricks and fragments of
shell-case clattered in the empty street. The reverberating
echoes seemed like a groan from the agonising town. The
explosions seemed to hit Winterbourne in the chest.

"Heavies," said Evans very calmly; "eight-inch, probably."

ZWIIIING, CRASH, CRASH! CLAAANG! Four more.

"Seems a bit unhealthy here. We'd better push on."

Winterbourne was silent. For the first time he began to
realise the terrific inhuman strength of heavy artillery. Whizz-
bangs and even five-nines were one thing, but these eight- or
ten-inch high-explosive monsters were a very different matter.

ZWIIIING, CRASH, CLAAANG!

Minute after minute, hour after hour, day and night, week
after week, those merciless heavies pounded the groaning
town.

ZWIING, CRASH! CRAASH! CLAAANG!

It was too violent a thing to get accustomed to. The mere
physical shock, the slap in the chest, of the great shells exploding close at hand, forbade that. They became a torment, an
obsession, an exasperation, a nervous nightmare. Unintention-
ally, as a man walked through M——, he found himself tense
and strained, waiting for that warning "zwiing" of the approaching shell, trying to determine by the sound whether it
was coming straight at him or not. Winterbourne's duties during the next two and a half months necessitated his walking
through M——, often alone, twice or four times every twenty-
four hours.

The real nightmare was only just beginning. There had been
the torment of frost and cold; now came the torments of mud,
of gas, of incessant artillery, of fatigue and lack of sleep.

Under the swift thaw the whole battered countryside seemed
to turn from ice to mud. It was deep on the *pavé* roads, deeper
round the billets, deeper still on the unpaved tracks, and deepest of all in the trenches. In Winterbourne's hallucinated memories, where images and episodes met and collided like
superimposed films, that Spring was mud. He seemed to spend
his time plodging through interminable muddy trenches, up to
the ankles, up to the calves, up to the knees; shovelling mud
frantically out of trenches on to the berm, and then by night
from the berm over the parapets, while the shells crashed and
the machine-gun bullets struck gold sparks from the road
stones. When he was not doing that, he was scraping mud with
a knife from his boots and clothes, trying to dry socks and
puttees and to rub some warmth into his livid, aching feet. He
had not known that wet cold could keep one's legs so achingly
dead for so long. He had not known how wearisome it could
be to drag tired legs and carry burdens through deep, sticky
chalk mud, where each step was an effort, where each leg
stuck deep as the other was laboriously pulled from the suck-
ing mud. He had not known that one could hate an inert thing
so much. Overhead it might be sunny, with innumerable little
fleecy puffs of exploded shrapnel pursuing a darting white airplane high in the misty blue March sky. Underfoot it was mud.
They had no time to look at the sky as they dragged along,
toiling their bent way along those muddy ditches.

He remembered a week of blessed respite which he spent in
an underground gallery, squatting twelve hours a day by a
winch and interminably winding sandbags of chalk to men in
the trench. These galleries—which were never used—were
being dug to conceal two or three divisions before a surprise
attack. They seemed to extend for miles. The cutting and picking at the advancing end was done by R.E.'s, skilled miners
who cut with astonishing rapidity and accuracy. The Pioneers
filled the chalk into sacks and dragged them along the galleries, where Winterbourne incessantly wound them to the top.
The Engineers had better rations than the infantry and the
Pioneers, whose lunch was bread-and-cheese. They had huge
cold beefsteaks and bottles of strong tea-and-rum for their

lunch. Winterbourne, during his half-hour's midday rest, one day wandered up to their end of the gallery, just as they were eating. He could not help glancing rather wolfishly at their meal. One of them noticed it, and, pointing to his steak, said with his mouth full:

"Ah reckon tha doesn't get groob the likes o' this in thy lot, lad."

"No, but the stew's very good—only, you get a bit tired of it every day."

"Ay, that tha does. But we're skilled men, we are, traade union. They're got to feed oos well, they 'ave."

Half-kindly, half-contemptuously, the miner cut off a hunk of his steak and held it out to Winterbourne in his large dirty hand.

"Here tha art, lad, tak a bite at that."

"Oh no, thanks, it's very kind of you, but . . ."

"Nay, lad, tha's welcome; tak it, tak it. Tha looks fair fammelled and wore out. Tha's na workin' chap, ah knows."

Torn between his feeling of humiliation, his desire not to reject the man's kindly-meant offer, and his hungry belly, Winterbourne hesitated. He finally took it, with a rather ghastly feeling of animal humiliation. The cold, tender meat tasted delicious. It was the first unsodden meat he had eaten for weeks. He gave them his last cigarettes, and returned to his winch.

Winterbourne detested "berming." Hour after hour standing in wet, chilly mud, shovelling the stuff away to prevent its sliding back into the trench from which it had been laboriously thrown, and widening the space between the top of the trench and the parapet. The machine-guns from the slag-hill constantly rattled away at them. One night Winterbourne and the man next him dug up the bones, tunic, equipment, and rifle of a French soldier, who had been hastily buried in the parapet many months before. His cartridges fell from the mouldering pouches and still looked bright in the dim star-dusk. Winterbourne dug up the skull; it was large and dome-shaped, a typical Frenchman's head. They tried to find his identity disc, but failed. Pemberton, who was on duty that night, made them rebury what was left in a shell-hole. They stuck a cross over it next day, marked "UNKNOWN FRENCH SOLDIER."

The best nights were those when Evans was on duty, but often the urgency was so great that the officers' runners and the officers themselves worked and carried burdens. The most awkward burdens were the long sheets of corrugated iron used for revetting. They had to carry these along the road, since they were too large to get round the traverses. It was impossible to keep the metal sheets from clanking against rifles or the sheet of the man in front in the darkness. The machine-guns from the slag-hill opened out, and they could see the spurts of gold sparks on the road come towards them. Winterbourne felt his piece of corrugated iron violently hit and half-wrenched from his hand; the man in front went down with a clatter. Somebody yelled "Stretcher-bearer!" The men dumped their burdens and cowered on the ground. It was an awful confusion. Only Evans and Winterbourne were left standing on the road. Evans cursed the N.C.O.'s, and made the men form up again behind Winterbourne. It took a long time to find all the sheets of metal in the darkness, and the machine-guns went on rattling pitilessly. They were hours late in getting back to billets.

As March dragged on, more and more heavy guns arrived, clattering up behind their tractors in the darkness. A tank and its crew were hidden not far from the Pioneers' billets, and there were others further from the line. A new infantry division was pushed into the line on their right. Other divisions were said to be in readiness close behind. The sector became more and more lively, but no big attack was made. Winterbourne questioned Evans, who said it had been postponed to give the mud a chance to dry. What hopes!

The Germans had excellent observation posts on Hill 91, and their aircraft were constantly over the British lines and back areas. They were perfectly aware that an attack was being prepared. Every night they shelled M——, shelled the cross-roads leading to M——, shelled any artillery positions they had spotted, shelled the wrecked village where the Pioneers were billeted. The cellars were good enough protection against shell splinters, but far too flimsy to resist a direct hit. Every day or night huge crumps were flung at them, exploding with concussions which shook the ground and made sleep impossible. In the daytime Winterbourne sometimes crouched at his cellar-entrance and watched the explosions within his view. If one of these big shells hit a half-ruined house, almost every vestige disappeared in a cloud of black smoke and rosy brick-dust.

And there was gas, a good deal of gas. It was the beginning of the intensive use of gas projectiles, which later became so greatly perfected. Their experience of it began one March night on Hill 91. A smart local attack had driven the Germans out of their advance positions and carried the British line forward—at a cost—about two hundred and fifty yards on a front of eight hundred. Evans explained to Winterbourne that these local attacks were being made all along the line to deceive the Germans as to the exact position of the coming offensive. Since the Germans would have needed to be blind or lunatic not to see where the guns and troops were being massed, Winterbourne thought this an over-subtle and over-costly bit of policy. However, his not to reason why.

The Pioneers—three platoons of them—under Evans, Pemberton, and Hume, were to dig a new communication trench from the former British Front line to their present Outpost line of hastily-interlinked shell-holes. Evans told Winterbourne not to carry any tools:

"I expect it'll be rather a sticky do. The old Boche is pooping off whizz-bangs all day and night up there. And I'm hanged if I can find out exactly where our new Front line is supposed to be. It's a network of Boche trenches up there, and we don't want to go barging into their line."

They struggled up Southampton Row and skirted M——, which was being shelled heavily and reverberantly. They got into another trench on the fringe of Hill 91. Whizz-bangs kept cracking all round them, in little masses of about a dozen— several batteries firing together. Evans and Winterbourne were leading. Winterbourne paused:

"There's a curious smell about here, sir" (sniff, sniff), "like pineapple or pear-drops."

Evans sniffed the air.

"So there is."

The smell rapidly became stronger after another salvo of whizz-bangs.

"By Jove, it's tear-gas!" said Evans. "Pass the word along to put on gas-goggles."

The line halted, while the men fumbled in the darkness for their goggles, and then slowly stumbled on. Winterbourne found he was practically blinded by his goggles in the darkness; they kept going dim with perspiration. He took them off.

"We shall be here all night at this rate, sir. May as well be blinded with tear-gas as goggles. I'll keep mine off and reconnoitre."

Evans pulled off his goggles, and the two went on ahead, telling the Sergeant to follow straight on until he came up with them. Tears poured from the two men's eyes as they toiled up the muddy trench. They kept dabbing their eyes with pocket handkerchiefs, like a couple of mutes at their own funerals.

Crash, crash-crash, crash, crash-crash-crash-crash, came the whizz-bangs; and the pineapple smell became stronger than ever.

"It'll be a jolly look-out for us," said Evans, "if they poop over poison gas too. We shan't be able to smell it with all this stink of pear-drops. Peuh! It's like being in a sweet factory."

They laughed. And then dabbed their streaming eyes again.

In ten minutes they came up to the largest of the mine-craters. The wind was fresh on the hill-crest and there was no gas. Their smarting eyes began to recover.

"Here we are," said Evans, "and there's the old No Man's Land; but where in hell our Front line is, I don't know. You stay here, Winterbourne, and tell Sergeant Perkins to halt until I come back. I'll go and reconnoitre."

"I'll go back, sir, and bring them up."

"All right," and Evans vanished in the darkness. Winterbourne returned to the line of men, dismally groping their way through the gassy trench. They waited for Evans, who led them over the old No Man's Land to a very deep trench. They turned to the left. Evans whispered to Winterbourne:

"There's nothing here but a network of Boche trenches; look

how deep they are. I couldn't see a soul, and there are still Boche trench-notices up. I'm hanged if I know where we are. For all I know we're in the Boche lines."

Winterbourne unslung his rifle and bayonet, and walked in front of Evans. Verey lights went up occasionally, but most mysteriously seemed to come from all sides, behind them as well as in front and to the flanks. The trenches were immensely deep and dark, except when lit dimly by the glow of Verey lights or the abrupt flashes of whizz-bangs. They went on and on, constantly passing cross-trenches, completely lost, probably returning on their footsteps. They could hear the men muttering and cursing behind them. At another cross-trench they halted in despair. Winterbourne stood on a large hummock in the middle of the wide trench, peering ahead through the gloom. Evans looked at his luminous wrist-watch.

"Good Lord! We've been wandering in these blasted trenches for nearly three hours. It'll be too late to do any work unless we get there at once."

Winterbourne grabbed his arm:

"Look!"

Several shadowy figures were silhouetted against the skyline, coming along the trench toward them. Too dark to distinguish the helmets. English or German?

"Challenge them," whispered Evans. Winterbourne threw his rifle forward:

"Halt! Who are you!"

"Frontshires," said a weary voice.

"Ask which company."

"Which company?"

"A, B, C, D—what's left of 'em."

They were now close enough for Evans and Winterbourne to see they were in British uniform. Evans passed down word to his men to stand to the left and let the outgoing party pass. The Frontshires staggered rather than walked down the bumpy trench.

"We 'ung on until nearly all of us was killed, sir," said one man huskily to Evans, as if apologising.

"When the Springshires were wiped out, we got enfiladed, sir," said another; "there's on'y one of our officers left."

About fifty men, the flotsam of the wrecked battalion, stumbled past them. Then came the Sergeant-Major and a young subaltern. Evans stopped him, and asked the way to the front line, explaining briefly their job. The subaltern seemed dazed with weariness. He kept swaying in the darkness.

"It's up there . . . up there . . . somewhere. . . ."

"But how far?"

"I don't know . . . not far. . . . I can't stop . . . mustn't leave the men."

And he stumbled on again. Evans turned to Winterbourne:

"Well, Winterbourne, you might as well get off the body of that dead Boche you're standing on, and we'll push along."

Winterbourne sprang away with a sensation of horror, and saw that he had indeed unconsciously been standing on a dead German.

They wandered about until nearly dawn, without finding the Front line. They came on a couple of wounded Germans, whom Evans put into stretchers. Just about dawn they found themselves back at the point where they had entered the old German trenches, and recrossed to familiar ground. The wounded Germans groaned as the stretcher-bearers stumbled and bumped them on the ground.

The remnant of the battalion of the Frontshires very slowly made their way into M——. ZWIIING, CRASH! CLAANG! went the great crumps, but they hardly heard them. They were too tired. They went through the town in single file. On the straight road the subaltern halted them, formed them roughly into fours, and took his place at their head. They shambled heavily along, not keeping step or attempting to, bent wearily forward under the weight of their equipment, their unseeing eyes turned to the muddy ground. They stumbled over inequalities; several times one or other of them fell, and had to be dragged laboriously to his feet. Others lagged hopelessly behind. Time and again the young subaltern and the R.S.M. paused to allow the little group to re-form. Hardly a word was spoken. They went very slowly, past the slag-hill, past the ruined village, past the Pioneers' billets, past the soldiers' cemetery, past the ruined château, past the closed Y.M.C.A.

canteen; and just as the fresh clear Spring dawn lightened the sky they came to the village where they had their rest billets. The firing had quieted down, and the larks were singing overhead in the pure, exquisite sky. In the pale light the men's unshaven faces looked grim and strangely old, grey-green, haggard, inexpressibly weary. They shambled on.

Outside of Divisional Headquarters a smart sentry was on duty. He saw the little party wearily stumbling down the village street, and thought they were walking wounded. The young subaltern stopped about thirty yards from the sentry, and once more re-formed his men. The sentry heard him say, "Stick it, Frontshires."

Already the news had reached the back areas that the Frontshires had been nearly wiped out in a desperate defence—fifty of them and one officer left, out of twenty officers and seven hundred and fifty men.

The sentry sprang to attention and took one pace forward. Sloped arms—one, two, three, as if on parade—and remained rigid. As the little group drew level, he sharply brought his rifle and fixed bayonet to the "present arms."

The young officer wearily touched the brim of his steel helmet. The men scarcely saw, and did not comprehend, the gesture. The sentry watched them pass, with a lump in his throat.

There was still nothing to report on the Western front.

8

After a few hours' sleep and a hasty meal, Evans and Winterbourne started for the Front line again. Evans was very much ashamed at having lost his way the night before, and the Major had strafed him for incompetence. Evans had not replied, as he might have done, that since the Major knew so well where they ought to have gone, he might have taken the trouble to lead them there.

It was about two on a sunny, cold afternoon. They skirted M—— with its everlasting, maddening Zwiiing, crash! claaaang! In the trenches on the edge of Hill 91 they met two

walking wounded, unshaved, muddy to the waist. One had his
head bandaged and was carrying his steel helmet; the other
had his tunic half off, and his left hand and arm were bandaged in several places. They were talking with great gravity
and earnestness, and hardly saw Evans and his runner. Winterbourne heard one of them say:

"I told that muckin' new orfficer twice that some mucker'd
get hit if he muckin' well took us up that muckin' trench."

"Ah," said the other, "moock 'im."

Evans and Winterbourne paused at the old Front line on the
crest of the hill to take breath, and looked back. The blue sky
was speckled all over with the little fleecy shrapnel bursts from
Archies, pursuing three different enemy planes. The heavy
shells fell reverberantly into M—— at their feet. They looked
over a broad, flat, grey-green plain, dotted with ruined villages, seamed with the long, irregular lines of trenches. The
wavering broad ribbon of No Man's Land was clearly visible,
blasted to the white chalk. They could see the flash of the
heavies, and enemy shells bursting on cross-roads and round
artillery emplacements. A Red Cross car of wounded bumping
its way from the Advanced Dressing Station in M—— was
shelled all down the road by field artillery. They watched it
eagerly, hoping it would escape. Once or twice it disappeared
in the smoke of the shell-burst and they felt certain it was done
for; but the car bumpingly reappeared, and finally vanished
from sight in the direction of Rail Head.

"God! What a dirty trick! I'm glad they didn't get it," said
Winterbourne, as they scrambled out of the trench.

"Ah, well," said Evans, "Red Cross cars have been used as
camouflage before now."

They easily found the new Front line in the daylight. Directions in English had been hastily scrawled on the old German
trench notices, and they wondered how on earth they could
have missed the way the night before. The Front line was full
of infantry: some on sentry duty, some sitting hunched up on
the fire-steps; many lying in long, narrow holes like graves,
scooped in the side of the trench. They found an officer, who
took them along to show them where the new communication

trench was wanted. Winterbourne, turning to answer a question from Evans, struck the butt of his rifle sharply against a sleeping man in one of the holes. The man did not stir.

"Your fellows are sleeping soundly," said Evans.

"Yes," said the officer tonelessly; "but he may be dead for all I know. Stretcher-bearers too tired to take down all the bodies. Some of 'em are dead, and some asleep. We have to go round and kick 'em to find which is which."

The new trench they were to dig had been roughly marked out, and ran from the old German front line to the lip of Congreve's Mine-crater, now used as an ammunition dump. A salvo of whizz-bangs greeted them as they went out to look at it.

"I don't altogether envy you this job," said the Infantry officer; "this is about the most unhealthy spot on Hill 91. The Boche shells it day and night. Your Colonel had a hell of a row about it with the Brigadier, but our fellows are too whacked to do any more digging."

Over came another little bunch of whizz-bangs, in corroboration—crash, crash-crash, crash. The grey-green, acrid smoke smelt foul.

"They're going to call it Nero Trench," he added, as they left him, "because the ground's so black with coal-dust and slag. Well, good-bye, best of luck. And, by the by, look out for gas."

The Nero Trench job was an intensified nightmare. The Germans had it "taped" with exactitude, and shelled it ruthlessly. Five minutes was the longest period that ever passed without salvoes of whizz-bangs. Evans and Winterbourne, Hume and his runner, walked continually up and down the line of men, who toiled hastily and nervously in the darkness to make themselves a little cover. When the shells came crashing near them, they crouched down on the ground. It was found after the first night that each man had simply dug a hole for himself instead of regularly excavating his three yards of trench. On some nights the shelling was so intense that Evans withdrew the men for a time to the shelter of a trench. They had several casualties.

And then the Germans began a steady, systematic gas

bombardment of all the ruined villages in the advanced area. It began on the second night of the Nero Trench job. They had noticed on Hill 91 that a pretty heavy bombardment was proceeding from the German lines, and all the way down from M—— they heard the shells continuously shrilling overhead. It puzzled them that they could not hear them exploding.

"Must be bombarding the back areas," said Evans."Let's hope it gives 'em something to think about besides sending us up tons of silly papers."

But as they came nearer their village they could tell by the sound in the air that the shells must be falling close ahead of them. Soon they heard them falling with the customary ZWIIING, followed by a very unaccustomed soft PHUT.

"They can't all be duds," said Winterbourne.

A shell dropped short, just outside the parapet, with the same curious PHUT. Immediately a strange smell, rather like new-mown hay gone acrid, filled the air. They sniffed, and both men exclaimed simultaneously:

"Phosgene! Gas!"

They all fumblingly and hastily put on their gas-masks, and stumbled on blindly down the trench. Winterbourne and Evans scrambled out on to the road and got into the edge of the village. A rain of gas shells was falling on it and all round their billets—zwiing, zwiing, zwiing, zwiing, PHUT PHUT PHUT PHUT. Each took off his mask a second and gave one sniff—the air reeked with phosgene.

Evans and Winterbourne stood at the end of the trench to help out the groping, half-blinded men. As they filed by, grotesques with india-rubber faces, great, dead-looking goggles, and a long tube from their mouths to the box respirators, Winterbourne thought they looked like lost souls expiating some horrible sin in a new Inferno. The rolled gas-blankets were pulled down tightly over the cellar entrances, but the gas leaked through. Two men were gassed and taken off in stretchers, foaming rather horribly at the mouth.

The gas bombardment went on until dawn, and then ceased. Winterbourne fell asleep, with his gas-mask just off his face. Hitherto they had slept with the box respirator slung on a nail or piled with the other equipment; after the experience of this and the subsequent nights, they always slept with the respirator on their chests and the mask ready to slip on immediately.

The heavies began again soon after it was light. Winterbourne was awakened by one which crashed just outside his cellar. He lay on the floor for a long time listening to the ZWIIIING, CRASH, of the shells. He heard two ruined houses clatter to the ground under direct hits, and wondered if the cellars had held firm. They hadn't. But fortunately they happened to be unoccupied. Presently the German batteries switched off and began bombarding some artillery about five hundred yards to the left. Winterbourne profited by the lull to wash. He ran out of the cellar in his shirt-sleeves and gasmask, with the canvas bucket in which he washed; and found that a shell had smashed the pump outside his billet. He knew there was another about three hundred yards to the right, although he had never been there.

It was another cold but sunny morning, with the inevitable white shrapnel bursts all over the sky. He was now so accustomed to them that he scarcely noticed their existence. Occasionally a very faint rattle of machine-gun fire came from the war in the air, of which he was nearly as ignorant as people in England of the war on land.

He took off his mask and sniffed. A fresh wind was blowing, and, although there was plenty of phosgene in the air, it was not in any deadly concentration. He decided to risk leaving the mask off. The ground was deeply delved with the conical holes made by the big shells thrown over, and pitted everywhere by the smaller holes of the gas shells. He found a dud, and examined it with interest. A brownish-looking shell, about the size of a five-nine.

The cottages were rather scattered, and unused as cellar-billets in this direction. The top storeys had gone from nearly all, but in several the ground floor was fairly intact. He looked into each as he passed. The wallpaper had long ago fallen and lay in mouldering heaps. The floors were covered with broken bricks, tiles, smashed beams, laths, and disintegrating plaster. Odd pieces of broken furniture, twisted iron beds, large rags which had once been clothes and sheets, protruded from the mass. He poked about and found photographs, letters in faded ink on damp paper, broken toys, bits of smashed vases, a soiled satin wedding-gown with its veil and wreath of artificial orange-blossom. He stood, with his head bent, looking at this pathetic debris of ruined lives, and absentmindedly lit a cigarette, which he immediately threw away—it tasted of phosgene. "La Gloire," he murmured, "Deutschland über alles, God save the King."

The next cottage was less damaged than the others, and its rough wooden shutters were still on their hinges. Winterbourne peered through, and saw that the whole of the inside had been cleared of debris, and was stacked with quantities of wooden objects. He shaded his eyes more carefully, and saw they were ranks and ranks of wooden crosses. Those he could see had painted on them R.I.P.; then underneath was a blank space for the name; underneath was the name of one or other of the battalions in his division, and then the present month and year, with a blank space for the day. Excellent forethought, he reflected, as he filled his bucket and waterbottle. How well this War is organised!

About nine, Evans's servant told him to report immediately in fighting order. Wearily and sleepily he threw on his equipment, re-tied the string of his box respirator, and slung his rifle and bayonet over his left shoulder. He waited with the officers' servants, who gave him a piece of bread dipped in bacon grease to eat. Presently Evans came out and they started off.

"I've got to see an R.E. officer," said Evans, "about a new job on Hill 91. It's a bit further to the left of where we've been working, and it'll take us half an hour longer to get there."

Winterbourne seized the opportunity to put forward one or two ideas he had been thinking over:

"I hope you won't mind, sir, if I say something—it's not an official complaint at all, you understand, only what I've been personally thinking."

"Go ahead."

"Well, sir, I assume that the reason we are kept in billets instead of in the line is to give us more rest so that we come fresh to work. But here it doesn't work out that way, especially in the past fortnight; and it's likely to get worse instead of better. It seems to me that we should be much better off if we were in dug-outs in the reserve line. We have that long walk through the mud twice a day; we get all the shells meant for the transport and ration parties; we get an all-night strafing in the line; we're shelled all the way down; we come back to gassy billets, which are shelled with heavies twenty hours out of twenty-four. The cellars are no real protection against a direct hit. They're damper than dug-outs, and just as dark and ratty. There are far more whizz-bangs and light stuff in the line, but far fewer heavies; and if we had even fifteen-foot dug-outs, we'd get some sleep, instead of starting awake every ten minutes with a crump outside the cellar entrance. We're getting a lot of useless casualties, sir. I passed the cook-house as I came along, and the cook told me one of his mates had just gone down with gas from last night. And the S.M. looks as green as grass. Can't you get us put in the line, sir?"

Evans cogitated a moment or two:

"Yes, I think you're right. No, I can't get us moved. I haven't the authority. I wish I had. I'll ask the Major to put it before the Colonel. It's quite true what you say. In the past week we've had eight casualties in the line, and twelve here or going up and down. But with this show coming off I expect every trench and dug-out will be packed."

Winterbourne felt enormously proud that Evans had not snubbed his suggestion. Evans went on, after a pause:

"By the way, Winterbourne, have you ever thought of taking a commission?"

"Why yes, sir; it was suggested by the Adjutant of my battalion in England. I believe my father wrote to him about it. He, my father, was very keen about it."

"Well, why don't you apply?"

It was now Winterbourne's turn to cogitate:

"I find it rather hard to explain, sir. For many reasons, which you might think far-fetched, I had and still have a feeling that I ought to spend the War in the ranks and in the line. I should prefer to be in the Infantry, but I think the Pioneers are quite near enough."

"They often come round for volunteers, you know. If you

like, I'll put you down next time and the Major will recommend you to the Colonel."

"It's kind of you, sir. I'll think about it."

One night, two nights, three nights, four nights passed, and still there was no big battle. And they were not moved. Every night they were shelled up the line, shelled in the line, shelled on the way back, and arrived in a hailstorm of gas shells. They had to wear their gas-masks for hours every day. And sleep became more and more difficult and precarious.

Winterbourne's intimacy with Evans and his own "education" put him in rather an ambiguous position. Evans trusted him more and more to do things which would normally have been done by an N.C.O. And Winterbourne's feeling of responsibility led him to take on and conscientiously carry out everything of the kind. One night there was supposed to be a gas-discharger attack by the British in retaliation for the heavy German gas bombardments. All the officers wanted to see it; and since it was staged for an hour before dawn, that meant either that one officer had to take the Company down or that the men had to be kept up two hours longer, exposed to artillery retaliation. Evans solved the problem. He sent for Winterbourne:

"Winterbourne, we want to stop and see the fun up here. Now, you can take the Company down, can't you? I'll tell Sergeant Perkins that you're in charge; but of course you'll give orders through him. Come back here and report after you get them back."

"Very good, sir."

There was no British gas attack, but the Germans put up what was then a considerable gas bombardment. They sent over approximately thirty thousand gas shells that night, most of them in and around the village where the Pioneers were billeted. The Company had to wear gas-masks over the last half-mile, and Winterbourne had a very anxious time getting them along. He had discovered a disused but quite deep trench running through the village almost to their billets, and he took the men along there instead of through the village street. It was a little longer, but far safer. The shells were hailing all round

them, and Winterbourne didn't want any casualties. Sergeant
Perkins and he managed to get the men safely into billets.
Winterbourne turned and said:

"Well, good-night, Sergeant; I must go up the line again and
report to Mr. Evans."

"You ain't going up agen, are you?"

"Yes, Mr. Evans told me to."

" 'Struth! Well, I'd rather it was you than me."

Winterbourne fitted on his gas-mask, and groped his way out
of the Sergeants' cellar. The night was muggy, a bit drizzly,
windless, and very dark—the ideal conditions for a gas bombardment. What little wind there was came from the German
lines. He hesitated between taking the long muddy trench or
the more open road; but since he was practically blinded in the
darkness with his goggles, he decided to take the trench, for
fear of losing his way. It was rather eerie, groping his way
alone up the trench, with the legions of gas shells shrilling and
phutting all round him. They fell with a terrific "flop" when
they came within a few yards. He stumbled badly two or three
times in holes they had made in the trench since he had come
down. For nearly half a mile he had to go through the gas barrage, and it was slow work indeed, with the mud and the darkness and the groping and the stumbling. Interminable. He
thought of nothing in the darkness but keeping his left hand
on the side of the trench to guide him and holding his right
hand raised in front to prevent his bumping into something.

At last he got clear of the falling gas shells, and ventured a
peep outside his mask. One sniff showed him the air was
deadly with phosgene. He groped on another two hundred
yards and tried again. There was still a lot of gas, but he
decided to risk it, and took off his mask. With the mask off he
could see comparatively well, and travelled quite rapidly.
About an hour before dawn he reported to Evans.

"There is a devil of a gas bombardment going on round the
billets and for half a mile round, sir," said Winterbourne;
"that's why I'm so late. The whole country reeks of gas."

Evans whistled.

"Whew! As a matter of fact, we've been drinking a bit in the dug-out with some Infantry officers, and one or two are a bit groggy in consequence."

"Better wait till dawn, then, sir. If you'll come up into the trench you'll hear the shells going over."

"Oh, I take your word for it. But the Major insists on going down at once. We've just heard that there isn't going to be a gas attack. You'll have to help me get them down."

"Very good, sir."

The Major was entirely sober; Evans was perfectly self-controlled; but the other four were all a little too merry. It was a perfect nightmare getting them through the gas barrage. They would insist there was no danger, that the gas was all a wash-out; and kept taking off their masks. They disregarded the Major's peremptory orders, and Evans and Winterbourne had constantly to take off their own masks to argue with the subalterns and make them put on theirs. Winterbourne could feel the deadly phosgene at his lungs.

Just after dawn they reached the Officers' Mess cellar, fortunately without a casualty. Winterbourne felt horribly sick with the gas he had swallowed. The Major took off his gas-mask, and picked up a water-jug.

"Those confounded servants have forgotten to leave any water," exclaimed the Major angrily. "Winterbourne, take that tin jug and go and get some water from the cook-house."

"Very good, sir."

The shells were still pitilessly hailing down through the dawn. It was a hundred yards to the cook-house, and Winterbourne three times just escaped being directly hit by one of the ceaselessly falling shells. He returned to the Mess, and left the water.

"Thanks very much," said Evans; "you may go now, Winterbourne. Good-night."

"Good-night, sir."

"Good-night," said the Major; "thank you for getting that water, Winterbourne; I oughtn't to have sent you."

"Thank you, sir; good-night, sir."

Outside the Major's and Evans's part of the cellar the other officers were sitting round a deal table by the light of a candle stuck in a bottle, which looked dim and ghastly. The place was practically gas-proof, with tightly-drawn blankets over every crevice.

"Win'erbourne," said one of them.

"Sir?"

"Run along to the Quar'master-Sergeant and bring us a bottle of whisky."

"Very good, sir."

Winterbourne climbed the cellar steps, lifted the outer gas-curtain rapidly, and stepped out. There was such a stench of phosgene that he snapped his mask on at once. The shells were falling thicker than ever. One hit the wall of the house, and Winterbourne felt bricks and dust drop on his steel helmet and shoulders. He shrank against what was left of the wall. Two hundred yards to the Q.M.S.'s billet. That meant nearly a quarter of a mile through that deadly storm—for a half-drunken man to get a few more whiskies. Winterbourne hesitated. It was disobeying orders if he didn't go. He turned resolutely and went to his own billet: nothing was ever said of this refusal to obey an officer's orders in the face of the enemy.

Winterbourne stood outside the entrance to his cellar, took off his steel helmet and folded down the top part of his gas-mask so that he could see, while still keeping the nose-clip on and the large rubber mouthpiece in his teeth. The whitish morning light looked cold and misty, and the PHUT PHUT PHUT PHUT of the bursting gas shells continued with ruthless iteration. He watched them exploding; a little curling cloud of yellow gas rose from each shell-hole. The ground was pitted with these new shell-holes, and newly-broken bricks and debris lay about everywhere. A dead rat lay in a gas-shell hole just outside the entrance—so the War caught even the rats! There had been a young, slender ash-tree in what had once been the cottage garden. A heavy explosive had fallen just at its roots, splintered the slim stem, and dashed it prone with broken branches. The young leaves were still green, except on one side where they were curled and withered by gas. The grass, so tender a Spring green a week before, was yellow, sickly, and withered. As he turned to lift the gas-blanket he heard the whizz and crash of the first heavy of the day bombardment. But the gas shells continued.

Inside the cellar was complete darkness. He took off his mask and fumbled his way down the broken stairs, trying not to wake the other runners. It was important to use only one match, because matches were scarce and precious. The air inside was foul and heavy, but only slightly tainted with phosgene. Winterbourne half smiled as he thought how furiously he had contended for "fresh air" in huts and barrack-rooms, and how gladly he now welcomed any foul air which was not full of poison gas. He lighted his stub of candle, and slowly took off his equipment, replacing the box respirator immediately. His boots were thick with mud, his puttees and trousers torn with wire and stained with mud and grease. A bullet had torn a hole in his leather jerkin, and his steel helmet was marked by a long, deep dint, where it had been struck by a flying splinter of shell. He felt amazingly weary, and rather sick. He had known the fatigue of long walks and strenuous Rugby football matches and cross-country runs, but nothing like this continual, cumulative weariness. He moved with the slow, almost pottering movements of agricultural labourers and old men. The feeling of sickness became worse, and he wanted to vomit out the smell of gas which seemed to permeate him. He heaved over his empty canvas bucket until the water started to his eyes, but vomited nothing. He noticed how filthy his hands were.

He was just going to sit down on his blanket and pack, covered by the neatly-folded ground-sheet, when he saw a parcel and some letters for him lying on them. The other runners had brought them over for him. Decent of them. The parcel was from Elizabeth—how sweet of her to remember! And yes, she had sent all the things he had asked for and left out all the useless things people would send to the troops. He mustn't touch anything except the candles, though, until to-morrow, when the parcel would be carefully divided among everybody in the cellar. It was one of the good unwritten rules—all parcels strictly divided between each section, so that every one got something, even and especially the men who were too poor or too lonely to receive anything from England. Dear Elizabeth! how sweet of her to remember!

He opened her envelope with hands which shook slightly with fatigue and the shock of explosions. Then he stopped, lighted a new candle from the stub of the old one, blew out the stub, and carefully put it away to give to one of the infantry. The letter was unexpectedly tender and charming. She had just been to Hampton Court to look at the flowers. The gardens were rather neglected, she said, and no flowers in the Long Border—the gardeners were at the War, and there was no money in England now for flowers. Did he remember how they had walked there in April five years ago? Yes, he remembered, and thought too with a pang of surprise that this was the first Spring he had ever spent without seeing a flower, not even a primrose. The little yellow coltsfoot he had liked so much were all dead with phosgene. Elizabeth went on:

"I saw Fanny last week. She looked more charming and delicate than ever—and such a marvellous hat! I hear she is *much* attached to a brilliant young scientist, a chemist, who does the most *peculiar* things. He mixes up all sorts of chemicals and then experiments with the fumes and kills dozens of poor little monkeys with them. Isn't it wicked? But Fanny says it's most *important* war work."

The sickness came on him again. He turned sideways and heaved silently, but could not vomit. He felt thirsty, and drank a little stale-tasting water from his water-bottle. Dear Elizabeth! how sweet of her to remember!

Fanny's letter was very rattling and gay. She had been there, she had done this, she had seen so-and-so. How was darling George getting along? She was so glad to see that there had been no fighting yet on the Western front. She added:

"I saw Elizabeth recently. She looked a little worried, but *very* sweet. She was with such a charming young man—a young American who ran away from Yale to join our Flying Corps."

The heavy shells outside were falling nearer and nearer. They came over in fours, each shell a little in front of the others—bracketing. Through the gas-curtain he heard the remains of a ruined house collapse across the street under a direct hit. Each crash made the cellar tremble slightly, and the candle flame jumped.

Well, it was nice of Fanny to write. Very nice. She was a thoroughly decent sort. He picked up the other envelopes. One came from Paris, and contained the *Bulletin des Écrivains*—names of French writers and artists killed or wounded, and news of those in the armies. He was horrified to see how many of his friends in Paris had been killed. A passage had been marked in blue pencil—it contained the somewhat belated news that M. Georges Winterbourne, *le jeune peintre anglais*, was in camp in England.

Another letter, forwarded by Elizabeth, came from a London art-dealer. It said that an American had bought one of Winterbourne's sketches for five pounds, and that when he heard that Winterbourne was in the trenches he had insisted upon making it twenty-five pounds. The dealer therefore enclosed a cheque for twenty-two pounds ten, being twenty-five pounds less commission at ten per centum. Winterbourne thought it rather cheek to take commission on the money which was a gift; but still—Business As Usual. But how generous of the American! How amazingly kind! His pay was five francs a week, so the money was most welcome. He must write and thank . . .

The last letter was from Mr. Upjohn, from whom Winterbourne had not heard for over a year. Elizabeth, it appeared, had asked him to write and send news. Mr. Upjohn wrote a chatty letter. He himself had a job in Whitehall, "of national importance." Winterbourne rejoiced to think that Mr. Upjohn's importance was now recognised by the nation. Mr. Shobbe had been to France, had stayed in the line three weeks, and was now permanently at the base. Comrade Bobbe had come out very strong as a conscientious objector. He had been put in prison for six weeks. His friends had "got at" somebody influential, who had "got at" the secretary of somebody in authority, and Mr. Bobbe had been released as an agricultural worker. He was now "working" on a farm run by a philanthropic lady for conscientious objectors of the intellectual class. Mr. Waldo Tubbe had found his vocation in the Post Office Censorship Bureau, where he was very happy—if he could not force people to say what he wanted, he could at least prevent them from writing anything derogatory to his Adopted Empire. . . .

George laughed silently to himself. Amusing chap, Upjohn. He got out his jack-knife and scraped away the mud so that he could unlace his boots. Outside the shells crashed. One burst just behind the cellar. The roof seemed to give a jump, something seemed to smack Winterbourne on the top of the head, and the candle went out. He laboriously re-lit it. The other runners woke up.

"Anything up?"

"No, only a crump outside. I'm just getting into kip."

"Where've you been?"

"Up the line again, for the officers."

"Get back all right?"

"Yes, nobody hit. But there's a hell of a lot of gas about. Don't go out without putting on your gas-bag."

"Good-night, old man."

"Good-night, old boy."

9

Three more nights passed rather more tranquilly. There was comparatively little gas, but the German heavies were persistent. They, too, quieted down on the third night, and Winterbourne got to bed fairly early and fell into a deep sleep.

Suddenly he was wide awake and sitting up. What on earth or hell was happening? From outside came a terrific rumble and roaring, as if three volcanoes and ten thunderstorms were in action simultaneously. The whole earth was shaking as if beaten by a multitude of flying hoofs, and the cellar walls vibrated. He seized his helmet, dashed past the other runners, who were starting up and exclaiming, rushed through the gas-curtain; and recoiled. It was still night, but the whole sky was brilliant with hundreds of flashing lights. Two thousand British guns were in action, and heaven and earth were filled with

the roar and flame. From about half a mile to the north, south-
wards as far as he could see, the whole front was a dazzling
flicker of gun-flashes. It was as if giant hands covered with
huge rings set with searchlights were being shaken in the darkness, as if innumerable brilliant diamonds were flashing great
rays of light. There was not a fraction of a second without its
flash and roar. Only the great boom of a twelve- or fourteen-
inch naval gun just behind them punctured the general pande-
monium at regular intervals.

Winterbourne ran stumbling forwards to get a view clear of
the ruins. He crouched by a piece of broken house and looked
towards the German lines. They were a long, irregular wall of
smoke, torn everywhere with the dull red flashes of bursting
shells. Behind their lines their artillery was flickering brighter
and brighter as battery after battery came into action, making
a crescendo of noise and flame when the limits of both seemed
to have been reached. Winterbourne saw but could not hear
the first of their shells as it exploded short of the village. The
great clouds of smoke over the German trenches were darkly
visible in the first very pallid light of dawn. It was the preliminary bombardment of the long-expected battle. Winterbourne
felt his heart shake with the shaking earth and vibrating air.

The whole thing was indescribable—a terrific spectacle, a
stupendous symphony of sound. The devil-artist who had staged
it was a master, in comparison with whom all other artists of
the sublime and terrible were babies. The roar of the guns was
beyond clamour—it was an immense rhythmic harmony, a
super-jazz of tremendous drums, a ride of the Valkyrie played
by three thousand cannon. The intense rattle of the machine-
guns played a minor motif of terror. It was too dark to see the
attacking troops, but Winterbourne thought with agony how
every one of those dreadful vibrations of sound meant death
or mutilation. He thought of the ragged lines of British troops
stumbling forward in smoke and flame and a chaos of sound,
crumbling away before the German protective barrage and the
Reserve line machine-guns. He thought of the German front
lines, already obliterated under that ruthless tempest of explosions and flying metal. Nothing could live within the area of
that storm except by a miraculous hazard. Already in this first

half-hour of bombardment hundreds upon hundreds of men
would have been violently slain, smashed, torn, gouged,
crushed, mutilated. The colossal harmony seemed to roar
louder as the drum-fire lifted from the Front line to the
Reserve. The battle was begun. They would be mopping-up
soon—throwing bombs and explosives down the dug-out
entrances on the men cowering inside.

The German heavies were pounding M—— with their
shells, smashing at the communication trenches and cross-
roads, hurling masses of metal at their own ruined village.
Winterbourne saw the half-ruined factory chimney totter and
crash to the ground. Two shells pitched on either side of him,
and flung earth, stones, and broken bricks all round him. He
turned and ran back to his cellar, stumbling over shell-holes.
He saw an isolated house disappear in the united explosion of
two huge shells.

He clutched his hands together as he ran, with tears in his
eyes.

10

Winterbourne found the other runners buckling up their packs
and fastening their equipment with that febrile haste which
comes with great excitement. Even in the cellar the roar of the
artillery made it necessary for them almost to shout to each
other.

"What are the orders?"

"Stand by in fighting order, ready to move off at once.
Dump packs outside billets."

Winterbourne in his turn feverishly put on his equipment,
buckled his pack, and cleaned his rifle. They stood, rifles and
bayonets ready, in the low cellar, ready to spring up the broken
stairs as soon as they were warned. In a moment such as this,
a kind of paroxysm of humanity, the most difficult thing is to
wait. They dreaded the awful storm thundering above them,
but they were irresistibly hallucinated by it, eager to plunge in
and be done with it. The German shells thudded continuously

all round them, muted by the vaster clamour of the attacking artillery. No orders came. They fidgeted, exclaimed, and finally one by one sat silent on their packs, listening. A large rat ran down the cellar stairs and began to nibble something. The beast was exactly level with Winterbourne's head. He shoved a cartridge into the breech of his rifle, murmuring, "Why should a dog, a horse, a rat have life, and they no breath at all?" He aimed very carefully and pulled the trigger; there was a terrific bang in the confined cellar, and the rat was smashed dead in the air. Not ten seconds later a red, perspiring face under a steel helmet was anxiously poked through the cellar entrance. It was the Orderly Sergeant.

"What the muckin' hell are you doing, down there?"

"Having a spree—didn't you hear the champagne cork?"

"Spree be mucked—one of you ******* fired his rifle and muckin' near copped me. Mucked if I don't report the muckin' lot of yer."

"Wow! Put a sock in it!"

"Muck off!"

"Ord'ly sergeants are cheap to-day!"

"Well, you muckers got to report to yer officers at once. 'Op it."

They ran up the broken stairs, pretending to poke their bayonets at him, and laughing, perhaps a little hysterically. The fat, good-natured little Sergeant went off, shaking his fist at them, shouting awful threats about the punishment awaiting them, with a broad affectionate grin on his face.

For Winterbourne the battle was a timeless confusion, a chaos of noise, fatigue, anxiety, and horror. He did not know how many days and nights it lasted, lost completely the sequence of events, found great gaps in his conscious memory. He did know that he was profoundly affected by it, that it made a cut in his life and personality. You couldn't say there was anything melodramatically startling, no hair going grey in a night, or never smiling again. He looked unaltered; he behaved in exactly the same way. But, in fact, he was a little mad. We talk of shell-shock, but who wasn't shell-shocked, more or less? The change in him was psychological, and showed itself in two ways. He was left with an anxiety complex, a sense of fear he had never experienced, the necessity to use great and greater efforts to force himself to face artillery, anything explosive. Curiously enough, he scarcely minded machine-gun fire, which was really more deadly, and completely disregarded rifle-fire. And he was also left with a profound and cynical discouragement, a shrinking horror of the human race. . . .

A timeless confusion. The runners scattered outside their billet and made for the officers' cellar through the falling shells, dodging from one broken house or shell-hole to another. Winterbourne, not yet unnerved, calmly walked straight across and arrived first. Evans took him aside:

"We're going up as a company, with orders to support and co-operate with the Infantry. Try to nab me a rifle and bayonet before we go over."

"Very good, sir."

Outside was an open box of S.A.A., and they each drew two extra bandoliers of cartridges, which they slung round their necks.

They moved off in sections, filing along the village street, which was filled with fresh debris and ruins re-ruined. It was snowing. They came on two freshly-killed horses. Their close-cropped necks were bent under them, with great glassy eyeballs starting with agony. A little further on was a smashed limber with the driver dead beside it.

In the trench they passed a batch of about forty German prisoners, unarmed, in steel helmets. They looked green-pale, and were trembling. They shrank against the side of the trench as the English soldiers passed, but not a word was said to them.

The snowstorm and the smoke drifting back from the barrage made the air as murky as a November fog in London. They saw little, did not know where they were going, what they were doing or why. They lined a trench and waited. Nothing happened. They saw nothing but wire and snowflakes and drifting smoke, heard only the roar of the guns and the now sharper rattle of machine-guns. Shells dropped around them. Evans was looking through his glasses, and cursing the lack of visibility. Winterbourne stood beside him, with his rifle still slung on his left shoulder.

They waited. Then Major Thorpe's runner came with a message. Apparently he had mistaken a map reference and brought them to the wrong place.

They plodged off through the mud, and lined another trench. They waited.

Winterbourne found himself following Evans across what had been No Man's Land for months. He noticed a skeleton in British uniform, caught sprawling in the German wire. The skull still wore a sodden cap and not a steel helmet. They passed the bodies of British soldiers killed that morning. Their faces were strangely pale, their limbs oddly bulging with strange fractures. One had vomited blood.

They were in the German trenches, with many dead bodies in field grey. Winterbourne and Evans went down into a German dug-out. Nobody was there, but it was littered with straw, torn paper, portable cookers, oddments of forgotten equipment, and cigars. There were French tables and chairs with human excrement on them.

They went on. A little knot of Germans came toward them holding up their shaking hands. They took no notice of them, but let them pass through.

The barrage continued. Their first casualty was caused by their own shells dropping short.

Major Thorpe sent Winterbourne and another man with a written duplicate message to Battalion Headquarters. They went back over the top, trying to run. It was impossible. Their hearts beat too fast, and their throats were parched. They went blindly at a jog-trot, slower in fact than a brisk walk. They seemed to be tossed violently by the bursting shells. The acrid smoke was choking. A heavy roared down beside Winterbourne and made him stagger with its concussion. He could not control the resultant shaking of his flesh. His teeth chattered very slightly as he clenched them desperately. They got back to familiar land and finally to Southampton Row. It was a long way to Battalion Headquarters. The men in the orderly-room eagerly questioned them about the battle, but they knew less than the questioner did.

Winterbourne asked for water and drank thirstily. He and the other runner were dazed and incoherent. They were given another written message, and elaborate directions which they promptly forgot.

The drum-fire had died down to an ordinary heavy bombardment as they started back. Already it was late afternoon. They wandered for hours in unfamiliar trenches before they found the Company.

They slept that night in a large German dug-out, swarming with rats. Winterbourne in his sleep felt them jump on his chest and face.

The drum-fire began again next morning. Again they lined a trench and advanced through smoke over torn wire and shell-tormented ground. Prisoners passed through. At night they struggled for hours, carrying down wounded men in stretchers through the mud and clamour. Major Thorpe was mortally wounded and his runner killed; Hume and his runner were killed; Franklin was wounded; Pemberton was killed; Sergeant Perkins was killed; the stretcher-bearers were killed. Men seemed to drop away continually.

Three days later Evans and Thompson led back forty-five men to the old billets in the ruined village. The attack on their part of the front had failed. Further south a considerable advance had been made and several thousand prisoners taken, but the German line was unbroken and stronger than ever in its new positions. Therefore that also was a failure.

Winterbourne and Henderson were the only two runners left; and since Evans was in command, Winterbourne was now company runner. The two men sat on their packs in the cellar without a word. Both shook very slightly but continuously with fatigue and shock. Outside the vicious heavies crashed eternally. They started wildly to their feet as a terrific smash overhead brought down what was left of the house above them and crashed into the duplicate cellar next door. A

moment later there was another enormous crash and one end
of the cellar broke in with falling bricks and a cloud of dust.
They rushed out by the steps at the other end, and were sent
reeling and choking by another huge black explosion.

They stumbled across to another cellar occupied by what
was left of a section, and asked to sleep there since their own
cellar was wrecked. Six of them and a corporal sat in silence
by the light of a candle, dully listening to the crash of shells.

In a lull they heard a strange noise outside the cellar, first like
wheels and then like a human voice calling for help. No one
moved. The voice called again. The Corporal spoke:

"Who's going up?"

"Mucked if I am," said somebody; "I've 'ad enough."

Winterbourne and Henderson simultaneously struggled to
their feet. The change from candle-light to darkness blinded
them as they peered out from the ruined doorway. They could
just see a confused dark mass. The voice came again:

"Help! for Christ's sake come and help!"

A transport limber had been smashed by a shell. The
wounded horses had dragged it along and fallen outside the
cellar entrance. One man had both legs cut short at the knees.
He was still alive, but evidently dying. They left him, lifted
down the other man and carried him into the cellar. A large
shell splinter had smashed his right knee. He was conscious,
but weak. They got out his field-dressing and iodine and
dripped iodine on the wound. At the pain of burning disinfec-
tant the man turned deadly pale and nearly fainted. Winterbourne found that his hands and clothes were smeared with
blood.

Then came the problem of getting the man away to a dressing-station. The Corporal and the four men refused to budge.
The shells were crashing continuously outside. Winterbourne
started out to get a stretcher and the new stretcher-bearer,
groping his way through the darkness. Outside their billet he
tripped and fell into a deep shell-hole, just as a heavy exploded
with terrific force at his side. But for the fall he must have been
blown to pieces. He scrambled to his feet, breathless and
shaken, and tumbled down the cellar stairs. He noticed scared

faces looking at him in the candle-light. He explained what
had happened. The stretcher-bearer jumped up, got his stretcher
and satchel of dressings, and they started back. Every shell
which exploded near seemed to shake Winterbourne's flesh
from his bones. He was dazed and half-frantic with the physical shock of concussion after concussion. When he got back in
the cellar he collapsed into a kind of stupor. The stretcher-
bearer dressed the man's wound, and then looked at Winterbourne, felt his pulse, gave him a sip of rum and told him to lie
still. He tried to explain that he must help carry the wounded
man, and struggled to get to his feet. The stretcher-bearer
pushed him back:

"You lie still, mate; you've done enough for to-day."

I I

The battle on their part of the Front died down into long snarl-
ing artillery duels, gas bombardments, fierce local attacks and
counter-attacks. Further south it flamed up again with intense
preludes of drum-fire. What was left of the Pioneer Company
returned to more normal occupations. So far as they were concerned, one great advantage of the battle was that the Germans had been driven from the long slag-hill, and from a large
portion of Hill 91. By fierce counter-attacks the Germans
regained much of the lost ground on Hill 91, but they never
came anywhere near recovering the slag-hill. The ground they
had lost further south made that impossible. Consequently,
some of the worst features of the salient were at last obliterated, and they were no longer under such close observation or
enfiladed by machine-guns.

They had a day's rest, and were then put on the cushy job of
building a new track up to the southern fringe of Hill 91 across
the old Front lines and No Man's Land. They were outside the
range of vision of the German observation posts, and it was
two days before the German airplanes discovered them—two
days of comparative quiet. Then, of course, they got it hot and
strong.

In clearing away the wire they made a number of gruesome discoveries, and examined with great interest the primitive hand-grenades and other weapons of 1914–15 which were lying rusting there in great quantities. Winterbourne took an immense interest in building this track, an interest which puzzled and amused Evans, especially since this was the first time he had ever seen Winterbourne show any enthusiasm for their labours.

"I can't see why you're so keen on this bally old track, Winterbourne. It's one of the dullest jobs we've ever had."

"But surely you can see, sir. We're making something, not destroying things. We're taking down wire, not putting it up; filling in shell-holes, not desecrating the earth."

Evans frowned at the phrase "desecrating the earth." He thought it pretentious, and with all his obtuseness he had an instinctive resentment against Winterbourne's unspoken but unwavering and profound condemnation of War. Evans had a superstitious reverence for War. He believed in the Empire; the Empire was symbolised by the King-Emperor; and the King—poor man!—is always having to dress up as an Admiral or a Field-Marshal or a brass-hat of some kind. Navydom and Armydom thereby acquired a mystic importance; and since armies and navies are obviously meant for War, it was plain that War was an integral part of Empire-worship. More than once he clumsily tried to trap Winterbourne into expressing unorthodox opinions. But, of course, Winterbourne saw him coming miles away, and easily evaded his awkward booby-traps.

"I suppose you're a *republican*," he said to Winterbourne, who was innocently humming the Marseillaise. "I don't believe in Republics. Why, Presidents wear evening dress in the middle of the morning."

Winterbourne nearly burst into a cackle of laughter, but managed to restrain himself. He denied that he was a republican, and admitted with mock gravity that Evans had put his finger on a serious flaw in Republican institutions.

But his joy in constructing the track was short-lived. As they were finishing their second day's work he saw a battery of Field Artillery cross the old No Man's Land by the road they had built, and then bump its way over shell-holes to a new position. So even this little bit of construction was only for further destruction.

They went on to night-work again, and Winterbourne distinguished himself by pulling out of the ground a dud shell which the other men refused to touch, in case it went off. They crouched on the ground while Winterbourne tugged and strained to get it out, and Evans stood beside him urging him to go easy. Suddenly Winterbourne went into a series of gasping chuckles, and in answer to Evans's questions managed to jerk out that the alleged shell was a stump of wood with an iron ring round it. The men returned sheepishly to their work. In reward for his heroic conduct Winterbourne was allowed to join a gang who were pulling up real duds embedded in the *pavé* of the main road, which had become available through the German retirement. They levered and tugged the shells up very gingerly, since the oldest duds are liable to explode if treated roughly. Winterbourne was glad when that little job was done.

The nightly gas bombardments became worse than ever, and Winterbourne sometimes spent twelve hours a day in his gas-mask. They used their respirators so frequently that a new set had to be issued.

Since Evans was now temporarily in command and had only Thompson to help him and about forty men available for work, they did only one shift, which Evans and Thompson took on alternate nights. As company runner, Winterbourne carried all messages between the Company and Battalion H.Q. On the other hand, Evans always let him rest on the nights when he himself was not on duty. Winterbourne was profoundly thankful for these nights off. His winter cough, aided perhaps by microbes communicated by lice, had evolved into a sort of tertian ague. Every third night he had alternate fits of sweating and shivering. It was much pleasanter to lie down even in a damp cellar than to go up the line feeling utterly weak and feverish.

He was sleeping soundly alone in the runners' cellar, oblivious to the zwiing, PHUT, of the gas shells outside, when he was awakened by Henderson, the other surviving runner, who came stumbling down the cellar stairs in the darkness. Winterbourne lit a candle for him. Henderson had just taken off his gas-mask, and stood with rumpled hair and a pale, scared look.

"What's up?" said Winterbourne; "what's the matter?"

"Thompson's killed."

"Good Lord! The only other officer! How?"

"Whizz-bang."

"How did it happen?"

"The Boche put up an attack to-night. Thompson took us off work, and told us to line a trench. He was standing on top, and told me to get into the trench. A whizz-bang burst just beside him. He died in five minutes."

"O God! Did he say anything?"

"Yes, he was perfectly conscious and calm. He told me how to get the men back. He sent best of luck to Evans and you and the S.M. And he made me take a couple of letters from his pocket to send to his wife and mother. He was horribly mangled—right arm and right leg smashed, ribs broken, and a great tear in the side of his face. He made me promise to make Evans write home that he was shot through the heart and died instantaneously and painlessly."

"Damn! He was a nice chap. One of the best officers we had."

The inner gas-curtain was lifted, and Evans's servant stumbled in, taking off his mask.

"Report at once, fighting order, Winterbourne."

Winterbourne hurriedly put on his boots and puttees, struggled into his equipment, snapped on his mask, and jog-trotted over to the officers' cellar through the now familiar hail of gas shells. He was amazed and distressed and ashamed to find how much his flesh instinctively shrank when a shell dropped close at hand, how great an effort he now needed to refrain from ducking or cowering. He raged at himself, called himself coward, poltroon, sissy, anything abusive he could think of. But still his body instinctively shrank. He had passed into the final period of War strain, when even an air-raid became a terror.

Evans was laboriously writing. The large cellar looked very

cellar-like and empty, with one man in place of the six who had lived there less than a fortnight before.

"You know Mr. Thompson's killed?"

"Yes, sir. Henderson told me."

"I can't carry on as a Company by myself with less than forty available men." Evans spoke bitterly: "There's a chit from Division complaining that we are doing far less work than a month ago. They don't seem to know there's been a battle, and that we're worn out and reduced to a third our strength."

He was silent, re-read his despatch, folded it, and handed it to Winterbourne.

"Take this down to Batt. H.Q. I've marked it Special Urgency. Make them get the Colonel up if he's asleep. If he questions you, tell him our position. I haven't seen him for three weeks. And refuse to leave without an answer."

"Very good, sir."

"And, Winterbourne."

"Sir?"

"There's another chit here somewhere urging us to get two volunteers for Infantry commissions in each Company. Henderson's going—he's a stout little tyke. The other volunteers are that filthy cook's-mate and the sanitary man. Idiotic. I won't recommend them. But I want you to volunteer. Will you?"

Winterbourne hesitated. He didn't want the responsibility; it was contrary to his notion that he ought to stay in the ranks and in the line, take the worst and humblest jobs, share the common fate of common men. But then, he had consented to be a runner. And then, he was sorely tempted. It meant several months in England, it meant seeing Fanny and Elizabeth again, it meant a respite. He was amazed to find that he didn't want to leave Evans, and suddenly saw that what he had done in the past months had been chiefly done from personal attachment to a rather common and ignorant man of the kind he most despised, the grown-up public-school boy.

"What are you hesitating about?"

"Well, sir," said Winterbourne whimsically, "I was wondering how you'd get on without me."

"*****!" said Evans. "Besides, at this rate I shan't last much longer. Now, shall I put your name down?"

"Yes, sir."

He afterwards regretted that "Yes."

Evans's sharp note brought an abrupt change in their lives. They exchanged places with one of the other Pioneer companies in a quieter section of the line. Evans marched his forty men down as one platoon, and they passed successively the four platoons of the relieving Company. The men exchanged ironical jibes as they passed.

Their new quarters were a great improvement. They were joined by a Captain, who took nominal command, and two subalterns. But no men. There appeared to be no men available. They lived in shelters and dug-outs in the Reserve line. Winterbourne, Henderson, and two other runners lived in a two-foot shelter just outside the officers' dug-out. Winterbourne was now officially Company runner. He lived one fortnight in the line, and one at Battalion H.Q. The sacking bed at H.Q., the comparative absence of shelling, the better food, the rest, made it seem like paradise. He did not know that his application for a commission had been passed at once, and that he was being looked after.

Two days after they got to their new quarters, in the line, Evans's servant poked his head excitedly into the runners' shelter.

"Winterbourne!"

"Yes."

"You're to come at once. Mr. Evans is sick."

"Sick!"

Winterbourne found Evans leaning against the side of the trench, a ghastly green pallor on his face.

"Whatever's the matter, sir?"

"Gas. I've swallowed too much of the beastly stuff. I can't stand it any longer. I'm off to the dressing-station."

"Shall I get a stretcher, sir?"

"No, damn it, I'll walk down. I can still stand. Take my pack and come along."

Every few yards Evans had to stop and lean against the trench wall. He heaved, but did not vomit. Winterbourne offered his arm, but he wouldn't take it. They passed two corpses, rather horribly mutilated, lying on stretchers at the end of the communication trench. Neither said anything, but Evans was thinking, "Well, gas is better than that," and Winterbourne thought, "How long will it be before some one puts me there?"

He finally got Evans to the dressing-station, supporting him with his right arm. They shook hands outside.

"You'll get your commission, Winterbourne."

"Thanks. Are you all right, sir? Shall I come down with you further?"

"No; go back and report that you left me here."

"Very good, sir."

They shook hands again.

"Well, good-bye, old man; best of luck to you."

"Good-bye, sir, good-bye."

He never saw Evans again.

When Evans had gone, Winterbourne's interest in the Company suddenly evaporated. He did not know the new officers, rather disliked the Captain, and of course was not on the same footing with them as he had been with Evans. Henderson left for England to be trained as an officer. Winterbourne felt lonelier than ever. And he realised with disgust and horror that his nerve was gone. His daily trips were really very easy—about a mile and a half, a few gusts of machine-gun bullets and about thirty or forty crumps on the road each way. The Germans had discovered some tanks hidden behind a slag-hill round which he had to pass. They shelled it with heavies. Winterbourne now found that he had to force himself to walk forward to them and through the area where they were bursting. It was worse at night. One night he did what he had never done before when carrying a message—waited ten minutes for the shelling to quiet down.

That ten minutes, curiously enough, saved his life. He heard several shells fall in and around Company H.Q. just as he came along the trench. One of them had fallen plump on their fragile shelter and blown it to pieces, instantly killing the runner, Jenkins, a boy of nineteen, who was lying there. If

Winterbourne had not lingered that ten minutes on the road, he would inevitably have been killed too. He felt very guilty about it. Perhaps if he had come back the boy would have been sent back with a return message. But no, if there had been a return message it would have been his job.

He lost his blanket, ground-sheet, and pack. The runners were transferred to a similar shelter twenty yards further on. Winterbourne hated to pass the smashed shelter. He always thought of Jenkins and his absurd boyish grin. Jenkins had been errand-boy and then assistant to a grocer in a small provincial town. A most undistinguished person. He had a solemn respect for *John Bull* and its opinions. Otherwise he wasn't solemn at all, always cracking rather pointless jests, and grinning his boyish grin, and hardly ever grousing. Winterbourne regretted him.

At Battalion Headquarters, Winterbourne tried to read, and found it impossible. He discovered an old number of *The Spectator* with an article on Porson, written by a man he had known. He had to read the article before he remembered who Porson was, and found himself puzzling over quite ordinary sentences like a ploughman. He threw the paper down in despair, and got permission to go to an estaminet. They had no wine, and spirits were forbidden. He sat there drinking the infamous and harmless French beer, and droning out sentimental songs with the other Tommies. He got into the habit of bribing the Q.M.S.'s clerk to give him extra rum. Anything to forget.

At the end of one of his fortnightly periods at Battalion H.Q., Winterbourne went as usual to the R.S.M.:

"Winterbourne, D Company runner, returning for service in the line, sir."

The R.S.M. turned over some papers, pursing up his lips:

"Let me see, let me *seeee*. Yes, yes. Yes, yes. Here we are: 31819 Private Winterbourne, G. Yes. You're returning to England on Friday for the purpose of proceeding to an Officer Cadet Corps. Report to the Orderly-room at four (pip emma) on Thursday for your papers, and draw iron rations from the Q.M.S. Will report to R.T.O. at Rail Head before eight (ack emma) on Friday, and will be struck off the strength. Got that?"

"Yes, sir. Will you give me a chit to show them in the line, please?"

"No. To-day's Wednesday. You'd better stay here, and I'll send up the runner who is taking your place."

"Very good, sir."

The boy who was taking Winterbourne's place was delighted to get the job. He was a quick-witted youth who had been trained as an elementary-school teacher, and thanked Winterbourne as if the new job had been his gift. He was killed by a bullet as he climbed out of the communication trench with his first message. Winterbourne began to feel as if he had made a pact with the Devil, so that other men were always being killed in his stead.

For the remaining two days he was virtually excused duty. He was allowed to go to the baths each day, and got himself clean and free from lice. He received absolutely new under-clothes, not the worn, soiled garments full of dead lice usually issued at the baths; was given new puttees and trousers in place of his soiled, torn ones, and handed in his rent leather jerkin. He had a sacking bed, and slept twelve hours a night. Already he was a different being from the dazed and haggard man of the Hill 91 days.

He wanted very much to go to England, and yet his chief feeling was that of apathy. Now that his orders had come, he felt he would just as soon have stopped where he was. Why prolong the agony? If he stayed, he would either be hit sooner or later, or become a battalion runner, a much better and less anxious job than that of an Infantry subaltern. Still, it might be worth while, just to see Elizabeth and Fanny again. . . .

It was hot midsummer weather. He wandered out along the straight French road, with its ceaseless up and down of mechanical transport and military traffic. The Military Police and armed pickets suspiciously turned him back. He found a little hedgeless field of poppies and yellow daisies, and sat down there. The heavies were firing with regular deliberation; overhead the white shrapnel bursts pursued an enemy plane;

from the far distance came a very faint "claaang!" as a shell
smashed into M——. It was so strange to have unmuddy
boots, to sit on grass in the sun and look at wild flowers, to see
one or two undamaged houses, not to be continually on the
alert. He sat with his elbows on his knees and his doubled fists
under his chin, staring in front of him. His body was rested,
but he felt such an apathetic weariness of mind that he would
have been glad to die painlessly there and then, without ever
going back to England, without ever seeing Elizabeth and
Fanny again. His mind no longer wandered off in long coher-
ent reveries, but was either vaguely empty or thronged with
too vivid memories. It seemed incredible that only seven
months or so had passed since he had left England—more like
seven years. He felt, not so much self-contempt as self-indiffer-
ence. He did not despise George Winterbourne; he merely
wasn't interested in him. Once he had been extremely interested in himself and the things he wanted to do; now he didn't
care, he didn't want to do anything in particular. Directly the
military yoke was lightened and he was left to himself for a
few hours, he was aimless, apathetic, listless. If he had been
told there and then that he was discharged from the Army and
could go, he wouldn't have known what to do expect to stay
there and stare at the poppies and daisies.

The night before he left, the runners and officers' servants
got rum and beer and champagne and made him drink with
them. They exhorted him not to forget his old pals, and not to
be a swine to his men when he was an officer. He promised,
regretting all the time the subtle difference which was already
dividing him from them. "Fancy 'avin' to salute old George!"
said one of them. Fancy indeed! He wished so much he had
stayed with them. He drank a good deal, and for the first time
in his life went to bed tight.

He got to Rail Head just before eight, hot and perspiring from
a rapid walk in full kit under a July sun. An immense drum-fire
was thundering from the north. The Division was under orders
to proceed there in two days. There was to be another great
offensive at Ypres. He shuddered, thinking of the showers of

bursting metal, flogging and churning the ground, shearing and rending human flesh; the immense concourse of detonations hammering on human nerves.

The R.T.O. gave him directions and he got into a waiting train. It was empty, except for a small group of leave men at the other end. Glad of a little solitude, he did not join them.

The German heavies gave him a last amiable farewell. They began dropping shells on Rail Head. That sickening apprehension of the explosion came on him, and he felt sure that a shell would fall on his carriage before the train left. He fought the apprehension savagely, as if the only thing he wanted to do in life was to repress his fear reflex. The shells came over, one at a time, at regular intervals of a minute. He listened for them, sweating, and gripping his rifle. Either let the train start or get it over. The train waited interminably. Zwiiing, crash! to the right; Zwiiing, crash! to the left; Zwiiing, crash! to the right; Zwiiing, crash! to the left. He sat there alone for thirty-five minutes—thirty-five Zwiiing, crash! It was somehow more awful than drum-fire, a more penetrating torture.

At last the train started and puffed slowly out of the station. Winterbourne sat quite still, listening to the crashes growing fainter and fainter as the train gathered speed. At last they disappeared altogether in the rattle of wheels. In place of the long, slow crawl coming up, the train clattered along at great speed. He passed undamaged stations, thronged with French peasants, French soldiers on leave, and British troops; he saw the lovely Corot poplars and willows shimmering in the sun as they wavered in the light breeze; there were cows in the fields, and he noticed yellow iris in the wet ditches, and tall, white hog's-parsley. A field of red clover and white daisies made him think of the old days at Martin's Point. An immense effort of imagination was needed to link himself now with himself then. He looked almost with curiosity at his familiar khaki and rifle—so strange that ten years later that boy should be a soldier. Then he noticed that he had forgotten to sheath his bayonet. It had been fixed so long that he had to wrench it off. There was a little ring of rust round the bayonet boss. He got out his oil rag and anxiously cleaned it. The bayonet sheath was so full of dried mud that he had to clean that too.

At Boulogne he sent a telegram to Elizabeth. The R.T.O. told him to leave all his kit on the quay, and to take only his personal belongings. He slipped off his equipment and laid his rifle beside his dinted helmet, feeling as if he were carrying out some strange valedictory rite. He went on board ship, holding his razor, soap, tooth-brush, comb, and some letters, wrapped in a clean khaki handkerchief. He managed to scrounge a haversack and strap on board.

The troop train from Folkestone to London was filled with leave men and others returned from France. As the train puffed up to the junction, the men crowded to the windows. Girls and women walking in the parallel street, standing in the doorways, leaning out the window, waved pocket-handkerchiefs, cheered shrilly, and threw them kisses. The excited men waved and shouted to them. Winterbourne was amazed at the beauty, the almost angelic beauty, of women. He had not seen a woman for seven months.

It was dark when they got to Victoria, but the station was brilliantly lighted. A long barrier separated a crowd from the soldiers, who thronged out at one end. Here and there a woman threw her arms about the neck of a soldier in a close embrace which at least at that moment was sincere. The women's shoulders trembled with their sobs; the men stood very still, holding them close a moment, and then drew them away. At once the women made an effort and seemed gay and unconcerned.

Many of the men were proceeding elsewhere, and were not met.

Winterbourne saw Elizabeth standing, in a wide-brimmed hat, at the end of the barrier. Again he was amazed at the beauty of women. Could it be that he knew, that he had dared to touch, so beautiful a creature? She looked so slender, so young, so exquisite. And so elegant. He was intimidated, and hung back in the crowd of passing soldiers, watching her. She was scanning the faces as they passed; twice she looked at him, and looked away. He made his way through the throng toward her. She looked at him again carefully, and once more began scanning the passing faces. He walked straight up to her and held out his hands:

"Elizabeth!"

She started violently, stared at him, and then kissed him with the barrier between them:

"Why, George! How you've altered! I didn't recognise you!"

12

Winterbourne had a fortnight's leave before reporting to his Regimental Depot. He came in for two or three air raids, and lay awake listening to the familiar bark of Archies. The bombs crashed heavily. It was very mild—all over in half an hour. Still, the raids affected him unpleasantly; he had not expected them.

He spent his first morning wandering about London by himself. He was still amazed at the beauty of women, and was afraid they would be offended by his staring at them. Prostitutes twice spoke to him, offering him "Oriental attractions." He saluted them, and passed on. The second girl muttered insults, which he scarcely heard. There seemed to be a great many more prostitutes in London.

The street paving was badly worn, but looked marvellously smooth and kempt to Winterbourne, accustomed to roads worn into deep ruts and reft with shell-holes. He was charmed to see so many houses—all unbroken. And buses going up and down. And people carrying umbrellas—of course, people had umbrellas. There was khaki everywhere. Every third man was a soldier. He passed some American marines, the advance-guard of the great armies being prepared across the Atlantic. They had wide shoulders and narrow hips, strong-looking men; each of them had picked up a girl. They walked in London with the same proprietary swagger that the English used in France.

A military policeman stopped and roughly asked him what he was doing. Winterbourne produced his pass.

"Sorry; thought you was a deserter, old man. Don't go out without yer pass."

The second night after his arrival Elizabeth took him to a Soho restaurant to dine with some of her friends. Fanny was not there, but the party included Mr. Upjohn, Mr. Waldo Tubbe, and Reggie Burnside. There were several people Winterbourne had never met, including a man who had made a great hit by translating Armenian poetry—from the French versions of Archag Tchobanian. He was extremely intellectual and weary in manner, and took Winterbourne's hand in a very limp way, turning his head aside with an air of elegant contempt as he did so.

Winterbourne sat very silent through the meal, nervously rolling bread pills. He was amazed to find how remote he felt, how completely he had nothing to say. They talked about various topics he didn't quite follow, and titteringly gossiped about people he didn't know. Elizabeth got on wonderfully, chattered with every one, laughed, and was a great success. He felt very uncomfortable, like a death's-head at a feast. He caught a glimpse of himself in one of the restaurant mirrors, and thought he looked ludicrously solemn and distressed.

Over coffee they shifted seats, and one or two people came and talked to him. Mr. Uphohn dropped clumsily into the next chair, thrust out his chin, and coughed.

"Are you back in London for good now?"

"No. I've a fortnight's leave, and then go to an Officers' Training Corps."

"And then will you be in London?"

"No; I shall have to go back to France again."

Mr. Upjohn irritatedly clucked his tongue—tch, tch!

"I mildly supposed you'd finished soldiering. You look most grotesque in those clothes."

"Yes, but they're practical, you know."

"What I mean to say is that the most important thing is that the processes of civilisation shouldn't be interrupted by all this war business."

"I quite agree. I——"

"What I mean to say is, if you get time, come round to my studio and have a look at my new pictures. Are you still writing for periodicals?"

Winterbourne smiled.

"No. I've been rather busy, you know, and in the trenches one——"

"What I mean to say is, I'd like you to do an article on my Latest Development."

"Suprematism?"

"Good Lord, NO! I finished with *that* long ago. How extraordinarily ignorant you are, Winterbourne! No, no. I'm working at Concavism now. It's by far the greatest contribution that's been made to twentieth-century civilisation. What I mean is . . ."

Winterbourne ceased to listen and drank off a full glass of wine. Why hadn't Evans written to him? Died of the effects of gas, probably. He beckoned to the waiter.

"Bring me another bottle of wine."

"Yessir."

"George!" came Elizabeth's voice, warning and slightly reproving. "Don't drink too much!"

He made no answer, but sat looking heavily at his coffee-cup. Blast her. Blast Upjohn. Blast the lot of them. He drank off another glass of wine, and felt the singing dazzle of intoxication, its comforting oblivion, stealing into him. Blast them.

Mr. Upjohn grew tired of improving the mind of a cretin who hadn't even the wits to listen to him, and slid away. Presently Mr. Waldo Tubbe took his place.

"Well, my dear Winterbourne, I am very happy to see you again, looking so well. The military life has set you up splendidly. And Mrs. Winterbourne tells me that at last you have received a commission. I congratulate you—better late than never."

"Thanks. But I may not get it, you know. I've got to pass the training-school."

"Oh, that'll do you a world of good, a world of good."

"I hope so."

"And how did you spend your leisure in France—still reading and painting?"

Winterbourne gave a little hard laugh.

"No, mostly lying about, sleeping."

"I'm sorry to hear that. But, you know, if you will forgive

DEATH OF A HERO

my saying so, I always doubted whether your Vocation were really toward the arts. I felt you were more fitted for an open-air life. Of course, you're doing splendid work now, splendid. The Empire needs every man. When you come back after the Victory, as I trust you will return safe and sound, why don't you take up life in one of our colonies, Australia or Canada? There's a great opening for men there."

Winterbourne laughed again.

"Wait till I get back, and then we'll see. Have a glass of wine?"

"No-oeh, thank you, no-oeh. By the way, what is that red ribbon on your arm? Vaccination?"

"No; company runner."

"A company runner? What is that? Not runner away, I hope?"

And Mr. Tubbe laughed silently, nodding his head up and down in appreciation of his jest. Winterbourne did not smile.

"Well, it might be under some circumstances, if you knew which way to run."

"Oh, but our men are so splendid, so splendid, so unlike the Germans, you know. Haven't you found the Germans mean-spirited? They have to be chained to their machine-guns, you know."

"I hadn't observed it. In fact, they're fighting with wonderful courage and persistence. It's not much of a compliment to our men to suggest otherwise, is it? We haven't managed to shift 'em far yet."

"Ah! but you must not allow your own labours to distort your perspective. The Navy is the important arm in the War; that and the marvellous home organisation, of which you, of course, can know nothing."

"Of course, but still . . ."

Mr. Tubbe rose to move away.

"Delighted to have seen you, my dear Winterbourne. And thank you for all your interesting news from the Front. *Most* stimulating. *Most* stimulating."

Winterbourne signed to his wife to go, but she ignored the signal, and went on talking earnestly and attentively with Reggie Burnside. He drank another glass of wine, and stretched his legs. His heavy hobnailed boots came in contact with the shins of the man opposite.

"Sorry. Hope I didn't hurt you. Sorry to be so clumsy."

"Oh, not at all, nothing, nothing," said the man, rubbing his bruised shin with a look of furious anguish. Elizabeth frowned at Winterbourne, and leaned across to get the bottle. He grabbed it first, poured himself another glass, and then gave it to her. She looked angry at his rudeness. He felt pleasantly drunk, and cared not a damn for any one.

Coming home in the taxi she reproved him with gentle dignity for drinking too much.

"Remember, dear, you're not with a lot of rough soldiers now. And, please forgive me for mentioning it, but your hands and fingers are terribly dirty—did you forget to wash them? And you were rather rude to everybody."

He was silent, staring listlessly out the taxi-cab window. She sighed, and slightly shrugged her shoulders. They did not sleep together that night.

Next morning at breakfast they were both preoccupied and silent. Suddenly George emerged from his reverie.

"I say, what's happened to Fanny? She's not out of town, is she?"

"No, I don't think so."

"Why wasn't she at dinner with us last night?"

"I didn't ask her."

"You didn't ask her! Why ever not?"

Elizabeth looked annoyed at the question, but tried to pass it off lightly.

"I don't see much of her now—Fanny's so popular, you know."

"But why don't you see her?" Winterbourne pursued clumsily. "Is anything wrong?"

"I don't see her because I don't choose to," replied Elizabeth tartly and decisively.

He made no reply. So, owing to him there was fixed enmity between Fanny and Elizabeth! His mood of depression deepened, and he went to his room. He picked a book from the shelves at random and opened it—De Quincey's *Murder*

Considered as One of the Fine Arts. He had entirely forgotten the existence of that piece of macabre irony, and gazed stupidly at the large-type title. Murder Considered as One of the Fine Arts. How damned appropriate! He put it down and began to look over his painting materials. Elizabeth had taken his sketching-blocks and paper and all his unused canvases except one. The tubes of paint had gone hard and dry, and his palette was covered with shrunken hard blobs of paint just as he had left it fifteen months before. He carefully cleaned it, as if he might be sent before his Company officer on the charge of having a dirty palette.

He turned up some of his old sketches and looked through them. Could it be that he had composed them? They were undoubtedly signed "G. Winterbourne." He looked at them critically, and then slowly tore them up, threw them in the empty fire-grate, struck a match and set fire to them. He watched the paper curl up under the creeping flame, glow dull red, and shrink to black fragile ash. Numbers of his canvases were stacked in little neat piles against the wall. He ran through them rapidly, letting them fall back into place as if they had been cards. He paused when he came upon a forgotten portrait of himself. Had he painted that? Yes, it was signed with his name. Now, when and where had he done it? He held the small canvas in his hands, gazing intently at it with a prodigious effort of memory, but simply could not remember anything about it. The picture was undated, and he could not even remember in which year he had done it. He deliberately put his foot through it, tore away the strips of canvas from the frame and burned them. It was the only portrait of him in existence, since he had always refused to be photographed.

In the line they had been forbidden to keep diaries or to make sketches, since either might be of use to the enemy if they got possession of them. He shut his eyes. In a flash he saw vividly the ruined village, the road leading to M——, the broken desecrated ground, the long slag-hill, and heard the "claaang" of the heavies dropping reverberantly into M——. He went to Elizabeth's room to get a sheet of paper and a soft pencil to make a sketch of the scene. She had gone out. As he rummaged at her table, he turned over and could not help seeing the first lines of a letter in a handwriting unknown to him. The date was that of the day on which he had returned to England, and the words he could not help seeing were: "DARLING,—What a bore, as you say! Never mind, the visitation can't last long, and . . ." Winterbourne hastily covered the letter up to avoid reading any more.

He went back to his room with paper and pencil and began to sketch. He was astonished to find that his hand, once as steady as the table itself, shook very slightly but perceptibly. The drink last night, or shell-shock? He persisted with his sketch, but the whole thing went wrong. He got tired of blocking lines in and irritatedly rubbing them out. And yet that scene existed so vividly in his memory, and he could see exactly how it could be formalised into an effective pattern. But his hand and brain failed him—he had even forgotten how to draw rapidly and accurately.

He dropped the pencil and rubber on the half-erased sketch and went back to Elizabeth's room. She was still out. The room was very quiet and sunny. The old orange-striped curtains had gone and were replaced by long, ample curtains of thick green serge, to comply with the regulations about lights. There were summer flowers in the large blue bowl, and fruit on the beautiful Spanish plate. He remembered how the wasp had come through the window, like a tiny Fokker plane, almost exactly three years ago. To his surprise he felt a lump in his throat and tears coming to his eyes.

A church clock outside chimed three-quarters. He looked at his wrist-watch—a quarter to one. Better go somewhere and have lunch. He dropped into the first Lyons' Restaurant he came to. The waitress asked if he would like cold corned beef— thanks, he'd had enough bully beef for the time being. After lunch, he rang up Fanny's flat, but got no reply. He walked in her direction, strolling, to give her time to return home. She was not in. He scribbled a note, asking her to meet him as soon as she could, and then took a bus back to Chelsea, lay down on his bed and fell asleep. Elizabeth came into the room about six and tiptoed out. At seven she woke him. He started up, fully awake at once, mechanically grabbing for his rifle.

"What's up?"

Elizabeth was startled by this sudden leap awake, and he had unconsciously jostled her roughly as she bent over him.

"I'm so sorry. How you started! I didn't mean to *frighten* you."

"Oh, it's all right. I wasn't frightened—used to jumping up in a hurry, you know. What time is it?"

"Seven."

"Good Lord! I wonder what made me sleep that long!"

"I came to know if you'd dine with me and Reggie to-night."

"Is he coming here afterwards?"

"Of course not."

"I think I'll have dinner with Fanny."

"All right; just as you please."

"Can I have the other key to the flat?"

Elizabeth lied:

"I'm afraid it's lost. But I'll leave the door unlocked as I did to-day."

"All right. Thanks."

"Au revoir."

"Au revoir."

Winterbourne washed, and worked desperately hard with a nail-brush to get out the dirt deeply and apparently ineradicably engrained in his roughened hands. He got a little more off, but his fingers were still striated with lines of dirt which made them look coarse and horrible. He rang Fanny up from a call-box.

"Hullo. That you, Fanny? George speaking."

"*Darling*! How are you? When did you get back?"

"Two or three days ago. Didn't you get my letter?" Fanny lied:

"I've been away, and only found it when I got back just now."

"It doesn't matter. Listen: will you dine with me to-night?"

"Darling, I'm *so* sorry, but I simply can't. I've an appointment I simply must keep. *Such* a bore!"

Such a bore, as you say! Never mind; the visitation can't last long, and . . .

"It doesn't matter, darling. When can we meet?"

"Just a moment; let me look at my memorandum-book."

A brief silence. He could hear a faint voice from another line crossing his: "My God! you say he's killed! And he only went back last week!"

Fanny's voice again:

"Hullo. Are you there, George?"

"Yes."

"To-day's Wednesday. I'm awfully busy for some reason this week. Can you see me on Saturday for dinner?"

"Must it be as late as Saturday? I've only a fortnight, you know."

"Well, you can make it lunch on Friday, if you prefer. I'm lunching with somebody, but you can come along. It'd be nicer to dine alone together, though, wouldn't it?"

"Yes, of course. Saturday, then. What time?"

"Seven-thirty, the usual place."

"All right."

"Good-bye, darling."

"Good-bye, Fanny dear."

He dined alone, and then went to a Circassian Café, which he had been told was the new haunt of the intelligentsia. It was very crowded, but he knew nobody there. He found a seat, and sat by himself. Opposite him at a couple of tables was a brilliant bevy of elegant young homosexuals, two of them in Staff Officer's uniform. They paid no attention to him, after a supercilious stare, followed by a sneer. He felt uneasy, and wondered if he ought to be there in his Tommy's uniform. Perhaps the Café was out of bounds. He paid for his coffee and left. After wandering about the streets for a time, he dropped into a pub in the Charing Cross Road, and stood beside a couple of Tommies drinking beer. They were home-service N.C.O.'s—instructors, he gathered from their conversation, which was all about some petty way in which they had scored off an officer who did not know his drill. Winterbourne thought he would stand them a drink and get into talk with them, but his eye fell on a notice which forbade "treating." He paid and left.

He dropped into a music-hall. There were numbers of War

songs, very patriotic, and patriotic War scenes with the women
dressed in the flags of the allied nations. All references to the
superiority of the Allies and the inferiority of the Germans
were heartily applauded. A particularly witty scene showed a
Tommy capturing several Germans by attracting them with a
sausage tied to the end of his bayonet. A chorus of girls in red
pre-War military tunics sang a song about how all the girls
love Tommy, kicking up their trousered legs in unison, and
saluting very much out of unison. There was a Grand Finale of
Victory to the tune of:

> "When we've wound up the watch on the Rhine,
>   Everything will be Potsdam fine."

At the end of the performance the orchestra played "God
Save the King." Winterbourne stood rigidly to attention with
the other soldiers in the audience.

Eleven o'clock. He thought he would go and sleep at his Club.
The place was dimly lighted and empty, except for three or
four elderly men, who were earnestly discussing what ought to
have been done in the hand of bridge they had just played.
There were notices everywhere urging members to be economical with light. The servants were women except the head
waiter, a pale little spectacled man of forty-five, who informed
Winterbourne that no Club bedrooms were available. They
had all been commandeered for War purposes. Winterbourne
found it odd to be addressed as "sir" again.

"I've got me papers too, sir," said the waiter; "expect to be
called up any day, sir."

"What category are you?"

"B 1, sir."

"Oh, you'll be all right. Keep telling them you're a skilled
club steward, and you'll get an Officers' Mess job."

"Do you really think so, sir? My wife worries about me
something dreadful, sir. She says she's sure I'll catch my death
of cold in the trenches. I've a very weak chest, sir, if you'll par-
don me mentionin' it, sir."

"I'm sure they won't send you out."

The little waiter died of double pneumonia in a Base Hospital early in 1918. The Club Committee made a grant of ten pounds to his widow, and agreed that his name should appear on the Club War Memorial.

Winterbourne felt sleepless. He was so much accustomed to being alert and awake at night and sleeping by day, that he found a difficulty in breaking the habit. He spent the night aimlessly wandering about the streets and sitting on Embankment benches. He noticed that there were very few occupants of the benches—the War found work for every one. Odd, he reflected, that in War-time the country could spend five million pounds sterling a day in trying to kill Germans, and that in peace-time it couldn't afford five million a year to attack its own destitution. Policemen spoke to him twice, quite decently, under the impression that he was a leave man without a bed. He tried to explain. One of them was very fatherly:

"You take my advice, my boy, and go to the Y.M.C.A. They'll give yer a bed cheap. I've got a boy your age in the trenches meself. Now, say you was my boy. I wouldn't 'ave 'im goin' with none of these London street women. 'E's a good boy, 'e is. An' they've treated 'im cruel, they 'ave. 'E's been in France nearly two year, and never 'ad any leave."

"No leave in nearly two years! How extraordinary!"

"No, not even after 'e was in orspital."

"What was he in hospital with?"

" 'E wrote us it was pneumonia, but we believe 'e was wounded and didn't want to fret us, because he wrote afterwards it was pleurisy."

"Do you happen to know the number of his Base Hospital?"

"Yes, Number XP."

Winterbourne smiled sadly and cynically; he knew that was a venereal disease hospital. Pay was stopped while a man was under treatment, and he lost his right to leave. Winterbourne determined not to undeceive the policeman.

"How long is it since he came out of hospital?"

"Ten months or more."

"Oh, well, he'll certainly get leave before Christmas."

"D'you think so? Reely? 'E's such a good boy, good-lookin'

and well set-up. P'raps you'll see 'im when you go back. Tom
Jones. Gunner Tom Jones."

Winterbourne smiled again at the thought of looking for
Tom Jones in the swarming and scattered thousands of the
Artillery. But he said:

"If I meet him, I'll tell him how much you're looking forward to seeing him."

He pressed half a crown in the policeman's hand, to drink
the health of Tom and himself. The policeman touched his helmet and called him "sir."

He had breakfast at a Lockhart's—kippers and tea—and
washed in an underground lavatory. He got back to the flat
about ten. Unthinkingly he went into Elizabeth's room. She
and Reggie were having breakfast in dressing-gowns. Winterbourne apologised almost abjectly, and went to his own room.
He threw off the boots from his aching feet and lay down
clothed. In ten minutes he was fast asleep.

The meeting with Fanny was somehow a failure. She was
extremely gay and pretty and well-dressed and charming, and
talked cheerily at first, and then valiantly against his awkward
silences. Winterbourne did not know why he felt so awkward
and silent. He seemed to have nothing to say to Fanny, and his
mind appeared to have become sluggish—he missed half her
witty sayings and clever allusions. It was like being up for oral
examination and continually making silly mistakes. Yet he
was very fond of Fanny, very fond of her, just as he was very
fond of Elizabeth. And yet he seemed to have so little to say to
them, and found it so hard to follow their careless intellectual
chatter. He had tried to tell Elizabeth some of his War experiences. Just as he was describing the gas bombardment and the
awful look on the faces of men gassed, he noticed her delicate
mouth was wried by a suppressed yawn. He stopped abruptly,
and tried to talk of something else. Fanny was sympathetic,
but he could see he was boring her too. Of course he was boring her. She and other people got more than enough of the War
from the newspapers and everything about them; they wanted
to forget it, of course, they wanted to forget it. And there was
he, dumb and dreary and khakied, only awaking to any

appearance of animation when he talked of the line after
drinking a good deal.

He took Fanny home in a taxi, and held her hand, gazing
silently in front of him. At the door of her flat he kissed her:

"Good-night, Fanny dearest. Thank you so much for having
dinner with me."

"Aren't you coming in?"

"Not to-night, dear. I'm dreadfully sleepy—bit tired, you
know."

"Oh, all right. Good-night."

"Good-night, darl——"

The last syllable was cut off by the sharp closing of the flat
door.

Winterbourne walked back to Chelsea. The street lamps
were very dim. For the first time in his life he saw the stars
plainly above Piccadilly. In the King's Road he heard the warning bugles for an air raid. He got into bed, extinguished the
light, and lay there listening, wide awake. To his shame he
found the shell-fear come back as the Archies opened up, and
he started each time he heard the thud of a bomb. They came
closer, and one crashed in the next street. He found he was
sweating.

Elizabeth did not get back until three. Reggie and she had
taken shelter in the Piccadilly Hotel. Winterbourne was still
awake when she came in, but did not call to her.

His leave came to an end, and he spent five weeks of vague
routine at his depot. He hated coming back to barrack-room
life, and did not like the men he was with. They were all Expeditionary men, but strangely different from what they were in
the line. Most of the comradeship had gone; they were selfish,
rather malicious to each other, and servilely flattered the
N.C.O.'s who could get them passes. They seemed to think
about nothing except getting passes out, so that they could
meet girls or go to pubs. They grumbled ceaselessly. Some of
them occasionally told hair-raising War stories, which Winterbourne thought quite probable, though he refused to accept
their evidence as conclusive. He always remembered one story,
or rather episode, related by a Sergeant in the Light Infantry:

"We' ad a bloody awful time on the Somme. I shan't forget some of the things I saw there."

"What things?" asked Winterbourne.

"Well, one of our orfficers laid out there wounded, and we see a German run up with one of those stick-bombs, pull the string, and stick it under the orfficer's head. 'E was wounded in both arms, and couldn't move. So 'e 'ad five seconds waitin' for his 'ead to be blowed off by that bomb sizzlin' under 'is ear. We 'adn't time to get to 'im. Some one shot the German, and then some o' our chaps picked up a wounded German orfficer and threw 'im alive into a burning ammunition dump. 'E screamed something 'orrible."

From the depot he was sent to the Officers' Training Camp with two days' leave. He managed to get Fanny and Elizabeth to meet and lunch with him on the day he left. They both saw him off from Waterloo, and then parted outside the station.

The months of dreary training in the cold, dreary camp dragged by. He had two days' leave in the middle of the course, then "passed out" as an officer, and was sent on leave again, with orders to wait until he received official notice of his appointment.

Elizabeth and Fanny both admired the cut and material of his cadet's uniform, which was exactly like an officer's except that it bore no badges of rank and that he did not wear the shoulder-strap of his Sam Browne belt. He looked ever so much smarter in his new officer's clothes, with the little blue chevron, marking service overseas, sewed on his left sleeve. They both quite took to him again, and during his month's leave gave him a good time. Fanny thought him still an excellent lover. Only, instead of gay and amusing talk "in between," he sat heavily silent, or drank and talked about that boring, awful War. It was such a pity—he used to be such a charming companion.

This leave came to an end too. He was gazetted, and went to his new regimental depot, situated in wooden huts on a desolate heath in the North of England, a place swept by rain and wind, and deadeningly chill in the wet winter days. The other officers were sharply divided into two sections or sects.

Wounded survivors from the early days of the War, now on Permanent Home Service; and the newly-gazetted officers, with a sprinkling of wounded on Temporary Home Service. They ate in one large mess-room, but had two common rooms, which seemed to be tacitly reserved for each of the two groups, who scarcely ever mingled. Only the cadets from Sandhurst were admitted into the more exclusive room.

There was very little to do—parading with the Company, inspection, a little drill, orderly officer occasionally. There were so many new officers waiting to go overseas that the quarters were uncomfortably crowded, and there seemed to be almost as many officers as men on parade. He got the impression that infantry subalterns were cheap as stinking fish.

At last he got his orders to proceed overseas—France again, though he had hoped for Egypt or Salonika. He had two more days of leave and a quarrel with Elizabeth, who found him writing a loving note to Fanny on the morning he arrived. He went off in dudgeon and spent the time with Fanny. He saw Elizabeth again on the afternoon of the day before he left, and patched matters up with her. She was now furiously jealous of his spending nights with Fanny, but "forgave" him. She said that the War had affected his mind so much that he did not know what he was doing; and anyway, as he was going out again at once, they might as well be friends. They kissed, and he went off to keep a dinner engagement with Fanny.

His train left at seven the next morning. He got up at five-thirty, and kissed Fanny, who woke up and sleepily offered to get him coffee. But he made her lie still, dressed hastily, made himself some coffee, found he could not eat anything, and went back to the bedroom. Fanny had fallen asleep again. He kissed her very tenderly and gently, not to wake her; and softly let himself out of the flat. He had difficulty in finding a taxi, and was horribly worried lest he should miss his train and be suspected of overstaying leave. He got to the platform one minute before the train started. There was no porter to carry his large valise, but he managed to get into a carriage just as the train started. It was a Pullman, so crowded with officers that he hadn't room to sit down, and had to stand all the way to Dover. Most of them had newspapers. The news of the crushing defeat of the Fifth Army was just coming through. They were being sent out to replace losses. He thought of something which had happened the night before. . . .

Fanny had insisted on his coming with her for a couple of hours to a party of the intelligentsia given by someone with chambers near the Temple. As they passed Charing Cross Station, Winterbourne bumped into a man from his own Company who had just arrived by the leave train.

"Go on with the others, Fanny dear. I'll catch you up. Anyway, I've got the address."

He turned to Corporal Hobbs, and said:

"Are you still with the old lot?"

"No; I left 'em in November. Got trench feet at Ypres. I was supposed to be court-martialled, but that was washed out. I've got a job at the Base now."

"You're lucky."

"You've heard the news, I s'pose?"

"No; what?"

"Well, we heard there's a big surprise attack on the Somme. We're retiring, and our old Division is s'posed to have copped it badly—smashed to pieces, the R.T.O. said."

"Good God!"

"I think it must be true. All leave's stopped. I just managed to get away before the order came. There were only about ten men on the boat. Lucky for me I went down early."

"Well, so long, old man."

"I see you're an officer now."

"Yes, I'm just going out again."

"Best of luck to you."

"Best of luck."

He found the man's chambers. There were about ten people present. Winterbourne knew some of them. They had also heard the news of the battle through a man in Whitehall, and were discussing it.

"It's a bad defeat," he said. "I'm told that the highest authorities think it adds another year to the war and will cost at least three hundred thousand men."

He said it carelessly, as if it were a matter of casual importance. Winterbourne heard them constantly using the phrase "three hundred thousand men," as if they were cows or pence or radishes. He walked up and down the large room apart from the others, thinking, no longer listening to their chatter. The phrase "Division smashed to pieces" rang in his brain. He wanted to seize the people in the room, the people in authority, every one not directly in the War, and shout to them: "Division smashed to pieces! Do you know what that means? You must stop it, you've got to stop it! Division smashed to pieces!" ...

13

WINTERBOURNE listened intently. Yes, it was! He turned to his runner:

"Did you hear that, Baker?"

"Hear what, sir?"

"Listen."

A plane droned gently and distantly in the still air, and then very faintly but distinctly:

Claaang!

"There! Did you hear it?"

"No, sir."

"It was one of the heavies falling into M——. You'll hear them soon enough. But come on, we must hurry. We've a long way to go if we're to get back before dark."

A year, almost to the day, after he had gone into M—— for the first time, Winterbourne was returning to it as an officer in command of a company.

From London he had proceeded direct to Etaples, where he remained for several days under canvas on the sandy slopes among the pines. Large numbers of officers were being sent out, and they had to sleep four to a tent. Winterbourne thought this a luxurious allotment of space, but the other three subalterns, who had never been to France before, complained that there was not enough room for their camp-beds and that they had to sleep in their flea-bags. Winterbourne had not troubled to bring a camp-bed, knowing how few opportunities there would be to use it.

There was very little to do in Etaples, even with the more extended opportunities of an officer. They messed in a large, draughty marquee, but there was a camp cinema where he spent part of each evening. There were numbers of women at the Base, and he noticed that some of them were pregnant. Apparently there was no attempt at concealment; but then the birth-rate was declining rapidly in England, and babies were urgently needed for the Next War. He observed that the cemetery had doubled in size since he had last seen it from the train a few months before. That Ypres offensive must have been very costly. Such acres of wooden crosses, the old ones already battered and weather-stained, the new ones steadily gaining on the dunes. And now there was this smashing defeat on the Somme. Haig had issued his back-to-the-wall Order, there was unity of Allied command under Foch, and America had been frantically petitioned to send reinforcements immediately. And still the front daily yielded under the pressure of repeated German attacks. It looked like being a longer War than ever.

At Etaples he was allotted to the 2/9th Battalion of the Foddershires, and left to join them with about fifteen other subalterns, most of whom had never been in the line. He found the battalion on rest in a small village about twenty miles behind M——. They belonged to one of the Divisions which had been smashed to pieces, and the battalion had suffered severely, losing most of its officers (including the Colonel) and the greater part of its effectives. The new Colonel was an ex-regular Corporal who had obtained a commission early in the War, and by dexterity and martinet methods had risen to the rank of Acting Lieutenant-Colonel. He was not a fighting soldier, but an expert trainer. He had the bullying manner of the barrack-square drill-instructor, and his method of "training" was to harass every officer and man under his command from morning to night. After a week's "rest" under this commander, Winterbourne felt nearly as tired as if he had been in the line.

The subalterns who had never been under fire were exhausted and dismayed.

However, it must in justice be admitted that Colonel Straker was faced with appalling difficulties, and Winterbourne would have sympathised with the man if he had not so obviously been trying to push his own professional career in the Army at the expense of every one he commanded. The old battalion was a wreck. It had four of its officers left, one of whom was the Adjutant; a few of its old N.C.O.'s and a sprinkling of men were there, mostly signallers and headquarters men. Not a single one of the Lewis gunners remained. Two companies had been captured, and the remainder had fought a way out with terrific losses. The gaps had been filled chiefly by raw, half-trained boys of eighteen and a half, many of whom were scared stiff by the mere thought of going into the trenches. To secure an adequate number of N.C.O.'s the Colonel had to promote nearly every man who had any experience of the War, even transport drivers who could scarcely write their names.

Winterbourne had expected to go into the line at first as a supernumerary officer under instruction, and to pick up his duties by watching others and always going about with them. To his dismay, but also a certain amount of flattered vanity, he found himself immediately appointed as acting commander of B Company. But it was inevitable. Several of the new officers were mere boys; others volunteers from the Army Service Corps—perfectly competent at their own job but quite ignorant of trench warfare; and others again were "keymen" from business houses, reluctantly yielded to the "combings out" of 1917. Winterbourne had four subalterns under him—Hutchison, Cobbold, Paine, and Rushton. They were all good fellows, but three of them had seen no service whatever, and the fourth had been in Egypt only.

When Winterbourne inspected his company on the first day, his heart sank within him. He felt it was monstrous to send these scared-looking boys into the line without a proper stiffening of more experienced men. It would have been far better to spread them out. They cleaned their buttons perfectly, drilled very neatly, turned right or left with an imitation

Guards' stamp, and trembled when an officer spoke to them. But they were mighty raw stuff for the job ahead of them. Winterbourne thought of his own greenness when he had first gone into the line, and his heart sank lower as he thought of his own utter inexperience as an officer. He had a very sketchy idea of how a company was run in the line. Of course, he had heard and carried orders, and had been roughly schooled in company organisation—on paper—at the Cadet School. But that was very different from assuming the responsibility for a hundred-odd men, most of them frightened boys who had never seen any but practice trenches and never heard a shell burst. Well, the only thing was to carry on, and do his best. . . .

The Division was to take over part of the M—— sector from the Canadian Army Corps. Winterbourne had to occupy part of the Reserve line just to the left of M——. The four company commanders with their runners were sent on ahead in a lorry to reconnoitre the positions and arrange details of "taking over." The Colonel particularly impressed upon Winterbourne the necessity for obtaining and carefully reading the written instructions for defence which would be with the officer he was relieving.

They were to have met Canadian guides at a given rendezvous, but the guides were not there. Winterbourne, who could have found his way to M—— in the blackest darkness, and who had twenty times passed up and down the trench he was to occupy, decided to push on. The other three, mistrusting him, stayed. He set out with Baker, his servant and runner. Owing to the shortage of men, the officers' servants had to act as runners, with the result that they performed both jobs abominably. Baker had been allotted to Winterbourne by the despotic Colonel, who interfered in the minutest details and then held the company commander responsible for everything which went wrong. Thus he was in a position to take credit for every success and push off the responsibility for failure on someone else.

Winterbourne would certainly not have chosen Baker for himself, and wondered what possible caprice of the Colonel had forced the boy on him. He was a decent enough lad—a milliner's delivery boy—but timid, unintelligent, and lazy. Baker seemed to think that he had performed all his duties as a runner if he followed Winterbourne so closely that he continually trod on his officer's heels.

They passed many places familiar to Winterbourne—the cemetery (now much enlarged), the ruined village (now still more ruined), the long slag-hill, Southampton Row. Nothing had changed, except to become a little more desolate and smashed. He noticed that several large shells had fallen in the cemetery that morning or the night before, digging up the graves violently, scattering bones and torn blankets and broken crosses over the other graves. He turned in for five minutes, and walked down the long row containing the graves of his Pioneer companions. He stood a couple of minutes at Thompson's grave. A shell splinter had knocked the cross crooked. He set it straight.

Winterbourne found the trench easily enough, and asked the first Canadian sentry for Company Headquarters. The man was leaning very negligently on the parapet, chewing gum. Winterbourne, accustomed to perpetual "sir-ing" and heel-clicking and general servility, was almost shocked when the man very casually jerked his thumb over his left shoulder without saying a word, and returned thoughtfully to his gum-chewing. He found the company commander, a Major, democratically sitting in the trench on a double-seated latrine, talking humorously to one of his men. The British always had separate latrines for officers.

Winterbourne enjoyed this hugely, and liked the Canadians. They at once invited him to whisky highballs and bridge. He managed to evade this, and then explained his own situation; asked for the written orders of defence and to see all the positions. The Canadian officer stared and said they had no written instructions.

"Well, what do you do if you're attacked?"

"I guess you'd form a defensive flank—if they ever got past the machine-gunners in M——."

The Canadian officer walked Winterbourne round the

positions. He was bareheaded—strictly against orders—and his men greeted him as he passed with friendly nods and an occasional brief remark. Winterbourne noticed that they did not wait for him to speak first, and did not call him "sir." He reflected with amusement that the Canadians were easily the crack troops of the British armies, and were sent into all the hardest fighting. And yet they didn't even say "sir" to an officer!

This meeting with the Canadians was probably the last piece of enjoyment or tranquillity that Winterbourne ever had. From the moment he went back to his own battalion his life became one long harassed nightmare. He was deluged with all sorts of documents requiring information and statistics he was totally unable to furnish. The blunders, the mistakes, the negligences of his inexperienced men were legion, and all were visited upon him by the martinet Colonel. For days and weeks he got scarcely any sleep, and never once even took his boots off. He had continually to be up and down the trench, especially during the periodic six days in the Front line, and even in Support. He spent hours a day answering idiotic written questions brought by weary runners, and trying to puzzle out minute and unnecessary orders. He was always being told to report to Battalion Headquarters, where he was savagely attacked and reprimanded for the most piffling and unimportant errors. He went on patrol himself, contrary to orders, to make sure that at least one patrol a night was properly done— and was severely reprimanded for that. The boys, suddenly released from button-polishing and saluting and drill (which they had been taught to consider all-important), became deplorably slack in important matters. They lost portions of their equipment, dropped their ammunition, never knew their orders as sentries, went to sleep on sentry duty, shivered when ordered to go on patrol, cried when put in listening-posts in No Man's Land, littered up the trench with paper, bully-beef tins, and fragments of food, urinated in the trenches, and "forgot" perpetually everything they were told. While Winterbourne was at one end of his section of trench, desperately and sweatingly trying to get some sort of order and sense into them, others were committing all sorts of military abominations at the other end. It was useless to "take their names" for punishments, especially as there aren't many punishments as bad as being in the line. One day he did exasperatedly make the Sergeant-major "take their names," and by night-fall found he had collected forty-two. Ludicrous. The N.C.O.'s gave the job up in despair and let things drift.

He found most of the recruits were hopelessly slow in getting on their gas-masks, and appeared to be in such a state of hebetude that they did not realise that gas was dangerous. They did preposterous things. They would, for instance, entirely abandon a Lewis-gun post to get their dinners. It was ten days before Winterbourne discovered this. The subalterns had seen it, of course, but had not known that they ought to report it. Winterbourne "ran" the responsible N.C.O. as an example. He "ran" a boy for sleeping on sentry duty, and then washed out the charge when he reflected that the poor wretch might be shot for so serious a military crime. His Front line positions were an exhausting nightmare, too. His Front was over five hundred yards. He had an outpost line of four listening and observation posts with a section in each. Three hundred yards further back he had his main defence line and his own headquarters. Behind that he had various isolated Lewis-gun positions. All these were imposed upon him in spite of his protests. The defence scheme might be all very well on paper, and might have worked out with experienced troops, but it was hopeless under these peculiar circumstances. He realised after a couple of nights in the Front line that under any determined attack it would be impossible for him to hold his positions for ten minutes. He urged this on the Colonel, begging that the dispositions might be temporarily revised and the men brought more closely together under his own eyes. He was told that he was incompetent and not fit to be a lance-corporal. Winterbourne sarcastically replied that some people are born corporals and some are not. He offered to resign his command, and was ordered to continue it under threat of immediate arrest and court-martial for negligence and disobeying orders in the face of the enemy. Knowing how easily a court-martial can be "cooked," Winterbourne unwillingly carried on.

Most fortunately, he was not at first attacked, but he lost several men. Two were wounded on a ration party, having lost contact and wandered about half the night. One was shot through the neck by a fixed rifle, although Winterbourne had thrice ordered every N.C.O. to warn the men about it. At stand-to one morning the Germans bombarded them with mustard-gas shells. Winterbourne had warned them of the gas until he was sick of doing so. Two mustard shells fell just outside the parapet of a fire-step with six men on it. They ducked down when the shells burst, and then stood stupidly looking at the bright yellow shell-hole, wondering what the funny smell was. Three of them were gassed, and two died.

Winterbourne spent most of each night plodding up and down his immense area of trenches to see that every one was at his post. After dawn one morning, instead of trying to snatch an hour's sleep, he went up to inspect his listening-posts, feeling an uneasy intuition about them. There were four, about a hundred yards apart, isolated in what had once been the Front line. At the third listening-post he found six rifles leaning against the trench and no men. They had been captured by a silent raiding party in broad daylight! Probably all asleep. Winterbourne was furious, sent his runner back for another section, and remained on guard himself. The runner came back timidly after an interminable time, and said the Sergeant wouldn't come. Winterbourne didn't want the other posts to know that one had been captured, fearing a panic. It was useless to leave the runner on guard; he would simply have waited until Winterbourne's back was turned and have run to the other posts and spread an alarmist report. Winterbourne hurried back, and found that the runner had delivered such a garbled and incoherent message that the Sergeant had been utterly unable to understand, and had sent him back for precise orders. Of course, the Colonel put all the responsibility upon Winterbourne, and threatened him again with a court-martial. Winterbourne protested and they had a furious row; after which the Colonel redoubled his persecutions. When they went out for four days' "rest" after their first three weeks in the line, Winterbourne felt more exhausted and depressed

than he would have believed possible. He saw that the men got
into their billets, after infinite tramplings and shoutings in the
darkness, and fell on to a sacking bed. He slept for fourteen
hours.

Of course, Winterbourne had taken all this far too tragically
and responsibly. The situation happened to be one which most
disastrously fed his "worry" neurosis. A bitterly humorous destiny seemed intentionally to involve him in circumstances which
rent his mind to pieces and exhausted his body—unnecessarily.
It was a misfortune, due possibly to the fact that the initial of
his name made him come towards the end of a list, that he was
sent to a battalion so raggedly composed and so naggingly
commanded. We passed out almost together at the Cadet
School; but where everything ran comparatively easily and
smoothly for me, all went wrong with him. He brooded incessantly and saw all things in terms of the bleakest despair—
the collapse of his own life, his present situation, the continued retirement of the Allied Armies which seemed to promise
an indefinite continuation of the War, his feeling that even
if he came out alive he would never be able to rebuild his life.
It was unlucky to go straight back to M——, which had
such tragic associations for him and made it doubly hard to
repress shell-shocked nerves. His state of mind, what with
sleeplessness and worry and shock and ague—which came
back as soon as he was in the line again—and physical exhaus-
tion and inhibited fear, almost fringed dementia, and he
would have collapsed but for his strength of will and pride. He
was a wrecked man, swept along in the swirling cataracts of
the War.

The days passed into weeks, the weeks into months. He moved
through impressions like a man hallucinated. And every incident seemed to beat on his brain Death, Death, Death. All the
decay and dead of battlefields entered his blood and seemed
to poison him. He lived among smashed bodies and human
remains in an infernal cemetery. If he scratched his stick idly
and nervously in the side of a trench, he pulled out human ribs.

He ordered a new latrine to be dug out from the trench, and thrice the digging had to be abandoned because they came upon terrible black masses of decomposing bodies. At dawn one morning when it was misty he walked over the top of Hill 91, where probably nobody had been by day since its capture. The heavy mist brooded about him in a strange stillness. Scarcely a sound on their immediate front, though from north and south came the vibration of furious drum-fire. The ground was a desert of shell-holes and torn rusty wire, and everywhere lay skeletons in steel helmets, still clothed in the rags of sodden khaki or field grey. Here a fleshless hand still clutched a broken rusty rifle; there a gaping, decaying boot showed the thin, knotty foot-bones. He came on a skeleton violently dismembered by a shell explosion; the skull was split open and the teeth lay scattered on the bare chalk; the force of the explosion had driven coins and a metal pencil right into the hip-bones and femurs. In a concrete pill-box three German skeletons lay across their machine-gun with its silent nozzle still pointing at the loop-hole. They had been attacked from the rear with phosphorus grenades, which burn their way into the flesh, and for which there is no possible remedy. A shrunken leather strap still held a battered wrist-watch on a fleshless wrist-bone. Alone in the white curling mist, drifting slowly past like wraiths of the slain, with the far-off thunder of drum-fire beating the air, Winterbourne stood in frozen silence and contemplated the last achievements of civilised men.

A raiding party was sent out from his front. He watched the box barrage from the Front line. The Germans filled the night with Verey lights and coloured rockets. Their artillery and trench-mortars and machine-guns retaliated fiercely. Smoke and gas drifted across. After interminable waiting the officer and three of the men staggered back, bleeding, blackened with smoke, their clothes torn to pieces on the wire. The raid had failed.

A company of gas experts came up from the Base, and sent over some thousands of Stokes mortars loaded with a heavy concentration of poison gas. As soon as the last mortar was fired they were in a fearful hurry to get away. The German artillery retaliation smashed their trenches. Next morning, Winterbourne watched through glasses the Germans carrying out their dead on stretchers.

A British airplane fell in No Man's Land. Winterbourne saw the pilot, who was still alive, struggle to get from the wreckage. An enemy machine-gun was turned on him, and he fell limp across the side of the cockpit. The plane was smashed to pieces by British heavies to prevent the Germans from obtaining the model.

They shifted to another part of the line. The company were out in No Man's Land in the darkness strengthening their shattered wire against a threatened attack. Suddenly half a mile of German front leaped into a line of flame. There was a whistling roar of projectiles, and a thousand gas-containers crashed to the ground all about them. Men were killed outright by direct hits, and wounded by pieces of flying metal. Every man who took more than two breaths of the deadly concentration was doomed. All that night and far into the misty dawn the stretchers went down the communication trench carrying inert figures with horrible foam on their mouths.

The German attacks spent their force, and the huge Allied counter-attacks began. The starving German armies were hurled back to the Hindenburg Line, their impregnable defence. The Canadians miraculously stormed the Drocourt-Quéant switch line.

Winterbourne was back on the Somme, that incredible desert, pursuing the retreating enemy. They came up the Bapaume-Cambrai road by night, and bivouacked in holes scratched with entrenching tools in the side of a sandy bank. The wrecked countryside in the pale moonlight was a frigid and motionless image of Death. They spoke in whispers, awed by the immensity of desolation. By day the whole landscape was covered with the debris left by the broken German armies. Smashed tanks, guns with their wheels broken, stood out like fixed wrecks in the unmoving ocean of shell-holes. The whole earth seemed a litter of overcoats, shaggy leather packs, rifles, water-bottles, gas-masks, steel helmets, bombs, entrenching tools, cast away in the panic of flight. By night the sky glowed with the flames of burning Cambrai, with the black hump of Bourlon Hill silhouetted against them.

They drove the Germans from Cambrai, and pressed on from village to village, constantly shelled and harassed by machine-gun fire from their rearguard. The German machine-gunners, fragments of the magnificent armies of the early War years, died at their posts. The demoralised German infantry surrendered wholesale.

For three days in succession Winterbourne's company formed the advance-guard, and he led it in the darkness over unknown ground, by compass-bearing, in a kind of dazed delirium. Pressing on through falling shells in the blank night, with the ever-present dread of falling into a machine-gun ambush, became an agony. They fought their way into inhabited villages, which had been held by the Germans for over four years. The terrified people crouched in cellars or ran distractedly into the fields. They took the village of F——, after a brief but fierce bombardment, an hour after dawn. The roads leading in and out were encumbered with dead Germans, smashed transport, the contorted bodies of dead horses. Dead German soldiers lay about the village street, which was cluttered with fallen tiles and bricks. In a garden a war-demented peasant was digging a grave to bury his wife, who had been killed by a shell-burst. In the ruined village school Winterbourne picked up a book—it was Pascal's *Thoughts on Christianity*.

Part of Cambrai had been levelled to the ground in 1914, and stood a melancholy monument of neatly-piled wreckage. Part of the remainder was burned. In the undestroyed streets many houses had been looted. The furniture had been smashed, pictures and photographs torn from the walls, cushions ripped open with bayonets, curtains slashed down, carpets gashed into rags. The whole mass of desecrated objects had been flung into the centre of the floor, after which the Germans had urinated and dropped their excrement upon it. Winterbourne gazed into a dozen houses which had been treated in this way. The villages beyond Cambrai had not been sacked, but were

utterly filthy and swarming with buzzing legions of flies. Isolated cottages had sometimes been completely gutted of their
contents. In one place Winterbourne found an emaciated
Frenchwoman and two starved children living in a cottage with
nothing but straw—literally nothing but straw—in the place.
He gave them his iron rations and twenty francs. The woman
took them with a dull hopelessness.

They were approaching the Belgian border. On the evening of
the 3rd of November, Winterbourne with about twenty men
rushed into the village of K——, just as the Germans hastily
retreated from the other end. He had been ordered to occupy
the place if possible, and to arrange billets. He lodged his
Company, placed guards and pickets, and then went through
the cellars. The Germans were experts in placing booby-traps
which would explode if carelessly moved, and Winterbourne
did not know whether there might not be men concealed in the
cellars to take them unawares. He went down into cellar after
cellar with his electric torch, and was soon reassured. The
Germans had fled in such haste that they had left their rifles
and equipment in several cellars. The floors were strewn with
straw. On a table he found a half-finished letter, abandoned in
the middle of a sentence. In another a large black dog lay
dead—its owner had killed it with a bullet rather than leave it
to possible ill-treatment.

The Colonel explained over a map the dispositions for the
coming battle. The conference of officers took notes of the
orders, which were very elaborate, but precise and clear. It was
nearly half-past three when they had finished, and zero hour
was six thirty. Winterbourne had been on foot since five the
morning before. His eyes smarted with lack of sleep, and his
mind was so dulled that he could scarcely comprehend and
write down his orders. He mis-spelled words as be scrawled
down notes in shaking, deformed hand-writing. He puzzled a
long time over map-references, and irritated the Colonel by
repeatedly asking questions.
    They had an hour or so before they moved out to their bat-
tle positions. The other officers hurried away to snatch a little

sleep. Winterbourne felt utterly sleepy, but quite unable to
sleep. The thought of another battle, even with the dispirited
and defeated German rearguard, filled him with shrinking
dread. How face another barrage? He tried to write letters to
Fanny and Elizabeth, but his mind kept wandering away and
he could not collect his thoughts sufficiently to string together
a few banal sentences. He sat on a chair brought him by his
servant, with his head in his hands, staring at the straw and
the dead black dog. He had only one thought—peace. He must
at least have peace. He was at the very end of his endurance,
had used up the last fraction of his energy and strength. He
wished he was one of the skeletons lying on Hill 91, an anony-
mous body among the corpses lying outside in the street. He
had not even the courage to shoot himself with his revolver;
and added that last grain of self-contempt to his despair.

They assembled by platoons in the village street, and each officer marched off in silence to his allotted position. Winterbourne followed with his little knot of Company Headquarters,
and saw that each platoon was in its proper place. He shook
hands with each officer.

"Quite sure about your orders and objective?"

"Yes."

"Good-bye."

"Oh, make it *au revoir*."

"Good-bye."

Winterbourne returned to his own position and waited. He
looked at his luminous wrist-watch. Six twenty-five. Five minutes to zero hour. The cold November night was utterly silent.
Thousands of men and hundreds of guns were facing each
other on the verge of battle, and there seemed not a sound. He
listened. Nothing. His runner whispered something to a sig-
naller, who whispered a reply. Three more minutes. Silence.
He could feel the beating of his heart, more rapid than the tick
of seconds as he held his watch to his ear.

CRASH! Like an orchestra at the signal of a baton the thousands of guns north and south opened up. The night sprang to
flickering daylight with the gun-flashes, the earth trembled
with the shock, the air roared and screamed with shells. Lights

rushed up from the German line, and their artillery in turn flamed into action. Winterbourne could just see a couple of his sections advancing as he started off himself, and then everything was blotted out in a confusion of smoke and bursting shells. He saw his runner stagger and fall as a shell burst between them; then his corporal disappeared, blown to pieces by a direct hit. He came to a sunken road, and lay on the verge, trying to see what was happening in the faint light of dawn. He saw only smoke, and pushed on. Suddenly German helmets were all round him. He clutched at his revolver. Then he saw they were unarmed, holding shaking hands above their heads.

The German machine-guns were tat-tat-tatting at them, and there was a ceaseless swish of bullets. He passed the bodies of several of his men. One section wiped out by a single heavy shell. Other men lay singly. There was Jameson, dead; Halliwell, dead; Sergeant Morton, Taylor and Fish, dead in a little group. He came to the main road, which was three hundred yards short of his objective. A deadly machine-gun fire was holding up his Company. The officers and men were lying down, the men firing rifles, and the Lewis guns ripping off drums of bullets. Winterbourne's second runner was hit, and lay groaning: "Oh, for God's sake kill me, *kill* me. I can't stand it. The agony. *Kill* me."

Something seemed to break in Winterbourne's head. He felt he was going mad, and sprang to his feet. The line of bullets smashed across his chest like a savage steel whip. The universe exploded darkly into oblivion.

RÉPUBLIQUE FRANÇAISE

COMMANDEMENT EN CHEF DES ARMÉES ALLIÉES

Quartier Général.   G.Q.G.A., 12. 11. 1918.

OFFICERS, NON-COMMISSIONED OFFICERS, AND
MEN OF THE ALLIED ARMIES

After resolutely holding the enemy in check, for months you have repeatedly attacked with unwearied energy and confidence.

You have won the greatest battle in history and saved the most sacred of all causes: the liberty of the world.

You may well be proud.

You have wreathed your colours with immortal fame.

Posterity is grateful to you.

(Signed) F. FOCH,
Marshal of France,
Commander-in-Chief of the Allied Armies.

END OF PART III